For Sarai

Glass half-full

a novel by
Carey Rowland

Carey

Beginnings
1

Big bang. And so it began: the raveling of some little universe.

"What the hell do you think you're doing?" came a muffled yell, so rudely inserted into Daniel's perfectly-planned afternoon.

Electronic "chirp, chirp, chirp" was bleeping from somewhere. Releasing the brake pedal, he protested, "Why can't you make up your mind where you're going to turn?" Daniel felt his voice cracking, as if he were thirteen years old instead of an accomplished twenty-eight.

But there was this insane chirping noise *somewhere*. It was the voice of universal law bleeping in his head: *Thou shalt not dial thy cell phone while attempting to drive thy car.*

The other guy jumped out of his Dodge didgeridoo, *or whatever the hell it was*. Looking at a crumpled rear-end, the spiffy Dodger-driver shook his head as if he were about to accuse Daniel of a crime. "Man, I'd have given a hundred bucks for you not to have done that." Then he whipped out a cell phone, punched a number and let out an exasperated sigh.

The chirping noise was *still* there to annoy Daniel from somewhere to his right while he tried to open his door, but to no avail. *Turn off the key, you idiot.* The chirping stopped; now it was the drizzling rain that filled his ears.

Daniel, you're going to have to climb out through the passenger door. And so he did. As he stood and began to survey the bumperly mess that his inattention had inflicted, Daniel's portly, nattily-dressed, pink-shirted opponent was speaking into the phone: " Hey...yea, but it'll be awhile. Somebody just rear-ended me. Can you call Rialto and tell them that I'll get there as soon as I can. Then call Dewey and tell them that I need those signatures before the end of today business. But it looks like we'll have to postpone the closing....right...no, tomorrow, I'm thinking...I hope so. I think so. Okay." He snapped the phone shut with perturbed impatience constraining his ruddy face.

He looked at Daniel with an expression of arrogant impatience. "Well, are you gonna call the cops?"

"Call 'em your own damn self. You must have put your brakes on six times, trying to decide where to turn, I bet. Why couldn't you make up your mind? Pay attention to what you're doing."

But the voice of universal law was chirping in Daniel's head: *'Twas thou, O Daniel, who was not paying attention.*

***

A couple of sprawling blocks behind the unfortunate incident, Kaneesha Michot stepped onto the bus, swiped her transit card and took a seat about a third of the way back, next to Maudy, the elderly lady she visited with regularity in this spot two or three times a week.

"How you *doin'*, honey? You gett'n along like a spring chicken. Lookin' good. I know you're happy today, with *the Eagles* teaching Georgetown a lesson last night. Isaac was really shining. I think he made 22 points."

Maudy was beaming with pride. There was nothing more in the world that she'd rather talk about than her son, Isaac, point guard for the Lincoln University *Eagles*. "Yeah, Kaneesha, you know I was really happy to see it, but when I saw him stretched out on that floor after that foul in the first half, I was pretty worried about whether he'd be able to get up and get on with it."

"He's strong, Maudy, built like a lion. But he can take it. I know what you mean, though. I was sweatin' it too. As fast as they run up and down the court, and run into each other, it's a wonder there's not somebody spillin' out all over the court every couple of minutes. But there's no stoppin'

Isaac. It doesn't surprise me a bit, what he's doing. When we were at Roosevelt together, he would always be the spark plug. He'd always be the one to get those boys rollin', even when they were behind and didn't believe they could pull it out. Isaac always seemed to find a way to motivate the other guys to rally and go for it."

"I'm just so glad he's all right after that fall. How many more of those is he gonna have to survive in that crazy game before he makes it?"

Kaneesha was looking past Maudy's wrinkled, joyous face toward the *unfortunate incident* that was happening in the street just below them at that moment, as the bus was stopped. Two young fellows were looking intently at each other, straining their necks, veins popping, as their verbal exchange escalated into a confrontation beyond mere words. Suddenly, the one in the gray suit took a swing at the other, socked him right in the side of the face, sent him reeling back against the crumpled hood of the black Ford Esperanti.

"Oh no! Maudy, look. That guy just punched that other guy. They've had an accident, and I think the guy in the suit got a little worked-up about it." Kaneesha had a look of genuine concern on her face. She was a sensitive girl, compassionate to a fault; her heartstrings went out immediately to the man who stumbled backwards in the street below.

Maudy just gazed at the unfortunate incident, shook her head. "People are just so short with each other any more...everybody in such a hurry...just like that fellow that decked Isaac last night, playin' dirty...no consideration for the other guy. Men ought to play by the rules."

After a few seconds of quietly observing the *unfortunate incident* below, Kaneesha mused: "Who makes the rules, Maudy? Where do the rules...come from?"

"The good Lawd makes the rules, honey, but a lotta folks around don't seem to understand that the rules are for their own good."

In their ponderous silence, the bus began to move.

"It just all seems so random to me, Maudy...people with their lives seem like puffy lottery balls bouncing 'round, bumpin' into each other. Every now and then one pops out lucky, but most of them are just bouncing 'round without any rhyme or reason."

"Kaneesha." Silence.

"Kaneesha."

"What, Maudy?"

"There is an order in the universe."

"And how do you know that?"

"I know it because...I believe it."

"You believe it, and that makes it so? You believe it, and that makes for order in the universe?"

"Well, Kaneesha, there is a random quality to it. It's all in how you look at it. It's all about your perspective...*your* perspective. Is the glass half full? Or is it half-empty? If you say the glass is half empty, what advantage is there in that?"

"It's more realistic."

"Pessimistic, it's more pessimistic," said Maudy, feigning rebuke. "You've got to look at the positive in life. You've got to look at the bright side. Every cloud has a silver lining."

"There ain't no silver lining today. Just a lotta rain. I had a hard time getting out of bed this morning."

Maudy thought for a moment. "Kaneesha, as you were laying there in bed, could you think of a reason to get up?"

"Not much reason. Gotta go to work. That's about it."

"Do you like your work?"

"I like it all right. James and the Gang are pretty good to me, and I do all right in tips. But it's hard to get motivated every day, every night."

"Well, I know, Kaneesha, you come from a solid place. Your mama has done a good job with you, and your daddy loved you. Be thankful for that."

"Oh, I am thankful, Maudy. I'm just ready to move on to somethin' else. I'm ready to get on in life. Being a waitress gets old."

"Well, I'm glad you're here for me to talk to, coupla' times a week. We do have some nice visits on this bus, you know."

"I do know, and I thank you for it, Maudy. Your talk helps me see things, a *little* more clearly anyway...even if it is raining and dreary."

Maudy surveyed her young friend curiously for a few seconds. Then she spoke: "Do you believe in destiny?"

Kaneesha laughed out loud. "Are you talking about Manifest Destiny...what we learned about in high school history class: the idea that Americans thought they could rule the whole North American continent, take it away from the Indians and all that. Is that what you're talking about?"

"No, no, no. I'm talking about *personal* destiny...the idea that you were born for a reason, born for a purpose, to fulfill a special role in life."

"If I have one of those, I don't know what it is yet. I don't think its serving folks their dinner for $100 a night. There's got to be more to it than that."

"Kaneesha, I certainly don't know if that's gonna do it for you, but I can tell you this: My personal destiny began to come into focus when I had Isaac and Izzy. There's nothing more satisfying, nothing more important than bringing new life into the world, and then raisin' them up right."

Kaneesha was laughing. "Yeah, right, Maudy. It takes two to tango."

Maudy is laughing "Your ship will come in, honey. Your prince will ride."

"Oh, no, Maudy, there ain't no man that I've ever seen who knew anything about anything. And most of them surely don't know anything about destiny. Except they think its their destiny to roll in the hay with any girl they can--"

"Oh, they're not all like that."

"I'd like to see the guy that can prove your statement to be true."

Outside the bus window, the bullish world pawed its perpetual path through and around phalanxes of stopandgo traffic; the cumbersome bus trudged its laconic, jaggedly-circuitous route through Urdor's expanding galaxy of suburbanness. A curtain of silence descended on the pondering women. Rain, rain, rain.

Between glistening, rain-sleek gray, blue, green metallic floes of automotive hulk, Kaneesha noticed a riotously colorful patch of pansies and tulips in a bed that was a little higher than the sidewalk below them. Above the flowers, dark, naked dogwoods extended their plaintive, dripping wintry extremities skyward toward the gray plasmic atmosphere. What a contrast. Kaneesha thought about what the flowers had looked like last week, when she had noticed them on a day that was sunny and cold.

"Maudy, what about Izzy? How's he doing?"

"He'll be shipping out of Fort Wenning, I think, next week."

"To where?"

"Iraq."

Maudy's older son was an army sergeant, a brave man. A couple of years ahead of his brother Isaac, Izzy had opted for the rigors of army life, thus releasing himself from the onerous mediocrity of Urdor. Maudy's heart was smitten with compassion when she thought of him. He had been the one always working on the car. Izzy had spent hours, days at a time keeping their old Chevy on the road, while Isaac steadily and unceasingly developed at every available moment the fine art of basketball. The fine art of basketball, the fine science of automotive mechanics…these were the two reservoirs of productive activity that had propelled Maudy's two sons through adolescence and young adulthood. Now they had flown the coop. She loved, missed them dearly…Isaac the star, Izzy the soldier. Maudy had a lot to be thankful for. She knew that the two boys had turned out extraordinarly well, especially considering the departure of their father when they had been not yet ten years old. She had spent many a night in trepidation over where the boys might be, and when they might come home.

But they had done well. They were doing well.

"Maudy, do you think Izzy would appreciate a letter from me?"

"Why, yes, child! He would love to hear from you."

***

When travelers facing west from their seats on Delta flight 1477 looked down upon the city of Urdor, they may have seen, as the plane approached the runway, a bus opening its door so that Kaneesha could exit to the sidewalk. They may have seen a traffic cop asking questions of the two motorists who had just encountered each other in an unfortunate incident. They may have seen a thousand other cars, trucks, travelers, pedestrians, butchers, bakers, candlestickmakers traversing the city of Urdor going about their merry and not-so-merry ways.

But of course they didn't. The city below them as the plane landed was only a blur of urban sameness that they had all seen time and time again. Nothing special about it. But there was one observant young lady whose surveying eyes caught a glimpse of a little traffic accident involving two SUVs beneath the lowering plane. She didn't think much of it. Happens every day. It had happened to her, as a matter of fact, just a few weeks ago. Seeing the unfortunate incident below, Helen was reminded of her own recent experience with collision. It had happened, curiously enough, on the same street, Pretoria Parkway. She felt bad about it, even a little guilty. Another woman had run into the rear end of her Volvo when she had been slowing down to make a turn. Or, rather, slowing down while trying to decide if she wanted to make a turn…that is…trying to decide if the place where she would be turning would be the place where she had wanted to turn. And then it happened: big bang, then the unlucky woman behind her had gotten a ticket. No one was hurt.

Helen was dreading the tedious trip back to her apartment. It appeared from the air that traffic was pretty-well choked up, as was usual for this time of day. The wet, gray, late afternoon wasn't the sort of environment that could spark energetic catching-up into her return from three days of conferencing about cardiovascular health in Atlanta. She felt older than her 28 years; and it seemed that her own cardio had endured too much strain lately. The weather was lulling her too-soon inclination toward sleep. But Helen had miles to go before she could sleep...a laborious retrieval of luggage and then the 30-minute drive home. It looked as though the rain may turn to snow. She was seeing little splats of ice in the raindrops on the plane window. What little energy the weary nurse had was being drawn upon by a dependent 16-week old child who lay within her, lovingly nestled between her heart and her hips.

Helen thought about the man who had planted that child within her. Where was he now? She shouldn't have listened to him, shouldn't have allowed herself to be swayed by his impish smile.

A troop of ravens, scattered upon the grassy field next to the runway, took flight as the immense silver bird set its gear down upon the runway. Big bump.

***

As the tow-truck operator was attaching a winch cable to the little Ford, Daniel opened the rear door and retrieved the roll of blueprints that had been the center of his distracted, best-laid plans of mice and men when he had made the phone call that had led to the *unfortunate incident.* What distraction could be so important as to merit this sudden disarray upon his drawn-out day?

It was a restaurant...or, at least, the *concept* of a restaurant--a place where people could lose their cares while merrily dining, wining, visiting, laughing their way to frivolity and fullness. People would *escape* to it, forsaking the noise and haste, and be surrounded by generic memorabilia that would help them experience profound conversation in a sepia-photograph past while dining in an elegant, candlelit future.

It would be the restaurant they've been looking for. Daniel just knew it. He had drawn some sketches for the Jesse James Gang, the up-and-coming trendy place to eat and be on Saturday night in Urdor, Virginia. And he was delivering these sketches to the Jesse James Gang so that James could begin making plans for their new building. They were bursting at the seams with business, having somehow put together the right combination of food and ambiance that was now drawing people like flies. *No, not flies...bad metaphor for a restaurant...* drawing people like white on rice. Or brown on rice. Whichever way you like it. They had the oriental sticky rice; they had the brown rice for the whole foods crowd. The Jesse James Gang Grille would serve it any way you like it up and down and over and out...of the wok, the casserole dish, salad bowl, or sizzling steak platter. They could put it together for you, and your crowd. Aiming to please, they could make you feel right at home while serving up just enough exotic allure to make you wonder at how you may have magically time-traveled to Bangkok, Barcelona or Birmingham. Yeah, it was a happening place all right. And Daniel had the vision for the Jesse James Gang of what their new building would be. It would be an exquisite blend of pragmatic functionality and otherworldly out-of-the-ordinary mystery. A regular magical mystery tour of epicurean delight.

Daniel had been thinking about James, the founder of the restaurant—a middle-aged teacher whose encounter with *No Child Left Behind* had provided incentive enough for James to forsake his first love, teaching, in order to tend his second love, cooking. Teaming up with Hilda, his wife, James had been seeking gainful employment for his son, Jesse, and daughter, Joanna, when he had started the Grille in a hole-in-the-wall rundown edge-of-downtown building in Urdor, two years ago.

All romantic notions of quaint old-world, brick-and-crumbling-mortar restaurant ambiance aside, it had become apparent to James and everybody else that his culinary success had expanded beyond the capacity of its present hole-in-the-wall location and was currently being transported (in his mind) to a more accommodating new construction on the edge of town where diners (more diners) could get in and out more easily, dine more comfortably, and generally enjoy themselves and the James Gang food more profitably.

Daniel would be the guy to house all of this. He'd be the builder *par excellence* who could put it together for James and the Gang... the one that could make it happen for them...the one who could craft a building that would portray all the success of a chain-restaurant emphasis on service and style, while at the same time preserving the essentially American entrepreneurial element of balderdash and *in your face* serendipity blended with small-town Disneyesque dreamworld propriety and nostalgia that never really existed for the present generation but certainly did exist in the small-town bicycling memories of their grandparents. And his proposal package would prove it. It was in the back seat right now, waiting to be unveiled.

So Daniel had been thinking of James' up-and-coming enterprise, had in fact been punching James's number on his cell phone on this Friday afternoon when the rain, the Dodge didgeridoo and Daniel's careless disregard for place, space and time in the present world had brought about the unfortunate collision of interests and vehicles that constituted his present situation.

So he inserted the blueprints under his raincoat, crossed the street and caught a bus home. Bopping along in unexpected bliss at having been released from the chore of driving through rain-choked traffic, he was at last able to resume the thought processes, but not the schedule, that had occupied his mind before the unfortunate incident had inserted its inconvenient traffic-laden tyranny upon his urgent itinerary. Had it not been for this, Daniel's proposal for the Jesse James Gang Grille would have been by now in James' sagey hands, under review by the master chef himself. It had been Daniel's attempted phone call under the duress of driving demands on his attention span that had unfortunately and unpredictably thrust a completely new set of circumstances into what would have otherwise been Daniel's perfectly planned presentation. But that was all water under the bridge now, or rather water under the hood, since the hood of his Ford was now crumpled past repair and care.

So the raveling of Daniel's little universe was assuming a slower pace, somewhat like that of the near-gridlock that his inattention had inflicted upon his neighbors' progress toward greater prosperity and self-fulfillment.

Daniel had to chuckle at himself. He had been calling James to tell him that he would be late. *Right.* But James, in his productive, crowded kitchen seven miles away, didn't care. Merrily at that moment raising a large colander of pasta from a pot of boiling water, he was whistling the Mayberry tune and meandering his way from one kitchen station to another, preparing cuisine for good people who would later that evening put good money into his good pockets. He was happy to be in the restaurant business, riding a big wave of *coup de maitre* that had been propelled by the scrumptious success of his menu-planning perfection, hospitably mated with the twinkle in his wife's eyes whenever she ceremoniously ushered diners into their culinary adventure in the now-too-small bistro accommodations.

Faults
2

A pretty girl was selling poppies from a tray. Marcus Derwin could see her outside beneath the large fixed-glass window. From his position on the scaffold, he could easily see the little collection of red silk flowers that she offered to passersby. Marcus thought she must know someone in the American Legion...*maybe her father, uncle, grandfather. Maybe her dad was a disabled veteran. Or maybe she didn't have a dad. Maybe he was dead.*

The girl's neatly-cut unnaturally black hair framed a cheerful face. She had thin lips, very fair skin, dark eyes. Just below the high left-cheekbone, he could see the faint suggestion of a scar. *Wonder what that was? Every person has a history...a tale to tell, a tale of woe, or a story of success. What must hers be? She couldn't be much on the ball if she's out selling silk flowers to a bunch of jaded suburbanite shoppers. Or maybe she's really doing it as a labor of love, a service to mankind, a true service of providing revenue for the Disabled Veterans. Maybe she's got a job somewhere at night. Or maybe she doesn't even need a job. Maybe she's an heiress, performing benevolent philanthropy.*

Ripping his gaze away from the unaware queen of poppies, Marcus set his chisel back to the tenon end of the collar beam that he'd been crafting. It wasn't quite there yet. The tenon, soon to be hidden forever within its own mortise, was the connecting end of a 20-ft long 8x8 cedar timber. This was the 30th tenon that he had so-shaped by using a chisel, having cut the logs back at the shop. It was in fact the last one. In the last few days, his crew had erected 15 beam trusses in the foyer of this once-fashionable Urdor mall.

Marcus's brother, Daniel, had designed the wooden beams as a retrofit project that would lend the mall entrance a more contemporary appearance, a trendier feel. Ironic...that ancient wood would be prescribed to augment concrete and steel after the fact, and then be deemed by popular whim more contemporary. Even though the bare timbers were a relatively primitive structural element, they were now viewed by 21st-century eyes to be more in line with the universe and more harmonic with the rhythm of life in a hip-flip city. Marcus wondered what had been so different about those 1970's mall-shoppers' eyes, that they had surveyed the narthex of this (at the time) brand-spankin' new mall and considered it a cool place to shop.

But it wasn't cool any more. Several other, newer shopping centers had overtaken Glenharden Mall in the race for public affection and dollars. The newer ones were, in fact, not even malls. It seemed that the newest trend was back to strip shopping centers. Go figure.

But Marcus was tired of figuring, tired of hammering his chisel into grainy wood, tired of standing on the scaffold. It was 6 o'clock, the end of another day in the life. This last collar beam insertion could wait until Monday morning. Marcus had hoped to get them all put together by the end of the day, but things don't always work according to plan in this life. The rain outside was turning to snow. What he needed was a cozy place to relax, have a brewski, and get in the mood for basketball. Thank God it's Friday.

The Rathskellar. *Funny name*, Marcus thought. Back in the old country, in Munich or wherever, there were probably Rathskellars that truly embodied by their very existence the very *biergarten* ambiance that this American version only aspired to obtain: Dark. Lots of wood. Shiny taps with Heineken and Guiness flowing frothily. Laughter. Swarthy people. Business people. Unwinding. *Basketball on the tube: that was the difference. What the Americans lack in authenticity we make up for in basketball, which wasn't quite on yet.* Tipoff would be at 7 o'clock. But the news was on. Marcus saw the Iranian president on the tube, criticizing Zionists and the US administration that supports them. *This is sad. What a messed up world. Is there any safe haven in the world for oppressed people? Is there any place in the world where people could build a government that would truly promote justice for all peoples?*

"Give me a Corona, Jack."

***

Across the airwaves and just a few miles away, a brown-orange leather basketball twirled between Isaac's hands, then descended to the floor as he skillfully arrested the sphere's spin and sent it downward. Back up it bounced immediately. He grabbed it again and sent a parabolic arc of cultivated precision sailing through the air of Ryerson Arena. Swish. Isaac was trying to decide if he could make good use of the 3-point option while being guarded by the infamous Blake Johnson, his nemesis in the contest that was at this moment brewing in the sweaty arms and minds of the two top Big 12 teams. Tonight's encounter would be Lincoln's first of two conference games against Jefferson University this season. Isaac thought himself to be in top form, except for a bruise that rendered his hip a little sore, no thanks to Tony Williams of Georgetown. But that was nothing new. A few battle scars along the way only make a man more determined. *Whatever doesn't kill you makes you stronger.* It was the dark badge of courage, albeit concealed by his green and gold uniform.

So far have we evolved, thought Marcus as he watched Isaac warming up for the game while sipping his second Corona and munching jalapeno peppers, *that our modern gladiators can portray their struggles on courts of wood with weapons of strategy and strength, yet no shedding of blood, no penetrating of flesh, no death, no spears, lances, nor swords. And the only nets are those tied to the hoops, which catch the balls, ten feet in the air. So civilized are we. See how far we've come since the days of Caesar and Nero.*

Yet that would not explain the Second World War, the Holocaust that lurked beneath it, the Korean, Vietnam or Desert Storms that inflicted their violent gesticulations upon mankind...the 6-Day, the Yom Kippur, 1967, Darfur, Somalia, Bosnia, Kosovo, and God-knows-what other horrors were/are going on...911.

But I wonder about that Iranian president, so intent on getting us out of Iraq, so critical of our support for Israel. Where would the Jewish people be, if not for Israel? What would Roosevelt think of this? Churchill? Eisenhower?

The Lincoln University band was striking up the National Anthem. Isaac and his teammates were lined up, their opponents similarly arranged on the other end of the court, hands reverently positioned over their hearts. *Oh, say, does that star-spangled banner yet wave... o'er the land of the free and the home of the brave?*

Lincoln University outlasted Jefferson University, 102-99.

Helen was back in her apartment safe and sound, watching 24. The baby was having a cardiovascular workout in her womb, and she was getting into it. Too bad the kid's father wouldn't be around to help during the pregnancy. *Or maybe his absence is a blessing. Loser.* At least she had a helper in her suitemate, Rachel, who was at this moment entering the apartment.

"Yoo-hoo. How you dooooin, girl?"

"Happy to be here. This kid is really making a move. I think he's an athlete doing warmup exercises."

"Great, you're looking great, radiant. You're wearing the pregnancy like a crown. You're a regular princess. How was the conference?"

"It was about what I expected. I learned a lot...some good presenters, who really knew their stuff. Are you going back out? You seem to be in a hurry."

"Yeah, I'll be working tonight. It should be worthwhile, with the basketball game, the insurance convention and all that going on."

"How were your classes today?"

"Poldrianne is *so* weird, making us sling paint onto geometric shapes...doesn't he know that I'm a *realist*, for cryin' out loud? Well, not a realist, *per se*, but a ...neo-impressionist. I'm into cherry blossoms and sunshine."

"But there are no cherry blossoms now, Rachel."

"There aren't any paint dribblings over random lines, either. It's all in his mind. I honestly don't know what kind of abstract conspiracy he's trying to hoist on us. What ever happened to still-lifes? What ever happened to Monet in the park? Degas in the dark?"

"He probably considers it part of his job description to introduce you to different schools, different techniques, you know...You can always make those stylistic choices for yourself later on, after you've seen what the Masters did."

"I don't know what kind of Masters would dribble paint off the end of a brush and call it art."

"Lots of rich artists who've sold their designs to wallpaper manufacturers have probably done just that, and they dribble paint all over their checkbooks all the way to the bank. And their wallpaper designs are all around the beltway, at every Quality Inn and Homewood Suites between here and Quantico."

Rachel was changing her clothes...out of the student identity and into the wine stewardess role.

"I don't think so, Helen, I think those wallpaper companies have some 8th-graders in after-school programs in the back room, dribbling paint onto 9-ft. high easels, eating gummi-bears and drinking cokes."

They were laughing now, the twisted logic of their banter gaining more and more absurdity.

"Why don't you come by the restaurant tonight, Helen? It'll be on me."

"Oh, heavens no, I'm flat worn out."

***

Morris Schroeder, preparing to devour the hot lasagna that Kaneesha had just set before him in the midst of the Jesse James Gang Grille, used a knife to slice across the upper layer of the pasta creation. As he did so, the thought occurred to him that he could use this dinner entre to illustrate the geological history that he was attempting to explain to his companions.

"Some layers of continental plate slide under the advancing continent. Like this:" Morris used his silverware to push one slice of pasta beneath the other half that he had just cut. "Other layers crumple up, eventually becoming mountains." Simulating internal geologic forces with his knife and fork, the grad student demonstrated, in a crudely improvised culinary way, the formation of the Rocky Mountains.

He continued: "One of these 'crumples' had lifted some half-billion-year-old Cambrian shale deposits into an accessible position, called the Burgess shale, in British Columbia. Fossils discovered there by Walcott contain crustaceans with biological features (eyes and gills, jointed limbs and intestines) that are too complex to have evolved by random mutation before or during the Cambrian period. Random mutations could not have produced organisms of such complexity by the Cambrian era. What's indicated then, by the fossil record, is a burst of genetic design that occurred about half a billion years ago, across a multiplicity of animal types."

"Why couldn't those highly developed crustaceans have been present during the Cambrian period?" asked Shapur.

"They were present. That's what the fossil record attests. But according to the mathematical principles of probability, their existence could not have been randomly generated so soon in earth's history."

"A sudden proliferation of complex life forms half a billion years ago, could only have occurred by design, then...not by random mutation," said Shapur.

"That's the way I see it."

"What's the name for that?"

Morris laughed out loud. "Well, I call it creation. What do you call it?" Then he stabbed a chunk of the layered pasta and promptly ate it with gusto.

"You think, then, that all 34 phyla may have been present half-a-million years ago?"

" Yes. They show up much sooner in the geological record than conventional, suppositional evolutionary theory can account for them."

"Is gradualism, then, not a working principle in the development of life forms?"

"Only within each phylum, not *across* phyla. The basic body plans were all established at pretty much the same time. They each developed in their own way. Natural selection is a process that was applied, and can be inferred, within the evolution of each animal division, but not *across the board*. Vertebrates, for instance did not evolve from invertebrates. They were different body plans, created for different purposes."

"Well, where did these these body plans, or 'phyla' as you call them, originate?"

Morris laughed out loud. "God, I guess. Who else could have done such a thing?" He took a big swig of his beer.

"You're being so anthropomorphic!"

"Perhaps, but that's not such a bad thing to be. I'm a human being, aren't I? There's no escaping it. Every one of us is going to accept a hypothetical 'given' or axiom in the foundation of our mental processes. Mine is based on a leap to an original designer. Others leap to an assertion random process. When you get right down to it, you can't prove anything. It's the human condition. I can aspire to objectivity. I can even claim it in certain areas of inquiry, if I'm careful to document the work. But somewhere beneath the substrata of our knowledge and wisdom is a bedrock (or a shifting sand, if that's how you think about it) of supposition, or assumption, hypothesis, whatever you want to call it."

"Faith," inferred Phyllis out loud.

"You could call it that. Yes." I think every person, every discipline, has it in some form or fashion, whether they're willing to admit it or not."

Shapur was skeptical. "And you're willing to admit it. Well, I'm not...I believe there's a basis of reason for what we can really know, and that true knowledge can be acquired from it."

"You used the words 'I believe.' There's the leap of faith upon which your understanding rests. No way around it. There are all kinds of interpretable evidence suggesting what the mechanics of it might be. But, hey, Shapur, here's the real question: Has all this come about through random mutations, or is there some direction to it? Is *something* or *someone* orchestrating it?"

At that moment, a table full of avid basketball fans erupted in cheers and applause. Eyes on the TV in the corner and backslapping, they were celebrating the 3-pointer that Isaac had just put away with only 7 seconds left in the Lincoln/Jefferson game. Shapur looked beyond Morris at the tube and expressed his blessing over this most recent turn of events. There was a release in his jubilant voice: "I don't know, Morris, but I can tell you this: the *Eagles* have just pulled one over the *Rockets*, thanks to Isaac Jones 3-pointer from downtown."

As the excitement abated, Kaneesha breezed by with a big smile on her face and a pitcher of water in her hand. "What can I get you? More Sam Adams? More tea?"

"I'll have a decaf, please," said Morris.

"Same here," said Phyllis.

"Not me," Shapur spoke. "I've still got work to do tonight. Bring me some real coffee."

"You're kidding, Shapur. All work and no play makes Jack a dull boy, right?"

"I'll play on Sunday when I ride the 20 with the bike club."

"Sounds like more work to me," said Morris.

***

A sepia photograph hung on the wall; Marcus was looking at it. He often wondered, when viewing such pictures, about the men and women depicted in them: men and women frozen in time. The old photographs, those that had been taken 100 years ago or more, always portrayed such a seriousness, a gravity in those stony expressions...high cheekbones, resolute chins, stiff upper lips...*pain and suffering.* Were people more serious back then? Was life harder? Did they laugh and do goofy things like insult the opposing players on basketball teams? Did they kiss and make up after arguing with their spouses and then accelerate the blood as it passionately ran through their veins while they made love and conceived children whose children might now be alive? The lives of dead people fascinated Marcus. Such mystery in those hollow eyes. They were real people with hopes and dreams and spouses that loved them and children that depended on them. He would stare into the small eyes of those brown/black and white images, and he'd be struck with fear. *Although you look a little strange to me, sir, I fear that you are just like me. You're sitting there on that wooden barrel just as alive as I am right now...but **now** you're gone...dead, just like I will be one day. What can I see in your 120-year-old eyes that will give me a clue about what's on the other side? Because you are, undoubtedly, there. You're on the other side of death now. What clue can I read in your stony face? Is there balm in Gilead?*

Deadpan. Only pigment on old paper.

It was just a picture of a train. Men stood beside it; some sat on the train engine. Maybe exposure times for photographs were longer back then, and that's why the faces reflected such rock-hard sullennes, such scowling trepidation. The sullen men were trying to be still, as a courtesy to the photographer and to the group. Or maybe they were under duress, fearful. Maybe the photographer had said, "Okay, boys, now you've got to stay still for at least five seconds, or this here photograph will be plumb messed up." Then the photographer would have spit tobacco juice and reinforced his commandment of stillness: "And the first pig-headed bastard that messes up my photograph is a-goin' to get run outta town on a rail....*this* rail... this here rail. I'll personally strap him on the front of this here engine with his very own reins that I've taken off of his very own horse (and I'll keep the horse, mind ye, and sell him when I get to Chicago) and I'll make a deal with Mr. Rockefeller and Mr. Carnegie so that you'll never ever again be seen in these here parts cuz you'll be clear on t'other side o' the Missouri River So you better not even think about messin' up my pitcher. Okay you can breathe now. Thank ye kindly. I think we'll be all right on this one boys. Go on back to work now."

Then the photographer would take his film into a darkroom with a red light bulb in Cincinnati or Louisville or some such place and he'd dip it into some chemicals or some such thing and the next thing you know there'd be a black and white picture. And it would look just like the scene that he had seen when he snapped the shutter. His little image frozen in time would reflect all the seriousness of men who had been hard at work only minutes before...men who knew how to make a train go...men who knew how to shovel black coal into hot engines, sweat pourin' off of 'em like hogs, and glide along on steel horses that chugged along steel ribbons that were strung over prairies, precipices, promontories, peaks, canyons, rocks, ruts, roads and Sierras from here to San Francisco.

That now-deceased photographer would have walked out of that darkroom with a photograph in his hands. Those were the days of darkrooms, dark expressions, dark shadows that grow darker and longer as history carries them further back on the rails of time, ribbons of memory fading into darkness, past the clock that once was on the edge of a Missouri town, Kansas town, Sante Fe, past the clock that is now in the junk heap of history, having been replaced with an art gallery with McDonald's across the street and a man in a business suit who appears to be talking to himself animatedly about a business deal *Oh, he just turned around. He's talking on his cell phone.*

But he does look like the man in the picture, the one standing by the locomotive.

Yea, verily, those were the days of iron and steel...the days of timber and toughness. But they're not totally gone...this very day, Marcus had worked with timbers that resemble railroad ties. He had shaped them with the hollow-ground shank of a steel chisel. He had erected them into a position where they would appear to hold the roof up. They wouldn't actually hold the roof up, because the roof had been structurally integral and self-standing since 1973, but they would appear to hold the roof up. What was actually holding the roof up was steel I-beams (steel!) that had been covered with gypsum drywall.

People just wanted to see something different, in order to be convinced not to go around the beltway another mile or two to get to the latest/greatest new mall. They just wanted to see something different, like wooden trusses that would authenticate their experience by reminding them that they were entering a great public space, a great common area where people come to feel connected to the great stream of commerce and human productivity that enlivens this mall every day, and to make great consumer choices of import.

Actually, Marcus was waiting for a girl...just what girl he didn't know. Maybe the queen of poppies would walk into the Rathskellar.

***

Helen was so cozily sleepy. After 2 days in a nursing conference, sleeping in a hotel, the plane ride back to Urdor, she had allowed herself a long, hot bath and then made an appointment with her bed.

After slipping into her bright yellow flannel nightgown with the sunburst pattern, Helen turned down the sapphire blue covers; she tossed the round, white throw-pillow to the foot of the bed and slid between the sheets. She turned out the lamp. Drowsily she turned her head upon the pillow from one side to the other. Visible outside between the window curtains were a host of distant stars; their luminous photons of million-year-old light baptized her dark curly hair; it glistened upon the pillow.

Within Helen's womb, the baby slumbered with her. In just a few minutes, they drifted off to sleep.

Helen awoke with a start. Someone was in the room. Before she could do anything, the rude, clumsy bafflement of a big hand closed upon her mouth, and a heavy, stinking, clumsy weight was all over her. Pressure on her belly. *What about the baby?* The smell of pizza and beer upon his hands, upon his breath. Wet rag in her mouth. Searing pain in her arms. *What has happened to my arms?* The gruff warning from an unclear voice, deep, threatening, urgent, mad, a violent voice. Violence. She tried to struggle but could not. She heard the words but could not understand them, yet she knew what they meant. Clumsy, groping manipulation; heavy weight; clumsy, violent forcing; evil; thrusting, unwelcome penetration; dragon-scales of sweating; pulsing evil all over her violated body; frenzied, perverted ejaculation.

What? Wha..?

He was gone. *Oh, but mercy, but no, no,no...I'll put a stop to him. Respond. Reflex. Move. Jump. Roll.*

Suddenly Helen was on the floor. She felt like she had fallen off a bucking horse.

Go to the door.

Looking into the hallway, she could hear him thrashing; dimly she could see him thrashing on the floor. She didn't know why he was on the floor. Suddenly she knew: He had tripped over the chair at the edge of the living room. Without thinking, Helen grabbed the nightstand, forced herself into the hall and threw the nightstand right at his face.

The intruder began to stand up. Blood on the floor. Blood on his head, visible only by the dim light at the other end of the living room. Without thinking, Helen kicked him fiercely in the groin.

"Bitch!"

He had her leg, flipped her over onto the floor. Sudden pain in her head.

The intruder stumbled to the door and was gone.

Darkness.

Helen woke up in bed surrounded by pain and terribleness, but didn't remember how she had gotten there. She knew, like a bad dream, what had happened, but she didn't know what to do about it. She felt swollen, like a big, bloody contusion. She heard something in the living room. A dull kitchen knife was in her hand.

"No!" she screamed. "No!"

Suddenly the light was on. Rachel stood in the doorway, her mouth wide open, her eyes wide open. "Helen! Oh...Helen." Running over to the bedside, stopping, Rachel hesitated, then slowly lifted her hand, began to stroke Helen's damp hair away from her eyes, away from her forehead. Composing herself, the careful friend began to think about what needed to be done. She looked right into Helen's eyes.

"Helen...what do you want me to do?" "What...do you want me to do?" Brimming with tears, Helen's eyes were full of pain. She only wimpered. Rachel, wanting to comfort, started to embrace her friend. Then, Helen's woe erupted like flood gates. Wailing, she lost control. The resolve with which she had doggedly climbed out of bed to pursue the intruder, now spent, yielded to weakness. Collapse. But it was all right now. She was in good hands. She wailed. Rachel was amazed at the extremity of her sobbing...shaking uncontrollably. Crying, like a baby. Crying *for* the baby. Thus, Rachel's tender attention allowed Helen to begin a recovery.

"Is my baby all right?"

"I ...I think so, Helen." Quiet, slow sobbing. "Helen, what happened?"

Helen turned her head, wanting to bury her tears and trouble in the pillow. She cried some more. Rachel was in no hurry. She was beginning to understand. She thought about the splotch of blood that she had noticed on the carpet in the living room. She remembered the overturned chair, the disarray. Rachel was beginning to wonder if...

"Tattoo."

"What, Helen? What...tattoo?"

"He had a tattoo on the back of neck."

Get it together, Rachel; something terrible has happened here. "Helen, I'm going into the bathroom to get a washrag. Okay? I'll be right back." It only took a few seconds. Rachel quickly stepped into the bathroom, grabbed a towel, a washrag, and then ran warm water onto it.

Back in the bedroom, she began stroking Helen's face with the warm washrag.

"Who? Helen, who was it? Tell me what happened."

Silence, sobbing.

Once again, she looked right into her friend's eyes.

"Can you tell me what happened? Who was it? He...he had a tattoo? Is that what you're saying?"

Helen nodded slowly.

"Helen, you're going to be all right, now. I'm just going to clean you up a little."

Helen nodded slowly. For the first time, as she looked into Rachel's eyes, Rachel could see something beyond fear, something beyond suffering. It was reason, or understanding, or something like that. Helen was going to be okay.

"Helen, you know we need to call the police about this—"

"No, wait." She said it quickly.

Rachel didn't know what to say. She waited.

"Dragon...a dragon tattoo, on the back of his neck."

"Let's call the police now and tell them about this, so they can do something...so they can find the guy."

"I don't want to see him." Helen spoke quickly, a tone of vehemence now in her voice.

"I know, honey, but, we've got to call the police. We can't let this go."

"If I could see him dead, that would be sufficient." Anger was rising within her.

Such a sudden change, thought Rachel, from whimpering to rage.

Rachel needed to be the initiator now. The time for consolation was on hold. It was time to insert some control into the situation.

Gently, but resolutely, she spoke: "I'm going to call the police now. Just lie still and rest."

"I'm going to take a shower now." Helen was beginning to assert herself.

"Please, wait, Helen...wait, before you do that. Just rest. Take some time to recover. What can I get for you. How about a little glass of wine. It'll make you feel better."

"I need to take a bath."

"Please, don't do that now, Helen."

"Rachel!" Now she was mad.

Rachel had been moving toward the door to get to the phone in the other room. But she turned around, walked quickly back to the bed, lowered herself into a seated position on the side of the bed, placed her arms on Helen's arms. "Helen, please wait a little longer. We need to consider that there is...evidence."

"Okay, Rachel." Helen closed her eyes, and began to weep again.

Rachel stood up slowly, went into the living room, grabbed a phone, called 911. She went in the kitchen, poured a little glass of red wine, grabbed a couple of pieces of melba toast that were in a little box on the countertop.

Returning to the bedroom, she was surprised to find Helen's bed empty, wrinkled, the covers thrown on the floor, spots of blood on the sheet. The bathroom door was closed, and Rachel heard running water in the shower.

Stirrings

3

Long ago...in the ocean deep, upon its formless floor, the very hand of God had ripped a fissure. And from that craterous gash the earth bled profusely red and hot into the watery darkness. From tectonic clashing, like uterine thrashing, the quivering planet spewed forth its viscous, umbilical magma, separating, by its red-gold hotness, vaporous, life-giving air from dark water, and lavaic form from formless rock.

And so the glowing, growing *mauna* ascended upward from its origin beneath ocean void; higher and higher it bled and built upon itself. Replacing cold water with molten firmament, then cooling and condensing itself into continental solidity, at last the newly-extruded volcanic head poked its foldy face beyond sea-level concealment. Thus, from beneath ancient, amniotic nothingness emerged dry land, with primordial cries of sizzling steam. It was good.

Such were the thoughts of Lili Kapua as she surveyed the city of Honolulu, her home, from a jet-plane window. The steep Ko'olau range, Oahu's mountain spine, loomed majestically above the city's rumpled carpet of neighborhoods, Nestled like newborn pups upon her lower slopes, they seemed to suckle upon her rain-forested extremities. Further down, along Waikiki, glistening towers released millions of visitors and residents to lap sunshine and milky life from her cocoanut shores.

Seated next to Lily on the plane was her husband, David, whose prosperity had grown steadily from the storied cityscape, now 6,000 feet below them. He was reading a newspaper. She turned her head further toward the window, gazing down upon Le'ahi crater, better known as Diamond Head, as its prominence on Oahu's southern point rapidly diminished in the distance and the clouds. In just a few minutes, nothing was below them except royal-blue Pacific, specked with whitecapped points.

They were bound for San Francisco, and later on to Washington. David's primary business, *Ohana-lei* travel agency, thrived upon contacts at both of those points. Lili accompanied him on this trip because she loved to travel with her husband, but also because she would be attending a convention in Washington of the *Family Education Foundation.* She had been a member of that organization since its inception in 1972, At that time she was a science teacher. Now she served as Principal of Nu'uanu High School in the area known as *Punchbowl*, an historic neighborhood of Honolulu.

At last year's *FEF* convention, the 785 delegates who were present had elected her president. Why they would select her to lead a continent-wide educational organization from her island home in the middle of the Pacific Ocean was a mystery to her. Perhaps her leadership was a genetic trait inherited through her ancestor and namesake, Lili'uokalani, the last queen of the kingdom of Hawaii.

In the waning relevance of royal authority that had constricted and eventually ended Lili'uokalani's brief latter-19th-century reign, the deposed queen's thoughts and philanthropy had turned more and more toward education. Lili knew this, having read the queen's written account of her tenure as the last reigning monarch of the Hawaiian islands.

Back in those days, the 1890's, the world had been changing, as it always has, and always will. The ancient *noblesse oblige* that accompanied the pulsing of Lili'uokalani's royal blood was being stilled by the democratic and republican spirit of a new age—an age in which royalty was being eclipsed by constitutional government and entrepreneurship. Lili's forbear, Lili'uokalani, had not only witnessed that transition, but had experienced it firsthand. She had found herself surrounded and overcome by smart, prosperous American businessman who had systematically and quasi-legally supplanted her sovereign authority with brash political maneuvering and not-so-small military counterweight. A hundred and ten years ago, it had happened.

Lili had read amongst the lines of her ancestral queen's written legacy an earth-changing shift of direction. The constraints of diminishing royal power had diverted the alert queen's attentions away from inexpedient political intrigue. Her influence had been ostensibly extinguished, except in the hearts of her loyal, Hawaiian subjects. And so, in an effort to optimize the impact of her changing royal responsibilities, she had redirected her efforts toward the realm of education, where she had perceived continued potential in serving her people and extending their opportunities into the looming changes that would undoubtedly accompany a new century.

Ironically enough, Lili's present sojourn was an aerial retracing of the former queen's sea-and-land exploits 110 ten years ago, as she had sought to recover, for her people and her domain, the diminishing vestiges of royal authority over the Hawaiian Islands. Lili'uokalani had traveled to Washington and consulted two Presidents about setting a constitutional course that would protect the best interests of her people and their resource-rich islands. But the beating of a queen's heart for her subjects was not a rhythm that could be understood or accommodated by the bustling business and legal manipulations of an industrial age that carried with it a manifest destiny that barreled down upon unschooled native populations like a fully-loaded freight train rolling down the steep side of a Utah-red promontory.

The queen's brother, Kalakaua, whose name was now posted on every street sign along the principle boulevard of Waikiki's gleaming skyscraper beach-scape glitz, had died in San Francisco, where Lili and David were now headed at 30,000 feet. Now revered and idealized as the heroic, visionary king of a Pacific Paradise, his fateful gleanings of the monarchy's waning power to pursuade or govern had landed him in the California city in 1890. There he had undertaken medical treatments to extend his life, but the strategy proved futile. He died in San Fransisco, his last days shrouded in a 2000-mile spray of oceanic distance and an as-yet nonexistent telegraph technology. The Hawaiians had not known of King Kalakaua's death until the ship that bore his body appeared with mourning displays in Honolulu harbor.

Thus had her brother's demise thrust Lili'uokalani into that fateful position as last reigning monarch of Hawaii. And these historical events, reconstructed as they were, 112 years later in Lili Kapua's analysis of historical accounts and family legends, as well as numerous significant landmarks in the city of Honolulu which they had just passed over, occupied her fertile mind.

The regal channels of authority that had sustained societal order in an earlier age came tumbling down in the comparatively anarchic free-for-all of impending 20th century political eruptions. A gathering storm of democratic/republican zeitgeist was overpowering monarchical palaces throughout the "civilized" world in political and military cataclysms that would ultimately erupt in multiple revolutions and two world wars. The

Hawaiian dynasty, noble and protective as it was, was merely one whitecapped speck in an ocean of tsunamic events and volcanic changes that swept like lava across the face of a modernizing, democratizing world.

Now a century later, Lili Kapua's noble instincts—a sensitivity to the needs of her students and their families—had prompted her to follow the paths of leadership that had been laid out for her in this day and age. Such inclinations now pulsed through the veins of her regal heritage and identity. Caught up in these musings, she began to settle into the 5-hour flight that would land her in the city where her ancestor king had seen the last of his days on this earth.

David gently laid his hand upon her hand, resting as it was on the arm between their two first-class seats. Looking away from the newspaper, his eyes caught hers. They smiled at each other. This trip would be an adventure. It always was, when they traveled together. He had just finished reading an article in the paper about divorce rates in Honolulu county, and their supposed effects upon the lives of children in one-parent households. This had not been a problem for the Kapuas; they had stuck together through 27 years, three children, and numerous other developments. But it was a problem for the citizens of Honolulu.

David Kapua looked into the wizened face of his 52-year-old wife. He remembered her countenance as it had been before the years and wrinkles had set in, when Lili was a graduate student and he had courted her. Those joyful, brown eyes were still the same, though every feature that surrounded them had changed.

Lili's hips, about which he had been obsessively curious at the age of 27, had widened a little, having delivered three new humans into the world, but they still held the attraction and mystery they had demanded when he first laid eyes on her. As a young man, he had known little about the wifely aspects of womanhood, and even less about the wide spectrum of feminine sensitivities and aptitudes—attributes within a woman that would later, as he slowly discovered over 27 years, blossom and bear fruit like papayas, bursting with blood-red fertility on the inside, thereby adding decidedly feminine fascinations to his insufferably dull male existence.

So back then, when he had first noticed her in a *halau*, dancing the hula on Kuhio beach, Waikiki, his attention was naturally riveted upon those hips, and those hands that flowed with artistic expression and storytelling profundity, stirring his wild young male heart with unexplained passion that seemed to be broadcast from the stamen of the 'ilima flower that garnished her hair, or the veiled shape of her womanhood beneath that skirt of banana leaves, he wasn't sure which. Later, when he had moved closer to the platform, the bright attraction of those brown eyes, and her epic Hawaiian smile on full, fruit-like Hawaiian lips, and the skirted, modest mystery that Hawaiian hula dancers could project so boldly and yet so discreetly—had transfixed his attention away from other pursuits that proved to be less satisfying. He had wandered aimlessly over to Waikiki, mingling with the perennial tourists during the magic dusky hour in search of amusement or possibly a woman, and had found—Lili. Eleven months later, she became his wife.

Yes, initially it had been those swaying hula hips that demanded his attention. That was before he understood the true power and significance of womanhood. He thought he had found a woman worthy of his attentions in those hips, those eyes, those lips. Little did he know that these feminine attributes were only the titular apex of the volcanically-proportioned *mauna loa* of womanhood that would reveal itself to him during the course of their shared lives. He had had no understanding of the feminine perspective on life that would gradually, comprehensively, enrich, decorate, procreate, support, promote and extend his bland male existence. *Even though* his own mother, Eva Kapua, had provided such an exemplary picture of the great gift to humanity that was present in full womanhood, *even though* his own mother, Eva Kapua, had counseled him and prodded him along the path of human productivity and development, he had not seen the light. It was as if his eyes had been veiled in...stupidity. The stupidity of youth, the inability to focus on what is truly worthwhile and enduring in life. His eyes had been clouded by human limits. Clueless, he sauntered forth amidst the noise and haste, thinking that he knew something.

But then, that evening, at the *halau* on Waikiki, he knew...well, he *knew* those hips, or, to put it more succinctly, he *knew* that he *wanted* to know those hips, hungered to taste those ruby lips, yearned to look deeply into those brown eyes. He knew all that surfacey stuff. That was before he knew the oceanic depth of true womanhood, before he discovered during the next 28 years Lili's compass-like bearing that inexorably and unfailingly set their course continually upon and sustained all things *ohana*...all things *family*.

She seemed to have known all along the meaning of family. She understood, and manifested in all that she did, the essence of true love and community, toward her children, her students, her school and neighborhood, her church, her city, state and nation. All actions undertaken by her were for the express purpose of improving the lot of those whom she loved. *This* was the mystique that swayed so gently beneath the banana-leaf skirt. *This* was the treasure in a field...*this*, the true meaning of womanhood that had drawn him into her sphere of influence, a world that was destined, although he didn't know it at the time, to guide him through the exploits of their three offspring (as well as their own adventures) into an ever-widening world of wonder and incredibly rich experience.

He looked at her and smiled. "Thank you," he said.

"For what?" she cooed, although she knew the answer. She smiled back at him. Theirs was a bliss known only to those whose fidelity has survived the longevity of marital union...a deep satisfaction in truly knowing, and being known by, another human being.

"You know what."

"No, I don't know. You expect me to read your mind?"

"Sure. You do it all the time anyway."

She squeezed his hand, hard, as hard as she could. It was a game they played. But he allowed no reaction.

After a moment or two of the antics, he responded: "Okay. If you have to hear it out loud—thank you, Lily, for making my life bloom in a way that it never would have otherwise if you hadn't entered into it."

"Yep. I knew that's what you were going to say."

"You see—you read my mind. I knew you were doing it again."

"I can't read it, silly. But I do get lucky in my guesses sometimes."

"Okay, queen Lili. Here's one for you. I'm going to ask you a question. Tell me what question I'm going to ask you."

"You're going to ask me what Stu Alexander's address is in San Francisco."

"No."

"Well, that proves it. I can't read your mind."

"Yeah, you can. Go ahead. Try again."

"You're going to ask me how many of Alicia's volleyball games we'll miss while we're away."

"No, but since you mentioned it..."

"Three. We'll miss three games...Roosevelt, McKinley and Kuhio."

"There you go, now. While you may not be *reading* my mind, you are proactively helping me to keep priorities in order. Thank you."

"You're welcome. Guess again."

"Ah, c'mon , smartypants..."

"You're going to ask me what I plan to present to the FEF convention in Washington."

David laughed out loud. "That's it. That's what I was going to ask you about. You read my mind, and that proves it. How did you know?"

"Well, I knew you would be asking about something in *my* life, because you never tell me anything about what's going on with you."

"Oh, you're crazy as a mynah bird on a mowed lawn. I tell you stuff all the time."

"All right, Mr. Executive, give me an example of one important thing you've shared with me in the last week."

"I told you that Dole was going to make a deal with Kahuna Bank."

"Oh, big deal. I read that in the papers. Tell me something about what's going on inside of *you*, ya big kahuna."

"Nothing that's significant honey. And you haven't answered my question about what you're going to present to the FEF."

"You never asked me." She giggled, and looked out the window. The sun was going down behind them. It was a beautiful sight above the clouds.

He leaned over and kissed her. "Okay, Mrs. Kapua, what urgent educational issues are presently challenging the Family Education Foundation?"

"One problem, among many, is...the demands of single parenthood, and their effects upon students' learning processes."

He was surprised. Here was a serious answer, after their frivolous banter. He paused for a moment, reorienting his mind to the issue now at hand. "I was just reading about that in the paper."

"Oh yeah?" she responded. "Let me see."

He handed her the newspaper. She began reading the article.

Hhe continued, "But it doesn't really say anything that we haven't heard about already. The institution of marriage seems to be breaking down. Everybody knows that. And children suffer from its demise. Children of single parents have less parental support in educational pursuits, and so they perform at a lower level."

"Not necessarily. You can't make generalizations like that."

"Well, I know there are exceptions. But generally, it's true, isn't it? That's the statement that's being made in this article. Single parents simply don't have as much time for helping their kids with schoolwork."

"Educators need to be careful, David, not to affix a negative stigma upon those students from single-parent households."

"Well, certainly. But isn't it a core value of the Family Education Foundation that every student should benefit from the support of both parents?"

"Yes, David, but we don't live in a perfect world. Everybody knows *that*. The challenge presented to schools, and to families *within* those schools, is to maximize educational opportunities for all students, regardless of the parental circumstances in each household."

"It seems to me that it's just like business or anything else. The bottom line really comes down to distributing resources, and that means money. Are you going to use resources to support families, or to provide assistance to single parents and their children?"

"Our goal, which is stated in the FEF charter, (you may remember that I assisted in the writing of it in 1976) is to promote the well-being and freedom of intact families in educational institutions of all kinds—from home school associations to public schools and colleges."

David thought about that for a few seconds. Then:"With the inclusion of that phrase, 'intact families,' you are limiting your scope, and possibly stigmatizing parents and students whose family conditions do not meet the 'intact' condition."

"Yes, that's a risk we take. But times have changed since that charter was written. And we acknowledge that. Now we encourage families that stay together to support—morally, socially, and financially—families that cannot maintain unity."

"That sounds to me like a function of the churches."

"From our perspective, David, that's true, because we are members of a church, and we've benefited greatly from that association. But not everyone sees things the way we do, or shares our core values. Many people, especially these days, don't want to have anything to do with a church. And furthermore...if people *are* religiously inclined, they've got Jewish, Muslim, Buddhist, and all other faith associations to select from."

"If you ask me, honey, that's the problem right there...people have drifted away from religious belief. That's why so many families are falling apart."

"Well, I agree with you, dear. But we can't say that in public organizations. It's not politically correct."

"Why not? It's a private foundation."

"It's all about the children, David. What's best for *them*? And not just the children from families like ours."

The flight attendant, working her way down the aisle, smiled at the conversing couple and skillfully interjected a question. "Would you like something to drink?"

Lili looked up at the pretty Hawaiian woman, who was not much younger than she. Lili smiled back at her. "Cranberry juice for me, thank you." She wondered if this flight attendant was a mother, and thought for a moment about what must surely be the unique difficulties of raising children while working as a stewardess. It occurred to her to ask the woman a question about it, but she was obviously too busy dispensing drinks to appreciate such a personal inquiry at this moment in time. The woman poured cranberry juice into a plastic cup and carefully handed it to her.

"And I'll have the white wine, please," said David.

"Any way, David, the most critical task for Family Education Foundation is vigilance. We want to prevent the development in educational institutions of conditions or attitudes that work *against* family unity. We don't want to have programs in schools that damage or destroy family unity. The plight of single-parent families is just one subset within that larger agenda. The reason I'm addressing it at this convention is because it *is* a hot topic just now—the learning processes of students who are in broken homes. That's why you see that article in today's paper." She took a sip of cranberry juice and looked at him without expression.

David sipped his wine with melodramatic flair. "Ahhh...that's good thank you." He handed the stewardess a $5 bill. Then he smiled and spoke to her. "I'll bet you're a mother, aren't you?"

The stewardess couldn't stifle a healthy laugh. "Yes, as a matter of fact."

"How many times?"

"Three. They're all pretty much grown now. They're at home with my husband now. Or at least they will be, later tonight."

"That's good." David looked at her quizzically. "If you ever get tired of flying all over the place, you can come work for me at the *Ohana-lei* travel agency, on Beretania. We could use some good help."

The woman was flattered, but a little embarrassed.

Lili punched her husband playfully in the ribs. "David!" She looked at the flight attendant again and said, "Don't pay any attention to him. He just gets a little crazy whenever we're on the start of a long trip."

The friendly woman laughed and replied, "Oh, that's quite all right. I appreciate the offer. We *do* have a pretty good benefit package, you know." She pushed the cart a little farther along the aisle. "Robert will be coming in a few minutes with your meal. I hope you enjoy the flight."

Intentions

4

Beneath a cold, clear, azure sky the city of Jerusalem lay stretched upon the mountains and valleys like a fuzzy glove upon God's hand. People from all over the world had gathered here to unearth evidence of God at work among the people of the earth. Some sought a temple that no longer exists. Some sought a mosque where a prophet entered heaven. Some trod upon the cobblestones of ancient, holy real estate, pleading for reconciliation, seeking atonement for the human condition.

A man wandered beyond the dome, past the blocked-up eastern gate; curving around northward, he noticed a large open area beside the mosque. *Was this where the former temple had stood?* What a beautiful mosque.

Could not the owners of this hill sell the adjoining, vacant acre or two to those pilgrims who, standing daily at the wall below, were wailing for their wonderful temple? Why not make a deal? Such a deal. Cousin to Cousin. Temple and Mosque, Mosque and Temple...Mosque Shsmosque, Temple Shmemple. Such a deal. Everybody happy. You pray your way; I pray mine.

A man traveled outside the wall, beyond the ramparts of human religion-building, pushing the envelope of mortally human strife... through the Kidron Valley below, to the vanity-laden valley of struggle, along the groves of Gethsemane; he trod among the graves of the prophets; he ambled along the graftings of the profits. He wept. Mankind, like a flock of fluttering chickens in a barnyard, clucking, headless...*why can't we get it together?*

A man walked up the other side of the valley, through Arab neighborhoods, to a Jewish cemetery. *Oh wailing trail of human history, why allowest thou such holocaust?* Turning around, he looked back across the valley, to the mountain where he just had been, with tears:

Sons of Adam, argue all you want about real estate on your holy hill. "I'll be over here on the other side," thought he.

But the walk was over now. It was time to go to work. John Demos, reporter for XYZ, was scheduled to do a live broadcast three hours from now. The American Secretary of State and her entourage were in the ancient city to prevail upon, once again, the ancient brothers and sisters to settle their ancient differences. And John would be covering the event for XYZ.

***

Half a world away, John's face could be seen on the TV in the Jesse James Gang Grill.

He was reporting to the world about the latest official Middle East peace initiatives. Hilda Hightower interrupted her flower-watering chore for a few minutes to watch his report..

Hilda went back to pouring water from a pitcher into her begonias, rusty-red begonias that thrived in little planter boxes at the end of their rows of dining booths. Saturday morning is a good time to water flowers, a good time to get caught up in the restaurant business. Her young son, Jesse, was dutifully sweeping the place, while their teenaged daughter Joanna wiped everything down with mild disinfectant.

James was in the back washing dishes. Tim, the dishwasher man, was running late this morning. It's inconvenient, having to endure people's shortcomings, but Tim was worth it. He had worked for the James Gang for two years now, with a good track record. Tim was worth a lot more than minimum wage to this operation, and they let him know it. But this morning, he was making life a little inconvenient by his absence. Deliveries were coming in while James was busy at the dishwashing station. Hilda would just have to deal with it. Setting her waterpot down on a table in the entryway, she greeted the driver who was bringing vegetables.

"Good morning, Mrs. Hightower, do you have a busy day?" Gregarious Mr. Taylor, the vegetable man, was the James Gang's lifeline to good health and prosperity. Not only that, but he was a really cheerful guy.

"Good morning, Sid. Yes, it is a busy day. We had so many people in here last night...it's a wreck. It'll take a few hours just to get the place ready for the next batch. What have you got for me?"

"I've got olives, okra, oranges, onions. I've got celery, cilantro, salad greens and sage... there's basil, broccoli, bitter herbs and brussel sprouts. I've got lettuce, leeks, legumes... corn, cauliflower, and cucumbers. Not to mention parsley, potatoes, and tomatoes. If I ain't got it, lady, you don't need it on your salad bar. Seriously, though, what'll it be today, Hilda?"

Hilda's chuckle, which began at about the brussel sprouts, had erupted into uninhibited laughter by the end of Sid's spiel. He did this little litany once or twice a week, Hilda supposed, just to remind her and all the other merchants along his route that he had it all. Anything you need in the way of vegetables you could get from Sid, including...laughter, like vegetable soup for the soul. What a clown. But she loved him for it.

Smiling, she just looked at him. "Is there a serious bone in your body?"

"Yeah, there was at one time, but I broke it. I'm takin' up a collection for the doctor bill. Would you care to contribute?"

"Right, Sid...It's Saturday. I'll get the checkbook, you goofball."

As she reached under the register for the checkbook, Sid changed his tone a little bit:

"Did you see the demonstration down the street this morning?

"No...been so busy I haven't stepped outside. What is it?

"Animal rights activists, picketing Nayman's. They wanta do away with furs. They don't want people wearing furs, because of the cruel practices inflicted on the animals. There's a guy down there with fox stoles draped over his neck, and a sign that says 'My dead brothers.'"

"Oh."

Then they were aware of a crescendoing rumble. It seemed to be filling the little concrete canyon that was downtown Urdor with a deep, thumping sound...Harleys, a whole bunch of them, were riding through, past the restaurant, toward that area down the street where the friends of animals were conducting their vigil.

"Oh no, watch this," said Sid, "the bikers. Here they come. I don't think the friends of animals will be too pleased with their visit."

The bikers' leather jackets were glistening in the morning sunlight. They rode slowly up Main Street, high handlebars looking like Viking headgear, front-wheel chrome shock-absorbers glinting. Sid giggled. "I think it's funny."

"I hope it's funny, " Hilda retorted. " I hope neither group finds anything to confront the other about." They watched and listened as the bikers reached and passed the Naymun's department store with its gaggle of protesters down the street. Apparently there was nothing to worry about, no incident, both groups having made their statements to each other as the motorcycles strode royally between two phalanxes of animal-rights activists.

Democracy in action...both groups free to make their statements...peacefully, of course. Both groups exercising their freedom of assembly, freedom of speech, freedom of religion (it was religion to them) and both groups righteously eyeing the other as the Harley-Davidson procession thundered by with only mild taunts, with only subtly proud raising of the heads and smiles hidden behind grimaces that seemed to say *hooray for our side*, as the old Buffalo Springfield song once opined.

"It's strange, Sid, how people form themselves into groups, and then oppose other groups, everywhere, all over the world..."

"...the human condition," Sid observed, with a knowing nod. "Human depravity. It's what put Jesus on the cross."

Hilda looked quizzically at Sid. "Yeah, I suppose so. You may be right about that. I was just hearing the news about the peace talks in the middle east. I wonder if they'll ever get that settled. They've been going at it for a long time, ever since I can remember."

"Oh, it's been going on for much longer than that, much longer than you or I can remember. There's a lot of blood crying out from the ground: innocent blood, and guilty blood. Those offenses don't just go away; they get strung along from generation to generation, until violence erupts. Then they fight it out. Things might settle down a bit, but then the cycle starts over again, over and over again. Multiply that little scenario by the number of ethnic groups in the world, and you've got a real problem. And one of these days, somebody'll push the button on the technology that starts the chain reaction that puts a very unpleasant end to the whole business. It's the human condition, I tell ya, and it'll never be worked out until Jesus comes back."

"You think so, eh? Well, we'll keep an eye on it. You can put those crates in the usual spot, Sid. Thanks. I've still got a lot of work to do."

"No problem, Hilda," said Sid with a big grin. "Thank *you!*"

Sid's smiling face followed the direction of the man who just now was entering the restaurant. "How you doing?" said he.

"Doing all right, You?"

"can't complain: nobody'll listen." Sid was always ready to make a joke, even if the world was in such a perilous predicament. He went out to the truck and began rolling the crates of vegetables in on his dolly.

Hilda looked at Daniel Derwin walking in. "What happened to you yesterday?"

"Sorry I didn't make it Hilda; I had a little accident on the way over here. But I've got what you and James are looking for right here. Have you got a few minutes?"

"I think James is finishing some stuff in the back, and it'll be just a few minutes. You want a cup of coffee?"

"I'd love to have one. Thank you."

Daniel sat in a booth and amused himself with a menu, while keeping one eye on the XYZ news on the TV in the corner...a story about a woman who breeds Rottweillers.

Hilda brought the coffee and he added the cream and sugar. Good, dark coffee, but he liked to lighten it up quite a bit.

"So you had an accident yesterday?"

"Yeah, I rear-ended a car on Pretoria Parkway, by the Wal-Mart."

"Anybody hurt?"

"Nah...well, the guy did take a punch at me." Daniel laughed like it was no big deal.

"You're kidding." Following Daniel's lead, she laughed also. "Where did he hit you?"

"Uh, on the side of my face...right here. That's what this little bandage is." He mugged for her, still making a joke of it.

"Yeah, right. People are so nutso any more. What would make a guy so mad to do a thing like that? A little busted-up bumper?"

"I think he was just having a bad day. I picked a bad time to interrupt it. Of course, my timing wasn't so convenient for my agenda either. You see, I never made it over here. I called James and told him."

"Yeah, he said you had called. It's just as well. Last night was a zoo, and it was all we could do to get ready for it. I'm kinda glad in a way that you didn't get over here 'til this morning." Her eyes began to follow something on the other side of the booth. Hilda redirected her speaking, "Well, *hello*. Look what the cat dragged in."

Tim, the dishwasher man, limped over to the booth. "...not a bad idea to have a cat around in the restaurant business: it keeps the mice down."

"I think James was ready to skin you alive last night. Jesse had to wash dishes the whole night; eleven-year old boy just can't keep up with a professional, you know. We missed you. You buckin' for another raise or somethin'? There are better ways..."

"I'm sorry. I had an accident."

"You too? What is this, an epidemic of klutzes?"

"I fell off a mountain."

"Okay, mister wiseguy, and you're still in one piece? This is Daniel, our architect, by the way. Daniel, meet Tim. Speaking of rear ends. He keeps the rear end of this place going."

They shook hands and greeted.

"We were at Seneca Rocks yesterday, bouldering. I got a little sloppy and, the next thing I knew I was on the ground."

"Oh?" Hilda's expression changed to one of genuine concern. "How far did you fall?"

"About 20 feet, but it was kind of a slide down. I turned my ankle."

"I'm sorry to hear it, Tim. Well, thanks for showing up today. I do wish you had called though."

"I apologize for not letting you know. The cell phone got smashed, and then I just never got around to it. It took us a lot longer to get out of there, and then Claire made me go to the ER in Winchester and get it checked out. They X-rayed it and wrapped it with an Ace bandage."

"Thank God, and you can still wash dishes. You don't need to sprint in order to do that, right?"

"Right. Well, I'm right on it."

James walked out of the kitchen. "Right on what? The dishes? They're done, good buddy."

"Sorry, James. But I'm good to go now."

"Okay, glad you made it. Well there are plenty of potatoes back there that Sid just brought in. You can get right on it."

Tim limped toward the kitchen, sheepishly.

"And be careful on that leg. Stunts are for rock-climbers, not dishwashers. And you know which one you are when you're working for the James Gang. If you need any help tonight, let me know and I'll get Jesse to help you. He's pretty good at it now, learned a lot about efficiency last night thanks to your absence."

"Righto."

James turned his big strawberry-blonde frame toward Daniel. One task after another in the life of an entrepreneurial small-business cook-chief dishwasher. "Helloooo, Daniel" Welcome to the wild west. I've been waiting weeks to see what you came up with."

"It's a silk purse made from a sow's ear," offered Daniel, risking an editorial comment about the old building that would soon become home to the Jesse James Gang Grille."

"If anybody can do it, Daniel, I know you can."

"The main problem I've had so far is with the windows: there aren't enough of them."

"Can that be fixed?"

"Sure, we can do anything you want, and it probably will involve *fixed* glass." Daniel smiled at his own pun. And so did James, as he sat in the booth, opposite Daniel.

"I'll bring you some coffee, dear."

"Thank you, love."

"How 'bout a refill, Daniel?"

"Got any decaf yet, this time of day?"

"That can be arranged. You're a pretty special person."

"Thank you, Hilda."

At last, Daniel was able to offer the presentation that he had intended for yesterday afternoon, before the unfortunate incident had delayed it by about 14 hours. He spoke.

"James, as you know, there are plusses, and there are minuses to having glass in a public building where people gather. There's the energy factor; it'll cost you more to heat...the more glass you have. On the other hand, people love natural light. Especially these days, they want windows. A lot of this decision has to do with what time of day do you want to be feeding people? Are you going for the dinner crowd? I know you are. Are you going for the lunch crowd? Yes, okay." He drained his coffee cup. "So you want to be feeding people all day long.

Breakfast? Yeah, sure, why not? Okay. Some large windows will brighten the place up nicely, and provide just the feel of openness that active people like to have when they're having a good time. Then at night, they can cozy up and get intimate, with the candlelight and so forth, while there's still a perception that this is a happenin' place with the city lights coming in from outside.

Got it?

"Right, you're right on it."

"Now, this is gonna cost a little bit, because this old free-standing drug store was built 20 years ago. It's got 8-foot high masonry in the front wall, will little transome-type windows at the top. The windows are not what we're looking for, but they're a real blessing—because of them we have the support we need to knock the masonry sills out below, then extend the glass openings downward to afford us some nice, **big** windows, like so." Daniel whipped out the plans, the page already turned to the front elevation drawing, and laid it on the table facing James.

Daniel was making a point about the windows. But, in fact, he was at this moment making an essential *first impression* as he had known he would be, while James looked at the front of the building that Daniel had redesigned. The point about the windows was, as Daniel had anticipated, well-taken. But what he was really watching for in James' face, was the response to the whole concept...the frontal appearance of his new restaurant. Displayed in large sandblasted letters arched over the middle third of the building's face was the name: Jesse James Gang Grille, complete with cactus in the foreground, and "mountain" lines in the background.

"Looks good to me," said James. "When do we start?"

Daniel laughed out loud. "You're kidding, right? Is that all you have to say about it? You haven't even seen the rest of it."

"Looks good to me. I don't know anything about remodeling buildings. I'm the cook, remember?" James guffawed a hearty laugh. He knew what he was doing. He knew how to work with people. That was a large part of his success. "Really, though, Daniel, I think you've got the right idea. This represents in bricks and mortar exactly what we talked about. I know it'll work. The success of the business is really all about the food, anyway. My biggest concern is keeping the quality up when we're serving twice as many people every day."

Parties
5

Wanda saw a guy in the next parking lot over. He looked like a likely candidate, a gullible, kindly sort. He didn't notice her approach his car from the rear; he was taking something out of the back seat, had the door open. Wanda put on her best pained expression.

"Excuse me, sir, could you take a minute to help me an' my sister out. We're trying to get to Philadelphia and we're about to run out of gas. Our dad is in the hospital dying, in Philly. Lung cancer. We left Florida a couple of days ago and we're trying to get there to see him before he's gone. We haven't had anything to eat except doughnuts since yesterday. You think you could help us out with somethin'?"

The kindly man, saint or fool, took out his wallet and handed the thin woman a ten-dollar bill. He didn't think about it; he just did it. Saint or fool?

Wanda was lucky that way. "Thanks so much. God bless you." Scampering back to the old van that was parked beside a gas pump, she seemed anxious to seal the deal with an expeditious departure before the kindly man could, you know, change his mind.

After Wanda jumped in the passenger seat and closed the door, the other woman got the van going, turned onto busy street and drove a few blocks to a breakfast diner.

Bridget and Wanda went inside, ordered coffee and scrambled eggs with bacon, went in the bathroom, went back to the counter, ate their breakfasts, paid the bill, went back out in the parking lot, lit up cigarettes, got back in the van and headed out.

Out of the city of Urdor, past shopping centers, discount stores, gas stations, fast-food places, real estate offices, insurance agencies, tire dealers, bars, ice cream shoppes, convenience stores, thrift stores, auto dealerships, car-washes, lumberyards, palm readers, nurseries, specialty shops, auto-detailing places, a junkyard, a few farms, a stockyard. After about 12 miles, they made a right turn that took them another three miles on a country road. Then they made another right turn onto a gravel road, about a mile and then they were at home. It was a double-wide with a little porch built onto it, about ten years old. It had seen better days, but the roof was still good. Protruding from a galvanized metal window covering was a wood-stove flue with smoke coming out of it.

Wanda and Bridget got out of the van, cigarettes drooping from their mouths. Wanda walked around to the back of the van, opened the hatchback. She began hauling some boxes into the house, a bunch of boxes. Bridget helped her. The boxes were filled with cough syrup, cold medicines, and a few other selected products, just what Buzz would need for making the next batch of methamphetamine.

As soon as she had shut the car door, Wanda heard the wailing of her daughter inside the house.

The trailer door was open; she kicked open the screen door and entered into the chamber that mingled the sick-sweet smell of cooking crank, stale hot dogs, old diapers and cigarette smoke. six-year old Jonda was jumping on the sofa and yelling. Wanda walked over to the child, slapped her on the butt, told her to shut up. Jonda's volume increased; she jumped from the sofa to the floor and ran down the hall to her room. Then there was no more whining, only the muted roar of Buzz's heavy metal in the back room.

The place was dark, all the blinds shut. Bridget closed the front door; it wasn't supposed to be open. The two women tossed their cargo in a corner of the room and collapsed on the furniture. Bridget turned the TV on and began watching *Batman* reruns.

Wanda pulled out her cell phone, punched a number.

"When you comin' over here?"

The voice on the other end: "I'm not comin' there. You're comin' here."

"I just came from Urdor." Wanda was irritated. Gas wasn't cheap, and energy wasn't something she had a lot of either.

The voice on the other end: "You want what I got?...or not?"

"Come on, Blimp, don't make me..."

"You want what I got?...or not?"

"Yeah, right." She snapped the phone shut.

Wanda went in the kitchen, got a beer and a doughnut, returned to the living room and plopped on the sofa next to Bridget.

"Wanna go to a party?"

"Whose party?"

"Blimp, in a little while."

Buzz came out from the hallway, scratching his belly beneath a shirt that was too small for him. "Floo's comin' over in a little while to get a load. You got an empty box?"

"I'll have one in a minute, after I unload this stuff." She was watching Batman jump into his Batmobile.

Buzz grabbed one of the boxes that they had just brought in. He disappeared into the hallway, and into his special room, his lab.

After *Batman* and *I Dream of Jeannie*, Floo came in. He was a thin guy with long hair and short chains, tattoos. Buzz came into the room with a box, handed it to Floo.

"Thanks a lot, man. I owe ya."

"No, you don't owe me. You got what it takes...or don't you?"

"Yeah, man, I got it. I was talking about next week. I might be a little short next week."

"We'll talk about that next week, Floo." But you know you gotta be prepared." Buzz flashed a sinister, fakey smile. "You know what I'm sayin' to ya, man?"

"Yeah, okay, man. That's cool. I'll see you next week, my man." Floo gave a little sweeping flourish with his fist in the air, like a worn-out 'right-on' gesture. He hung his head down like a cool dude, opened the door and slid on out of the trailer.

When Floo was gone, Wanda looked at Buzz and said: "Come on, let's go to Blimp's. He's having a party."

"I don't want go to no party till its dark. Just chill." He went in the kitchen, grabbed a couple beers, handed one to her, then went back into his lab.

When it was dark, they all four got in the van and drove back into Urdor. Wanda drove the van to Blimp's place, a large house near the beltway, with rambling porch. It had once been a crown jewel of an affluent neighborhood. The house looked nice enough at night with candles in the windows, a bunch of cars parked outside, and revelers on the porch. A closer inspection, however, might reveal a house that was in dire need of a paint job and a little TLC.

When Buzz, Wanda, Bridget walked in with Jonda in tow, they encountered a diverse menagerie of Urdor's underground good-timing crowd: working stiffs, rednecks, hippies, bikers, and everything in between. The music was loud, but not loud enough to attract any neighbors' attention.

Finally, Bridget saw someone she knew: a girl she had worked with at Dollar World. But Bridget couldn't remember her name.

"Hey, how you been?"

"I'm still at the Dollar World. Rainey gave me a raise last week, and I still bowl a lot on the weekends."

"I never would've thought that anybody could get a raise out of that fella."

"He's been good to me. We got a huge shipment of Christmas decorations in, back in September. I stacked 'em all in the back, then got into a couple of boxes, made a display on the middle aisle using a little bit of everything we had, including the artificial tree and the blow-up Santa Claus. Rainey really like it. He gave me a 50-cent raise."

"Sweet."

"He's been doin' a lot for me. His wife got diabetes a coupla months ago, had to go in the hospital for two weeks. He spent so much time gone, I practically ran the place without him. He gave me keys and everything. I bought a car. It's a '87 Bonneville, emerald green, leather upholstery. It runs good. My brother Billy worked on it for me, put a new head on it. The old one was cracked. So I let him drive it whenever he wants to. But he doesn't need it much, on account of he lives so close to work. He works at the PayLo on Royster. He works all night. You can go in there any time of night, just about, and he'll be there. You ever been in there?"

"You ought to go sometime. You'd like Billy. He was in Iraq for a year. He knows 'bout everybody in the neighborhood. But did you know the city's getting' ready to run the new beltway loop through there? They're takin' a bunch of houses, all in a row...all along Poydras Street and Bosphorus, right in there, you know."

"Are they taking your house?"

"No, it's gonna come a couple blocks away from where we live. My momma lives there; my dad died three months ago, emphysema; we came here from West Virginia, you know. He had been in the coal mines for 30 years. I guess it got to him. But he was good to me; he's the one that taught my brother to work on cars..."

"Hey, 'scuse me. I got to go for a minute. I see someone I need to talk to. Nice talking to ya, okay. I'll see you in a little bit."

Bridget had seen her old boyfriend, Eddy, but he was with another girl. He had his arm around the girl in a dominant kind of half-embrace. In the other hand was a beer. Bridget didn't expect much from him, but she was warming up to the possibility of talking to someone besides DollarWorld girl. Extricating herself, Bridget went over to Eddy, slapped him on the arm and tried to greet him.

But he was obviously drunk. He snubbed her.

She took the hint, moved on, wandering around the large room trying to act cool. She needed a drink, something to take the edge off the meth that she was coming down from. She went in the kitchen and found some wine in the refrigerator. Then a guy started talking to her. He wasn't the type that she usually hung with.

"Hi, my name is Marcus Derwin. What's yours?"

Well, I didn't expect to meet Mr. America. Wuzzup with this guy? "I'm Bridget, Bridget Golden."

"What brings you here tonight, Bridget?"

Pretty blunt, asking personal questions right off the bat. "I'm here with a couple of friends of mine."

"Do you live around here?"

"Um, yeah." She didn't want to tell him that she wasn't quite sure where she was living right now. She had been sleeping on the sofa at Wanda's place.

"Where do you live, Bridget?"

Who wants to know, buster? Can't you do anything besides ask personal questions? "I live, uh, out by the river, with some friends."

Marcus smiled at her. "I've been working at the Glenharden Mall, doing some renovation. You ought to come check it out some time."

You want to start me a charge account at Bloom's while I'm there? Then I'd have a reason to be there. "Well, what is it you do there?

"I'm working with a crew of guys refurbishing the mall. We've been working on the east entrance, erecting wooden beams in the entryway. It adds a little pizzazz to the place. Updates it, so it doesn't look so...70's. We've also been upfitting a coffee shop in there, adding wainscoting and some other decorative wood. Same deal. Making the place look old, so it doesn't look so old, or...making the place look new so it doesn't look so old, or making it look old, so it doesn't look so new..." He busted out laughing.

Bridget found herself unexpectedly joining in his laughter. *What's he so happy about?*

"I'm really happy to meet you, Bridget."

Oh, so now he's a mindreader. You're not going anywhere, are you? "Well, Marcus, uh...what else do you like to do?"

"I like to...I like ...'blue satin sashes, snowflakes that fall on my nose and eyelashes, brown paper packages tied up with string. These are a few of my favorite things.'" He was laughing *again.* "Really, though, I like riding my bicycle. I ride around the city a lot. You wanna go riding tomorrow?"

He really is Mr. Clean. Next thing, he'll be opening the door for me.

"Let's go outside for a few minutes, Bridget. It's stuffy in here, all these cigarettes..."

I'll have to stop smoking.

"Come on, I won't hurt you or anything." Smiling.

He stepped over to the door that would open from the kitchen to the back porch. He opened the door. "Come on. Let's get some fresh air."

Bridget was starting to wonder if she had put on glass slippers. What could she do but step out with him into that placid, cool evening? For the first time, she really looked at Marcus. He wasn't the best looking guy. But he was no hunchback of Notre Dame either. The dark brown hair and greenish eyes made her think of her father, whom she had not seen in at least a year.

"I only knew one person, a fellow I work with, at this party before I met you, Bridget."

"I just kinda ended up here by accident myself, Marcus. Or maybe it wasn't an accident."

"Hey, there aren't any *real* accidents in life. Everything that happens, happens for a reason."

"And what do you suppose is the reason for your coming here tonight?" Her mind was starting to wake up a little now. It seemed like she'd been in a fog for the last year or so. Bridget surprised herself at even asking such a question. She hadn't known herself to be so philosophical. It must be Marcus. *He's philosophical.*

"Well, Bridget, the only conclusion I can come to is that I came here tonight so that I could meet you."

Yeah, right. What book did you pull that line from? But she wanted it to be so. She wanted to agree with him. She could think of no clever response, nothing to say except: "Yes."

"Where did you come from?"

"Cleveland."

"What brought you here?"

"I started at Lincoln a couple of years ago, but dropped out."

"I just, uh, I don't know, just...I wanted to make some money, get a job, you know."

"So, what did you do when you dropped out of school?"

"Not much, really, I just worked." She looked around the back yard. She dimly discerned unidentifiable junk lying around in the darkness. "Um...at Dollar World."

"Did you like working there?"

"No." *Why is he so persistent?* "No. Who's asking all the questions around here? What about you? Where'd you come from? Don't you have a life?"

"Dallas, Texas. My brother came up here to study architecture at Lincoln, and I followed him. I did a couple of years of school too, but had no direction in it, so I've been doing construction work for him."

There was a silence, except for the noise of the party inside. *He's got it together.* "What's your brother's name?"

"Daniel. He's an ambitious type. Me, I'm just along for the ride."

"Well, Marcus, you seem pretty focused to me."

He laughed, looking up at the sky, then started gently kicking a smooth stone that happened to be on the deck. He looked directly at her. "Oh yeah? And what would you think I'd be focused on?"

"Well, you focused on me, started asking me all these meddlesome questions."

"Oh, I'm sorry--"

"No, it's nothing really. It's kind of nice, actually."

"Surely you know, uh," He looked down at the little stone. "Bridget, that you're a woman who could easily draw a man's attention."

"But I don't like attention."

"Right." He laughed again. "You just want to be ignored by the universe, and all the men in it."

"I had too much attention growing up."

"You're kidding, right? How could that be a problem? I think the world is probably screwed up mostly because kids don't get enough attention while growing up. And you're complaining about getting too much of it?"

"I guess that didn't come out right. Maybe I, uh, just didn't have enough space of my own."

"Oh, so you shared a room with a sister who got on your nerves. Is that it?"

"No, my sister kept to herself, and we had separate rooms. She's an achiever, though; I wasn't. I guess that's what I'm trying to say. She was always doing school meetings, or violin lessons, or some productive activity."

"Yeah, welcome to the club. That sounds like my brother. "
He paused, looked up at the eerily-glowing urban night sky. "But, did you find anything to occupy yourself with while growing up?"

"I like taking pictures." She paused for a few seconds. A calico cat approached Bridget's feet and began caressing her legs with its fur. She bent down and petted it. The cat began meowing. "...and making collages. I like putting images together with color."

"So I bet you studied art, or photography, at the university."

"Yes. I started to."

"And then what?"

"I guess I, school just wasn't as important to me as I had thought it would be."

"And you dropped out?"

"It's not that I dropped out. It's just that, I didn't go back last fall."

"I hear ya. That was pretty much the same for me, except it's been a year and a half ago that I didn't go back. What did you do then?"

"Well, I was kind of messed up. It's a long story."

"I'm listening." He looked into her eyes and smiled.

"Yeah, you would be. You're too polite."

"I can be mean if you like. Would you prefer to meet a mean guy at a weird party on a Saturday night?" He stepped back, spread his arms dramatically, gently mocking her jaded attitude. She could see his raised eyebrows in the moonlight. He had big ears.

Someone had turned up the music inside. The bass was thumping through the house walls.

"I'm a spoiled princess who left a jeweler father and a doting mother to come here and... and, I don't know what. You ask too many questions."

But she wasn't mad, just a little exasperated with herself.

"And you haven't answered all of them yet." He smiled, again looking right at her. As far as he was concerned, the interview was just beginning.

"I **wanted** to work at Dollar World." She raised her chin, nodded melodramatically, as if pretending to convince him.

Marcus thought she looked like a grown-up Shirley Temple. "Yes, Bridget. Everybody wants to work there." lol.

"Well, I did. It was time for me to generate some funds of my own. I needed a job, and that's the best I could do at the time."

"OK. So you worked at Dollar World. What was that like?"

"Oh, it was an education, believe me." She laughed, feeling refreshed. It had been a long time since she had been so relaxed in conversation with another person.

"What did you learn?"

"You're so persistent, Marcus." She slapped his arm playfully. "What's your last name again?" She was loving his penetrating questions.

"Derwin."

" Let's just say, Marcus Derwin, I learned things that I wouldn't have learned at the university."

"Like for instance..."

"People are gullible. They're like sheep; you can lead them around by the nose and make them buy stuff that they don't need, just by, um," Bridget laughed and extended her arm in a vaguely rhetorical waving gesture. "...by sticking a display in front of them in the aisle where they'll be shopping." She took a sip of wine from the plastic cup in her hand.

"I understand. That reminds me of the renovation thing I was telling you about, how fickle people are. If you just rearrange the mall every few years, they think they're going to a cool place, and so they'll spend money."

"Yes, fickle. That's exactly right. People are fickle and gullible."

They had reached a little point of agreement about life in a world populated by human beings. Somewhere in the dark disarray of this unfamiliar back yard, a nightingale began to sing.

"How long did you work there? And you are talking about the Dollar World on Westside Avenue, right?

"Yes, about three months. Then I went over to Mama Lu's Diner, just down the road from there. I worked there until, oh, just two weeks ago, actually."

"And then what happened?"

"Well, Marcus, if you must know, it got back to the 'attention' thing again. This time, it was too much attention from the manager. He kept wanting to hit on me. Finally, I just left the place rather suddenly one night, with a broken bowl of spilt chili on the floor." She covered her mouth, laughing. "...and him practically chasing me around the tables."

"Good for you."

"Yeah, I made the break. But there I was back at Go again, but without the $200."

"Where were you living?"

" I had a little upstairs dive just a few blocks from there. "

"*Had* a dive? Where do you live now?"

"I'm staying with some friends, uh, out by the river--" She stopped talking for a second, then turned her head and faced him directly for the first time. As she did, wavy brown hair swung loosely across her shoulders. "But that's enough about me, buster. What about you? Do you have a life? Where did you come from? I'm halfway expecting you to step into the nearest phone booth and change clothes before disappearing."

She is beautiful. "What?"

"...a phone booth, you know, like Superman."

They laughed. Marcus felt his ears getting hot, and his heart speeding up. "Oh, yeah, Lois Lane, I mean, Clark Kent, or..."

"Where'd you **come** from, silly?" She lowered her head to try and get his eye contact again, as he hung his head in embarrassment. She smiled largely. "Krypton? Mars?"

"Dallas, Texas." He looked up at her again, reveling with the mirth he had found in her brown eyes. "...er, well, we had come from Philadelphia originally, but we moved to Dallas when I was nine."

"And what kind of home was yours?"

"It was, er, comfortable. My dad was a lawyer, mom, a schoolteacher. Nothing special about it. They loved me and my brother; they loved each other. I played basketball in high school, and, when I graduated, followed Daniel up here to go to Lincoln. He was studying architecture."

"And what did you study?"

He was loving her eyes. "er, just general college stuff. I guess I'd have become a business major if I had stayed with it."

"So, you could always go back and finish if you want to?"

"Yeah." He was stroking the cat, which was up on the deck rail now, purring for them.

"So, Marcus, do you like working with wood?"

"Yeah, it's great. I like it more than studying. In wood, you get immediate results."

"...like taking pictures and making collages."

"Right." He sighed, looking up at the dark trees, which had just rustled in a faint breeze. Then he had a crazy thought from nowhere about making children.

There was a very pleasant silence, except for the little wind, the dull thumping of the party inside, and the cat's meow. Bridget was meditating on something.

In a quiet, ponderous tone, she asked him, "Marcus...what keeps you...going? What motivates you to...to get up in the morning and go to work or whatever?"

Marcus was surprised by the question. "Do you want an honest answer?"

"Well, no, *duh?*" She laughed. It felt good to laugh. This was like puppy love. "Yes., I do want an honest answer, Marcus." They were playing a game now, but they both were starting to know what the object of the game was. It was exciting.

He looked up, breathed deeply, thought he'd make the game a little more playful. Lately, he had gotten into a rather sarcastic mode of talking about and relating to the world. It was because of the guys he was working with. "What keeps me going is," He stopped, and straightened his body. "...crack." He spoke it with a deadpan expression.

Bridget seemed to freeze. Her eyes turned away, signaling some tidal change inside her head.

She didn't get the joke, and it was a bad one anyway. "No, no, no. Just **kidding**," said Marcus, trying to restore those prior moments of quiet glee.

But something had captured her mirth, and seemed to have taken it, and her, as prisoner. He gently put his hand on her shoulder. And, after a moment, he was aware that she was weeping. Without knowing it, he had somehow pierced deep inside of her. Without knowing it, he had reached down into the soft, vulnerable flesh of her heart, and he had touched her. He had penetrated some hidden wound with his probing questions, but especially with his stupid, ill-timed little joke.

How could he have known? Was he trying to imply something? And, what, what the hell have I been doing with my life? This person I have become--it is not **me**. *What happened to me?* What had happened to Bridget?

"Bridget, I'm sorry if I..."

"It's all right. It's nothing, really." She was wiping her eyes.

"I didn't mean to, well, I hardly know you." He was desperate to repair whatever breach he had inflicted. "Bridget, let's get out of here. Let's go somewhere. You hungry? You want to go get something to eat?"

She was afraid of him, not afraid of what he might do to her, but afraid of the power that he already had over her... whatever it was, her *heart*. She could not go with him now. She was falling apart inside, afraid of what might happen. She was still crying a little, but suddenly found herself captivated, strangely, by an intense joy, an intense hope that she had not known for a very long time, if ever.

"Marcus."

"What?"

"Marcus, I need to go with my friends now."

"What?" It couldn't end like this. *Wilt thou leave me so unsatisfied?* "Well, Bridget, we...." He was stammering. "Let's do something tomorrow."

She wiped her eyes again, then gently picked up the calico cat. Her response was torturously slow, but finally it came: "That would be good, Marcus."

"Er, what do you want to do?"

"Oh, I don't know." She tossed her head back, and he was surprised when she released a little laugh that seemed to have surfaced from some deep well within her.

"We'll go for a bike ride." Marcus was grasping at straws, but he did feel better. Her laugh had brought them back to the place of repose that had been cracked by his ill-timed venture into sarcasm.

"Yes, that would be good." First grasp worked.

"I'll pick you up."

"No." She hesitated. "No. I'll meet you. Where do you want to meet?"

"Sanderson Park, by the bear habitat. What time?"

"One o'clock?"

"One o'clock it is. Are you sure you don't want to get something to eat now?"

"I'm sure."

But he was waiting for something to change. *Surely she's hungry right now.*

She was thinking about something else. "Marcus."

"What?"

"I don't have a bike."

He breathed a sigh of relief. "Is that all? I've got an extra one you can use. I'll meet you with the bikes at 1 o'clock."

"Okay." Bridget was giggling now. She felt so silly. Nothing like this had ever happened before.

"What do you want me do to now, Bridget, before I leave here? Is there anything I can do for you now?"

"Nope. I'll be fine." Gazing downward, she released a little droplet of joy.

She's resolute. There's something pithy and substantial down there inside of her. "Okay, Bridget, I'm going to leave now," he said slowly, still waiting for something to change. It was back to being a game now: *Slowly I turn, step by step, inch by inch.*

"Go, you wild man, I'll see you tomorrow." She was blowing her nose. She hadn't done or felt anything like this in so long.

"Okay, Bridget. I'm outa here." He smiled, and raised his hands in mock surrender; he started backing away toward the porch steps.

Suddenly, she stretched her neck out. Without touching him, she kissed him on the cheek, then stepped away.

Yes. Now he was wondering at her; he felt drunk with the mystery of her femininity, which was so boldly, so suddenly, rearranging his head. But he was managing a recovery from this unexpected little gift. Slowly, he said, "One o'clock, then, tomorrow. You'll be there?"

"I'll be there," she said.

Gingerly, he stepped off the porch. There was no need to go back inside. He had discovered what he had been looking for when he came to this strange party.

And then, as quickly as he had appeared, he was gone.

Twenty minutes later, Bridget was still standing on this back porch where she had never been before. The night was quiet, except for the thumping of music from inside the house, and the muffled sound of partying that accompanied its monotony of noise. Bridget knew what she needed to do. It was time to extricate herself: she needed a *shabat* from the self-effort that she had gotten herself into.

Bridget spoke to no one, but simply stepped off the porch and began walking...around the back of the rambling, ramshackle house, past a garage; she walked along the row of cars and trucks that were parked in the driveway like silent metallic dragons. When she got to the sidewalk, Bridget made an abrupt right turn; staying on the sidewalk, she sojourned along the dark residential street, quiet except for the distantly faint murmur of traffic several blocks away. *Who are all these people, that live in these contented houses? What do they do?* The sedate character of this neighborhood was fascinating. It was alien to her, but then it wasn't really. It wasn't really. She had originated in a place like this, although not nearly as shabby. There was no reason, really, to have alienated herself from this. It wasn't so bad. These people in these houses were probably decent people; there was evidence of their decency— swingsets and bicycles in the yard. Somehow, to Bridget, the children's toys in some of these small yards represented something very decent, very *natural.* There was an order here; it was not alien to who she was. It was alien only to what she had become, or to what she knew she was becoming. She needed a *shabat* from the self-effort that she had gotten herself into.

Bridget walked seven blocks until she reached Commonwealth Avenue. Then she turned left and went another four. When she reached Venture Boulevard, she waited at the bus stop for fifteen minutes or so. She got on the Westside bus, rode for twenty minutes or so through the bright, traffic-laden night. She knew where she wanted to go.

There were eleven people on the bus, spread apart. With no one very near to her, Bridget raised her right leg and crossed it over her left, like a man might do. She discreetly reached inside the hem of her jeans and retrieved, from a hidden pocket that she herself had sewn into the garment, a white plastic card. The name embossed on the debit card was: Bridget Golden.

Upon arriving at her intended destination, Bridget stepped off the bus and walked over to an ATM about 30 yards away, inserted the card, punched some numbers, obtained what she needed. She walked through a large parking lot to an all-night Target. It had been a year or more since she had done anything like this. The recovered familiarity of it was starting to envelope her like a warm glove. Grabbing a cart, she walked around the store, in no hurry. She chose a stylish backpack, flannel nightgown, new underwear, a couple of pretty blouses, belt, running shoes, new jeans, even a dress...toothbrush, toothpaste, shampoo, deodorant, skin lotion, etc., two plastic bowls, coffee mug, a box of granola, small bunch of bananas, and a quart of milk. Then she checked out. Outside, she stuffed most of the stuff in the backpack and carried the rest in one of the plastic bags.

Bridget walked along Westside Drive for about five minutes. She came to a motel, the *Traveler's Inn*. She went inside, told the night clerk she wanted a room for a week, displayed her Ohio driver's license and a credit card, and checked in. After walking up a flight of stairs, she found room 207, inserted the key card, entered what would be her domicile for the next week. The backpack and bag she tossed on the bed. Grabbing the ice bucket, she walked down the hall, found an ice machine, filled the bucket, returned to the room. She opened the box of granola, sliced a banana into little discs and dropped them onto the cereal. After opening the milk and pouring an ample amount into the cereal bowl, she placed the quart container in the ice bucket.

Bridget ate her granola and milk. She slipped into the new flannel nightgown, then between the cool sheets. She slept like the baby she was.

Conflicts
6

On the first day of the week, things slow down a little bit in America. Likewise, James Hightower. He never tried to operate his restaurant on the first day of the week. It was just too much work; there had to be a break in the action somewhere.

He walked out in the yard and got the newspaper. Coffee was brewing in the kitchen. Nobody else was up yet. Back in the kitchen, he was sitting at the table with coffee and toast with marmalade. He noticed a headline in the paper: *School Board: Annual Scores Down.* He began reading the article.

James had chosen the restaurant business because he could get immediate results from it. If you cut up enough vegetables, made a good selection of meat and threw it in a pot, you could make a pretty good batch of soup, if you didn't get in a big hurry. Good results. Put the right stuff in— get something good out of it.

The truth is, he had not *chosen* the restaurant business; it had chosen him. Really, he drifted into it, for the aforementioned reason: results. It seemed more productive than, say, *teaching*, which had been his first choice for a profession. James had started out as a high school English teacher, and had done that for two years. As it turned out, though, there was incongruence between his way of approaching the task of teaching, and the actual practice of it.

In James' view, what kids really need to do is learn how to read. And that was a prospect that each one could approach on his/her own terms. The teacher would act as a coach, equipping each student with skills, the basic knowledge of the alphabet with all its millions of possibilities. And what kids really needed do, in order to learn how to read, was, well...to read. They just needed to read. He wanted to find a way to motivate them toward that activity. He wanted to divert their delicate attention spans away from TV and other passive electronic stultifiers.

Over the course of a couple years, however, it seemed that teaching, as it existed in the system, had become too complicated for its own good. In some ways, it was backwards. Instead of encouraging a child to read and comprehend texts on a level appropriate to the child's proficiency, a teacher was expected to arrange adult-generated analytical concepts in a convoluted world of literary analysis and conventional grammar.

Then, the child was expected to extract all of the intangible ideas and principles from what would otherwise be interesting stories, and to arrange those extractions into little conceptual boxes like *irony, metaphor, and personification.*

Certainly, James had concluded, these analytical disciplines were valuable for some students, those who were inclined toward such conceptual regimens. But then there were other groups of kids whose motivations, whose attributes and aptitudes, whose *intelligences*, were imminently practical, experiential, not so analytical. And many of these kids were smart. *Couldn't they read a book and just enjoy it? Talk about it with their classmates? Couldn't a teacher then, judiciously, place a new book in their hands and say, "Here. Now see what you think of this one."*

James did not by any means claim infallibility or any special knowledge in these matters. He just discovered that it was not for him. He would leave the literary analysis, *and* the plethora of grammatical corrections, to other adults who were better suited for it than he. But this dilemma wasn't even the primary determinant of his egress from the teaching profession. There were a few other reasons: students' rudeness, inattentiveness, lack of respect, disdain for discipline, apathy, terrible home situations, neglect from parents, neglect *of* parents, need for continual repetition, eternal defaulting to sentence fragments and run-on sentences which he was supposed to somehow correct, constant use of the word *like*, pierced tongues, sexual obsessions and junk-food dependencies, among other things.

So James had decided to cook for people, and feed them. It was easier, and, he later discovered, more lucrative. On this particular Sunday morning, as he sipped coffee, he noticed that the price of tea in China was up. Interesting.

After a little while, Hilda, Jesse and Joanna got up. The family ate breakfast and went to church.

***

At about noon, Bridget woke up. What a glorious sleep it was. She took a shower, dressed in new clothes, and walked three quarters of a mile to Sanderson Park. Along the way, she stopped at a deli for lox cheese and a bagel.

The day was bright and blustery, and cool, about 45 degrees. It wasn't the best day to ride a bike, but was certain to be *invigorating*. At the appointed time, Bridget was at the appointed place, feeling a little self-conscious. It was likely that bright sunshine would afford Bridget's newfound friend a more complete revelation of just who she was.

The thought was intimidating her, but she understood that appearances were only a small part of what life really is, or should be.

On a day like this, one could almost taste spring.

Marcus drove up in an old Toyota station wagon with two bikes strapped on a rack in the back. He eased out of the car, stood up to his full 6 feet, smiled, and said "Hi."

"Hi." *What now? Should I check my feet for glass slippers?* She almost pinched herself to make sure it wasn't a dream. The difference between today and yesterday at this time was so extreme.

"Are you ready for a little ride...Bridget?"

"I haven't been on a bicycle in several years."

"Well this is a perfect day to get back on one."

She felt herself smiling. *Already? So strange...this joy. "Which handle is the brake?"* Putting one hand gingerly on the handlebars, she squeezed the brake. It seemed like the thing to do.

"They're both brakes. The one on the right is your front brake; the left," He squeezed the handle opposite of the one she was holding. "the rear brake." Marcus unstrapped the two bikes, one red, the other a silvery-grey, and lifted the silver one off the rack, set it on the pavement and knocked down the kickstand with his foot. Then the other. "Where do you want to go?"

"We can ride over by the duckpond, or...just wherever you want to go."

"How 'bout...wherever *you* want to go. You lead, I'll follow."

It had been, in fact, so long since she had done this, that Bridget had to pay close attention to her movements. It was an effort to keep the thing on the asphalt path, which was a generous 6' wide, and not run into anybody.

But it was fun. *It was liberating. How, or why, had she ever gotten away from it...riding a bicycle?* And it was true: you don't forget how to do it.

Bridget had gone to London once, with her parents and her sister, when she was sixteen. She had a vivid memory of some of the parks in that great city. St. James Park was one that stood in her memory. They had sat on the grass and listened as a brass band played beneath a large gazebo. And there were ducks there, which is what called the memory to mind: the silly little ducks, quacking, waddling. *What would life be without ducks? What a silly thought. She had gone for years never even thinking about silly ducks.* This whole day was inebriating. She was drunk with pleasure.

But what had been so captivating about the London parks was...their unexpectedness. She had walked along on a city street with her family, and then, like a pearl among stones, there it was: an island of green escape, a harbor of placidity with daffodils and tulips. This park was somewhat like that, but not exactly. It was more like a *string* of pearls, a ribbon of sylvan calm that embraced a little rocky stream. Then it widened into the duck pond.

Up and down the path they rode several times, and around the pond. After a while, Bridget became brave and ventured beyond the safe haven of Sanderson Park. Confidently navigating over city sidewalks and streets, she gravitated to a quaint neighborhood with quiet streets, modest but well-kept houses, front porches with people on them, children playing. Then she was back on Westside Drive, and there was a Starbucks. Boldly she wheeled up to the front door and parked the bike. *Coffee would be appropriate, more civilized than meth. What a crazy thought. How could she have gotten so close to what surely would have been disaster? And today...how could she have traveled, so quickly from one world to another?*

Marcus, joining her, declared: "It's getting hard to keep up with you, girl."

Laughing, "Oh, right. I'm *so* speedy."

They went inside, drank coffee, and on a whim, decided to go across the river to Washington. Improvising, the serendipitous duo took their leave of Starbucks, hopped back on the bikes, rode directly back to the parking lot by the bear habitat where they had begun their sojourn, now expanding and taking on new dimensions. Also adventurously enlarging was the newly-grafted bond between them, a friendship unfolding like the delicate petals of a cherry blossom; And so it was that the sap of their two lives was stirring beyond the two barren wintry branches that they each were, and finding union at a bough beneath: a metamorphosis from lonely separateness into long-sought familiarity with another human being. It was an unexpected, but welcome epiphany. Together, though they understood it not, they sought the trunk and root of existence..

Marcus removed the bike rack from the hatchback, removed the front wheels from both bicycles, carefully laid them in the flattened rear compartment of the station wagon. Bridget was amazed at him. She knew herself to be amazing, but in ways that were different from his. All in good time, he would know her.

Marcus locked the car. They walked three blocks to the Metro station , then boarded a subway bound for Washington. Thirty minutes later, they walked out of the Foggy Bottom Metro Station. As they emerged into a golden afternoon, Bridget Golden noticed on the station clock that it was 4:30.

A lot of people were out having the same experience as they. Why not? If life could get any better than this, it must just disappear in a cloud of hope. A communal savoring of the day's rarified air enveloped a multi-hued flock of gatherers; now they were spread out like manna upon the here and now of a rambling portico. The reflecting pool below witnessed their reverie.

Children were running up and down the steps; parents were shepherding. All around, they heard the buzz of human motion and drone, laugh and groan, reminding Bridget of a beehive she had once seen. All kinds of people, from everywhere. This was America.

Marcus knew what hallowed figurehead seemed to keep stony, silent vigil at the apex of these steps. It was a favorite appointment for him-- this reflection upon the life and death of a sculpted ancestor. Certainly the whole place was nothing but marble and mortar, but a promise of freedom indwelt the hearts of those pilgrims who came here, or so it seemed to Marcus.

They walked up the steps of the Lincoln Memorial.

When they reached the top, Bridget was gazing, like most everyone else who ascends here, with rapt interest at the seated statue. But Marcus, holding Bridget's hand, gently prodded her to keep moving, slowly to the left, through the myriad of ambling visitors.

They came to an inner sanctum. Carved on the white marble wall in front of them were the words of the slain President's Gettysburg address.

Marcus stopped, taking in the enormity of it, both physically and philosophically. He was looking at the speech intently. Bridget was looking at him.

After a few moments: "Isn't that amazing?

"Yes." She could see that he was thinking hard about something. The great chamber echoed a murmur of humankind.

"Supreme irony." The longing of a nation's soul reverberated through the memorial... in the soundings of children, the whisperings of passersby. Deep within Marcus' soul, something sacred was stirring, and she could see it coming forth.

"The world will little note, nor long remember, what we say here, but can never forget what they did here." He was reading aloud Lincoln's words on the white wall.

But for the echoes of a million people who had passed through this place, there was silence. After a moment, Bridget responded. "...and yet, there it is carved on the wall, for all to see: 'the world will little note what we say here....'"

"Right, Bridget. Isn't it amazing?"

Suddenly, amid the noise was a loud shouting.

Marcus could hear where it was coming from. He moved quickly away, toward the noise, to see what was happening. Bridget felt the sudden coolness of air on her hand, in the absence of Marcus' gentle grip.

As soon as he emerged from behind the marble column, Marcus was puzzled by an incongruous, glistening wet flash of red upon the feet of Lincoln's statue. *What the hell?* Instinctively, he ran over to it. He could still hear a constant shouting; it was a ranting. Then his attention settled on the man who was yelling. He had a bucket in his hand, dripping with red paint. The rant went on, and suddenly Marcus was comprehending it: "...you sonofabitch see if you can get that off and then rub it on your white ass, your sorry white ass that destroyed what this country could have been you're a traitor to your race."

This must be a dream, a very bad dream. Marcus was noticing the speaker's bald head, goatee, his moving mouth spouting insult. Then Marcus was deciding to do something. It seemed to him that it was someone else speaking when he asked, loudly, "What the hell do you think you're doing?"

The stranger, startled, turned to Marcus and looked at him. Then he opened his foul mouth: "I'm gonna make things right. There's a lotta things need to be made right. It's gonna start now."

A bad dream. Marcus could feel his ire rising. His voice must have quivered with "You better leave now. You've defaced national property. You better find a park ranger and turn yourself in. If you don't, *I'll* turn you in." Marcus found himself yelling, as his challenge escalated through the marble edifice.

The man turned and began to walk down the steps.

Impulsively, Marcus thought, and shouted: "Who are you, anyway?"

Marcus began following the man down the steps. "They oughta bury you under this place." Marcus was right behind him.

Suddenly the vandal turned and punched his assailant in the face. Marcus reeled. There was blood and pain in his awareness. Impetuous, he jumped on the guy with a vengeance and tackled him. They spun downward through midair, landed with a bonecrunching impact on the steps, rolled and stopped, still lost in a fierce, flailing embrace of sudden hatred.

A crowd of people tore them apart. Then there was a D.C. cop. He arrested them both.

Bridget had run down the steps, following, startled by the suddenness of it all. Now a huge, loathing fear took a violent bite out of what had been idyllic day. Although she had come to know so much about Marcus, and she felt that he had allowed her to peer deep into his soul, she realized with alarm that she hardly even knew him. She had been falling in love with a prince who was now...arrested? No, no, no. He was no criminal. She knew that much.

She started to run up to him, but the policeman stopped her.

"Stay away, ma'am, or I'll have to arrest you."

"Go ahead. Arrest me, then."

The policeman ignored her. He was too busy. She cowered, not knowing what to do . Nothing like this had ever happened before.

The policeman, joined now by another, began directing the two men away, down the steps. Marcus was reeling with pain and confusion. *Surely this is not happening to me now. It must be a dream.*

Recovering somewhat, Bridget resumed her following. She would have to try a different strategy to communicate with her friend.

She started talking slowly, but firmly, to the cop as he was doing his job. "Sir, my friend Marcus here has done nothing wrong. He was trying to prevent any further damage from occurring." Bridget was encouraged that others in the crowd were attesting to the truth of her statement. She was aware of a murmur of consensus. But she didn't have much time. The cop car was just below the steps, off to the left side.

"Ma'am, I'm arresting this man for breaching the peace in a public place. The other fellow's going in for breaching the peace and desecration of public property You can make a statement at the station."

Duty-bound, the cop was rushing them into the backseats of two different squad cars. Just before Marcus disappeared inside, Bridget was able to catch his eye, which was already swollen beside what appeared to be a broken, bloody nose. His voice cracking: "Thank you, Bridget, I'm sorry...." Her friend ducked into the car. The officer closed the door, got in the driver's seat. Behind glass, she saw him make a call on the radio. Then, he sped away, the crowd parting before the vehicle like the Red Sea. As suddenly as it had started, it was over.

Sitting in the backseat in handcuffs, Marcus' puzzled awareness started to take inventory of the fact that he had seen something strange while approaching the car. It was an image that stuck in his consciousness. *What was it? Where had he seen it? On the back of the guy's neck: a tattoo, a dragon tattoo.*

When they got to the station, Marcus was ushered, without force, out of the car. The cop who had arrested him asked him, using the word "please," to come inside and follow him. They ushered him into a small, featureless room with a table and two chairs.

The door was closed; he sat at the table for two or three minutes. A uniformed woman walked in with a pitcher of water and a glass, which she set on the table in front of him. From a small goretex bag she extracted some gauze, ointment, and other medical items.

"Mr. Derwin, my name is Rita." She spoke very clearly and precisely. " I am a police officer and a nurse. I'm going to clean up your wounds a little bit, if you would like me to. In a little while, we'll have a doctor here to treat your nose, which appears to be broken. I have some acetaminophen here to ease your pain until the doctor comes. Would you like to take a couple of them?"

"Yes, ma'am. Thank you."

She began stroking his eyebrow with hydrogen peroxide.

She was businesslike, but pretty, with bright, green eyes and a disarming smile.

"Rough time at the Lincoln Memorial today, eh?"

"Yeah...did you hear what happened?"

"No...What happened?" Somehow he didn't believe her, but it seemed okay. She began unwrapping gauze.

"That guy threw red paint on Lincoln's feet."

He was waiting for her reaction. She seemed to be busy, taking care of him. "Was there anybody else with him?"

"I didn't see anyone."

"What *did* you see?"

"I didn't see it happen. I was standing with my friend reading the Gettysburg address when all of a sudden I hear this guy yelling...something about white ass, or white people, or something...I walked around to where he was and saw what he had done. He *had* red paint on his hand—"

At that moment, the door opened. In stepped the arresting officer. Walking to the table, he looked directly into Marcus' eyes and spoke to him in a low voice: "Mr. Derwin, please tell us what happened."

" I was just telling this kind lady here..." and he restated it up to the point of seeing red paint on the man's hand. There was a bandage over his eyebrow now. The lady officer, without ado, withdrew her medical ministrations. She stepped behind him, but said nothing. Marcus turned his head gingerly (his neck was stiff with pain) as if to thank her. Then he resumed. "He was ranting and raving, spouting some trash about Lincoln being a traitor. He had a foul mouth. Suddenly I just felt that I didn't particularly want to hear what he had to say. It was just trash-talking. I interrupted him...don't remember what I said." Incredulously: " Then he *starts to walk away,* like this is a Sunday walk in the park..." Marcus shook his head. Now that he thought about it, *what audacity.* "...which it was, come to think of it...a walk in a national park, that is."

Behind him, Rita let out a low chuckle. The other cop allowed a very faint smile, but he put a lid on it. Marcus had an unexpected sense of victory; he had done a good deed, and he knew it. He had nothing to be ashamed of. *Now, whether these two know it or not...*that's another matter. But he didn't feel threatened by them. It seemed that he would convince them of the truth of his statement. He was, it occurred to him, giving a statement, just like the cop shows on TV. Nothing like this had ever happened to him before.

"So, he's walking away, down the steps. And I had this thought: he can't just walk away after desecrating a national monument. And I wasn't going to let him get away with it. I went down to where he was. Next thing I know...he whacks me across the face. I don't really know what happened after that, but the next thing I knew we were rolling down the steps together. It hurt like hell." Marcus couldn't think of anything else to say about it, so he rested from his accounting. He was feeling pretty tired; it had, after all, been a long day.

The cop looked at him for what seemed like a long time.

"Mr. Derwin, do you know the fellow's name?"

Marcus hadn't even thought about it. "Uh, no." I don't even *care* what his name is. They oughta lock him up and throw away the key." He chuckled to himself.

"In his statement, he says that you came there with him, but that you chickened out when it came time to do the deed."

"...say What?"

"You heard me."

Marcus was about to get real mad, but unexplainedly, he felt himself laughing.

"Yeah, right. I have witnesses, probably a hundred of them who can testify that I had nothing to do with it. That's ridiculous."

"Name one witness."

"There was a girl with me there, Bridget Golden. Ask her about it."

"Okay, Mr. Derwin. We have talked to her already."

"Well, then, you know what happened."

"I think the pieces are starting to fall into place, Marcus. Is there anything else you'd like to add to your statement?"

"Not right now. If I think of anything else later, can I let you know?"

"Okay. And the doctor is here now. I'm going to send you into the medical room with him; then you'll be free to go. You may be called into court as a witness. We're going to drop the charge against you, but he'll be booked for desecrating public property and breach of peace."

"He oughta be. What about assault? He punched me, you know.

"Do you want to file charges? You'll want to see the judge about that, and maybe a lawyer."

"We'll see. So, you've talked to Bridget. Is she here?"

"She is."

Then Marcus had a remembrance that jumped in his mind like a steel trap.

"There is one more thing, sir."

"And that is...."

"The man had an unusual tattoo on his neck...a dragon. Did you see it?"

"We did. It probably doesn't mean a thing. We see that kind of thing all the time. You'll get a letter about his court date. Now, it's time for you to do some paperwork before you get out of here."

He offered a mild smile; officer Rita offered a big one.

Holocausts
7

Not too much happening on Monday morning. People are slinking back into the scheme of things, slipping through the routine, slurping their way toward coffee break. Productivity is at all-time median level. On 14th Street, the welcome winter sun is stealing across the tops of limestone, concrete and brick buildings, starting to warm passersby below and brighten the day for a small crowd of citizens who have come from all over to visit the Holocaust Memorial Museum.

Lt. J.D. Joadson walked at a leisurely pace along the sunny side of the street, with his eyes wide open, his ears tuned to the familiar background of traffic and voices. A police officer in this type of work could not generally expect to know what he was looking for, except to be aware of the possibility that *anything out of the ordinary* could indicate a threat. The officer took his job as a protector of people in public places seriously. During his three years in this type of law enforcement, he had developed a sharp eye for persons who might pose a threat to the safety of others. On one occasion he had successfully disarmed a mentally ill man who was attempting, at gunpoint, to steal his children from his estranged wife.

Just like every morning at this hour, visitors waiting to obtain entrance to the Museum were forming an orderly line that steadily lengthened, minute by minute, as the 10 o'clock door-opening hour approached. J.D. was an amicable fellow; one of his favorite activities was talking to people while they waited in line. This morning he noticed a boy of about 12 years with his father; the kid was reading, with great interest, a brochure, apparently scoping out the territory before entering the museum. As J.D. passed, the boy looked up and asked him a question:

"Officer, can you tell me if the exhibit about the Polish kids is open today?"

"You mean the one about the Lodz ghetto?

"Uh...yes, sir." The boy was looking at his brochure to confirm this reference.

"As far as I know, you can see it today. Have you been here before?"

"Yes, sir. We were here a couple of years ago. This is my dad."

The man grinned, nodded his head. "Good morning, sir."

"Good morning...and what did you see when you were here before?"

"We saw a lot of pictures and things set up. We saw the inside of a railroad car, and we saw a room from a house in Germany where a guy named Daniel lived."

"And so you're hoping to see some rooms today that you didn't see before."

"Yes, sir."

"Can you help us get tickets for the Wizards' game?"

J.D. laughed. "Son, I don't have any tickets, but if you go to the Verizon Center, they can sell you some. Do you know where the Verizon Center is?"

"No, sir."

"Well, young man, (what's your name?)"

"Joey."

"Well, Joey, when you get done here this afternoon, you might want to go over to the other side of the Mall. You know the Mall, right? Right. On the other side over there, at the corner of F Street and 6th Ave.NW, is the Verizon Center. You can go there and ask them, and they'll sell you a ticket. If you go there tonight, you can see the Wizards beat the Pistons."

"I don't think so," said the boy, with a surprisingly serious tone.

"Oh no?" said the policeman, raising his eyebrows, "and why not?"

"We're from Michigan."

The good-natured cop laughed. "Oh, excuuuuse me. Well, you might find yourself disappointed tonight, then. But hey...welcome to our nation's capital, Joey."

The banter was interrupted by the deep voice of a man who was standing behind them in line. He had a thick African accent. "Sir...you say that the Verizon Centa is on the other side of the National Mall. Is that correct?"

"Yes, sir, at F Street and 6th Ave NW."

"And how much do these tickets cost, sir?"

"You can see a game for about $30, or, you can get a good seat for...as much as you want to pay...$50...$100, depending on where you want to sit in the arena."

"Thank you."

"You must be from Africa, right?"

"Yes, sir, I am originally from Sudan. I have now been in the US for three years. I am a US citizen." He smiled largely.

"Congratulations, Mr..."

"Leng, Aleph Leng. I am pleased to meet a policeman of the city of Washington."

They shook hands happily.

"Congratulations, Mr. Leng. Welcome to our nation's capital., I am Lt. J.D. Joadson. And what, may I ask, brought you here from the Sudan?"

"I fled that country when government troops raided my village and stole everything we had. I and my three friends escaped through the desert to Kenya. From there, I came to Los Angeles. That is where I now live."

"I've heard a little bit about the refugees from southern Sudan. How long did it take between when you left your village and when you arrived here?"

"It took seven years, sir."

The officer's jaw dropped. For a moment, he was at a loss for words.

"Seven years?"

"Seven years, sir. For five years I evaded the government troops in Sudan. Then I escaped to Kenya, where I stayed in a United Nations camp for two years. At last, I was selected to come to the United States. I was grateful for the opportunity...then, and now. I am most happy to be a United States citizen."

It was now past 10 o'clock. The line was moving inside the building. As the officer approached the building, he noticed a brown duffel bag on the pavement near a corner of the building, where the round façade entry of the building joined the main structure. The bag was in an odd position, standing upright behind a trash receptacle. He had not noticed it until just this moment. Lt. Joadson walked toward the duffel bag.

It exploded.

The officer had come within three feet of the bomb. A cloud of flying debris and smoke obscured the scene. The people nearby began running away. Aleph Leng, staggering away and toward the street, peered through the haze. When the smoke had cleared, Joadson lay on the pavement, his upper body a bloody mess. He did not appear to be moving. A part of the building had collapsed onto the policeman's body. Aleph was not sure of what he should do. But as the dust drifted away in the morning breeze, he approached the man who lay sprawled on the ground beneath rubble.

He shouted. "Lieutenant."

Again: "Lieutenant, can you hear me?" There was no sound but the screaming of people nearby. Aleph Leng pulled out his cell phone and dialed 911.

Chances
8

Julius Jamel collected three pairs of shoes from their disarray on the carpet, inserted them into their respective boxes, walked into the stockroom and returned the boxes to their places in inventory. Happy to have just made a $108 sale, he sauntered back onto the sales floor, smiling, eyes alert for his next prospect. He was having a pretty good day for a Monday. He bent down, picked up a gum wrapper and a small motel-bottle of shampoo that were laying on the floor beneath a seat. The place needed to be neat and orderly. He surveyed the familiar interior of Brill's shoe store; the afternoon sun was beginning to brighten his showroom which was situated on the east side of 3rd Street in Urdor. This was the time of day where work got a little easier. He was over the midday hump; it had been a productive morning. He could have minimal business in this after-lunch time and still have a good day. So it was profit-time—the gravy train! In the midst of Julius' silent calculations, he noticed an attractive dark-haired middle-aged woman looking at a pair of Italian dress shoes on the rack.

"Good afternoon."

"Hi."

"Are you looking for anything in particular, ma'am?"

"Yes." A forced smile jumped on her face and promptly off again. "I'm looking for some leather shoes with a medium heel to match an outfit that I'll be wearing to a graduation."

"I hope we have what you're looking for. Do you have the outfit with you?"

"Yes." She had been carrying a Nayman's bag. Opening it, she produced an elegant, dark green lady's suit. It had impressive olive-wood buttons and a fur collar.

"I see you have your sights set on a pair already. Would you like to see that in your size?"

"Yes, a size 6AA, thank you."

"Do you see any others that I can bring you at this time, ma'am."

"No, not yet." She put on the fake smile again. This time it had a little more authenticity; the eyes registered a fleeting agreement with her upturned lips.

"I'll be right back with this. Have a seat, if you like."

Hot diggetydog! I'm on a roll now. This great day is getting even greater!

Back in the stockroom, Julius collected four boxes. He understood that a woman of this type would expect to make a choice between two or more pairs of shoes. Providing the choice, and his skillful selection of the samples from which the lady would form her decision, would practically *assure* a purchase from her. *Practically a done deal. The lady had class written all over her demeanor, and she was ready to expand her impressive wardrobe.* He found the shoe in 6AA; then grabbed a similar style in the same dark brown, and pulled also the same shoe in a different shade of brown. Master salesman that he was, Julius went one step further: he selected a totally random shoe that had nothing to do with the woman's buying objective at this time. This practice of including a "wild card" was a strategy that he had learned eight years ago from his first boss, Mr. Picou. The little game often resulted in a second sale. Yet, even if that did not happen, the presence of the "wild card" was sometimes known to work a little unaccountable magic. Surely, the lady would buy a pair of shoes today.

Stooping to serve as he did countless times every day, Julius slid the leathers on her feet, as easily as putting gloves on his own hands. She turned one leg aside to get a view of the shoe on her foot, then stood up to walk.

Julius smiled at her. "Excuse me. Let me know if I can get a different size, although that one seems to be right, doesn't it?" Without waiting for an answer, he slipped away. Another customer had come in and was looking around.

The woman was pretty scruffy compared to his well-heeled customer. An equally scruffy child was lingering beside her. The mother's mascaraed eyes were tired, a little bloodshot. The wrinkles on her face looked premature for a woman who must be in her late 20's. The hair was wiry bleached-blonde, brown at the roots. Blue jeans. She smelled of cigarette smoke, with a raspy voice to match; she was nervous. The child seemed sedate, but there was something about her that implied neglect. Maybe it was the oily stain on her worn gingham dress.

Julius smiled at her anyway. "Can I help you ma'am?"

"I'm just lookin' thanks."

"Let me know if I can help you. We've got a 2-for-1 sale on athletic shoes today."

Not wanting to bother his prime prospect just yet, he walked over to the sales counter, began tidying up a mild disarray that his employee, Brad, had left before going to lunch. He was busying himself with this insignificant task when a man walked in. With a very serious look on his face, undisguised cruelty on his mouth, he went straight over to the mother and child.

"Come on. We need to get going."

"No."

"Wanda, we can't get there in time if you don't get your ass in gear. Let's go."

The child was cowering behind her mother. "Just go on, Buzz. I'll see you at home." Her voice was starting to break. This was the middle of a discussion that the couple must have been having before she walked in.

"You're comin' with me, now."

"No, Buzz. You go on now, " raising her voice.

He *lowered* his voice. No need to make a scene. Then he got very close to his frantic wife, put his face right up to hers and growled a threat.

"No! No!. Buzz. Go." And then her voice lowered, with tears: "Please."

He gave her a little push. She started to back up, but a rack of shoes was behind her. She was trapped. He pushed her again, like a bully on a playground. She stumbled. Suddenly the large shoe-rack, 8-feet long, 6-feet high, fell over to the floor with the woman on top of it, her jeaned legs flailing in the air. She was in a vulnerable, humiliated position. But only for a few seconds. The man wasted no time; he grabbed both her arms, brusquely pulled her up. "Goddammit, git your ass in gear, woman." When she was up, he grabbed the child's arm and dragged them both, protesting and whining, over to the door and out of the store. Before he knew what to do, Julius caught the last glimpse of them trudging away on the sidewalk outside. So glad to see them gone, he didn't bother to pursue.

He just walked over to the fallen shoe rack, dumbfounded Such entropy baffled him. *It was going to be such a great day...and now this.* He was still trying to put it together in his mind what had happened.

Then he was aware that the elegant lady was speaking to him

"I'll take these two," she said.

He walked over to her, a little shocked that his sales plan had actually worked under such conditions. His head was spinning. "Yes...Yes, ma'aam...Thank you."

She smiled at him. "I hope you don't have to put up with that kind of thing every day."

Such a relief. She could have walked out of here mad. Now he felt himself happy again. *What a wonderful lady.* "Ha, ha...no ma'am. I can assure that doesn't happen every day. In fact, it's never happened before. It was...very strange, don't you think?"

"To say the least. I don't know what's happening to people today. That poor child...that man...she needs to ditch him, any way she can. He's a loser.."

He was putting her two shoe boxes in a bag, and ringing up the sale. "I wonder if she even *can* get rid of him. He seemed so dominant, possessive. If I ever find a wife, I'll think I'll be treating her better than that."

"I know you will, Mister...?"

"Jamel, Julius Jamel. Pleased to meet you. Sorry it had to be in these circumstances. Like I said, this really has never happened before." He was shaking his head and smiling about it. Thank you, Mrs...?"

"Stuart , Margaret Stuart. Can I help get that display back up?"

"Oh, no. My helper will be back in here in a minute. We'll get it. No problem."

"Well, okay then." She tossed her head back, looked him in the eye, smiling.

"You know what? Mrs. Stuart, just so you'll know that I appreciate your business, please pick out another pair of shoes. I want you to have another one, no charge...any one you like."

"Oh, no, Mr. Jamel, I'll be fine, really, you needn't do that."

"Mrs. Stuart, I insist."

She paused, ever so graciously. "Well, maybe I *could* take that little handbag over there, for my niece.".

"It's yours. Thank you." He walked over to the little purse and tossed it in the bag. I hope she likes it."

The front door opened. A couple of young mothers and their four children were being ushered in by Brad, Julius' helper. When they had entered the store and started to look around, Brad looked over at the fallen display and asked, quizzically, "What happened here?"

"Long story, Brad."

Mrs. Stuart was moving toward the door. "How about keeping that open for Mrs. Stuart. She just picked up some shoes to wear at her niece's graduation."

"My *daughter's* graduation."

"Well, there you go. (How are you ladies today?) May your daughter have a successful graduation, and a productive life. Thank you, Mrs. Stuart."

"Bye, now." She stepped out the door, smiling. Brad was holding it wide open for her.

As an afterthought, she added: "Oh Mr. Jamel, I think the Lord is looking out for you."

"Amen, sister."

***

Marcus hadn't even gotten to work Monday morning until 10 o'clock. After Sunday night's fiasco at the Lincoln Memorial, Bridget had enlisted the aid of a helpful witness, and his willing wife, to bring them from downtown all the way back to Urdor. And there had been a gaggle of people outside the police station who wanted to talk to him last night, even a couple of reporters. He had told them all the same story he'd given the police. In the third telling, however, he was adding a little bit along the way, like for instance how the whole thing had started, when he realized the terrible insult that was being inflicted on the nation by this disrespectful, paint-wielding *idiot*. He had just pointed out to Bridget, for cryin' out loud, that Lincoln had not expected that his comments at Gettysburg would be any big deal: "The world will little note, nor long remember, what we say here…but can never forget what they did here." And yet *there the words were*, carved in stone. How ironic it was (he had said to them) and then at that moment there was this *desecrater* throwing red paint on Lincoln's feet. (It's not really Lincoln; we all know that) And how ironic was it that the paint was *red*, for Christ's sake, and that in strange kind of way it was appropriate, although of course he didn't condone the insult. It was just ironic that the paint was red, and represents the blood, perhaps, of those men of whom Lincoln was speaking, and maybe even the blood of many other men and women who had given their lives in service to our common cause, which is, by the way, freedom and justice for all men and women.

In fact, there was really nothing a man could do to defame Abraham Lincoln. His reputation was pretty well set in stone.

So then they had gotten back to Sanderson Park, and he took Bridget to her hotel and she kissed him and by that time it was almost midnight. He had eaten a bowl of cereal and gone to bed.

So at 10 o'clock he climbed back on the scaffold to fix the tenon that hadn't quite fit in its intended mortise on Friday afternoon. Then he positioned the collar beam with a hydraulic jack and the aid of his helper, Jake. Then they got down, the job being complete, and spent the rest of the day cleaning up, moving tools to Daniel's warehouse, and generally moving stuff around at the warehouse getting ready for the next job.

*** *** ***

Kaneesha loved the dinner hour. There was always so much going on, and she was pleased to be a part of it. She loved feeding people, and this was a great place to do it—with a mellow clientele. With an armful of dishes headed for the dishwasher, she stopped to check on a couple of regulars.

Shapur, the handsome Iranian who just happened to be one of Kaneesha's favorite customers, was engaging in one of the frequent dialogues that he had in this place with his friend and colleague, Lambert. Kaneesha hated to interrupt. But with this armload, she wasn't going to hang around for a long time waiting for their requests.

"What can I get you guys?"

Shapur: "I'll have apple pie and decaf."

Lambert: "Carrot cake for me, and some more water."

Shapur continued: "...so the molecules are repelling each other...their electron clouds preventing them from forming a bond."

Lambert: "Yeah, they need a third party, if you will, to overcome their repulsion to each other. They're both in relatively stable states."

Shapur: " ...activation energy, usually some kind of heat."

Lambert:"Yes, and in the Big Bang expansion, there seem to have been some mysterious 'potential energy wells' that protected the newly-forming matter particles instead of destroying them. In a sense, these forces were working against entropy. They were analogous to that *activation energy* in molecular bonding, And this constructive principle (whatever it was) somehow enabled the stabilizing of fundamental matter components--protons, neutrons, etc. As a result, matter could become a stable, real entity, even in the presence of *enormous* Big Bang force.

Shapur: "Energy separated itself into matter."

Kaneesha, who was accustomed to their dialogues, overhead this, set desserts on the table, and inserted: "Or, maybe it was more like: energy *was separated* from matter...like, somebody did it."

Lambert: "Thank you, Kaneesha. Yes, you could say that."

Kaneesha smiled broadly, put her hand on her hip and looked at Lambert, teasing him. She quipped: "Maybe it was like: 'God separated the light from darkness, matter or whatever you want to call it, and said 'yeah, it was, like, pretty good.'"

Shapur busted out laughing.

And Kaneesha chuckled. She raised her eyebrows and started to walk away, tending to her duties. Shapur laughed quite a lot about it, while Lambert's eyes registered genuine amusement and a sense of well-being.

Shapur lassoed their levity back to discussion: "Well, then...back to the Second Law...the effects of it are really more general than some folks suppose: the original concentrated energy of the universe expanded, diffusing, and slowing down, and thereby sort of 'condensing' into matter as it went."

Lambert was pleased to resume his discourse: "Fusion of protons and neutrons, etc, eventually formed the elements of the physical world. But then there were some variables that resulted in conditions like... hydrogen being compressed. In those circumstances (and God only knows what they were) the fusion didn't stop—it became a sun, or whatever. From there, the Second Law of thermodynamics continued working itself out...in a way that was unique, I guess to each star."

James Hightower, proprietor *extraordinaire* of the Jesse James Gang Grille, was passing their booth. Grinning, he stopped to capitalize upon the jovial conditions that his skillful restaurateur's perception had ascertained were present here for an excellent dining experience.

"Good evening, gentlemen. How are we doing? Did you get enough to eat?"

"Oh, yeah," chuckled Shapur, "plenty enough calories to keep our universe expanding for awhile."

"Great. Thanks for dropping in. Say, I want y'all to meet Daniel Derwin, who will soon construct our new place. Daniel, this is Shapur Kabir...and Lambert Newton. They spend a lot of time here."

The men shook hands. Shapur asked: "So you're going to build a new restaurant?

Where will it be?"

"The old Rite-Aid drug store building at the corner of Pretoria and Edgerton. We'll renovate the building, and upfit it for restaurant use."

"How long will that take?" asked Shapur.

"I'm hoping we can knock it out in three or four months, depending on how the inspectors handle us. Maybe more like six months."

Shapur looked over at James. Jokingly, he said: "When James hits the big time, we'll come in and have to wait for a hostess to seat us, then wait in line."

James had a quick retort: "You guys will always be first in line. You know it. If it wasn't for you, we wouldn't be in a position to do this."

Lambert tossed his two cents of banter: "You'll have little 'comments' cards with questions about how to improve the place. We'll write things like you should have free refills on beer, and continuous Sam Cooke on the soundtrack, and Hilda's apple pie should be free on odd-numbered dates...."

"You got it, Lambert. Write it down on a napkin. We'll consider it at the board meeting."

Daniel was saying goodbye. "Nice to meet you fellows. Just keep givin' James a hard time and maybe he'll stay on his toes. I'm ready to sample some of this grub, so if you'll excuse me, have a good night."

Smiling and moving away, he sat in the next booth. Joining him were his brother, Marcus, and a young lady whom he had not yet seen but had heard about in the brothers' phone conversation an hour ago.

"Bridget, meet my brother, Daniel. Daniel, this is Bridget Golden."

"Hi."

"Hi."

Daniel hardly knew where to begin. "Marcus, what in the world have you been up to? One little weekend passes by. We finish the Mall job, then I see your picture in the paper on Monday morning. I didn't even know about what happened at the Lincoln Memorial. Now you come in here with this beautiful lady...."

Marcus was grinning like a good dog. "For starters, my brother, there's really nothing more important than the fact that Bridget and I had a great time yesterday, riding through Sanderson Park. Wouldn't you say, Bridget?"

"Definitely," agreed Bridget, demurely. "Then we took the Metro over to Washington. We weren't expecting that Marcus would be assaulted by a paint terrorist on the steps of the Lincoln Memorial. It sure took me by surprise. I was just getting to know your brother when, next thing I know, he was being arrested for disturbing the peace." Marcus put his arm around the diminutive woman, and was playfully squeezing her while they giggled together, recalling his unexpected detention, an event that would forever seal the memory of their first day together.

"You must have been wondering what kind of wild man you'd gotten yourself connected to?" contributed Daniel.

" Oh, I had my suspicions about him. He had been so forward with me the night before, asking all these probing questions." She was laughing without inhibition. Daniel was impressed with a quality that he sensed in her—a genuine innocence that shone brightly in her green eyes and mirthful exchange with his brother. Their joy lifted him up.

Kaneesha breezed in, introduced herself, deposited menus, took orders for beers.

Then she said: "I hear you guys are going to build us a new restaurant."

"You got that right," affirmed Daniel.

"That sounds great. I'll be back in a minute."

"What *was* the deal with that guy at the Lincoln Monument? What was he up to?"

"Strange bird," replied Marcus. "The whole incident happened so fast, I hardly had time to think about what he might have been up to, other than just generally making trouble. He must be a racist...ranting about white this and white that, and yelling that Lincoln was a traitor. I don't know...he might have been on somethin'. Wasn't very agreeable. I discovered that the hard way. What did you think, Bridget?"

"He was definitely on a racist trip, an extremist. I don't think there was anybody there who was agreeing with his action or the statement that he intended to make by it."

"When I was at the police station," recalled Marcus, the cop who arrested me said that he had claimed that I was there to help him, but that I had 'chickened out.' Everything about that guy indicates that he's about one brick shy of a load."

"Do you think he was alone? Was there anyone with him?" asked Daniel.

"We never saw anything or anybody to indicate that he had a confederate."

Bridget reported: "There were *so* many people who spoke to me afterward, Daniel, expressing support for what Marcus had done. After the policeman took them away, I found myself surrounded with people asking me about Marcus and all.."

Kaneesha brought their three beers, set them on the table. She took their food orders after Daniel instructed her to add it all on his check. Then Daniel asked her:

"What is this *awesome* music you've got playing tonight? I've never heard anyone play a clarinet like that."

Kaneesha was happy to inform: " It's a klezmer group from Germany. There's a story behind it. Hilda loves to tell people about it, so I'll ask her to come over here, okay? and I'll go get your order going in the kitchen."

"Thank you," Daniel replied.

Bridget continued. "Those people were *very* supportive of what Marcus had done. And the Metzgers, that couple that later brought us back to Urdor, offered immediate help. It seemed as if they adopted me right away. They brought me to the police station and waited with me there until Marcus was released."

"They went out of their way for us, a really nice old couple. They live in Gaithersburg. We had left my car, with the bikes in the back of it, at Sanderson Park here in Urdor. So their assistance saved us quite a bit of time at the end of an exhausting day."

A perky redheaded woman stopped at their booth.

"Hi. I'm Hilda Hightower," she said, looking at the young couple. "Hello, Daniel. It's nice to see you here, and your brother, and his friend."

"Marcus, and this is Bridget."

"I guess we'll be seeing a lot of you in the next few months."

"It looks like it. We're gonna have a great time building you a restaurant," declared Marcus.

" I was excited to see the plans that you brought on Saturday, Daniel. It looks like we're off to a good start, as far as planning goes anyway."

"I think we'll have a permit tomorrow. We should be able to start right away. Have you shown it to all interested parties? Gotten all the necessary opinions about the layout and so forth?"

"It's basically up to James and me, and it looks just fine."

"Good."

"James might have a few changes in the kitchen, and I may get some input from my sister about the decorating...but it looks like a go."

"We've got some liberty in the kitchen, depending on the size of the closets, coolers and so forth. The plan we're working with now is, I was sure, close enough to the final outcome to submit it to the city for purposes of obtaining a permit. We can make adjustments as we go."

"Sounds good. Now...Kaneesha said that you had expressed an interest in the music that's playing right now.

"Yes."

"A couple of years ago, James and I went to Germany. It was summertime. We were in Munich. Walking through a large, public square, the *Odeonsplatz*, we heard this music. It was around the corner from where we were when I first heard it, so it kind of drifted in and out of our hearing as we walked around the square there. I was reading a plaque that commemorated the lives of four policemen who had been killed right there in 1923. It was in that place that the Nazis made their first attempt to seize power in Germany. One night in November, there were thousands of people gathered there to hear a bunch of Nazi speakers. Hitler and his crew got the people really worked up about terrible shape that Germany was in— blaming all their troubles on the Allies, and the way World War I had ended."

Kaneesha brought them salads to eat.

"Hitler and his thugs tried to take advantage of the situation; they launched a *coup d'etat,* called a *putsch* in German. But it failed, and they ended up getting arrested. The event has been named *the beer hall putsch of 1923.* Well, I was reading about these police officers who were killed by the Nazis that night. And I was reading in my guide book some information about the incident. I kept hearing this beautiful music, really *spirited* music. We walked in the direction of the music. We turned a corner...and there they were, five musicians playing five instruments: clarinet, violin, accordion, cello, a drummer. I could tell they were Jewish right away. I considered their courage: *to stand there at the Odeonsplatz where the Nazis had made their first move to try and take over the world*, and declare, with their music, that Jewish people, along with their music, were alive and well in the 21st century. They inspired me. We must have listened to them for an hour...the Bridge Ensemble."

Across the restaurant's sound system, an illustrious fountain of sound expressed musically exactly what Hilda had said. Clear clarinet legato flowing from one intense note to another, sliding between winsome minor phrases that led to triumphant major cadences, undergirded by irrepressible klezmer rhythm. Its melancholy passion summoned the soul of hundreds, thousands of years of Jewish struggle in melodies hauntingly beautiful, sorrowfully exuberant, but victorious in their raw energy and fortitude. One could imagine Miriam dancing after the parting of the Red Sea, accompanied by such strains, had there been a clarinet, or any other kind of woodwind, on that miraculous occasion.

Bridget was crying.

Marcus eased his arm around her. "Our Bridget is Jewish."

Kaneesha brought dinner: steak and potato for Daniel, sirloin tips with peppers and onions for Marcus, chicken *cordon bleu* for Bridget. Daniel asked for a bottle of Merlot. Marcus began eating.

Daniel, looking curiously at this woman who was suddenly having such impact on his brother's life, slowly asked: "Where are you from, Bridget?"

"I grew up in Cleveland." She was wiping tears from her eyes, but smiling as she gained composure. "My grandmother was an Auschwitz survivor. When Hilda was talking about the beer hall putsch of 1923, I was reminded of some family history."

"Thinking about your grandmother, and how she must have suffered?"

"That's part of it. I've been hearing about it ever since I was very young. What upset me, though, was thinking of all the times...times when I could have heard from her about it. But I was too young and foolish to pay much attention... in too much of a hurry being a stupid kid to bother with hearing anything from her. She was just an old lady to me, kind of odd."

"What was her name?" asked Daniel.

"Maria Einstein."

Changes
9

Mt. Ebal stood warm, dry, and high in the morning sun. The red, gold hues of its boulderous ridges projected starkly into whisper-blue sky. On a soil-laden saddle nestled within the lower, rocky welts a man was digging.

Yesterday, the man had tilled the sandy soil and thrown in manure, which he had gathered from the sheep field. Today, he was hoeing trenches in the dirt.

Setting the hoe aside against a nearby shrub, Yahya Najah lifted his arm, moved the forearm across his sweaty brow, thanking God for another beautiful day. In order to give a moment's respite to his aching back, Yahya stood up straight, looked southward across the valley to Mt. Gerizim. He drew a deep breath, and drank water from a plastic bottle.

He had lived here since he was a child. Today, he was extending the stewardship of this land that his father had acquired and developed for olive-growing over thirty years ago. Yahya's father, Hassan, moved to this valley in the late '60s after the old Mughrabi quarter, just below the Western Wall in Jerusalem, had been demolished. His family had been planting, cultivating, and harvesting olive trees since his father's arrival here.

He reached into a burlap bag, pulled out several short lengths of olive branch that had been cut the day before, tossed them into the trench he had just dug. Then he grabbed the hoe and covered them with dirt. He moved to the next section of trench and repeated the procedure. Several times he performed the task, until his burlap bag was empty. Having placed this collection of propagation-stock in the dry ground of Mt. Ebal, Yahya watered the new rows with a water sprayer. When the tank was empty, he picked up and strapped the tank on his back, picked up the empty bag, grabbed the hoe, and walked down a rocky path to the garden patch. He would be going into Nablus today to sell vegetables at the market.

After harvesting a truck-full of vegetables, Yahya and his brother, Kader, drove the fifteen miles into Nablus, backed the truck into the usual stall and unloaded their produce for sale.

They spent the rest of that day selling vegetables. In the evening, after most of the produce had been sold, Yahya left Kader to finish their day's enterprise while he took a stroll up the street to get some supper for them. Satisfied to have gathered the increase of their labors, Yahya enjoyed the evening sun as it bathed the busy West Bank cityscape with golden light. As he ambled along, he noticed an American news reporter speaking into a microphone. While passing the scene, and curiously surveying the camera as it turned silently upon a cameraman's shoulder, the farmer's face was projected to television sets around the world. But he wasn't thinking of that; he was looking for a good falafel.

The American spoke into his microphone.

***

Half a world away, Rachel Vinnier saw, for a couple of seconds, the face of a handsome middle eastern man on the TV in the corner of the restaurant.. She had glanced up at the TV while inspecting a case of French wine that had just been delivered to the Jesse James Gang Grille. As she watched, the cameraman in Nablus panned the busy streetscape, and ended his movement with a focus on John Demos' serious face.

"...Mr. Ramra's escape from prison confounds authorities' attempts to monitor a tense situation on the West Bank. His jihadist activism in Cleveland had led to an American investigation in 1994. Subsequently, the imam had been deported from the U.S. when it was discovered that he had lied about his links to Islamic Jihad. Israeli and Palestinian authorities are now searching for Mr. Ramra, whose public statements have included, in the past, references to Jewish people as 'sons of monkeys and pigs.' Nevertheless, as you can see here in Nablus, peace in the West Bank remains intact this evening, while the alleged terrorist-supporter's apprehension is undertaken by Israeli and Palestinian authorities. This is John Demos, XYZ News, Nablus."

Rachel continued her wine-gathering chores, opening crates and unpacking them, then removing some bottles to racks in the cellar, and others to special places in the restaurant.

At about 2 o'clock on this Tuesday afternoon, her suite-mate, Helen, came in for lunch. Rachel led her to the back corner of the dining room, where they could talk without being disturbed. Rachel had also arranged with Hilda that Rachel herself would serve them, instead of a waitress, even though that would be a hassle. They were going to discuss Helen's second interview with the police, which had just taken place this morning. Four stressful days had passed since the rape had occurred.

After Rachel had seated Helen, she brought a pitcher of iced tea, with a dish of lemon slices; and a couple of salads. They began eating. Rachel asked:

"How are you feeling?"

"Pretty rough."

"Did they come to the apartment?"

"Yes. They had asked me to go to the police station, but gave me a choice about it, so I asked them to come to me. It was very different from the first interview. This officer was a woman, Ruth Maybin. She was very professional...works on rape cases all the time. She was sensitive...but persistent. I had to tell the whole story again. Her emphasis was more...how can I say it...more therapeutic. Instead of probing for facts, her questions were directed more toward helping me cope...I guess, with the whole ordeal of it."

"Well...did that happen? Was there anything about it that helped you cope?"

"Nothing really." Rachel could see her friend's eyes welling with tears. This thing that had happened, this *terrible* thing, was not going to go away. It seemed to be hanging over Helen like a dark cloud, or worse, like a *knife* hanging from a string, that could, at any moment be cut and render Helen useless, incapacitated by the trauma of it. Rachel knew that Helen was a good nurse, diligent and exacting, faithful to her profession. But nothing in the last couple days even remotely suggested the possibility of her friend returning to that world. It seemed as though Helen had been reduced to a bundle of torn-up nerves, a far cry from the competent, cheerful woman that Rachel knew her to be. Rachel didn't know what to say, so she didn't say anything. Eating the salad in silence, she began to wonder if this event may have rendered some irreparable damage. Surely, this was *not* some kind of fatal blow to Helen's functioning as a nurse, as a human being, a future wife, mother.

Helen was looking past Rachel, out the window at State Street. Finally, she said, "I may just...leave here. I may just...go back to Florida, live with my mom."

"What can I do to help, Helen? Is there anything?"

Helen's attention was slowly redirected toward the woman sitting across from her. A hint of smile turned up the corners of her mouth. She was beginning to appreciate, again, the consolation that her friend had to offer.

"I don't want to be insensitive, Helen, but...the hospital needs you. Maybe...if you could get back to work, you could find something there...."

"You *know* I've thought about that, but I just don't see how..."

"I know, I know, I'm sorry I mentioned it. It's too soon to talk about that now."

"Rachel...I just keep thinking about...that guy, whoever he was...that bastard. He was on the floor in the living room. He had tripped over the chair in the dark. If I could have found a way to kill him at that moment, I would have done it. The only thing I could do was get the nightstand and throw it in his face. If I could have killed him..."

"Helen...."

"Then he rolled over. He was trying to get up. I saw that tattoo on back of his neck. It was like...I had been attacked by a damn *dragon*. It's...blasphemous. I felt...I don't know...crucified...like, I'm *innocent*, for Christ's sake, and I'm having to...."

The troubled woman broke down for a minute or two.

Rachel, at a loss, gazed out the window, herself breaking, bearing the burden with her friend, waiting. There was a robin with a worm in its mouth on a the tree outside the window. People were walking past them on the sidewalk, unaware of the trauma that existed just a few feet away from them, inside. The robin flew away. She felt the need to redirect their attention; she had the thought that, as insensitive as it may seem, it was time to go on to something else.

"Helen, have they got any clue about his identity?"

The question startled Helen. A sudden rage penetrated her countenance: "I don't care who the hell he is."

Rachel spoke gently. "They have to find him. Justice has to be done."

Now Helen was bitter. "Who cares about justice? They should just kill him and be done with it."

Suddenly Rachel had the thought she'd been waiting for: there is, after all, a baby inside of her friend's womb, a baby that the doctor had said was still alive and well.

"What about the baby? You know, you're half-full of another human being, Helen."

"The doctor said it looks okay. Seems like a miracle to me, after what *I* went through."

"As far away as it is, you've got something to look forward to: a brand-new life."

"Yeah, that's one reason I was thinking of going to live with my mom. It might make things a lot easier."

A call came out across the dining room. It was Hilda's voice: "Rachel, there's a call for you, line one."

"Thank you," said Rachel, as she turned in that direction. Slowly, she stood up. *It's too early for her to make any moves, or decisions. She's in a kind of shock.* "I'll be back in a minute, Helen."

The injured woman sat in the restaurant booth, silent, looking out the window. A robin landed on the bare branch of the tree outside the window. Helen watched it, curiously, *with a worm in its mouth. That mama bird had just found a meal for its hatchlings; she was about to take it to the nest and feed it to the little ones.*

The robin twitched, with jerky little motions. Then it flew away.
What a miracle.

***

Special investigator Derrick Trent connected his laptop to a digital projector. Two other detectives, one man and one woman, joined him in the projector room. Together, they viewed the video files from a camera that was mounted on a light-pole in front of the Holocaust Museum. He played the selected segment of video for his co-investigators. Then he replayed it, stopping it at a specific point

"Here—three people—two men, one woman, enter the area where people are lined up. They walk over to the trash-can and stop. The woman pulls out a cell phone and appears to make a call. The man on the left lights a cigarette; the other man drops something in the trash. Then they pause, just hanging there, like he's just smoking, thinking about something; she's biding her time on the phone. The other guy—you can't see very well; he's hidden, maybe intentionally. After 17 seconds, they walk away, and out of the camera's range. Now, let's take another look."

"Okay, brainstorm time. Tell me what you see,." Said Trent to his colleagues.

The video file began to roll again.

"They're overdressed. It's 45 degrees, but they're wrapped up for freezing weather," said Rufus.

"They may be protecting the middle man from the camera," said Jan.

"Yeah, and he's the one that's most wrapped up," said Rufus. "Play it again."

Trent started the video again.

"The middle man *is* bulky, and when the other two stop, he's in a position near the backside of the trash can. He may be dropping the IED behind the trash can. See, he lingers for a few seconds; he's moving, but not going anywhere," said Jan.

"The other two are doing a pretty good job of shielding him from the camera," said Trent. "Now, they walk away. Can you see any difference in the trash can?"

"No."

"The middle man might have dropped it into the trash-can."

"Or behind it," said Trent. Here's the clip from nine minutes later."

Trent punched some buttons on his laptop. "Here...."

Visible in the camera's range was an erratic line of people, waiting to enter the building, and a seemingly-insignificant trash-can, which appears to explode. "I can't tell a thing about that explosion," said Jan.

Trent replayed it again. "Maybe I'm just reading too much into this, but, its seems to me that the trash can is not the actual point of explosion. See how it moves just before the blast is visible, like it's being overturned. The IED may be behind it."

"True," said Rufus. "Either way, it's obvious they planted the bomb—that team of three people planted the bomb. Now, I want to show you something about the people in line."

This time, Trent played a longer segment of the video record, beginning with the point in time of the trio's entry. "Look at the line of people waiting to get into the museum. There's Lt. Joadson, who was killed in the blast. He's talking to that kid, and the adult who must be the kid's father. His back is turned to the trash can. Unfortunately, he wasn't the

90

perfect police officer. He failed to notice the bombers as they approached. Or, if he did notice, he didn't suspect anything. It's easy for us to say, looking at it now, that he missed an opportunity to call an alert. God rest his soul. Anyway, do you see the guy standing in line behind the kid? The black guy...yeah.

That man has come to us and has given an eyewitness statement. He has identified himself as Aleph Leng, a naturalized citizen, originally from Sudan, now living in Los Angeles. He claims to have noticed the bombers as they approached the trash can. Of course, at the time, he didn't know their significance, so he didn't mention anything to Lt. Joadson. Lt. Joadson's proximity to the trash-can, which was brought about because he was approaching the trash-can when the bomb exploded, is why he did not survive it. Mr. Leng has given a rough description of those three. You can read it in the report. But here's the basic: two white males, fair complected, one, maybe...with red hair. The woman...bleached blonde hair, thin. This is confirmed by the view that we get when they're walking away from the trash-can. I'll replay that for you. Here, look at this. What's special about this view, even though it's not much better than their approach to the trash-can is...there...the guy on the left. He lights a cigarette. There's a spot on the back of his hand, see, a tattoo?"

***

Lucido Gutierrez took his wife, Maria, and his two children, Victor and Alexandra out to eat. He walked into the Jesse James Gang Grille on Tuesday evening, crowded with diners and people waiting to dine. Hilda greeted him with a smile, and told him it would be a few minutes before they could be seated. Maria and the children squeezed onto the long, wooden bench where others were waiting. Lucido looked around the restaurant. Noticing a sign hanging on the wall to the left side of the front door, he walked over and began reading it:

Hold your horses, partner.
Don't be thinking that this here establishment has anything to do with the infamous Jesse James gang that robbed banks back in the old days. This here grille is named for James Hightower, who founded it in 2000, with

his son, Jesse, not to mention the Mom of this outfit, Hilda, and their daughter, Joanna. We are good people, not robbers.

Although James' mama told him when he was a boy that the bank robber of infamy was a distant relative, we don't want to have anything to do with the guy.

So while you're in our Grille, don't be getting any wild ideas about gunslinging. Just leave 'em outside. Also, horses left outside the Grille must be tied up. No smokin', and no spittin' on the floor. Poker antees larger than a nickel will be confiscated by the proprietor.

The Management.

Lucido chuckled. Then he looked around some more. The place was decorated in an old West style. Tables, chairs, and booths of Ponderosa pine. High wooden bar with mirrored background. Stucco on the walls. Waitresses with gingham dresses, white aprons and red scarves at their necks.

And lots of people eating. He could see why they wanted to get into a larger building.

Hilda approached him and said: "Mr. Gutierrez, your table is ready." She issued them to a table by the window. A minute later, a thin, blonde waitress brought menus and ice water for the family, and announced: "Buenas noches. Mi nombre es Bridget. Les voy a servir esta noche. ¿Puedo traerles algo de tomar?"

"Gracias," replied Lucido. "Me gustaría una Corona, por favor."

"Y para mí, té." said Maria.

Victor and Alexandra ordered cokes.

"Bueno. Vuelvo en seguida." Bridget offered a large, genuine smile. This was Bridget's first night on the job. It had been three years since the last time she worked as a waitress.

Mrs. Gutierrez looked at the eyes of her son and daughter, sitting across the table from her and her husband. "How was school today, my young ones?" She was a flamboyant woman, and she *loved* her children.

Alexandra volunteered first: "In world history today, we talked about how World War I started. In 1914, The Archduke of the Austro-Hungarian empire was assassinated in Sarajevo, Bosnia. That's how it started."

Bridget brought their drinks, set them on the table. She handed out menus, announced that she would return in a minute or two. They surveyed the menus.

When Bridget got back to the table, Lucido ordered steak and potato. Maria ordered trout almandine. Alexandra asked for a grilled chicken sandwich, and Victor wanted a hamburger with fries. They all ordered salads. Bridget took their orders and the menus.

"Okay, Alexandra, then what happened? How does one man getting shot start a world war?"

" A few weeks later, the Austrians and Hungarians (they were together in an empire) attacked Bosnia, because their Archduke had been shot. The Germans were allied with them."

"The Germans were allied with whom?"

"The Austrians and Hungarians."

"And then what?" prodded the mother.

"Germany declared war on Russia, but they attacked Belgium and France."

"And why in the hell did Germany do that?" inquired the father, incredulously.

"Well, there were a bunch of old treaties. It confuses me. And Britain declared war on Germany. I can tell you more about it tomorrow."

"So Germany, Austria and Hungary were fighting against Bosnia, Russia, and France." Lucido was seeking clarification.

"...and Britain and Belgium. Britain and Belgium also declared war against Germany and Austria-Hungary,"

"Things really got out of hand, didn't they? What a crazy world...*loco*."

"Yeah, papa, I think my teacher's a little loco too." Alexandra raised her eyebrows and rolled her eyes.

Lucido chuckled. "Oh, yeah? Why?"

"He's so *into it*. I think all he does is read books about history. He's a dork."

"Well, you can learn a lot from that *dork*, *Senorita*, so you just keep listening to him and reading what he gives you to read." Education was important to Lucido. He had not gotten enough of it to suit him, but his children would.

Victor was curious. "Where is Bosnia, anyway?"

"Bosnia is in eastern Europe, above Greece."

"That's right, Alexandra," added her mother, "and there was another war there a few years ago...Bosnians fighting Serbs."

"Serbs..." Alexandra pondered the word. "It was a Serb who killed the Archduke in Sarajevo in 1914."

"It's a big, big mess, my children. This world is a dangerous place," warned their mother. "Be thankful that you live in the United States, where people live in peace together."

"I'm not so sure about that, Maria. There are people here who would just as soon send us back to Mexico," Lucido complained.

"But we have laws here, Lucido, that protect us from harassment from such people," said Maria.

Then Bridget was there with salads.

The family prayed, then began eating.

After a minute or so, Lucido asked, "What about you, Victor? What did you learn in school today?"

"We studied adjectives in English. In algebra, we learned about the reflexive and commutative properties of equations."

"Explain them to me."

"Explain which?"

"Both of them, wise guy."

"An adjective is a word that describes a noun. Like...this is a *busy* restaurant. Or, this is *red* tomato."

"Okay, good."

"The reflexive property is simple: $a=a$. The commutative property is $a+b=b+a$."

"Okay. Sounds good to me. What are you going to do with that?"

"I don't know yet. I'll let you know tomorrow."

Bridget was passing by and smiling at them. Lucido said to her, "Senorita, "¿Es Sr. James Hightower el dueño aquí?"

"Si, senor."

"¿Le puedes preguntar que si puede venir él, ahora que tenga un momentito?"

"Si. Uno momento."

Lucido resumed. "Victor, I am happy to see you doing well in math, because it is a skill that you will need all the time when you are doing business, like I do."

"Si."

"Every day, I order blocks and other material. After the blocks are delivered, our helpers set them in a certain way so the masons can set them into the wall. After they are laid into the wall, the number of them, after they are counted, is the same number that was delivered to us. A=a, comprende?"

"Si."

"And the English as well. I want you to be proficient with the language."

"Yes, sir."

"Many of our guys don't speak English, or they don't speak it so well. We want to help them. That's going to be part of our mission as a company. Our people learn to use English. Everybody knows and understands English—fewer mistakes are made. You understand?"

"Yes, sir."

"That's *if* you want to stay in the business, Victor. I don't expect you to be a masonry contractor if you decide to go on to something else, like general contracting, or something else entirely...architecture, law or whatever."

"I am glad to hear you say that, Papa."

James Hightower walked over to the table, smiling, and introduced himself.

He asked: "Are you enjoying dinner tonight?"

"Yes, sir," responded Lucido. "We like your place here." Then he paused, stood up and held out his hand to James. "I am Lucido Gutierrez. I do masonry work for Daniel Derwin."

"Excellent, Mr. Gutierrez. I am happy to meet you. You'll be helping us with the new restaurant then?"

"I think so, yes. We do all of Mr. Derwin's masonry work, and the concrete, and drywall."

"I guess we'll be seeing a lot of you, then, over at the new place."

"I hope so...This is my family...Maria, Alexandra, and Victor." They nodded and smiled happily.

Bridget brought the food, set it on the table. James moved smoothly aside as she set the plates down. He helped her by taking the water pitcher and refilling glasses.

"Me avisan que si les puede traer algo más, ¿ok?"

James smiled at them and spoke. "Thank you for choosing our restaurant tonight. Bridget will be here to serve you. Mr. Gutierrez, I will surely see you later on." He looked around the table. "Nice to meet you. Enjoy your meal."

When James got back to the kitchen, he instructed Bridget, "When the Gutierrez check is ready, just bring it to me. I'll take care of it."

Deeds
10

In spite of the cold and the rain, the man was wearing a black tee-shirt. Beneath the short sleeves, both arms were covered with tattoos, blue, green, red.

The content of them was not a subject on which Kaneesha wished to dwell, but she did notice them. *How could you not notice them?* That's the point, right? *Express yourself. Life as art. Be a colorful* person. Well, she did not want to be a *colorful* person. *I'm perfectly happy, thank you, to be a person of color.*

Rain dripped from the roof of the bus stop. Just watching it made her feel cold. Whoever said that April was the cruelest month must have slept through March. Seeing the guy with tattoo arms made Kaneesha a little uncomfortable. Then, thank God, there was the bus.   She   stepped through the raindrops, onto the bus, swiped her transit card, walked back a few rows and sat next to Maudy.

Of course, they were smiling at each other.

"How you *dooooin'* girl?"

"Fine as wine"

"Me too."

"You been hearing anything from those fine boys of yours?"

"Well, you know Isaac's on top o' the world, honey. What else could I say? A mama couldn't ask for no more."

"Right. I heard he was a good spark plug in that Seton Hall game, had the team running like a well-oiled machine...a lot of assists."

"Too bad they lost."

"You can't win 'em all, Maudy. Hey, wait a minute...didn't *you* tell *me* that last time we sat here?

"I don't know, honey, but it sure is the truth. You can't win em' all."

"How 'bout Izzy? What have you heard from him lately?"

Maudy's expression changed suddenly. She pursed her lips, raised her eyebrows, but said nothing. She turned her head to look directly at her young friend, then turned back forward.

"What is it, Maudy? What happened?"

"It's just...sad...too sad to tell."

"He's not hurt, is he?"

"No, no." Silence.

Kaneesha lowered her voice, and spoke tenderly to the old woman. "What is it, Maudy? You can tell me."

"Kaneesha, it's not that I don't wanta tell you, it's more...maybe I shouldn't?"

"What's it about, Maudy?" Kaneesha knew how to wield the age-old technique of probing for information that must be obtained slowly, indirectly. Persuasively, she persisted in her small, loving inquisition. "Is he going to combat?"

"He hasn't been assigned yet. We don't know yet where he's going. But there's been some bad talk. He heard some bad reports at Fort Wenning. I can't just tell you about it. It might be secret stuff."

"It couldn't be too secret if he told you, could it?"

"Well, that's just it. I don't know if he was *supposed* to tell me?"

"Whatever it was, Maudy, he *did* tell you. And I don't think Izzy is a snitch. He's a brave man, and he knows how to do what's right."

"Yes."

"Besides, what could be wrong about telling your own *mother* about what's going on in your life."

"He was talking to another army man who had just returned from Iraq. The man told Izzy about some terrible things that were going on."

"War *is* terrible. I can't imagine what those boys have to go through. God bless 'em. They ought to put medals on every one of 'em."

"That's true, honey. But if Izzy has to take his turn at it, I'd just as soon he'd get back in one piece, as to see a bunch of medals on him."

"I hear ya."

"But this fella that Izzy was talking to...he had been at a prison."

"Did he get out of prison?"

"No, no. He was stationed at a prison, where they keep prisoners"

"Where they keep Iraqi prisoners?"

"Yeah, or whatever those insurgents are. He was at this prison working."

"A guard? A prison guard?"

"I don't know...but he said they were very cruel to the prisoners."

"Some of those prisoners probably getting exactly what they deserve."

"...if they're guilty."

"Right. If they're guilty. But some of the things he said they did...shouldn't even be done to *guilty* people."

Kaneesha looked around. Tattoo man was four rows behind them. She didn't say anything for a minute. She looked out the bus window, through the rain. They were passing a little nightclub, a place where heavy metal freaks hung out. A sign, posted in plastic letters on a portable frame, read: *Tonight—Slasher—Ladies no cover.*

"*What* things, Maudy?"

"What?"

"*What* things do they do to the prisoners that shouldn't be done?"

Then Maudy looked out the window. She said nothing for awhile.

"Sexual things, cruel things."

Kaneesha thought for a minute. "It's right that you told me about it, Maudy. People need to know what goes on."

"Don't tell anybody."

"I won't tell anybody. What did he say about it?"

"He said that that fella said that there were some guards there who would strip prisoners naked and force them to have sex...and even sometimes the guards would use them for sex."

"I can't believe American soldiers would do that sort of thing."

The bus stopped. Tattoo man walked down the aisle, and out of the bus.

"Thank God, Maudy. That guy was giving me the creeps."

Then Maudy turned her head toward Kaneesha, looked into her eyes. She spoke, seriously and slowly: "That's the kind of things Americans were doing back in the days of *slavery*." Suddenly, there was fire in Maudy's eyes. Kaneesha was surprised at the conviction she heard in the voice of the old woman--this old, harmless woman--her friend.

"You don't know what evil lurks in the hearts of men."

Kaneesha pondered for a few seconds. She didn't want to believe it.

"Has this been proven?"

"I don't know a thing about it, honey. All I know is what Izzy told me on the phone a couple nights ago. He said some guards would tie them up with ropes, naked, make them parade around and climb on top of each other. Some guards would piss on them. It's disgusting."

They were again quiet for a few minutes.

"See...things have gotten worse in this country, girl. It used to be...kids were trained to do things right...brought up in church...they may not always *do* right, may not always *be* right, but kids were, most of 'em, *trained* to be decent."

The rain beat with newfound force on the bus roof.

"But these days, you can't tell what they're gon' do... *everyone doin' what's right in his own eyes*...many of 'em not even thinkin' that there is a difference between right and wrong."

Kaneesha was quiet, as if she must endure a parental lecture. Yet, she was listening intently.

"And then they send these boys overseas to represent America..."

Now Maudy was crying.

Kaneesha was at a loss. She didn't know what to say. So she didn't say anything, and Maudy didn't either. They rode along in glum silence, except for the swishing of rain on the bus windows, and the muffled groans of traffic that punctuated their quiet contemplation of a malevolent world. When it was time for Kaneesha to get off the bus at her usual stop near the restaurant, she gently took Maudy's hand in hers, leaned over and kissed her older friend on the forehead.

"Maudy, I pray for Izzy. I want you to know that. I pray for the Lord's protection over him, wherever he goes."

"Thank you, honey. And ask the Lord for wisdom for him, in the decisions that face him."

"Most of those decisions are made for him...in the army...like where he has to go...Iraq, or wherever they send him."

"Yeah, honey. But he needs to make good decisions about who he trusts, and who he spends time with."

"Sure, Maudy. I'm off for work now. I'll see you on our next ride. Maybe the sun will come out before then."

"Whether it rains or shines, it's all the same to me. Make a lot of money tonight ya hear?" She smiled up at her young friend, now walking away toward the bus door.

"Bye, now."

Fifteen minutes later, when Maudy arrived home, she folded the umbrella, left it on her little front porch to drain. As she stepped through the front door, and entered her quaint, comfortable (dry) living room, the phone rang. She set the bags down, sat in her favorite wing chair, picked up the handset from its position on the doilied end table.

"Hello."

"Hello, Maudy. This is Lili Kapua."

"Lily! It's so good to hear from you. I've been looking forward to seeing you next week at the FEF convention."

"As I look forward to seeing you, dear friend. How have you been?"

"Life has been good to me this year. I'll not complain. Are you at home, in Hawaii?"

"I've been working at the Oakland office for the last few days, trying to get organized for all that's going to happen next week."

"I can't imagine, Lili, how complicated it must be to arrange a national convention that will take place here in Washington, while you're on the west coast."

"Well, it's probably easier than doing it from the middle of the Pacific Ocean."

Maudy laughed out loud. "I hear you, honey."

"There isn't much to it now, really. Nancy and Frank and the other officers have done a fabulous job right there in your area. And the convention is pretty well set up now. We should be in good shape, come Thursday night next week. I'm just working out a few last-minute details. How are your boys doing?"

"They're doing well. Izzy will be shipping out to Iraq next week. He's a sergeant now."

"He's a fine young man, Maudy. I have a lot of confidence knowing that he's working on our behalf in that uniform."

"Thank you, Lili. And Isaac...he's a basketball star."

"I know! He always has been. I've been reading about him in the sports section, and I think I even saw him on ESPN last week. They're expected to win their conference tournament next week. Is that right?"

"That's right, honey. How about you and yours? How are you all getting along?"

"David and I are spending this week at the home of his business partner in San Francisco. It's been a great arrangement. He's taking care of business, and I've just crossed the Bay Bridge to Oakland these last three days. Peggy Sweetwater in our office here has made all of my tasks and to-do lists very easy to accomplish. This morning I'm taking a little break. We're actually walking across the Golden Gate right now. It's one of our favorite things to do whenever David and I are in the Bay area."

"I know it must be a beautiful sight. It's sunny there, right?"

"Yes. It's a beautiful spring day here."

"What about *your* three children? How are they?"

"Alicia stayed in Honolulu, at a friend's house. We can't tear her away from volleyball. She's a senior now, and captain of her team. The other two are going to meet us at the convention. Lee will be coming from Rhode Island, where he's studying architecture. Margarite will be joining us next week for the flight to Washington. She's at Southern Cal studying communications."

"Lord, what a collection of young'uns," pondered Maudy.

"But I was going over one of my little to-do lists, here, Maudy. I need to get your opinion on something."

"And what is that, dear?"

"Thursday night next week, we've got the opening session with dinner, at the Belmont in Urdor. You'll be there, right?"

"I wouldn't miss it for the world."

"After the opening session, I'm thinking about sending all the students, about 200 of them, to a keynote session of their own, while the parents and educators have a different program in the main ballroom."

"Right."

"Well, I need a guest speaker for those young people...someone who can motivate and serve as a role model at the same time. Frankly, I couldn't think of a better speaker for that bunch than your Isaac. I'd like to ask him to speak to the 200 young people who are present at the opening of our convention. What do you think?"

"Oh, honey, I think he'd jump right on that one, like a loose basketball. I'm sure he'd love to do it."

"I'm going to call him today and ask, but I noticed that he's not registered to attend the convention."

"It may be an oversight. He's very busy, especially since the conference tournament will be starting two days later. The coach may have something to say about that."

"I should think that any competent college coach would fully support a player's leadership role in a gathering of this type."

"Oh, I don't think it'll be problem. But he will have to get permission from Coach Brown. Go ahead and call him. Do you need his number?"

"Hold on a second. We're right in the middle of the bridge now. I'm getting a pen. Okay."

Maudy called out two sets of numbers—one for Isaac's dorm room, the other for his cell phone. Lili wrote the numbers on her address book, using the bridge rail as a support. "Got it. I'm going to call him now."

"Sounds great, Lili. Are you going to ask him to speak about something in particular?"

"Well you know, Maudy, our foundation's emphasis has always been on preserving family unity in educational institutions. But times have changed. This year, 25% of our students attending are from single-parent homes. And the same percentage is true for the 350 educators and parents attending. Isaac has some amazing accomplishments to his credit. And I know he's a young man of solid character. You've done a great job raising both of your boys, Maudy. I'll probably ask him to address, indirectly, the challenges of growing up in a single-parent home. But I'll basically leave it up to him, what he wants to talk about. I should probably ask you to speak in the other session about *raising* children and educating them."

Maudy laughed. "No, thank you. I'll be in there with the kids listening to Isaac."

"Right. I think that's what I'd be doing if I were you. Anyway, the main keynote speaker is a real fireball—teacher of the year in North Carolina. Between those two sessions, I think our convention will be off to a great start."

"Sounds like it, Lili. I'm looking forward to it. Is there anything I can do to help you on this end?"

"I'll be calling Isaac today. If you talk to him in the next day or two, and can help him get direction for the speech, or logistics or scheduling kinks worked out, please do anything you can to get him there and ready to speak to 200 youngsters who probably think the world of him anyway."

"I'm right on it, honey. Don't you worry about a thing."

"Oh, and one more thing, Maudy. Your situation is so poignant, with two boys, one having taken the university route, the other military. We want to develop support strategies for students like Izzy who choose the military. So you might want to consider that in anything that you say to Isaac about the content of his speech."

"That's great, honey. I'm glad you mentioned it. Isaac's in the limelight, while Izzy's doing the dirty work somewhere to protect our freedoms. His is a very important role."

"Exactly. I'll get back to you in a few days after we've talked to Isaac. Otherwise, I'll see you at the Belmont Hotel in Urdor, a week from tomorrow. Okay?"

"See you then. Thanks for calling."

"The pleasure is mine. See ya in a week or so. Bye."

Lili closed the cell phone, then opened it up again. She punched the number that Maudy had given her for Isaac's cell phone. She was surprised when he answered on this, her first attempt to call.

"Hello. This is Isaac Jones."

"Hi, Isaac. This is Lili Kapua, president of the Family Education Foundation."

"Yes. What can I do for you?"

"First of all, Isaac, I want to congratulate you on a great season with the Lincoln Eagles, and I want to wish you well in the upcoming tournament."

"Thank you."

"Your mother and I have been friends for the last twenty years or so. She has followed my teaching career, and I have kept up with hers."

"Yes, ma'am. I remember talking to you a few years back at one of the conventions. I think it was the one in Chicago."

"Right. Well, you know, your mother and I have corresponded over the years, and talked whenever we could get together. I'm principal of a high school in Honolulu."

"A great place. Our team went through there a couple of years ago on the way to the Maui tournament. It must be a great place to live."

"It certainly is, Isaac. Anyway, the reason I'm calling you is I would like to ask for your help at our FEF convention next week. Would you be willing to speak to a group of 200 people your age and younger?"

"Whoa!" He laughed. "I think that can be arranged. What do you want me to tell them?"

"Well, what wisdom could you offer them? As you probably know, the purpose of our organization is to promote and preserve families in educational institutions of all kinds. That involves motivating people toward high levels of educational accomplishments. Your record speaks for itself. I think you could come up with some sound advice for a bunch of students. They need motivation and direction. You probably know all about those dynamics, being a point guard, right?"

"Sounds good to me. When is this exactly, and where?"

"Thursday night, a week from tomorrow, at the Belmont Hotel, right there in your hometown of Urdor. You also get, by the way, a very good meal with the deal, and a free registration for the convention if you like."

"I'd love to do it. That's two nights before our conference tournament starts. I'll have to clear it with Coach Brown."

"I understand. Would you like me to call him?"

Isaac thought for a moment. "Yes. That would probably be a good idea."

"I'll call him today."

"So, Mrs. Kapua, you don't have a more specific topic for me than motivation and direction?"

"Well, Isaac, we do have a special emphasis this year on the educational challenges that are unique to single-parent households. If there were any disadvantage to not having a dad around while you were growing up, it certainly wasn't much of a factor in your life. You've done very well in school, and in basketball. I don't want to limit you to this topic. But...there are a lot of kids out there who don't have one parent or the other to help them get through school...and through life, you know. Your experience may yield some special advice for those students. But I'm leaving it up to you, how you want to handle it. If you can get them thinking like your guys are playing on the basketball court, it will be a successful session."

"I'd probably like to mention my brother, Izzy, who is a sergeant in the Army."

"That would be excellent. I know a little bit about Izzy, what your mother has told me. And there are plenty enough kids who have military inclinations, whether they plan to go to college or not. It would be very appropriate for you to talk about Izzy's life direction, as well as your own."

"Thank you for this opportunity, Mrs. Kapua. I'll start working up a message for those kids today. Tell you what. I'll send you an email in the next hour or two, and it'll have Coach Brown's phone number, so you can call him. I would appreciate you doing that. And then you'll have my email address. You can send me specific information about where to be, and what time to be there."

"Okay. But that part is simple. Just be at the Belmont Hotel on Thursday night next week, ready to talk. And...come hungry. It will be a meal you won't forget. My email address is Lkapua@fef.org. Don't hesitate to request any help that you may need between now and then to accomplish this. Got it?"

"Yes, ma'am. Thanks for calling."

"Thank *you*, Isaac. I'll be talking to you later on. Bye now."

***

"I'll have a Guinness stout," said Matthew Brady. Rachel drew it out for him. Rachel was having to work this Wednesday night for Rudy, the regular bartender. She could handle it all right, but it certainly didn't compare favorably with serving *vino*, which of course was her *forte*. Every now and then, however, someone would order a glass of wine; she'd take the opportunity to educate them a little about what it was that she had brought them, be it *Merlot, Beaujolais, or Bordeaux, Liebfraumilch, Chianti, or Shiraz.*

Matthew, enjoying his Guinness, was getting a discourse from Morris Schroeder on how God probably breathed an immortal soul into the life of a Cro-Magnon creature whom Moses later named "Adam." He was listening, but then he said, "Morris, have you ever been to a football game?"

"Why, sure, I've been to a football game."

"Morris, you're the kind of guy who sees a lesson in everything. Any football game that you've ever been to...what did you learn from it?"

Morris, a good-natured fellow always willing to talk as long as there was someone interesting, or interested, on the other end, replied, "The quarterback calls the play in the huddle. The center snaps the ball. The quarterback either a.) runs with the ball, b.) hands it to a teammate who then runs with it, or c.) passes the ball to a teammate. While this is taking place, the opposing team does everything it can to put a stop to whatever it is that the quarterback and his guys are trying to put across. Right?"

"That's it, Morris. You've got it. Now, another question: Do you know who the greatest coach was that ever coached in football?"

Morris cocked his head and thought for a minute. "Uh, Matthew...that would be Joe Gibbs, with the Redskins."

"No, no, no. You mean to tell me...you don't know who the greatest coach in football was?"

"Well, Matthew, I've given you my opinion. What is your opinion? Who was the greatest coach that ever was in football?"

"Vince Lombardi."

Morris took a swig of his beer. "Vince Lombardi. I should have known."

"Vince Lombardi led the Packers to 5 NFL championships during the 9 years that he coached them. Is that amazing, or what?"

"Amazing, Matt."

"No coach has *ever* been able to, and no coach will probably *ever be able to* do such a thing in such a short period of time. Because, you see, Matthew, the game is different nowadays. The players have got it all tied up with their contracts; they're free agents. It'll never be the same. There will *never be* another Vince Lombardi."

"By Jove, Matt, I believe you're right."

"Listen...December 31st, 1967. The Packers are playing the Cowboys for the NFL championship, at Green Bay. The field is terrible...snow, ice. Packers have the ball on the Cowboys's 1-yard-line, down by three. They could go for the field goal to tie. What do they do? Bart Starr calls the play to handoff to Mercein, but instead of handing it off, surprises everybody, *including his teammates*, with a sneak—right into the end-zone. Lombardi had called the play—*instead of a field goal that would have tied it*. What balls that guy had. Then they went on to beat Oakland in the Super Bowl. There will never be another Vince Lombardi, Morris."

"You got that right, Matt."

"You know where football came from, don't you Morris?"

"Nah, I never knew...never thought about it. Where did it come from, Matt?"

"Ireland."

"Yeah? Well, that makes sense...."

"Some people'll tell you it started in England. But...that was later. *Originally* , it was the Irish who came up with it. My people came from Ireland, Morris. Did I ever tell ya that?"

"No."

"County Cork, Ireland. Catholic, none of this Protestant stuff. My great-great-grandfather Patrick Brady stepped off the boat in Boston, 1855. After that, four generations of hard work and determination in the land of the free, home of the brave... and here I am. You know what, Morris?

"What?"

"We need to set up a time to talk about your insurance needs."

"I've got plenty of that, Matt."

***

Footfalls cannot easily be heard on wet grass.

Nor can dark figures, clothed in dark clothes, be easily seen. Dark deeds, perpetrated by dark figures, treading upon dark, wet grass, cannot be detected. This was their deception.

Two dark figures slithered stealthily through slick dark night. Dark letters, sprayed upon white walls, across menorah in bas-relief, denoted desecration, demon-designed. Dark figures, done with their denigration, prepared to flee.

Bright lights: Police, protectors of the people, pursuing desecrators. They apprehended those denizens of the dark.

Bright lights revealed their denigration: "Holocaust is Lie from Zionist Jew-pigs." Black paint was dripping down the wall, slick and wet. What a mess. What a lie.

Officer Rashad Torres was out of breath. He had chased those denizens of the dark for two blocks before catching them. His partner, Michael Zwick, had assisted by driving the patrol car along the street, keeping the pressure on, assuring that the dark figures would not escape. Torres arrested them, slapped the handcuffs on them. Just young kids they were...17, maybe 18.

"Take 'em to the station." Dark deeds discovered desisted.

At the station:

"What's your name, kid?"

No answer.

"I've got ways of getting your name that you never even dreamed of."

No answer.

"You want to make it hard on yourself?"

Silence. "I'll be back."

Next room, next dark-deed-doing kid.

"What's your name, kid?"

"Who cares?"

"Your mother cares. She doesn't want you out on a night like this, especially when she finds out what you were up to."

"I don't have a mother."

"Were you cloned from a chimpanzee?"

"Greg Burst."

"That's your name? Greg Burst."

"Yeah."

"What about your buddy? What's his name?"

"Leo Zollinger."

"Thank you. Things are getting better for you already. But you *are* under arrest, and you will be charged with malicious vandalism. There's a little lesson about life that you should have learned a long time ago, boy. 'Do unto others as you would have them do unto you.' Would you appreciate it if someone spray-painted your house with insults like that?"

No answer. The kid just hung his head.

A few minutes later, Officer Zwick had written a report. Greg Burst and Leo Zollinger, both of Urdor, Virginia had vandalized Temple Beth Shalom in Georgetown. They had yielded the names of their parent/guardians. Greg Burst's father, Fred Burst, and Leo Zollinger's mother, Ruby Ross, and stepfather, Jack Ross.

The parents were called but could not be contacted. The denizens of the dark spent a long night in a dark jail.

Plans

11

Thursday morning, America woke up, time zone by time zone.

This is the nation whose legacy, and hope for the future, is to be an example of liberty, justice, and enterprise for all the nations of the world. It's a tall order.

This Thursday morning in America meant a lot of things to a lot of people.

In the city of Washington, Senators, Congressmen, Congresswomen woke up thinking about, among other things, legislation they would debate today. Some of them had headaches; some had troubles back in the home district. Some had agendas that were dear to them. Most had appointments to keep. They all had places to go, people to see. Each Senator, each Congressman showered, shaved, put his pants on one leg at a time, then went out to face the day. Each lady Senator, Congresswoman showered, put on makeup, chose an outfit and put it on, then went out to face the day. Most of them headed for their place of business: the Capitol of the United States.

Across the street, Justices of the United States Supreme Court assembled to consider how the laws passed by Senators and Congresspeople could be constitutionally interpreted by judges and other legal bodies across the breadth and width of America. Today's docket included, among other things, appeals by counsels pertaining to decisions in lower courts about the legality of wiretapping for law enforcement purposes, reverse discrimination in state applications of civil rights laws, freedom of expression as exercised by hate-groups, equitable administration of health and welfare entitlements, tort reform, objections to the death penalty, and partial-birth abortion. No small task-list for nine Justices.

Farther west, on the other end of official Washington, the President of the United States began his day, presumably with breakfast and a cup of coffee, accompanied by international intelligence reports, perhaps a newspaper or two, and requests from a host of aides, each of whom had a whole list of items that could, would, should require the President's attention.

Beyond the four manicured borders of the White House, thousands of men and women streamed into the nation's capital to do what they do five days every week: keep the government of the Unites States going. From four directions—north, south, east, west—from three states and the District, they came in cars, trains, motorcycles, airplanes, even boats. Some may have ridden to work on roller skates.

A diverse legion of workers finding their respective stations at desks and kiosks throughout the District of Columbia and beyond, they were patiently, predictably traveling toward their to-do lists this Thursday morning. Every day, their destinations include a myriad of departments in the federal government: Agriculture, Treasury, Commerce, Justice, Health, Education, Welfare, Housing, Urban Development, Interior, Army, Navy, Air Force, Marines.

Beyond the halls and edifices of official Washington stretches a metropolitan area. Like any major city of the world, it supports a hundred or more bedroom communities, villages, towns, neighborhoods, fringe cities, all populated with those men and women whose routes and paths are trod repeatedly every morning as they stream inexorably toward the central focus of their existence.

In the center of it all stands a white dome, and a lone obelisk.

Beyond and among the households of governmental workers is another city. It is a city within a city: a metro area within a metro area, an overlay of infrastructure and services. And it is populated by the thousands, millions who provide groceries, glass, and gasoline. It is kept humming by the industry and entrepreneurship of countless butchers, bakers, candlestick-makers, doctors, lawyers, accountants, technicians, attendants, superintendents, cashiers, cooks, waitresses, dishwashers, plumbers, electricians, carpenters, architects, engineers, bus drivers, jet pilots, trash collectors, road-builders, truck-drivers, farmers...you name it, they're in there somewhere. Their offices and work stations are slung out across a great city like stars in a galaxy.

Across the river, in one of that host of fringe cities, an industrious man is traveling, was traveling, will be traveling like the million or so others around him, to the place where he performs his work. He hums along with a tune on the radio.

On this particular Thursday morning at the corner of Pretoria Parkway and Edgerton Street in Urdor, Virginia, Lucido drove his twin-cab Dodge pickup into the parking lot of the vacant Rite-Aid drug store. Behind him were two more pickup trucks, each containing a crew of his employees. The three vehicles parked in the back corner of the lot, and began unloading equipment from the trucks.

Lucido spoke authoritatively to his men. "Unload the floor-saw here and take it through the back door. The rest of it goes into the front of the building. Juan, you come with me."

He walked through the back door and over to an area that would soon become a kitchen for the restaurant. Daniel Derwin was there. Standing next to him were an electrician, a plumber, and his brother, Marcus. His hands gesturing toward a set of blueprints that lay on a tilted plan table, Daniel was explaining to the men what the general sequence of work would be.

Having worked with Daniel, Marcus, and the plumber, Ed, Lucido knew them. Daniel introduced Lucido to the electrician.

"Lucido, this is Bryan Hall, our electrician for this project. Bryan, this is Lucido Gutierrez. He'll be doing the masonry, concrete and drywall."

Lucido smiled. The two men shook hands.

Daniel continued giving instructions. "Where we now stand will become the kitchen. These spray-painted lines that Marcus and I made indicate areas of the slab that will have to be cut for plumbing and electrical rough-ins. Ed and Bryan, Lucido will cut the slab today, along with any other cutting that you may need done. You guys are welcome to work in here today. I don't know what kind of dust problem we'll have. The floor saw has water to keep the dust down. But the cutting up at the front of the building will generate some dust. Is that right, Lucido?"

"Yes. We will have dust in here for the first couple of hours. Then it should settle. We'll try and get all the dirty work done as soon as possible."

"Okay. Let's go up there now and mark those window sills according to the plan. Marcus, I want you to help Lucido's guys get the glass out so they can get started cutting." Daniel looked at Ed and Bryan. "You guys have a look around. Do whatever you want to get started, running conduit and pvc overhead, or whatever…I'll be back in a minute and we can talk more about the rough-ins."

Using the blueprints, Daniel, Marcus, and Lucido marked lines to establish which sections of the front wall would be removed in order to make the windows larger. When they were done, Lucido's men began drilling holes in the masonry walls, and transferring the cut-lines to the outside face of the building. A couple of them also started removal of the metal frames that surrounded glass panels in the existing window openings. The old glass units, essentially 8 feet wide by 2 feet high, would be replaced new, bay-style units, 8 feet high by 6 feet wide. Marcus assisted them. He wanted to recover the old windows intact, because they would be useful to a friend who grows vegetables and spices in greenhouses.

Lucido and Daniel walked back to the kitchen area to monitor the start of floor-cutting. Eduardo would be the man to operate the floor saw, with which he would slowly walk the floor, using its circular diamond blade to make a deep incision in the 4" concrete slab. The machine stood on its own, looking much like a large vacuum cleaner with wheels. It also had a water tank that sprayed water onto the surface of the concrete to minimize dust in the air. Eduardo cranked the machine up, began the task.

Until Eduardo and his two helpers were done, there was little work to be done by plumbers and electricians in the kitchen area. There were plenty of other tasks, however, that could be initiated. The electricians would be installing, later on, several new panels to handle new electrical functions inherent to operating a restaurant. Overhead electrical conduits would have to be reworked and expanded. The lighting for the restaurant would be very different from the system that the drug store had utilized. There was a lot of work to be done. Ed, the plumber, decided he would return tomorrow after the floor-cuts had been completed. Bryan instructed his two employees to begin renovation of the existing electrical conduits and cables that were strung above the ceiling grid.

Mackie Heist, an electrician, climbed up on a rolling pipe-scaffold that he and his helper had just assembled. With wheels underneath and walkboards suspended 5 feet from the ground, they could easily work above the ceiling grid just about anywhere in the building. They could remove old wiring, conduits and fixtures that would not be required for the new plan. They could install new conduits and raceways in preparation for the lights and other electrical fixtures to be installed later.

Mackie knew what he was doing with electrical installations, but he had a dark side. He didn't like Mexicans. In the last ten years or so, he had seen too many of them moving into his neighborhood, and his work environment. Too many Mexicans were getting jobs that had formerly been done by white people. He wished that they would go back where they had come from.

Mexicans are hard workers in America. Mackie resented it. In fact, he was obsessive about it. As the morning wore on, he couldn't help noticing that all the Mexicans spoke to each other in Spanish. Mackie's opinion was that people in America should speak English. Their gibberish was upsetting him. After about an hour of working, he descended from the scaffold, went out to his van. He moved a few items and containers around until he found what he was looking for. It was a coffee can that contained special items that he used only on rare occasions—simplex nails, a type of roofing nail that has a one-inch square metal head fixed onto its shank; it will stand straight, upside down. He pulled a half dozen of the sharp objects out of the can and set them gingerly in his tool pouch. The pudgy electrician unlocked and opened the front door of the van, reached in and pulled a soft-drink out of a small cooler. He closed the door. He lingered by the van, swigging the plastic bottle, surveying the back parking lot of the store. No one was around, everybody inside busy. Casually, he walked over to the old truck that the Mexicans had driven, dropped a pencil, bent down to pick it up. As he did so, the begrudging man slipped an upright simplex-nail directly beneath a front tire of the truck. This nefarious feat he stealthily performed, four times, each the same, at each front tire of the two trucks. He ambled away, re-entered the building, walked back to his scaffold, and climbed upon it, as if nothing had happened.

***

Over on Westside Avenue, Bridget walked out of her motel room and down the steps. She would be catching a bus for work, but first she needed to walk down the street a ways to pick up a few personal items. She walked into the Target, grabbed a small shopping basket, headed for the interior of the store.

Bridget was going her merry way when a familiar face suddenly appeared.

Wanda, the woman on whose sofa she had slept for three nights, stood at the end of the sundries aisle, looking directly at her. Beside the scraggly woman was her young daughter, Jonda. Wanda's face registered nothing more than the chaotic life by which she was entrapped; she did not smile. It was that needful look, that look of seeking sympathy. Bridget was pierced to the soul by it—the sudden reminder that it might have been her own face reflecting that limp desperation, had it not been for her decision to escape it.

"Bridget, where did you go?"

Bridget put on a fake smile. This was what she had dreaded. *Just when I was getting set up in a new life.* Forcing a response from herself, she droned, "Wanda, how have you been?" Although Bridget knew in her heart how Wanda was doing, because Wanda had been headed for nothing but trouble, living with that meth-freak, Buzz. When Bridget had realized what was going on in that trailer...*that's when* she had made her move.

The awkward silence was short-lived. "Bridget, honey, can you help us?"

Wanda's raspy cigarette voice irritated her. "I'm on my way to work, " Bridget stammered.

"Oh, where? Where are you working?

"I...at a restaurant. What do you need?" As if she didn't know. Actually, Wanda's situation was worse that Bridget thought.

"I took Jonda and left Buzz. It got to where I couldn't stand his meanness any more. We need a place to stay."

Dammit. Why couldn't I get away from this woman? But this woman had taken Bridget in when she needed a place to go. Bridget was now cornered between her own desire to be free of a destructive lifestyle and the personal obligation she felt to return a merciful favor.

"Look, Wanda. I've got to go. Here's $20. That ought to help you."

"Oh, thank you Bridget." But it was not appreciation that she heard in Wanda's voice; it was more need. Bridget started backing away.

"Okay. I...I'll see you later. I've got to go now."

"Where you working?"

"I'll call you, Wanda."

"You can't call me. I'm not going back there. I mean it."

"Well, that's good."

"Where you working, Bridget? Do they need any help?"

"I've gotta go, Wanda. It's the Jesse James Grille." Now she was trotting. "I don't want to be late. Bye."

Bridget hurried to the checkout. Wanda and Jonda moved to the end of the aisle and watched Bridget as she left the store. Bridget wasted no time getting to the bus stop. Five minutes later, when the bus arrived, she climbed on, greatly relieved to be headed for a place where people were happy and productive.

***

At 4:30, Kaneesha and Bridget were wrapping silverware in napkins. "What courses did you take at Lincoln, Bridget?"

"Just some general college...English, math. I'm halfway through being a sophomore. The psychology class was pretty interesting. That was something that I could get into...don't know what I'd do with it though...be a shrink? The world is crazy enough as it is. I'd probably make it worse."

They laughed.

Kaneesha thought for a moment. "That's one reason I haven't made a move toward college yet. I don't know what I'd do. I do like to paint, though. James has said that he'll let me paint a mural in the new place before we move into it."

"Cool."

"I suppose we'll be picking up a lot of business from the University when we get into the new building. It'll be so close. Say...you know about Isaac Jones? The point guard for the Lincoln basketball team?"

"I've heard of him." Sports was not a prominent area in Bridget's radar.

"His mother is a good friend of mine. Most of the time when I come to work, I ride the bus with her. She's a wonderful lady...kinda like a mama to me. Not really, but you know what I mean."

"Yeah. She's older, probably seen a lot.."

"I went to school with her son, Isaac, the basketball star. I didn't really know him in high school, but since I've been getting to know his mother, I've been thinking about getting into college. I wouldn't mind getting to know Isaac. He's a man that I could take some interest in. Well, I suppose if I had been interested in him at the high school, I might have done something about it."

"Maybe it's because he wasn't interested in you."

"Well, he had any number of girls that he could give his attention to. And I had a boyfriend anyway."

"Oh? What happened there?"

"Not much. We graduated. Now he's at Virginia Tech. What about you, Bridget?"

"Not much to tell there, Kaneesha."

"Oh, come on. There must be something."

"Well, there was a guy back in Cleveland. We dated for awhile."

There was silence between them. Then, they could hear the sports announcer on TV talking about Isaac Jones and the Lincoln *Eagles*.

"See, Isaac, Isaac, Isaac. Every time they talk about the *Eagles*, they talk about Isaac. But you know what? Isaac is really, kind of a kid, compared to his brother, Izzy."

"Oh yeah? What's he like?."

"Soldier boy. He's going to Iraq any day now."

"Where is he now?"

"Fort Wenning, South Carolina."

Hilda approached the two women and said, "Bridget, phone's for you. Line one."

Bridget dreaded the call. It could only be one person. She went to the phone.

"Bridget, thanks for the 20. It's really helped me a lot. Do they need any help there?"

Bridget had been thinking about this. Remembering how Wanda had taken her in had softened Bridget's heart. "No. They don't need any help now. But if you need a place to stay for a night or two, I'm at the Traveler's Inn on Westside. I'll be there about eleven, or you can come by in the morning, but not before ten o'clock."

"Thanks, Bridget. Jonda and I really appreciate it. You'll probably see me there tonight." Then Wanda hung up.

Bridget walked over to where she and Kaneesha had been wrapping silverware. But now it was time to help Tim in the back, stacking glasses and cups. And there were menus to wipe. Suddenly, Bridget was sad. Her new world was about to be invaded by the presence of a someone whom she really didn't know very well, and who had a connection to a dark world of drugs and God-only-knows what all. This could only be a *disturbance* in the neat little life that she thought she was building. But then...it had always been so. At least now there was Marcus. With him around, things couldn't go too wrong.

At 9:30 Wanda and Jonda walked into the restaurant. Bridget was alarmed at the sight of them. Before she could do anything, though, Hilda had greeted them and seated them. Bridget walked over to their table unsure of what to expect. She set two glasses of water on the table and smiled. It wasn't her fake smile this time, just...strained.

"Hi" she said. "What's up?"

"Hi." Wanda looked up at Bridget, trouble in her eyes. She looked at her daughter and asked: "Jonda, can you say hi to Miss Bridget?"

"Hi. Can I get a hamburger?"

The simple honesty of the child's question surprised Bridget. She laughed.

"Why, sure you can, honey. Do you want some fries with it?" She smiled at Jonda, a child unaware of the reasons for her mother's chaotic lifestyle. Her innocence called for a little tenderness. A sudden burst of generosity pricked Bridget's heart. She looked Wanda in the eyes and said, "The same for you, Wanda? Or would you like something else? We've got an extra ribeye back there. How 'bout it? Would you like a good steak?"

"That sounds great, Bridget, thank you."

"With baked potato?"

"Sure."

They were both lightening up now. Bridget felt silly with generosity, as if giving had suddenly released her from all fear of what this encounter might mean. "And I'll bring you a salad, okay?"

"That would be nice."

"What kind of dressing?"

"Uh...thousand island."

"Back in a minute."

Bridget went back to the cooler, poured a glass of milk. Then she went by the bar, drew out a draft beer, and delivered the two drinks to mother and daughter.

A few minutes later, Bridget brought their food out. Mother and daughter ate voraciously. When they were about done, Bridget visited them. She spoke quietly:

"So...I take it you'll be needing a place to sleep tonight?"

"Yes, Bridget. That would help us a lot."

"Okay. Just hang here for a little while. We'll leave here in an hour or so. A friend of mine will pick us up and take us to the motel."

"Thanks."

Bridget brought desserts for them. Mother and daughter sat contentedly and watched TV. Bridget performed the nightly cleanup and closing duties. Kaneesha had left early. Bridget paid Wanda's check out of her tips.

At 10:45, Marcus came to take Bridget to her motel. Bridget made introductions. They crowded into his truck, Jonda on Wanda's lap, Bridget in the middle. It thrilled her to sit so close to him. They smiled at each other and kissed. He started the truck and turned onto Pretoria Parkway, headed west.

Marcus, never one to beat around the bush, began asking questions.

"So Wanda, you're going to stay at Bridget's room tonight?"

"Yes, and I appreciate it so much, Bridget."

"Well, what's your situation, Wanda?"

"What do you mean—my situation?" In Wanda's paranoid world, open inquiry was not an everyday occurrence. She was accustomed to cautious, equivocal speech in which decisions and judgments were postponed as long as possible. People's personal circumstances were guarded by their intentions not to readily involve others.

"I had to leave my boyfriend."

"Why?"

Bridget was amused at Marcus' by-now predictable forthrightness. But she was a little concerned at what this conversation may lead to—what Marcus' probing inquiries may uncover.

"Well, he's a mean bastard, if you want to know the truth."

"What did he do that was mean?"

Wanda was evasive. "He's just always been that way. In the two years that I've known him, he's always been mean."

"Well, what do you mean? Does he beat you? Lock you up? What?"

She hesitated. "He doesn't really beat me...Maybe he slaps me now and then...He just...well, I don't know what's going on."

Marcus didn't say anything for a few minutes. He knew when to slack off.

"Is Jonda in school...first grade?"

"I haven't put her in yet."

"Where have you been living?

"Out in the Pressley area. We were living in his trailer."

"You mind me asking his name?"

"Billy Townsend, but everybody calls him Buzz."

"Well, Wanda...what's your last name?"

"Smith."

"Wanda...Is there anything I can do for you? You got some plans about what you're gonna do?"

"I don't know. I've got a sister in Staunton, but I'd like to stay around here if I can get somethin' goin'."

"You done any cleaning?"

"You mean like cleaning houses and businesses? Uh, yeah." She was lying, but it was something she thought she could figure out.

"I know someone who runs a cleaning service. I'll ask her if you can help."

"That'd be great. Thanks."

"What about Buzz? Is he looking for you?"

"I don't know. I hope not." But she knew better.

Marcus stopped the truck at the motel. Wanda and Jonda got out, waited awkwardly in the parking lot. Jonda was falling asleep. Bridget lingered in the truck with Marcus for a minute, then got out. They waved goodbye. Bridget led the mother and daughter up to the room, opened the door. She had a nagging thought that in opening that door for Wanda, she may be opening her life to influences that could prove difficult to control. For she had caught a glimpse, a murky discernment, that the trailer where she had stayed with Wanda for three days concealed something destructive. Maybe it was methamphetamine, or maybe it was something more destructive than that.

Wonders
12

The explosion that Aleph Leng experienced at the Holocaust Museum had torn him up inside. His insides were not torn up; nor were his outsides torn up. But inside, he was torn up about it. The police officer who had been killed in the blast, J.D. Joadson, had been calmly speaking to Aleph less than a minute before he was so rudely blown into eternity. Aleph was, in fact, the last person to whom Joadson had spoken. The funeral would be tomorrow, Saturday; Aleph was planning to attend.

Today, he was wandering in Washington, trying to sort out his thoughts. Having spent his young years evading hostile militia in Sudan, Aleph was accustomed to the violent, malicious ways of *homo sapiens*. This latest explosion of human depravity had pierced his soul with a terrible awareness that, everywhere on the face of the earth, human existence is incomplete in and of itself. There is something lacking. Aleph wept; it was a *Gethsemane* moment.

The African had walked through the Capitol building. Exiting from the east side, he had continued eastward, across the street to the Library of Congress. Entering the majestic structure beneath a granite archway, Aleph found himself at the base of a grand, white marble staircase. He ascended. The steps led him to the focal point of the building—the middle of the Great Hall. Centered upon its marble floor, he stood over a large brass inlay shaped like the sun, on which the four points of the compass had been inscribed. Wandering between two bronze liberty ladies, the African turned around, looking straight up, beholding, within a rotunda ceiling 75 feet above, a cupola bright with sunshine and stained-glass magnificence. His attention then shifted from the grandiose that was above and all around him to the miniscule. On either side of him were solid marble railings that enstoned the next flight of stairs. They had been intricately carved. One detail caught his eye: an electrician holding a telephone. This figure, crafted in marble represented him...himself...for Aleph was himself an electrician.

He pondered.

Then, circumambulating the stairway base, southward he ascended; eastward he continued. Halfway up, he saw Africa, the land of his birth, represented on a marble globe.

Aleph stepped slowly; he perused the vaulted, mosaic-laden ceilings. In a semi-circular area below the ceiling, his studious eye landed upon a series of paintings. In 1897, John White Alexander had labored upon these images, and rendered them *The Evolution of the Book*. Aleph stood looking into the Great Hall, noticing the progression, left to right, from human memory to the spoken word, then the written word, and the *printed* word. *This is, after all, a Library.* But, unlike any library that Aleph had ever seen, it embodied much more than the storied record of human expression and knowledge. It was a masterpiece of architecture. More than that...it was a masterpiece of *Art*. The building itself was a work of art.

Even as Eurocentric as this art obviously was, the African was moved by its grandeur and uninhibited declaration of human possibility. His eyes rested upon Johann Gutenberg, one of the figures depicted in Alexander's *Book* mural. The world's first printer was shown reading from a white paper, presumably with newly-printed words on it. With him were two assistants, one of whom was operating the printing press, by applying pressure to a long wooden handle.

Aleph studied the painting. *Is there any invention, besides the wheel, that could have changed the world more than the Printing Press?* The only one he could think of was, perhaps, the telephone, which earlier he had seen included in the detailed carving on the stair railing. *Maybe the automobile...nah, it's just a glorified horse buggy.*

Beneath the arched painting of Gutenberg was a memorial to the men of the Library of Congress who died in World War I.

As Aleph walked through the East Corridor, he discovered a display case containing a *Gutenberg Bible*. He stood amazed at the first printed edition of a Bible. Childhood memories of his mother reading the Scriptures to him streamed into his consciousness. Upon that foundation she had mortared the building blocks of her love, forming a solid structure of truth. His faith in a God who saves us from trouble and error later grew like a vine around that framework. The immensity of this revelation reverberated at this moment deep within his eternal soul.

Aleph felt his cell phone vibrate in his pocket. Discreetly, he moved toward the exterior wall and answered it. "Hello."

"Mr Leng?"

"Yes."

"This is Jan Wokowski with the Washington Police Department. When would you be available to give a statement about the bombing at the Holocaust Museum?"

"I am available now."

"Would you come to our headquarters?"

"I can be there in one hour if you wish."

"That would be fine. Do you know where it is?"

"I know where it is. I will see you about two o'clock then?"

"Right. I'm detective Jan Wokowski."

"Yes, thank you. Goodbye."

Aleph walked down the stairs and out of the Thomas Jefferson building, the Library of Congress.

***

Detective Jan Wokowski led Aleph into a room with a table and a few chairs. A glass of water was on the table.

The policewoman, gray-haired and businesslike, smiled politely and spoke. "Mr. Leng, thank you for providing information that pertains to this terrorist act. We have watched a video file that confirms the statement which you gave us on Monday, the day of the bombing. Your proximity to the explosive device, and your conversation with Lt. Joadson just prior to the explosion have been noted. Upon review of the evidence we have, we have just a few more questions for you. Okay?

"Yes, ma'am."

"Please give us in your own words a description of the scene, and what happened there."

"I was standing in line waiting to enter the Museum. I was talking to Lt. Joadson. He was asking me questions about my life in Sudan and Kenya, and immigration to Los Angeles, California, USA. Suddenly, his eyes fixed on something near the building. He interrupted me, excused himself, and began walking toward the building... toward a trash can that was by the building. Then, the explosion...all hell broke loose. I jumped to the ground, or was thrown to the ground...I don't know which. There was smoke everywhere. After it cleared a little, I went over there to where the trash can had been, but it was gone. I saw Lt. Joadson lying there. He was obviously dead. Then I called 911."

"Before the explosion occurred, while you were standing in line, did you see anyone near the garbage can?"

"I did see three people near the garbage can, but I didn't pay much attention to them. I think they had put something in the trash."

"Did you get a look at their faces?"

"No...I'm afraid not. I was not paying much attention. And it was cool; they were wrapped up to keep warm." Mr. Leng's eyes flashed with remembrance. "Wait...one of the men...there were two men and a women...the man in the middle had a baseball cap on, with a confederate flag on the back of it."

"Did you notice any other characteristics about him, or about the other two?

Silence.

"Hair color?"

"No."

"Thank you, Mr. Leng."

***

At 2:45 Friday afternoon, Detectives Jan Wokowski and Rufus Ray drove over the river in order to visit the home of young Leo Zollinger, investigating the possibility that there may be a connection between anti-Semitic vandalism and the bombing at the Holocaust Memorial. The two plainclothes officers arrived at 745 Winchester Street in a neighborhood of medium-sized, mostly brick, 40-year-old houses in Urdor. After stepping onto the low, uncovered front porch, Lt. Ray knocked on the aluminum storm-door. A woman of about 50 opened the front door, but looked at them through the screen.

"Mrs. Ross?"

"Yes, sir."

"I'm detective Rufus Ray, with D.C. Police. This is Lt. Jan Wokowski. We'd like to talk to you about Leo Zollinger."

"What do you want to know?"

"Is Leo your son?"

"Yes."

"Did you know that he was arrested Wednesday night in Washington?"

"No sir. I did not. What did he do?"

"He and another boy, Greg Burst, were caught vandalizing a building. They've been charged with malicious vandalism."

"What did they do?"

"They were caught in the act of spray-painting a hate message on a synagogue in Georgetown. The bail has been set at $1000."

"My husband will probably want to bail him out, but he's not here right now. He's still at work. But he oughta be here soon. He's off at three."

"Where does he work, ma'am?"

"He works over at the Reddy-mix plant on Raynor Road."

"Do you mind if we wait for him?"

"No. Come on in."

Mrs. Ross opened the door, then went over to the TV, turned it off. She removed some items from the sofa.

"Have a seat, if you like."

The house smelled of cigarette smoke and burnt bacon. Opposite the sofa was a fireplace with insert, dusty, not having been used in a while. Two large vases of artificial magnolias were set on the brick hearth. The mantle had family pictures. Above the mantle was a mirror with a large confederate flag decal on it. The furniture was neat, a little worn.

The lady detective ventured into further questioning. "Were you surprised to hear that Leo was arrested?"

"Yes. We let our phone go about six months ago. We just use the cell phone now. So this is the first I've heard about it. I guess he didn't give you the cell number?"

"No, ma'am."

"Really, though...Leo doesn't live here any more. I can't really keep up with him these days. He's been working days. He dropped out of school. I think he's been doing some construction work."

Rufus asked: "What company do you think he'd be working for?"

"Probably Lickety-Split Drywall...Wendall Foggerty."

Jan made a note of it.

"Do you know where he's been staying?"

"I think he and Greg have been living with a fella out in Pressley somewhere."

"And who is that?"

"Moa...I think it's...Moa Grindell."

"Mrs. Ross, have you ever known your son to get upset about political issues?"

"No. He mostly likes to hunt and fish. I've never known him to get worked up about much of anything."

"You've never heard him make any statements about hating people...shocking statements?"

"No. Well...some of those friends of his...I don't know what all they might come up with. They get a little crazy I think when they've been drinkin'."

A pickup truck drove into the driveway. Jan could hear the radio blasting country music. Immediately it was turned off. They heard the truck-door slam. A few seconds later another door was opened in the house, then closed. Then a pudgy middle-aged man with reddish hair walked in through the door that must have led to the kitchen.

The man didn't say a word; he tossed a disappointed look at his wife. After pausing for a second, he leaned against the door-frame.

"What can I do for you fellas?"

Rufus Ray introduced himself and Jan Wokowski. Then: "Leo was arrested Wednesday night."

"What happened?"

"He and Greg Burst were caught in the act of vandalizing a synagogue in Georgetown."

Jack Ross didn't say anything for a few seconds. He registered no surprise.

"Has bail been set?"

"$1000."

"Goddam. What did he do? Rob the place?"

"He spray-painted a hate message on the front wall of the building. The oil paint has done serious damage on white limestone."

"Goddam. I don't know why he'd wanna tangle with a bunch of damn rich Jews."

Rufus was surprised that the man didn't inquire about what message had been painted on the wall. "Do you know why he would do that?"

"Hell, I don't know. It's none of your damn business anyway. I've got another job to go to. I'll go to the jail tomorrow and post bail." He walked out of the room.

Mrs. Ross, a little puzzled, wanted to put an end to the encounter. "Thank you for tellin' us about Leo. We'll pay the bail tomorrow."

The two detectives stood, thanked the woman for her time, and left.

***

After seriously considering the advice of her friend Rachel, Helen Olei decided to give it a try going back to work. She had discussed her situation with the Head Nurse of the Emergency Room where she worked. They had agreed that the best schedule for Helen would be 3-11 pm, four days a week. So she was back on the job at Wessex County Medical Center.

Part of the rationale behind getting back to work was that assisting others to overcome medical problems would enable Helen to forget her own. Only two people, both of them supervisors, knew what had happened to her just one week ago. Her first task was to function as a "normal" person, with no hint of trauma seeping through the professional exterior. After treating a couple of light-duty patients, Helen understood that her first priority was still the same as it had always been: caring for and healing people.

At 4:30 on Friday afternoon, a man named Mackie Heist came to the emergency room with a nail in his butt. Someone had shot him with a nail gun. Helen helped him heal.

The shift proved to be routine, uneventful, even though it was a Friday night. At 11:15 Helen emerged from the behemoth hospital building, under a canopy of stars. Clothed with a sunny disposition and a healthy weariness, she had once again found her place in the great tide of human endeavor. She had bounced back into the great career of human health care.

And her baby was still within her, alive.

***

Saturday morning, Aleph Leng attended J.D. Joadson's funeral.

It's a good thing he got there early. Zion Grace Temple was overflowing with mourners and rejoicers alike. The death of one dedicated cop had focused the attention of a straining city upon one life, well-lived, that had made a difference. People loved the man.

J.D.'s widow sat in the first row. She had borne no children, but she had borne the pains and tribulations of a man who had given himself to public service. Herself a busy nurse, she had stood by her man for seventeen years. Amazing accounts of mayhem and mirth she had been told: truth tales whispered in desperation, declared in triumph. Oh what a frail, faithful man of strength he had been; and the burden that had been laid upon him was this: to patrol the sidewalks of purgatory, perchance to storm the gates of hell, and yet never fail, never fail, to hold heaven in his heart.

A coterie of distinguished guests for this solemn occasion included not only J.D.'s dear friends and family, but also: the menagerie of friends who had known him on the street, the brigade of law enforcement officers who had served with him, 212 members of Zion Grace Temple, administrators and employees of the Holocaust Museum, a handful of Muslim neighbors, and the Honorable Cedric Douglass, Mayor of Washington.

From deep within the Abrahamic breast of a robed choir the rumble of grief and dignity came forth, slow and resonating at first, without words, then clear and loud: *Amazing Grace, how sweet the sound...hmmmmm..*

Tears. Such a life he had lived.

Voices raised, eyes glazed, souls amazed.

> *Through many dangers, toils and snares*
> *we have already come.*
> *'Twas grace that brought us safe this far,*
> *and grace will lead us home.*

The words had been written 150 years ago by a former slave-trader who had renounced his wicked ways. *Grace...that saved a wretch like me.*

A shroud of tears veiled many eyes, blurring utterance of words, bleeding their hearts dry of further sympathies expressed, until the honorable mayor took his place at the podium of embattled human dignity. He said:

"We have come together today to honor and remember a man whose life represents the best in us...whose death was suffered because of the worst in us. J.D. Joadson was a man well-loved by this community, and by this city. He died...stemming the tide of human hate. His life was not in vain. His *death* was not in vain.

"Go to 14th Street today, or any other place within his beat, any other place that knew the beating of his heart, and ask people about J.D. You will not wander far, before encountering the testimony of some person or other who has known him...some person who has seen the dedication with which he protected the citizens of this city, and the citizens of many cities and nations around the world who came here. He was a *great* man.

"The conviction with which he spoke sternly to those who would violate our peace...and gently to those who would preserve it...was resident within him all his life. J.D. was never known to have strayed from the principles of honor and justice to which he devoted himself...until, by the hand of some foul and ignoble enemy, it was extracted from him: the last full measure of his devotion.

"No...J.D. Joadson did not live in vain. His life goes on in the hearts, the hands, the minds, of those men and women who are inspired by his example. Could that be *you* this morning? Could it be *you* who has been inspired by his courageous example?

"Yes. It could be you.

"And, no...J.D. Joadson did not *die* in vain. His death defeats the dark deeds of those who would seek to rob us of our peace and security. His death defeats those dastardly attempts by malicious haters to make us relinquish our remembrance of the past.

"We, a people whose eyes peer expectantly into the future...we, a people whose minds are informed by the knowledge of those struggles that comprise human history...we, a people who deplore the Holocaust assault upon human life and dignity...we honor him today. May J.D. Joadson be remembered as a man who loved mankind... a man whom mankind loved.

"And I believe today...he's in a better place, raised from death to life, in Jesus Christ."

Violations

13

Sunday morning, Moa Grindell punched in at the convenience store where he worked. He had a hangover and a headache. But he got started on his duties anyway. A little hangover wasn't anything that a couple cups of coffee couldn't fix. Comfortably situated in the fort-like enclosure behind the checkout corner, he could do what he had to do to get through the next eight hours: keep an eye on the eight gas-pumps, not too hard to do now that half the folks used credit cards at the island and didn't bother to come in anyway. The gas-pumps were the main deal—where most of the money rolled in. Not his money, but at least he got a chunk of it.

So he was situated in the little convenience kingdom behind the counter, selling cigarettes, soft-drinks, donuts, and little packaged sausages that stayed on the counter all the time...candy, potato chips, porno magazines, milk, beer and key-chains, all kinds of little afterthoughts, trinkets and whims, whistles and bells that folks might decide to get on the spur of the moment while gassing up. It took a lot of skill to keep this little show running; couple cups of coffee and he'd be okay.

His buddy John-boy came in, paid for gas, cheese crackers and a green drink. John-boy hung around for a few minutes waiting for another customer to leave. Then he said: "You been layin' low, I take it."

"Can't complain, cool as a cucumber in a hot taco."

"Nothin' happening?"

"Nothing that I can see. I'm good."

"I saw Jack yesterday. He said the DC cops came to his house asking questions. Then he went and bailed Leo out of jail."

"Cool."

"Yeah, well...Leo and his buddy Greg still have to go before the judge."

"They can plead guilty and walk, pay a fine. They did it, didn't they? They just shouldn'a got their asses caught."

"Young idiots...don't know their asses from a hole in the ground."

A man walked in, then another man and a kid.

"I'll talk to ya later. I might see you tonight."

"Okay, John-boy, take it easy."

Moa kept the show on the road for a few hours. About 1:30 John-boy came back in the store. He hung around for a few minutes until there was no one in the store again. Then he said: "Jack said the Jews would drop the charges if he'd pay the fine and they clean the mess up."

"That's a crock of shit. The kid can't be out there cleaning a wall for a bunch of damn Jews."

"You got any better ideas?"

"Hey...It's not my problem to solve, Johnny boy. And it ain't yours, either."

Marcus Derwin entered the store. The little bell on the door rang. He walked back to the cooler, pulled out two Gatorades. At the counter, he said: "I've got this, and the gas on #7." He smiled at the two men.

"$27.45."

Marcus handed a credit card to Moa, who swiped it, retrieved a receipt from the machine and set it on the counter. Marcus signed the receipt. He took the drinks and left. Out at the gas pump, he checked the secure position of two bicycles on a rack on the back of his station wagon, then he drove away.

Sitting in the passenger seat, Bridget watched Marcus as he eased the car out into traffic. Then she said: "I've prepaid for another week at the hotel. Kaneesha has said that we could get a place together, but I don't know what to do about Wanda and Jonda."

"You probably ought to stay where you are until Wanda figures something out. Then you can work something out with Kaneesha, right?"

"That's what I would hope to do. But, looking at Wanda's situation, I don't think there's any way she can get on her feet right away. It'll probably be months."

"Well, maybe you'll want to take her as a third roommate, and Jonda."

"Do you think she can pull her share of the load working part-time for Stevens?

"Not likely. You'd probably have to carry her for awhile. You've been doing that anyway, right?"

"Yeah, but I was hoping to work into some other arrangement."

"You sure can't put her in a position of having to go back to that meth freak."

Marcus pulled the station wagon into the parking lot at Sanderson Park. He parked, lifted the bikes from the rack, inserted Gatorade in the drink-holder on his bike, inserted a bottle of water in the drink-holder on her bike. They rode to the trail. They rode on the trail, back and forth for an hour or so. Then they went around the duck pond, along city streets, and stopped at Starbucks just like last week.

Drinking coffee, he said, "You want to go to Washington?"

She said: "You want to stay out of trouble this time?"

They laughed, and looked out the window. Clouds were moving in.

Back outside, he said: "You never answered my question."

She said, "It's not the right question."

They laughed. He threw his arms around her, kissed her. They had a thing going on. They rode back to the Park. He locked the bikes in the car, and they walked to the Metro Station. This time they got out at the Smithsonian.

***

"Mitsitam." Bridget pronounced the word slowly, as she read it on a sign in the American Indian Museum.

"It means 'Let's eat!' in the native language of the Delaware and Piscataway peoples who lived in this area before white folks got here."

"I say we go for it."

While seated in the Mitsitam café, they shared a meal of food prepared in the way of Seminole. Marcus was looking out a big window at a little waterfall.

Bridget was reflecting on her life. She was pondering a certain time period that wasn't so long ago, and yet it seemed worlds apart from where she now sat. *How was it that she had landed in that disgusting little trailer that always smelled like cigarettes and old cat litter?* She had decided, stubbornly, not to accept any help from her dad. She had fallen out of his favor when she dropped out of school. Although he had been displeased, he still had offered financial help. *But I had insisted on being independent. Look where it got me.*

Wanda had taken her in. Wanda, hardly knowing Bridget, had opened her humble home to her. Why? *Wanda had wanted company...that's it. She had wanted someone to commiserate with. She could probably see and feel the warning signs about Buzz and the direction his life was taking. Wanda was having premonitions about the collapse of her relationship with Buzz.*

But after she had been there three days, Bridgit had awakened one morning with the understanding that she was in the middle of a sinking ship, or sinking *trailer*, as it were. Then she decided to get out. Seeing Wanda lie her way into gas money from a naïve guy who was too generous for his own good...seeing *that* had been the last straw. That's when she got out.

Alas, she didn't get out completely. Wanda had come back to haunt her. And the child, Jonda. Bridget must consider the life of the child in whatever decision she made about handling Wanda. *But Jonda is not my responsibility.*

"Bridget, I think you should go ahead and do it. Give Wanda a break. She gave you a break."

"I don't even like her."

"Hey...I understand. On the other hand, you could fling her out, toss her out to the manipulations of her cranked-up boyfriend."

Bridget began to cry.

"Come on, Bridget. Let's go. Let's take a walk." He threw some trash in the nearby receptacle, picked up their coats, took her hand gently. "Come on, you don't have to get it all figured out now. Have a little faith, huh?"

"Faith in what?"

Marcus just laughed. "Come on. I want to show you something."

They walked out of the building. The March evening was getting chilly and cloudy. Marcus put his arm around her. They began walking along the Mall side of Jefferson Avenue, back toward the Smithsonian.

A strong voice called out to them: "Hello. Hello, sir, madam."

Was someone calling us? The wind was picking up.

"Sir, you dropped a wallet."

Marcus definitely heard that part. He turned around.

A tall black man was walking swiftly toward him, waving Bridget's wallet.

"You left this under the table."

"Thank you. Thank you," blurted Bridget.

"I am happy to have been able to help you."

"You are so kind." Bridget opened the wallet, took out a $10 bill, and offered it to the man.

Aleph just looked at it and laughed. "If you must give that away, give it to someone who needs it more than I do."

"Are you sure?"

"Oh, yes."

Marcus sensed something strong and unusual about the man. He extended his hand. Aleph took Marcus' hand and shook it.

"I am Aleph Leng. I am pleased to meet you. Is there anything else I can do for you?" His smile seemed as genuine as driven snow.

"I'm Marcus Derwin, pleased to meet you. I think the question should be 'What can *we do for you?*'"

"There is nothing that I need. But perhaps you can answer some questions for me about Washington?"

"Sure."

Aleph thought for a moment. " Ah...Do not let me detain you. Would you like to continue walking? I am also going in that direction."

"Sure, if you prefer."

"I am visiting here. I live in Los Angeles."

"But you're originally from Jamaica, right?"

That was *very* amusing to Aleph. He just let a big laugh fly out. The he said: "I was born in Sudan. I came here to this country two years ago. I am now an American citizen."

"Congratulations. We're glad to have you." Marcus chuckled.

"Just this week, however, I have decided to move here, to Washington. And I am looking for work to do."

"What kind of work do you do?"

"I am an electrician."

"A licensed electrician?"

"Yes, in the state of California."

Marcus thought for a minute. *This was getting interesting.* He was about fed up with Mackie Heist and his cranky, hateful attitude. And Mackie's boss, Bryan, wasn't any great example of cooperation either. But that was Daniel's problem, Nevertheless...Marcus spoke slowly: "I *might* have some ideas about that...Where are you staying now?"

"I have some friends here in the city. They work at the Kenyan Embassy."

They had reached the corner of 14th and Jefferson, by the Smithsonian. Aleph changed the subject. "Have you got a few minutes? I would like to show you something?"

"Yes. We're in no hurry. This is what we like to do anyway...walk around."

Aleph continued: "About a week ago, there was a bomb planted at the Holocaust Museum. Did you hear about it?

"Yes." Marcus and Bridget answered at the same time.

"It is right up the street here." They turned left and walked on 14th Street.

"Yes."

"When that bomb exploded, I was standing in line waiting to enter the Museum."

Bridget was surprised. "Thank God it didn't kill you!"

"I did thank God. But there was one man killed there, a police officer..."

"Lt. Joadson, wasn't it? I heard about him."

"That's right. Just before the explosion, I was talking with him. Then, he interrupted our conversation, and started walking away. A few seconds later, he was dead."

They were now approaching the Holocaust Museum. The building was closed and barricaded. But the destructive power of the bomb, as small as it had been, was obvious. A large chunk of the semi-circular face of the building had been blown out.

They looked at the scene for a moment, in the dim light of a streetlamp.

"I was standing there." He pointed to the spot.

"You are fortunate, sir, to be alive," said Bridget. "You must have been the last person to hear him speak."

"That I was, madam. That I was." The African hung his head solemnly. He seemed to be lost in thought.

After a while, Bridget spoke, tenderly: "Mr. Leng, this place is very special. Do you know why?"

He looked directly at her, a serious expression still on his face.

"My grandmother survived Auschwitz."

***

From the darkness outside the convenience store, Moa saw a familiar van pull up to an area behind the store. But no one got out of it. About 10 minutes later, when the store was empty of customers, he opened the back door. Working very efficiently, he wheeled a dolly with four cardboard cartons out. He slid the side door open. Moa tossed the four cartons into the van and threw a blanket over them.

"It'll be five," said Mo, flatly.

Buzz had five hundred-dollar bills ready for him. Moa took them.

Then Buzz drove off with his lifetime supply of cold medicine.

But he didn't go home. He drove for about 5 minutes on Dolphus Road, then turned south onto Westside Drive, went another 10 minutes. He turned into the *Traveler's Inn*. He parked the van behind the motel, in the darkest spot that he could find. Then he walked around the side of the old, 60's-era motel, up an exterior steel stairway to the second floor. Walking quietly, he found the room that he'd been looking for, the room that he had previously been watching: 207. He knocked gently on the door. Wanda opened it.

She tried immediately to shut it, but Buzz was ready. He rushed in forcefully and closed the door behind them. Wanda backed away, but Jonda began whining. He knew how to deal with her. Buzz slapped the child across the face and told her to shut up. Jonda whimpered. She had been through this before; she knew the routine.

"Pack your shit. We're goin' home."

"No."

Buzz suddenly decided to ease off a bit, now that he had established control. Lowering his voice, he said, "What is your problem?"

She didn't answer right away. "You. You're my problem."

"I'm gonna take care of us."

She didn't say a word, just looked at him. He didn't know what to do, hadn't thought this far ahead. Looking at her in that defenseless posture, he remembered how beautiful she was. He tried to kiss her.

She pushed him away. It took all of her strength. His insistent advances were not yet violent. "I'm going to take care of us." Reaching in his pocket, he pulled out two hundred-dollar bills. "Look."

"That don't mean shit to me, you idiot. Get out of here and don't ever come back." Jonda whimpered.

Wanda could see his rising frustration. It was a familiar pattern, Having failed with the sweet-talk, he was getting desperate. But she had decided she would not allow it. Without warning, she reached down, opened the bureau drawer, and withdrew a pistol. Directing the point of it at him carelessly, unskillfully, she shouted at him, like a cornered wildcat: "Go...Go...away, Buzz." She was hysterical.

Buzz didn't believe she would pull the trigger, and he needed to shut her up. He moved on her. She did pull the trigger, but not before he had grabbed the gun and turned it away from himself.

The bullet destroyed her abdomen. Hysteria turned to moaning. Jonda's whimpering turned to wailing. Buzz panicked. He pulled the gun out of her hand, ran out of the room and closed the door. Running as fast as he could, down the stairs, across the parking lot, he reached the van, fumbled clumsily with the keys, could not get the key in the lock. He began sobbing, couldn't see straight, leaned his head against the van, didn't know what to do. He ran into the dark night.

***

Marcus and Bridget didn't know it, but they had traveled from one crime scene to another. When they entered the parking lot in Marcus' car, the blue lights seemed uncomfortably close to Bridget's motel room. Then unexpectedly, Marcus understood that the blue lights were *all about* her room.

A deputy sheriff was waiting for them, but he did not yet know for whom he was waiting. The officer held up his hand, halting the vehicle. Yellow tape was suspended all over the place. The blue light flashed surreally through chaotic dark. Marcus stopped the car immediately. The deputy sheriff approached the vehicle carefully, with his arm extended in a prolonged 'halt' gesture, that also shielded his eyes from the glare of Marcus' headlights.

"Can I help you, sir?"

"I'm bringing this lady to her room in the hotel, sir."

"Please turn off your engine and step out of the vehicle, sir." The deputy's voice was alarmingly urgent.

Marcus did as he was told. The young deputy, keeping an eye on Marcus, cautiously shone a flashlight inside the station wagon, illuminating Bridget's fearful face.

"Please step out of the vehicle, ma'am."

Bridget opened the door and got out.

He walked around to the passenger side. Then he spoke to Bridget, but now in a softer tone: "May I see your identification, ma'am?"

Bridget was shivering. "It's in this pocket of my coat."

"I need to see it, please."

Bridget reached into the pocket slowly, but as she did so, she began her own inquisition: "What is happening, sir? Has something happened here?"

"I need to see your identification, ma'am...driver's license, if you have one."

Bridget fumbled with the plastic cards in her wallet. She managed to separate the Lincoln University ID card. She handed it to the officer. He looked at the name on the card.

"Miss Golden? Bridget Golden?"

"That's me, sir."

"Your room is 207. Is that correct?"

"Yes."

"Are you sharing that room with anyone else, Miss Golden?"

"Yes. Has something happened? What's going on?"

"Who is staying in the room with you, ma'am?"

"Wanda Smith. Is she all right?"

The deputy lowered his flashlight and turned it off.

"She's been shot, ma'am. She's dead."

"Oh, God..." Bridget broke down, wailing.

The deputy walked quickly around to Marcus.

"Do you have any weapons, sir?"

"No."

"Step over to your vehicle, sir. Raise your hands in the air and lean on the hood of the vehicle."

Marcus did as he was told. The deputy frisked him. Satisfied that Marcus was unarmed, the deputy released him. Marcus walked around the car and embraced Bridget.

Deficiencies
14

Cruel, cold Monday morning, Bridget woke up in the guest room at Marcus' house. Jonda lay next to her, sleeping soundly.

A shroud of nightmare was wrapped around her attempts at wakefulness. Blood. She remembered seeing blood on the floor, lots of it, and Wanda's legs twisted in a final expression of disarray.

"Yes, sir. That's Wanda," she had said, numbly.

The sheriff's procedures and inquisitions had lasted until 2 a.m. Jonda had clung to her; Bridget remembered, in the midst of the deathly chaos, an unfamiliar sense of being the provider of a child's well-being. *Sometimes I feel...like a motherless child.* She remembered the old mournful, spiritual tune.

Marcus had patiently remained with them until the end. Finally, he had brought the child and her newly-adopted mother (so it seemed) to his home and tucked them in.

Bridget lay there not knowing what to do. She had never awakened beside a motherless child before. She had never been a mother. She had never seen a dead person before last night, nor so much blood. The smell of the blood had bothered her.

***

Marcus had begun his day an hour later than usual. As he drove to the job, the image of Wanda's body was clinging to his brain like a spider web. He had listened to Bridget's account about what she knew of Wanda's life...about Buzz. *What a loser that guy must be. They ought to put him under the jail, if he did it. Who else would have done it?* Not that Marcus knew anything about Wanda's life, or Buzz's life. *But what other person...other than her abusive boyfriend, would even care enough about a derelict woman like Wanda to confront her about anything and then shoot her?*

But a man cannot comprehend, with reason, such a world of chaos as the one that Wanda had lived in. The world of Wanda and Buzz was in another universe, apart from the one that Marcus inhabited. His hazy Monday morning disorientation was a case of culture-shock, accompanied by first-time-ever awareness of so much blood spilled in one place, and on the floor of a cheap hotel room. An orderly, productive, reasonable, sane person had an unanticipated, sudden encounter with an undisciplined, purposeless meth-drenched world, as evidenced by the unforgettable sight of a dead body and too much blood.

Marcus had been aware of the deputy's radio reporting about the suspect, Buzz. He had overheard information about Buzz's van, which the officers had identified in the parking lot. At 1:45 a.m. when Marcus had taken Bridget and Jonda from the scene, the infamous Buzz had not yet been apprehended.

At 9:15, Marcus entered the building where he had people working. Lucido's crew was laying block, replacing the window sills with new masonry. The plumbers were installing drainpipe and water-supply pipe in the ground, where they would later be hidden by the concrete floor. There were no electricians on the job.

He made some phone calls.

***

Detective Lee Nguyen of the Wessex County Sheriff's Department got a written report about the murder of Wanda Smith. It included a full description of the scene, as well as all the facts and statements that had been collected so far. He went to the motel, inspected the crime scene, didn't notice anything that hadn't been properly documented in Deputy Greene's report. He also inspected the van, the ownership of which had been established. Billy "Buzz" Townsend, known boyfriend of the deceased, had not only neglected to remove his van from the parking lot, he had also abandoned a suspiciously large quantity of cold medicine inside the van. The over-the-counter remedy was commonly known to be a major source for the chemical isolation of ephedrine, a critical ingredient in methampetamine.

An arrest warrant had been issued for Buzz Townsend. Deputy Dan Linkletter accompanied Detective Nguyen as they drove into the rural area know as Pressley, and located the suspect's abode.

Nobody home. Having the arrest warrant and search warrant, they entered the trailer to gather evidence. The place was a wreck. It didn't take the officers long to find the meth lab. After a thorough look around, Deputy

Linkletter called for assistance in analysis of the meth lab and collection of evidence.

Two hours later, they drove away with a few boxes of drug paraphanalia, several rocks of crystal meth and crank, and a small collection of the suspect's personal effects. One item in particular caught Nguyen's attention: a recordable compact disc with a name written on it: Leo Zollinger. He called headquarters:

"Martha, you got anything on a 'Leo Zollinger'?"

"Hold on. I'll get back to you on that: Leo Zollinger, with a z as in zebra?"

"Right."

Deputy Linkletter spoke: "According to Bridget Golden's statement, Lee, Wanda had moved out of that trailer only a few days before Townsend went looking for her."

"Yeah. That seems to be the case."

"I can understand why. The place was a pig-sty."

"Yeah, and it probably got a lot worse after the lady moved out."

Nguyen thought for a moment. "Can you imagine a six-year old child having to live in that environment. I wonder what Social Services is gonna do with this one?"

"Nelly Greene said the kid was clinging pretty mightily to Bridget Golden, as if she were an aunt or some other relation."

"Could be. Golden didn't say anything about a blood relation between them. But...I imagine a kid in that situation would latch onto anybody familiar."

Nguyen's cell phone rang. "Yeah."

"Here's the report on Leo Zollinger: 17 year old, white, resides in Urdor at 745 Winchester. He was arrested last Wednesday night by DC Police for vandalizing a synagogue in Georgetown. His mother, Ruby Ross, lives at that address with her husband, Jack Ross. Jack Ross posted bail on Saturday for Zollinger. There was another kid with Zollinger in the vandalism incident...Greg Burst. He's still in the DC jail."

"Thank you, Martha."

"Okay, Lee. Here's something else for ya, if you're interested."

"Yep. Give it to me."

"Two DC detectives visited the Rosses last Friday. They picked up a couple of names that have Pressley addresses."

"Okay. We'll get that when we get to headquarters in a few minutes. We've got to unload some evidence at headquarters."

"Copy that."

***

Four thousand miles west of Urdor, Ben Stillman trod the sidewalk of Haight Street. When he reached the intersection of Haight and Ashbury, he stepped off the curb, went directly to the middle of the intersection. Formerly a meth-freak, now a Buddhist, he aspired to be a monk. But Ben's monk potential had been arrested in his own mind when he had arrived at a very special decision this morning. He reached inside his robe, pulled out a piece of yellow silk on which he had painted, in black, "Out of Iraq Now!" Calmly unfolding the fabric, he was aware that the attention he sought from passersby was riveted upon him. Cars had stopped. With trembling hands, he placed the message on the street in front of him. Again reaching inside his robe, the serious young monk-to-be grabbed, and raised above his head, a green plastic 2-litre bottle. Without further ado, he doused himself with gasoline, flicked a pocket lighter with his thumb. A holocaust of fire engulfed him.

Residents of San Francisco, and many other observers from distant lands who happened to be there that day, witnessed a conflagration unlike any that Haight-Ashbury had ever seen. Twenty-one minutes later, Sandy Ballew, reporter for XYZ network, was on the scene reporting Stillman's self-sacrifice to the world.

Hilda Hightower, setting sauce bottles and flower vases on tables in the restaurant, paused to hear Sandy's report. She listened as the blonde reporter described the conflagration and its effect upon persons nearby.

"...Stillman's act of martyrdom intensifies the awareness of many Americans who now actively protest U.S. presence in Iraq. At Haight and Ashbury, I'm Sandy Ballew, XYZ in San Francisco."

Hilda resumed her routine, getting ready for the day's lunch crowd.

The restaurant's front door opened; in walked a little girl with straight blonde hair. Just behind her was Bridget, with a troubled look on her face.

"Good morning, Bridget." She walked in their direction and stood gazing at the two. "Who is your young friend?" Hilda offered a hesitant smile; for she had heard of the previous night's events. *Oh, what a lamentable day it must be for this child.*

Jonda tarried, clinging to the hem of Bridget's jacket. Bridget had not yet spoken. Hilda thought she could see tearful eyes beneath the bill of Bridget's cap.

"You seem to have acquired a daughter, or niece...anyway...a little friend."

I haven't worked here a week yet, and already I'll be dumping excuses on Hilda. But Bridget mustered from somewhere inside herself the courage with which she might resume her life *and function and speak and serve tables and be a waitress, and be...a mother, no...not a mother...a sister.* She could be a sister. She could think of herself as a sister to Jonda.

"This is Jonda."

"How about some pancakes, Jonda? You want some pancakes and syrup for breakfast?" Lunchtime was imminent, but somehow pancakes seemed, to Hilda, just what was needed at this moment.

Bridget volunteered an answer for her shy young friend. "Wouldn't you like that, Jonda?...pancakes."

The child said nothing. Hilda, having raised two of her own, knew a little about what could help a child through troublesome times. "She extended her hand toward the girl. "Come sit over here, and I'll get you something to eat."

The child relented. She took Hilda's hand, allowed the woman to lead her and seat her at a nearby booth. Bridget went to the cooler and poured a glass of milk for her. *The last time I poured a glass of milk, it was the same situation, except now...there is no more Wanda, no more mother.*

Bridget set the milk on the table. Jonda gingerly partook of it. Then Bridget felt herself torn in three or four directions at the same time. *I should stay here at the table with Jonda. I should go to the back and start preparing to serve lunch. I should talk to Hilda and cry.* Then the choice was made for her. She began sobbing. Hilda did not yet know Bridget very well, but she embraced her troubled young friend, without hesitation.

In a world of woe, there was yet comfort for those weary with trouble.

After a minute or so of ministering, Hilda asked: "Bridget, what can I do for you?"

"Oh, I don't know."

The TV droned on: "...we'll have the weather with Paul West after the break, and it *might* include the word *rain.*"

"What's going to happen to this child?"

"Don't think about that now."

"Hilda...if you could only know *what she has seen.* I saw the scene myself—"

"Let's go in the back, Bridget. Rosa will bring the pancakes out here in a few minutes. Jonda will be all right. She won't go anywhere. Where would she go? Come with me." Taking the fearful woman by the hand, Hilda went to the silverware station and began assembling sets, wrapping them individually with napkins.

"Do you want to tell me what happened?"

Bridget began, haltingly, to give the account, again, of last night's horror. She instinctively began assisting Hilda, wrapping silverware. After a few more minutes, Hilda interrupted her: "Can you do me a favor?"

"What?"

"Tim has asked for the day off. Can you handle the dishwashing for him?... just for lunch."

"Yes, You'll have to show me a few things."

"No problem, and Jonda can stay back here with you, if you like."

Bridget was unsure, as if she were stepping onto a tightrope, but she was being slowly drawn into the cacoon of support that Hilda was weaving for her. "That sounds good."

"She might even want to help you a little. When we get through lunch, we'll go from there, okay?"

***

After having lunch at his desk, Detective Lee Nguyen drove to Winchester Street, hoping to discover what connection there may be between Leo Zollinger and Buzz Townsend, who had not yet been apprehended. But nobody was home. So he drove out to the Pressley area of Wessex County, seeking the two other addresses that dispatch had provided.

Nguyen eased his Dodge into the gravel driveway that bordered a grassy yard, starting to turn green. In the middle of an impresive lot was a quaint old-style-brick bungalow with a covered porch and a porch swing. Purple pansies were growing in a cement planter on the edge of it. A late-model Chevrolet was parked just in front of where he stopped the car. On a flagpole mounted by the front column the detective noticed a confederate flag. When he knocked on the door, it was answered by a mid-30ish woman.

Nguyen identified himself as a police officer and asked if this was the home of Wendall Foggerty. Although the lady was quite attractive, she was serious.

"Yes. He's not here. He's working now."

"That's drywall work, right?"

"Yes."

"I'm looking for a young man, Leo Zollinger. Leo's mother said that he sometimes does work for your husband."

"That's right. He's not in trouble, is he?"

"I can't really say, Mrs. Foggerty, but I need to talk to him."

"I haven't seen Leo, but he may be working today. I don't know."

"Do you happen to know where they might be working?"

"No."

Uncomfortable silence.

"Well, thank you, ma'am." He started to leave, then hesitated.

"There's another fellow I'd like to talk to. He lives around here...on Laird Road. Is that up here on the right just a ways?"

"Yes. Who is it you're looking for?"

"Moa Grindell."

A subdued alarm escaped from Mrs. Foggerty's eyes, but she immediately capped it. Then she said: "That's right. Up on the right there in a couple of miles. Is there anything else I can do for you. I'm kinda busy right now."

"No, ma'am. Thank you."

As he was walking toward the car, he noticed an old 50s model tractor next to a large Gambrel barn, about 50 yards behind the house.

He called out to her: "Would y'all be interested in selling that old tractor?"

"I don't think so."

"Would you mind if I take a look at it? My grandfather had one like it."

"You'll just have to ask my husband about it."

As he peered at the old barn, Nguyen noticed an insignia of some kind above the double doors on the side. It was difficult to see because of the obtuse angle. But there was something odd... He peered. Red and black...it was a small swastika.

"Well, thank you, Mrs. Foggerty. Have a good day."

***

Aleph stepped off the Metro at the Urdor station. He began walking. Walking did not bother him one bit. As a teenager, he had walked halfway across the hot sands of Sudan. His destination was the office of Hall Electrical, Inc. He walked through Urdor, two miles to the address that he had seen in the phone book.

In the course of this small sojourn, Aleph crossed over a small concrete bridge. He stopped in the middle and looked down. The structure was spanning a creek, a quite insignificant creek, by the looks of it. The water appeared stagnant, slime proliferating on the edges of it. Nestled against the muddy edge of what must have been at one time a life-giving stream was a rusted child-sized tricycle, several beer cans, paper litter of all shapes and sizes, a strewn plastic grocery bag here, another one there, two tires, an irridescent oil slick across the surface of the water.

Aleph lamented the passing of this place. This place, that had once been a home to trees and shrubs, squirrels and duck, foxes and deer...and fish. This place was now a mere oversight. A mere overlooking. Everyone overlooked it. No one looked at it. A mere overpassing. Everyone overpassed it. It was just an overlooked, overpassed sewer hole in the middle of a great, seething civilization. Once teeming with life, now it was collecting death. The African lamented. His eye settled on a styrofoam enclosure that had once been the home, for three minutes or so, of a cheeseburger. *Super Size* was splayed across its broken back.

He continued on his journey. What else could he do? Stop and clean the place? *A man is not saved by his works, but by the grace of God.* What kind of God would permit such a thing? *What kind of God would permit a Holocaust?*

God who had given freedom and choice. God created. Men chose.

Along the road: more of the same, the detritus of a civilization straining to relieve itself of trash.

A few more blocks down the road, and he had reached Hall Electric, Inc. It was a small metal warehouse with an office built into it. Parked outside was a white van with the company logo painted on the side. He saw a battered gray metal door.

Aleph entered.

A man with dark slicked-back hair sat behind a cluttered desk. Dusty light diffused through a dingy window. The man looked up from a magazine at him and said, "What can I do for you?"

"My name is Aleph Leng. I am looking for Mr. Bryan Hall."

His face showed no expression. "I am Mr. Hall."

"Mr. Marcus Derwin mentioned your name to me. I am a licensed electrician. Do you need any help, sir?"

"No, sir. We got everything covered."

"May I fill out an application?"

"Don't have any. I just hire people I know, or know about."

"Well, I thank you, sir. For your time. Have a good day."

Aleph paused for a moment, looking right into the man's eyes. Mr. Hall looked at his magazine as if to continue reading.

Aleph left.

He walked back across the bridge, across the ravine of human neglect.

The African had studied a map of Urdor, and he knew where he was, although he had never been there before. He knew how to get to the location of the old drugstore that was now being remodeled as a restaurant. Marcus had given him the address. So he set out for it. After walking for ten minutes or so, he came to Pretoria Parkway. Seeing a bus stop for westbound passengers nearby, he waited. In ten minutes he got on the bus, and got out ten minutes after that, at the corner of Pretoria and Edgerton.

He walked through the front door. Marcus saw him and waved, then walked over to a plan table, set blueprints down, and approached Aleph. They shook hands.

"Did you have any luck at Hall Electric?"

"No. He doesn't need anyone."

Marcus grunted. "I'm surprised. His main man just had a big screw-up. He hasn't sent anyone to this job yet." Marcus' cell phone rang. "Hold on a second, will ya?"

Marcus walked over to a sunny area by a big hole in the wall. He motioned to Aleph. He gestured toward a plastic deck chair that was sitting there in the sunshine that streamed through the hole in the wall. "Have a seat," he yelled out, in between phrases of the phone conversation. Aleph accepted his offer. Sitting down was a relief after so much walking. He watched.

Lucido's crew were laying block, to replace those that had been removed, setting finished sandstone sills at about three feet off the ground, in preparation for new, large windows. Back in other parts of the building, plumbers were talking to a hard-hatted city inspector about their rough-in. In and around all of that were scattered a few more of Lucido's men, erecting metal stud walls according to Daniel's floorplan.

For Aleph, it was a very familiar setting. He had spent many hours in projects just such as this in Los Angeles. His works had been almost entirely electrical.

He noticed that Marcus had gotten off the phone. He was standing at the plan table with Lucido, discussing the work. And then, *déjà vu.* This was so very much like his work environment back in California: Mexicans all around, and the same sounds and smells that he was accustomed to. Aleph was surprised at the sensation, sitting there in the middle of a construction project after he spent the last week doing nothing except touring national monuments. It was as if he was back home, with Washington on the other side of the continent.

Marcus walked over to where Aleph was sitting. Lucido was with him. Marcus had a funny smile on his face. "Aleph, I want you to meet Lucido, my masonry man."

Aleph stood up, extended his hand, and smiled broadly. For him, smiling was as easy as slicing butter. "I am Aleph Leng, glad to meet you."

The Mexican reciprocated, "Lucido Gutierrez."

Then Marcus, still displaying an amused look on his face, put his hand on Aleph's broad shoulder. "Have you ever installed a ceiling grid?"

"Oh, yes."

"Would you like to do one for us?"

"Oh, yes." He laughed at the unexpected opportunity. "I have no tools. They are in California."

"I've got a laser level and hand tools you can use."

Aleph was puzzled. "That's fine, but..." He pointed upwards. "You already have a ceiling grid, my friend." He laughed.

"Daniel says it's gotta come down. It's too low, for one thing, and for another, we're going to a 2'x 2' grid. The work would have probably gone to Lucido, but he says he can do better with his guys on other things. Isn't that right?" Marcus looked confidently at his masonry man.

"That's right," said Lucido. "And I can give you a helper if you want one."

"What about a scaffold with wheels?" inquired Aleph.

"That one right over there is mine," said Marcus. "You can use it. The electricians were using it, but they decided to inflict some bad luck (in the form of flat tires) on Lucido's trucks. So they've lost some privileges around here. And they may lose more than that if they're not careful."

Aleph was a very agreeable fellow, but there were some limits to his easygoing world-view, so he asked: "And what does this ceiling grid job pay?"

"Twenty dollars an hour, with a 1099."

Not bad for an electrician four thousand miles from home with no tool belt.

"Where do I start?" asked Aleph.

Cycles
15

Detective Nguyen had decided to recruit some company for the visit to Moa Grindell's place. So he had driven back to headquarters and prevailed upon Sergeant Luke Mendez for assistance. Something about the prospect of this housecall seemed to indicate that the word "backup" might be a more appropriate term for his associate's role.

His concerns were confirmed when they drove up to the address. The place was nothing special, just a nondescript brick ranch with no outbuildings. But it was surrounded by a wire fence and a locked farm gate. As soon as their Dodge approached, two Dobermans went streaking across the yard to make their presence known, ostensibly to discourage the presence of inquiring police officers or any other nosy people.

The two police veterans got out of the car, knocked on the fence loudly, as if they were knocking on a door. To no avail. The only response was a crescendo of barking from the two appointed denizens of discouragement. They stood for about five minutes, the dogs' noise incessant, and yelled "hello."

They got back in the car.

"I don't think this guy likes having visitors."

The Sergeant agreed. "What now?" he asked, as Nyugen backed the car into the road and headed in the direction from which they had come.

"I think we should visit the Foggerty farm again."

"That's where you saw the swastika?"

"Right. She said he's a drywall contractor. It's five o'clock now. Maybe he'll be home."

"Give me the scoop on this guy again," requested the Sergeant.

"Buzz Townsend had left a cd on the table in his meth lab. I think it was a copy of a heavy metal. Written on it was the name 'Leo Zollinger,' presumably the owner, right?"

"Right."

"Leo Zollinger, 17 years old, was arrested last Wednesday night in DC, for vandalism. He spray-painted a message on the front of the Temple Beth Shalom, in big black letters: 'Zionist jew-pigs lie about holocaust,' or some such thing. The DC detectives went to his house, talked to his mother. She said that Zollinger doesn't live there any more. He stays out here somewhere, in Pressley. And he works for this guy Foggerty. So if Townsend, the murder suspect, is linked into any kind of meth ring, chances are that Leo knows something about it. He may be a part of it, or maybe just a user.

"And you think there might be a connection between a meth network and Townsend's killing his girlfriend?"

"I don't know. It's just a hunch. But...from the looks of the motel room—it's just the kind of thing that a cranked-up fool would do. Then we found the van with the cold medicine. If there are any better leads, we've haven't found 'em yet. You got any ideas?"

"No. But I probably will have in a few minutes after we see this Foggerty guy."

Nguyen's cell phone rang.

"Yeah."

"We got Buzz Townsend, at an abandoned warehouse on Narnberg Street."

"Good work. You talk to him yet?"

"No."

"Okay, we're at Foggerty's place. Later." He closed the phone, glanced at the Sergeant. "They got Townsend."

They pulled into the driveway. Nguyen quickly got out and was looking intently at the barn about 50 yards behind the house. There were two vehicles parked right next to it—a large black twin-cab pickup and a maroon Jeep Cherokee about 12 years old. Nyugen decided to dispense with the niceties of being distracted by Mrs. Foggerty.

He started walking toward the barn, assuming that Foggerty was there. Trying to get himself into a position to see the swastika, just to convince himself that it was actually there, he was straining his neck, while steadily, cautiously approaching the barn. The big pickup was in his line of vision, so he could not see the spot where he had earlier spotted the swastika. A muscular, blonde man emerged from the barn, began walking aggressively toward them. From a distance of about 20 yards, he spoke, loudly:

"What are you looking for?"

"Wendall Foggerty."

"That's me."

"I'd like to ask you some questions. A woman has been killed in Urdor."

"I didn't kill her. I didn't kill anybody."

Nguyen stopped abruptly. "I didn't say you did. We're doing a routine investigation.   Do you know Leo Zollinger?"

"What's he got to do with it?"

"He may know the suspect—Buzz Townsend. Is he here? Is Leo here?"

"It's none of your damn business if he's here. You got a warrant?"

"I've got a warrant for the arrest of Buzz Townsend. Have you seen him?"

"I haven't seen him." Foggerty's strategy was adjusting to the situation now. His tone of voice had lowered, become less antagonistic.

"Could we sit down and talk? I'd like to ask you a few questions. Maybe you can help us find the murderer of this young woman."

Foggerty raised his chin, surveyed the detective coolly. "No, sir. I'm not getting involved."

Nguyen thought he'd try a different tact. "Your old Ford tractor there. My grandfather had one like it. Would you be interested in selling it?"

"No, sir."

That was a mistake...should have stuck to procedure.

"Does Leo Zollinger work for you?"

"What if he does? I think it's about time you get your chink-ass off my property."

"Sir—"

"Now."

"Okay. I'm giving you an opportunity to cooperate with a routine investigation."

Then Nguyen noticed something unusual. "Mr. Foggerty, there's smoke coming out of your barn. I think it's on fire. You better check it out."

The man's countenance changed. He looked back at the barn. There was smoke rising from behind the wooden sash that enclosed the upper story. The smoke was pouring faster as they watched it...and faster. There was some serious fire in there somewhere.

While Foggerty stood undecided, which seemed uncharacteristic of his bravado, Nguyen responded quickly: "Have you got a groundwater spigot back here somewhere? A hose? We can put it out."

Suddenly, the double doors flew open. A boy and three men came stumbling out. They looked toward the two policemen, made visual contact with them. Then they turned to the opposite direction, began running, stumbling and running, as fast as their smoked-out surprise would enable them, through an open field on the other side.

Nguyen began moving toward the barn. "Where's your water supply? We can stop this thing."

Foggerty regained his composure. "We won't stop it. It's time you got outta here." Suddenly there was a gun in his hand. He pointed it directly at the detective.

"Your barn's burning down," said Nguyen.

Suddenly a stabbing, searing pain in his left forearm. He had been shot. Nguyen instinctively hit the ground. Flames were engulfing the barn now. Sergeant was right beside him. Foggerty was nowhere to be seen. Not knowing whether to move forward toward the barn, or backward in retreat, he remained on the ground. He somehow sensed that a retreat would make him more visible, more vulnerable.

Grabbing the cell phone from his shirt pocket, he punched the single number that would call headquarters. They answered.

"We've got a fire here, Foggerty's barn burning down, and he shot me." The sergeant was moving stealthily toward the barn, gun drawn and ready. The shooter was still nowhere to be seen. "Send the fire guys out here. Repeat. Send the fire trucks."

The pain in his arm was overwhelming. Dark sky was overtaking the daylight, smoke and flames rolling out of the barn, getting out of control. He was losing blood. He was very near the vehicles now, although he had not remembered moving. Suddenly, Sergeant Mendez was there with some kind of fabric. He wrapped it tightly around Nguyen's injured arm and tied it.

"We better get away from these trucks right now. They're liable to blow. Can you get up?"

Nguyen didn't answer. He just got up. Together they began moving away from the fire, back toward the car. When they got back to it, Sergeant said, "I don't think there's any way we could find them now, with darkness coming on, and all that forest on the far end of the field. We better wait for backup."

The detective couldn't even think about pursuit now. The pain was excruciating. He had reported being shot. *Surely they would be here any minute with medical.*

Red flames roared upward into the dusky sky like insanity.

***

Kaneesha set a sizzling plate of sirloin tips with peppers and onions on the table for Aleph. Her curiosity about this tall, dark stranger was actively generating within her a nobility of questions. "Would you like some butter for the baked potato, sir?"

"No, thank you. But some olive oil, vinegar and chives would be nice."

She brought it to him. Looking at Marcus, she asked, "Would you like another beer with your meal, Marcus?"

"No. I'd like a glass of red wine, whatever Rachel recommends."

"And for you, sir?" She looked directly into the African's bright eyes.

"Not for me, thank you. Just water."

"What about you, Daniel?"

"I'll go with the wine, Kaneesha."

There was a solemnity overshadowing their fellowship. Marcus had just finished recounting the torrid drama that had led up to Wanda's death. He explained that the stressful string of events had culminated this morning with Bridget in a state of exhaustion. In spite of that, she had taken the bus, Wanda's daughter with her, to the restaurant this morning because she was scheduled to work.

Marcus continued, "But after lunch Hilda took them back to our house to get some more sleep. Bridget's predicament now is what to do about Wanda's daughter, who is six years old and, suddenly, motherless. She feels a burden of responsibility for the child, Jonda. And I can see why. From the moment we got to the motel, Jonda was all over Bridget, as if she were sovereignly adopting a mother for herself."

Aleph had been listening with interest. "I can tell you, my friend, as one who was separated at an early age from my own mother, the void that is left behind is huge. The child was seeking to fill that empty spot immediately, by clinging to the first person whom she could identify as a mother figure."

"Well, it was more than that," said Marcus, "more than just filling an empty space, I think. Jonda already had a little personal history with Bridget. Bridget was a familiar, and probably a comfortable, presence in her life."

Aleph was moved with compassion for the child. His heart of experience enabled him to see clearly into what emotional forces must now be stirring within the six-year-old.

"Maybe God has appointed Bridget to be mother to this child."

Daniel's interest now stimulated, he decided to contribute some wisdom of his own. "Um, if you want to look at it that way--God, fate, whatever you want to call it."

Aleph chuckled. "I call it God, my friend. God is a person who creates, and who cares for his people. Fate, on the other hand, is an impersonal force, like gravity. Which do you consider to be a stronger influence on life in this world?"

"Whoa!" Daniel laughed loudly and took a sip of wine. "I didn't know we were having a theology class here."

"Think about it. Suppose that there is a God who cares for us. Suppose he is a loving force in the universe, and he would want the child to have a mother. Then, he may allow circumstances where...one woman could replace another in that mother role."

"If you're talking about God *allowing* things, why would he *allow* an abusive boyfriend to kill Jonda's mother?"

"Perhaps she was unfit to be a mother," interjected Marcus.

"No second chances, huh?" Daniel's skepticism was showing.

Aleph continued, "It was Wanda's boyfriend who killed her, not God. God allows bad things to happen for the same reason he allows good things to happen. He gives men and women the freedom to choose, in every little decision they make every day. Wanda made a bad choice for a boyfriend. Buzz (is that his name? yes) made a bad choice when he killed her. Perhaps his bad choice was controlled by the drugs in his brain instead of God in his brain." Aleph laughed. "Ha. That's a funny thought. God on the brain. Actually, it's more like: God in the spirit. God in the spirit of a man, or woman."

Marcus added, "It appears that, after the dreadful incident, Jonda chose a new mother."

"Yes,"continued Aleph. "But here is the real question of the moment." The African smiled mischievously and lowered his head conspiratorially.

Marcus, playing along, raised his glass of wine, took a sip, and asked, "What is the question of the moment, Aleph?"

"Will Bridget *choose* to be mother to this orphaned child?"

Daniel had an opinion. "This is all speculation. The state is probably going to overrule all this personal decision stuff and assign the kid to a foster home somewhere."

"That would be tragic, if God had intended for Bridget to raise the child."

Daniel persisted. "Or...we don't even know who this woman was. Wanda may have a sister up the road somewhere who will come and take the child, or even Wanda's mother."

"That makes sense to me. It could happen that way," said Marcus. "And most likely, the law would favor that scenario."

"It certainly could happen that way," agreed Aleph. "We shall see."

"Or the father could show up," observed Daniel.

"Bridget told me that Wanda had said that Jonda has never seen her father."

"Not too likely, then, is it?"

"What about a father?" mused Aleph. "Every child should have a father." The African raised his eyebrows and looked around the room, as if he were looking for a volunteer.

"What are you looking at me for?" asked Marcus, turning red.

Daniel and Aleph laughed at the same time.

"Hey, I've only known Bridget for eight days. What are you talking about?"

"Who said anything?" Daniel smiled ryely and sipped the wine.

Marcus was embarrassed. He turned, for deliverance, to Kaneesha, who happened to be passing by. He spoke loudly to her, feigning exasperation, "Kaneesha, can you please bring me a piece of that cherry pie?"

The vivacious Afro-American waitress, appreciating any opportunity to serve, especially if the serving involved the tall stranger whom she had been observing, turned on her heel, and responded, "Yes, sir." Then she looked, again, directly into Aleph's eyes, looking for a sign that he somehow reciprocated her unspoken ministrations (which sign she thought she saw), and she asked, "And for your dessert, sir?"

"You."

He didn't say that. "Say what?" She reflexively covered her smiling lips with her hand, pencil between two fingers.

"I'll have you for dessert." He laughed uninhibitedly.

Totally unexpected. Totally out of character. But then, she didn't even know his character.

He was hunched over laughing. Then he straightened up, looked at her, and said:

"I am just kidding you. Don't pay any attention to me. I have traveled a long ways and I am out of mind." Still smiling. "But I will have some vanilla ice cream, please."

"Me too," said Daniel. "Vanilla ice cream for me, but not just yet."

Then Kaneesha's face assumed a curiously wise expression. She spoke, "I have some news for you gentlemen."

"And what is that?" asked Marcus.

"I have already told Bridget that she and Jonda can stay at my house for awhile."

"Praise God," spoke the African.

"Only my mother is there with me, and I know she won't mind. There is an extra bedroom that was my brother's before he moved out."

"See, Daniel, "said Aleph. "That's the God thing that I was talking about."

"It's something to think about," mused Daniel.

Marcus asked: "What about the child? What would your mother do with a child around?"

"My mother is pretty good with kids. I mean...I turned out pretty good." She smiled and curtsied.

"Yes, ma'am," agreed Aleph.

"And Bridget could pay my mother some rent. It's a win-win."

"It does sound like a win-win situation," agreed Daniel.

Then Marcus looked at Aleph. "Then you could take the extra bedroom at my place, until you get situated. It would be closer to where we're working than where you're at now, right?"

"That is a good arrangement. I would appreciate that very much," said the African. He meant it.

***

Helen knew what to expect, but she didn't know what to *expect.* The sheriff's dispatch had just called to alert the emergency personnel that a wounded officer would be coming in soon. But she didn't know how ugly the wound would be.

Sure enough, Nguyen's Dodge pulled into the emergency turnaround, driven by the Sergeant. Helen immediately wheeled out a gurney, and advised the detective to lay on it. He had emerged from the car under his own power.

She spoke to the Sergeant: "You must have done a good job on him. He's getting around well; maybe hasn't lost much blood."

Helen and another nurse, Laura, rolled him directly into a receiving room. Helen quickly unwrapped the blood-soaked shirt from around the hand.

It was an ugly wound. The bullet had gone through Nyugen's left hand, below the thumb, not quite in the middle of the palm. It must have been small...maybe a .22. Maybe a good orthopedist could save his thumb.

The doctor on duty came in, looked briefly at the wound, prescribed pain control medication and ordered the patient to be sent to the operating room for orthopedic surgery. Laura called the surgeon. Helen gave him a shot of morphine. She cleaned the wound. Thankfully, the bleeding had slowed to a trickle. The Sergeant's use of his jacket as a bandage had been skillful, tight, and effective.

Out in the waiting room, Sergeant Mendez spoke with Deputy Danny Greene about what had happened. Billy "Buzz" Townsend had been arrested in an abandoned warehouse in Urdor. Upon being interrogated, he had confessed, almost immediately, to the murder of Wanda Smith. Questioning about the contents of his van, specifically the large quantity of cold medicine, was still underway. Foggerty's barn had burned to the ground, the cause of the fire unknown. The forensics team would be sent to examine the remains. Foggerty and four unknown men, one possibly a minor, escaped and were yet to be apprehended, although pursuit was underway.

With Nguyen headed for surgery, and the Sergeant updated, the two officers each drove back to headquarters to check in before calling it a day.

Four deputies had been dispatched to the Pressley area to continue pursuit. Wendall Foggerty had neglected to consider, when he fired upon the sheriff's detective, that by so doing he had committed a crime. The deputies had already obtained a warrant, and were out to get him.

***

Deputy Rashad Williams had his cruiser parked on the side of a county road. He was studying a county map, while his partner Eddie Wheeler kept an eye on whatever might be happening beyond the range of their headlights.

"Look here, Eddie." Williams pointed at the map. Here's Foggerty's place, where they started out. "Now, see over here, the location of Buzz Townsend's trailer." He paused, running his finger over the map while his thoughts congealed. "A person could travel on foot between the two points without crossing a road." He grabbed a pencil, ran its point lightly along the surface of the map to indicate a possible route. "It would probably be worth our time to check out Townsend's trailer."

Wheeler replied: "If they've thought about heading for the trailer, they've probably decided against it. They know that Townsend was arrested today."

"Yeah."

They studied the map a little more.

"If they've got allies, or even acquaintances, in any of these houses nearby, they could be holed up in someone's house having dinner by now."

"True, but we don't know that. Even if that were the case, we wouldn't know which house to choose, and then we'd have to have a search warrant."

"I say we give it a look at Townsend's trailer. It's only a mile in that direction." Williams pointed toward a road that turned off to the left, just ahead of them.

"Can't hurt...I can't think of a better idea."

Slowly, Williams pulled the cruiser back onto the county road, carefully drove it along the route that they had decided, headlights illuminating their calculated pursuit.

A deer ran out in front of the car. Wheeler, a little edgy, jumped. After a second, he realized what it was, and relaxed.

"Deer in the headlights." Williams looked at Wheeler and gave a low, nervous laugh.

"Right."

About a minute later, they turned onto the driveway that would lead to Townsend's trailer. Slowly, they approached.

"Stop!" whispered Wheeler. "There's someone on the front porch."

Standing at the front door, hands high, was a boy with a red cap on, squinting.

Williams stopped the car, turned off the engine, left the headlights on. The two officers stood up, each partly protected by a car-door, their guns drawn.

Wheeler addressed the boy: "Step away from the trailer."

The boy took a few steps, off the front porch.

"Walk slowly in this direction until I tell you to stop."

The boy obeyed.

"Stop."

Williams frisked the youth, handcuffed him. "Is there anyone else here, son?"

"Yes, sir." The boy had a resentful, but fearful look on his face.

"How many people here besides you, son?"

"One."

"Where?"

"Inside the trailer. He has a broken leg."

"Where is he inside the trailer?

"Just inside that front door."

Wheeler trained his powerful flashlight on the front door. In a commanding voice, he spoke: "Open the front door. Come out with your hands up."

"He's got a broken leg, I tell ya," said the boy, a little testily.

Williams spoke to the boy: "What's your name, son?

"Leo."

"Leo what?"

"Zollinger."

Williams spoke authoritatively: "Leo, since your buddy has a broken leg, you'll have to open the front door for him. Go open the front door."

Williams was surprised at the youth's ready compliance. Leo turned around slowly, walked to the trailer door, opened it with his cuffed hands, and pushed it open.

"Now, Leo, step back slowly, back off the porch."

Wheeler walked slowly to the left, in order to get a better view inside the trailer. He shone his flashlight inside. "Come out with your hands up."

They heard a muffled voice respond, and a rustling on the floor inside.

"Speak louder, or come out with your hands up."

A weak voice replied, "I can't walk."

Wheeler spoke slowly. "Sir, I'm coming in there for you. If you, or if anyone with you resists, I *will* shoot to kill."

"There's no one in here with me."

Wheeler stepped cautiously onto the porch, took two steps, reached inside the trailer and flipped the light switch on. Splayed upon a grungy carpet, a man lay, wincing with pain, his head laid back in surrender.

"Who else is in here with you?"

"Nobody."

Outside, Deputy Rashad Williams locked the boy in the back of the car. Then, with gun drawn, he walked into the trailer and conducted a full search of the place while Wheeler kept an eye on the broken man.

Satisfied that no one else was inside, Williams opened the back door, shone his flashlight around the back yard and adjoining woods, then closed the back door.

Wheeler had frisked the man and handcuffed him. When Williams was done with the search, he pulled out a pocketknife and carefully cut the pantsleg, which revealed a leg obviously broken.

Williams went in a bedroom, pulled a bedspread, brought it into the front room. Carefully, the two deputies picked the broken man up, set him in the bedspread, carried him out to their vehicle. They laid him on the back seat. While Williams closed up the trailer, Eddie Wheeler arrested the two suspects, informed them that they were being taken under suspicion of arson and assaulting an officer with a firearm.

***

At 10:30 p.m., they arrived at the hospital to obtain medical care for the broken man. Nurse Laura Zenakis brought a wheelchair out to the car, then wheeled him in the emergency room entrance to be examined.

Five minutes later, the prisoner was seated in the wheelchair in an examining room. Deputy Wheeler was with him, asking questions, recording answers. Nurse Helen Olei entered the room. This would be her last patient of the night before leaving at 11. She shut the door of the examining room, turned to see who the last patient would be. A look of horror took sudden control of her face. Wheeler became suddenly alarmed when the broken man began to squirm in discomfort.

Helen commanded herself to be calm. She looked at Deputy Wheeler and spoke to him sharply. "Officer, would you please turn the patient around so he's facing the back wall."

"Yes, ma'am. The deputy did as he was asked to do.

As soon as Wheeler undertook the maneuver, Helen saw exactly what she had expected to see—on the back of the broken man's neck— dragon tattoo.

Helen began sobbing. She left the room, leaned upon the handrail in the hall, actively attempting to compose herself. Wheeler stepped out of the examining room. She looked at him and forced herself to speak understandably:

"Officer, that man should be arrested."

"He's already been arrested. He needs the broken leg fixed."

"Arrest him again for rape."

"Who did he rape?"

"Me. And you'll have to find somebody else to fix his leg, because I already tried to break both of them."

Helen walked away.

Memories
16

Between the void of space and the crumpled berm of blue-green, red-ribbed, rumbling earth, a wind blows, gentle and mighty. This firmament of birth, broad enclosure of our earth, whirls beyond our comprehension, yet within our hearing and our knowing, but beyond our grasp or grip. Rip, flip, trip it slips through our invisible atmospheric tide, bellowing, caressing, stirring mist within our breathing and our gentle, writhing ride.

There is a creature whose native country is that domain of air. Endowed with wings of quill, it compels every wisp and waft of atmospheric nuance to its own advantage. Thus the agile eagle soars nimbly between yon mountainous clouds and above our nimbus trees.

Her rising thermals o'erflown, her swooping secrets to us unknown, she at last settles upon her aerie rock, to tend her young...stupid eaglets still not grown. It is said among the wise, and yet it is a tale to tell, that she...with her younglets' comfort unimpressed, does up and kick them from the nest. Could such a tale be true?

It was just this question that fluttered through the curious mind of young Tim, dishwasher for the James Gang, this brisk Tuesday morning as he observed a mother eagle approach its aerie nest. *What ancient instructions synapsed through an eaglet's airstreamed wonder...to make it flap its feathered wings? What genetic code, or providential wake-up call, enacted the plummeting bird brain to fly? Yet there she was: a mother eagle, that herself had been a hatchling novice, newly kicked from its mother's nest.. The stirring of air must have provoked stirring of wings by the moving of some ancient mystery, too tall to tell.*

Such potent mystery may have stirred within the *mishama* soul of young Jonda when she suddenly found herself plummeting through life without a mother's hovering care. Detecting no explanation or example, she flapped her instinctual wings and lofted safely onto another matronly perch. Or so it seemed to her. Bridget's life had itself been in freefall when it briefly found confluence with Wanda's manic existence. Bridget's twenty-seven-year-old wings, newly- roused from their atrophy by the encounter with Marcus, had given flight to a new resolve, a new life. And that new lease was not yet a fortnight old when she felt the unfamiliar weight of a child, clinging desperately to the tailfeathers of her newfound free flight.

Upon their Tuesday waking, Jonda's winsome green eyes sought explanation for the tossed-together tumult of events that had resulted in their landing at Kaneesha's house. Yet the same question interfered in Bridget's numbed awareness of what was happening to them. So she had no answers for the child. She simply responded: when the child extended her small hand in need of something unexplained, Bridget gently held it, in need of something unexplained.

They had been thrown together by a simple twist of fate. Or was it? Could we not as easily say they had been tossed together by some design? Well...thinks the fatalist...*what Designer would arrange such mishap... murder of a young woman by her depraved boyfriend resulting in an orphan.* Yes, but...says the designed one...*a Designer who included freedom as a working principle in unfolding events... must tolerate such disruptive rapacity. By such discrepancy, choice for meaningful works, labors of love, is passed to others. To care for an orphan is true religion.*

But the call of such belief carried with it requirements that seemed, to Bridget, beyond the strength of her fledgling existence. Not that this thought had actually occurred to her as yet; it was just a dull, confounding presence in the tailfeathers of her mind.

Jonda held out her hand; Bridget held it. It was as simple as that. She was not a mother. She was acting as a comforter, or, *on behalf of*, a comforter, if there was such a presence in the universe.

And so everywhere that Bridget would go, would it be? Another *little* Bridget, a little Jonda, announcing, *I want some, too. I want to do that, too*...asking: *Can I have some, too? Can I do it, too? She's a little appendage to life, a clinging little dependent, and she sounds like a little Shirley Temple when she speaks* . But Jonda was much more than that.

A little ray of sunshine refracted through the stained glass ornament that hung in Bernadette's kitchen window. Kaneesha, Bernadette's daughter, set a cutting board on the table, precisely where the light had brightened up a little spot. She sliced a banana, then arranged the pieces atop a bowl of breakfast cereal. Jonda sat down at the kitchen table, fascinated by the sight of Kaneesha pouring whole milk on corn flakes.

"Jonda, here's some breakfast for you. Eat it all up while Bridget finishes taking her shower. She'll be in here in a minute. Okay?"

"Okay, Miss Kaneesha."

***

Beatrice Smith was hemming a pair of pants for her neighbor. She had thrown the little task in as a freebie along with a larger chunk of work that she regularly did for an interior decorator. For the last three years, Beatrice had been cutting and sewing the fabric elements of "window treatments." She had built up a steady stream of work that was, at long last, beginning to provide the income level that she had previously attained through 24 years at Conan Casuals in Greensboro.

Beatrice removed the pantsleg from her machine, snipped the thread and cinched it. She set the garment aside and decided to take a break. Standing up, she stretched, walked out of the sewing room, through a hallway and into the kitchen. She prepared a cup of coffee, walked through the back yard and entered the cabinet shop of her husband, Frank.

His shop was large, but not large enough. Its development had happened sporadically, each piece of equipment being acquired as funds would allow and the need for higher standards demanded it. Like his wife, Frank had undertaken the transition to independent business a few years ago when the furniture factory had shut down. Fortunately, his 31 years had been sufficient time to have earned an early retirement.

As Beatrice walked in, Frank was completing the rip phase of a set of eighteen cabinet doors of varying sizes. He turned the table saw off, began stacking the glued-up panels on a cart.

"Frank, I'm going over to Marge's office to get a check on this design before doing the rest of them. I'm going to stop at the post office and grocery. Can you think of anything we need?"

"How about that coffee? Is there any left?"

"Oh yeah, there's still a cup in there."

He brushed the dust out of his hair as they went back to the house.

Frank walked through the hallway to his office, picked up some sketches and a letter from his desk, put them in a manila envelope.

Back in the kitchen, he handed it to Beatrice.

"How 'bout dropping this in the mail while you're out? And don't forget we need eggs and milk."

"Okay, dear." She kissed him and was out the door.

Frank decided to make a sandwich for lunch. He heard Beatrice start the car and pull out of the driveway. As he was getting some bread out of the package, the phone rang.

"Hello."

"Hello. Mr. Frank Smith?"

"This is he."

"Are you the father of Wanda Smith, who has resided in Wessex County, Virginia?"

"Yes."

"Mr. Smith, I am Alex Bofa, with the medical office of Wessex County. I am sorry to inform you, sir, that last Sunday evening, Wanda was killed."

***

At 2:05 p.m. Bernadette was opening boxes in a closet. She was looking for children's books. After finding the box that she sought, she brought it into the living room and arranged some of the books on a low shelf.

Bridget and Kaneesha were preparing to go to work at the Grille. Bernadette took Jonda's hand, led her into the living room and directed the child's attention to the books.

"Jonda, do you see those books on the shelf?"

"Yes, Miss Bernadette."

"Have you read any of those books?"

"No."

"Take some of them out. Let's look at them and see which one we want to read first."

Jonda did as she was told. She appreciated being led, although her behavior reflected a certain reticence, a consequence of her life's unpredictability. And her life was still in a kind of shock. The child looked dumbly at several book covers. Her mother had never read to her. Finally, as if flipping a coin, she settled on *The Cat in The Hat*. Bernadette had just begun reading it to her when the phone rang.

"Hello."

"Mrs. Michot?"

"Yes."

"My name is Beatrice Smith. Hilda Hightower gave me your number. She said that Bridget Golden is staying at your house now. Is that right?"

"Yes."

"May I speak with her?"

"Yes."

"Thank you."

Jonda was looking at the peculiar Dr. Seuss drawings. Bernadette went to the guest room, which had once been her son's room, and handed the phone to Bridget.

"Hello."

"Hello, Bridget. I am Beatrice Smith, Wanda's mother."

This was not what Bridget had expected. In the brief season of her acquaintance with Wanda, she had never heard a mention of Wanda's parents. "Hello...yes...I'm Bridget Golden. I was there a little later...I mean, you're calling because you heard...."

"The coroner's office up there called us today with the news about Wanda," said Beatrice, on the other end of the phone.

Long pause. Neither woman knew what to say. This had never happened before.

"You have Jonda with you?"

"Yes, ma'am. I was the first one to...Did they tell you how it happened?"

"The coroner said it was a gunshot wound."

"Yes."

"And it was that guy she was living with that shot her?"

"Yes, Buzz...uh...Townsend. I really didn't know him very well."

"He was a loser, wasn't he?...and a now, a murderer."

"Wanda was trying to defend herself from—"

"I don't want to hear about it now. My husband and I are coming up there tomorrow. I understand you have our granddaughter with you?"

"Yes, ma'am...like I said...I was the first one to...be there for her after it happened."

"It happened in your motel room. Is that right?"

"Yes."

"So, Wanda and Jonda were staying with you?"

"That's right."

Long pause. Then: "How is Jonda doing?"

"As well as could be expected."

"So, she had nowhere to go, and you brought her home with you?"

"That's right."

"Thank you."

"Well, it was...she just latched onto me, and...we've been together ever since."

"Thank you for looking out for her."

"Although...I'm going to work now. She'll be staying here with Mrs. Michot."

"We would like to see Jonda tomorrow evening when we get there, if that is all right."

"Yes, ma'am. I'm sure Jonda would love to see you."

"She hasn't seen us in two years."

"Oh...well, it'll be good for you to get reacquainted. When will you be here?"

"About 5, I'd say. We're flying into Washington, arriving at 3. We'll rent a car. Can you give me an address?"

"Yes. Hold on a second please."

Bridget covered the phone, gently interrupted Beatrice's reading to Jonda.

"Would you mind if Jonda's grandparents come and see her tomorrow afternoon about 5 o'clock?"

"Heavens, no. Let me talk to them. You and Kaneesha need to catch the bus."

***

A spider was crawling along the floor. Emerging from an area darkened by the nearby toilet, it moved slowly along the base of the wall. From his position on the bed, Moa Grindell could see it. Quietly, he got off the bed, snuck up on the spider, and stepped on it. Then Moa sank back down on his jail-bed and continued digesting the jail-supper that he had just eaten.

He was thinking about his chances of beating the rape charge. That wasn't going to happen—too much evidence against him, including the DNA test. His thoughts wandered back to the first time he had ever done it. It had been so much easier then; there hadn't been any struggle, and no retaliation afterward.

What Moa remembered best about that insane little scenario in Kosovo was the point of his gun—everywhere he went it commanded respect. Albanians, Serbs, Romas—they all cowered when he would point the damn thing in their direction. Especially the women—they were like butter in his hands when he pointed the gun. Except that he had not yet gotten the chance to get his hands on one of those women. Then one evening he got his chance. He had been patrolling the place for about a week or so, securing houses and apartments, making sure that the way was clear for people to move back into their homes. But in the back of his mind, he had been working out a plan to get it on with one of these helpless women. Finally, the time and place were right to carry out his plans.

He opened the door of an apartment in—it must have been a Serb neighborhood—hell, he couldn't tell the difference between one group and another. He entered the place and there she was—a lone, unprotected woman with her child. Daddy was gone, probably killed off by the Albanians, or maybe still fighting, out in the woods somewhere. The first thing Moa did was assert the intimidating power of the gun. It was like a magic wand in his hands. It hadn't taken much wielding and waving before she got the message. He had laid the gun down and just had his way. The kid didn't even make trouble, just whined while he did what he had to do. It had been so easy...piece of cake.

Not like this one, which was the 6th time since that first. He had been keeping count. No...this one had been a real bitch, had caught up with him in the living room. And now she was gonna roast him in the courtroom. Moa didn't know what to do. He was stuck, like a cornered rat.

***

Aleph Leng was beginning to fall asleep on the bed that Marcus had provided for him. He was thinking about honor. In the recesses of his memory, Aleph could remember a man in the city of Nyala, Sudan, who portrayed himself to displaced children as a kind of saviour. He would recruit homeless children, talk to them about great ideas and adventures—escaping the chaotic streets and going to faraway lands. He would feed them, clothe them.

Then he would sell them. The children would be taken away willingly by a "friend" or "business associate." A few days or weeks later, they would discover the rude truth that they were now slaves, or military pawns. Aleph himself had been under the sway of this man—Maladi was his name—until he and another kid had decided not to risk the future that Maladi was preparing them for. To this day, Aleph could not remember exactly what it was that had initiated within him the distrust of Maladi's scheme. For whatever reason, he and his friend, Bakar, had decided to leave the vicious little fiefdom. Perhaps it was the wisdom that arrives in a young man's mind when he reaches the ripe age of 14, enabling him to see more clearly into the motives and deceptions of those around him. Or perhaps it was something greater than his own wisdom...something more potent and perceptive than his own wits, something providential that had persisted in his mind until eventually he had left it all behind. It wasn't until three years later that he learned the truth about Maladi's deceptive little empire. Aleph had met a girl in Juba who had escaped a prostitution ring. Maladi had sold her into the prostitution after caring for her for two months.

There was no *honor* in that. Maladi had presented himself to unsuspecting children as a protector, a provider. That's not a difficult role for a man to play, since many men are naturally endowed with that propensity. To a young child who has lost all relation to family or village, "friendship" with a strong man who is well-established seems a natural thing...like a moth is drawn to flame, until that association is proven to be an exploitation of the child by the man.

But such a "man" is not a man. He is a beast, a snake. There is no honor in that.

Having escaped the clutches of such men and their myriad bondages, Aleph had determined that he would be a man of his word, and he would be, by God's grace, a man of high character.

From the nether regions of Aleph's mind another memory emerged. He had befriended a Muslim in Khartoum—Ahmed was his name—whose death had come as a result of an explosion. Aleph had never known why or how the explosion had come about, but it had occurred in a marketplace. He had seen the face of his friend Ahmed in a crowd of people, and had wished to go over and speak to him. But then there was an explosion. Everyone fled the market. Pandemonium ensued. He ran as fast as he could, which had become his habit in any perilous circumstances. But he never saw Ahmed again.

But before his untimely death, Ahmed had imparted some wisdom. He had come on a boat from Iran. On one occasion, the two homeless boys were having tea at that same market in Khartoum. Ahmed was telling him about life in Iran. There were many Iranians who hated Americans, and it was because of these numbers of people that the religious ones were able to kick the Shah out and return the country to *Sharia*. A mullah had told Ahmed that the main reason Americans were hated was: pornography. *Sharia* in Iran, over hundreds of years had established an order in society. The order was founded upon the Qu'ran, and upon families who served Allah because of his great compassion. Families were founded upon the authority of men, and the proper role of women in relation to that authority. When the Shah had opened the country up to the influence of Americans and other westerners, there was a tide of moral decadence that flooded in from the west. That decadence was characterized by many new ideas about women and sexual relations. Although the Americans spoke of democracy and freedom, their real impact was a flood of pornography, liquor and other evils that poisoned the good people of Iran. The Iranians would not stand for it. They would not stand by and consent to their country being overridden with a tide of immorality and filth. So they had rallied behind Khomeini and thrown the Shah out.

Aleph was not a Muslim, but he had understood Ahmed's point. Aleph had himself seen some of these influences in Sudan. He could understand the revulsion that many held for Americans, who were in many quarters seen as immoral and hypocritical. He had seen and heard the reports of many who accused Americans of having no *honor*, no truth. They would sell one thing, but deliver another. They did not live up to the standards that they set for others.

Aleph had eventually achieved an understanding about Americans, and what their *real* problem was: they were human. They were no worse than, and in some cases, much better than a multitude of peoples whom he had encountered during his seven years of eluding danger.

And when an opportunity to come to America had presented itself to him in Nairobi, he had accepted it without hesitation. He would find out for himself about Americans. And would benefit from that experience by becoming, like them, rich, or free, or rich *and* free. Regardless of what anyone else might say about them, Americans *were* free, *too* free for their own good. They couldn't handle their own freedom. They flaunted it before the world, and the world hated them for it.

But Aleph was going to find out for himself about the land called America. And so he did. And when he got there, he found it to be a place, like any other, where many could aspire to, and live, *honorably*, authentically. *Or*, they could live, as many did, deceitfully and immorally. But it was America's freedom that made these two extremes *so* extreme. In America, you could kill yourself being free. *Or,* you could live a long, prosperous life filled with nobility and honesty. Either way, people would love you. You could find people here to agree with you on anything. Yep. America was too free for its own good, but then...its freedom was its strength. A paradox, America is a paradox: the best and worst of everything.

In America, you are free to love anybody, in any way you choose. You're also free to hate anybody, as long as you don't hurt them. If your hatred crosses the boundaries of injury or violence, the Law will come looking for you. Not someone seeking vengeance (that's the old world). No, In America it would be the Law to come looking for you. The law of the land protects those who are innocent and those who are minority. The Law protects them from injury. It also protects the right to hate, as long as that hate doesn't inflict *injury.*

Take Mackie Heist, for instance, the electrician. He's free to hate Mexicans. But he's not free to hurt them. So he decides to, instead of hurting *them,* damage their *property.* He knows he can't *steal* their property, because if he were to do so the long arm of the Law might come looking for him, so he damages their property instead. He inflicts, by malicious arrangement, flat tires upon their trucks. This enables him to register his hate in a way that he thinks he can get away with. But here's Mackie's problem (or one of them): while he is free to hate, he is also free to act in stupidity, which he does, in fact, do, when he places nails under Lucido's truck tires, because what he doesn't realize is that the Mexicans come from a country where justice is something closer to raw recompense or vengeance instead of complex litigation. The Mexicans, in this case, decided to take this little legal matter into their own hands, because they have not, as yet, accustomed themselves to, or benefited from, the multi-tiered judicial system that exists in the United States. So they revert to the "old country" justice system.

And that is why Mackie Heist got a nail shot in his butt. And also why he hadn't been to the jobsite since last week. His failure to uphold the standards of true *honor,* which includes *doing no unnecessary harm* to others as well as being honest and forthright and not lying about such things, *backfired* on him. The Mexicans had fired upon his backside. They were crafty in the art of under-the-radar war, having aimed just accurately enough with the nail gun to avoid life-or-limb-threatening injury, but just accurately enough to maim, and thus make their point in a most persuasive way: don't mess with Lucido's crew.

And it wasn't only Mackie's honor deficiency that Aleph thought of. It was also the work itself, that was yet to be done, because Mackie had not been on the job. And Bryan, his boss, the very same Bryan with whom Aleph had so briefly interviewed on Monday, had not sent anyone else out either. Today, Tuesday, Aleph had spent the entire day removing old ceiling grid, installing new, in close proximity to the electrical work that was as yet undone, but which he, Aleph, could do, if he had the contract to do. And he was wishing that he could do it. He was not *coveting* the other man's work, of course, because that would be a violation of the law of God...*Thou shalt not covet thy neighbor's contract.* He was simply noticing the fact that the work remained undone when it should, in fact, be done, and Marcus needed it done.

Aleph was pondering these things when, finally, he drifted off to sleep.

Exchanges
17

"Actions have consequences. You go messin' around with people's heads on my job, disturbing the peace, making flat tires, generally makin' trouble and displaying a bad attitude...and then not showing up for two days when I've got all this work to be done. I've got to do something, Bryan." Marcus was mad.

"I take it you wanta get that nigger to do it?"

"I want to get it done." Marcus calmed down a little.

"Are you gonna send Mackie over there to finish what you've *barely* begun?...one day's work— it's not 2% complete. And he lays out for two days."

"He didn't lay out. I had him on another job."

"You *what?*"

"I didn't want him to get hurt. Those Mexicans might kill him."

"Oh, bullshit. He *asked* for it, Bryan, by poppin' their tires with simplex nails."

"I can't be takin' the chance on somebody getting' hurt. My insurance will skyrocket."

"Well, if you don't want the work—"

"The hell with it, Marcus."

"Look, Bryan, we've got a contract. You want to make some money. I need to get my building done. I'll make a deal with you."

Bryan was sitting at his desk with a bent piece of copper wire in his hands, twirling it in his fingers. He wasn't into the discussion.

"Look, Bryan, I'll get the electrical work done, handle the inspectors, and still cut you your 10%."

"I always figure on at least 15."

"Come on, 10% for not doing *anything?* That's a pretty good deal."

"Nah...I'm not gonna have that nigger over there working under my license."

"Here's the deal, Bryan. When Daniel put together those blueprints, you know he had an engineer put stamps on the plans. So the design work is done—all the load calculations and that. I can get another electrical contractor on the job, and he'll work on my terms. It's your choice. You've got 'til tomorrow to decide. Either send me someone to get the job done, or the deal is off. If you don't send someone, I'll pay you for what you've got in the job and that's it. By tomorrow, I'll know what your decision is."

"I'll send my lawyer over in the morning."

"Bullshit. You don't even have a lawyer, and even if you did, you don't have a leg to stand on—three days with no one on the job. That's not getting the work done 'in a timely manner.' And there's the nails in the tires and all of that that will work against you in court. No. You heard my offer. Take it or leave it. I'm outa here." Marcus looked the man right in the eyes, then walked out of his office.

***

Margaret Stuart sipped iced tea while she waited for her friend to show up for lunch. She had one eye on the TV news. Senator Alligere was commenting on the failure of US troops to find weapons of mass destruction in Iraq. His remarks implied that there had never been any there to begin with, and that the President had merely used the weapons issue as an excuse to attack Iraq.

Her friend Rosalind appeared, escorted to the table by Bridget.

"Honestly, Marge, I can't get used to this traffic. There seems to be so much more of it these days"

Bridget set ice water and two menus on the table.

"Oh, it's not your imagination, honey. It has gotten worse."

"...a lot of people moving here these days."

"One wonders where they're all coming from, or why they choose this place to live."

"Federal government gets bigger and bigger. I guess one day everybody will be working for the government."

"God forbid...anyway...how are your grandkids doing?"

Bridget eased to the table. "Good afternoon. Do you see anything appealing on the menu?

"Ah, haven't even looked at it yet. Bring me an iced tea, please."

"Yes, ma'am" *Strange that I forgot to ask if she wanted something to drink.*

"June is probably going to be validictorian. Bobby's playing jv basketball, and Courtney can't get enough of gymnastics. How about yours?"

"Abby says she's going to spend spring break on the Gulf Coast doing Katrina relief. Miriam loves dancing more all the time, and Jake...well, I don't know. It's too early to tell."

"I think he's like my Ricky was...just taking longer to get it figured out."

"There are some hard choices out there. And sometimes college is not the best choice, at least not right away."

"Lord knows," said Margaret. "Ricky dropped out of one college, stayed out for two years, then went back to another. Once he figured out that he wanted go to medical school, he was focused from that time on. But he was thirty before he was practicing medicine."

Bridget brought iced tea for Rosalind and took their orders.

"I surely wouldn't mind if Jake took that route, even the roundabout way, as long as he's going somewhere."

"Young men will have to be careful, though. Every now and then I hear that some Congressman or another is talking about reinstituting the draft."

"I don't think it'll happen. War these days is so high-tech, they don't need as many soldiers."

"Well, that's a novel idea. Are you talking about conducting some kind of electronic war from a protected position...like in a video game?"

"I don't know what I'm talking about. I just know that with dictators like Saddam in power, it's a wonder we haven't had another world war already."

"Well, that's the point, Rosalind...we probably would have had one already if we hadn't gone into Baghdad and taken him out."

"Oh, you don't really think that, do you? It could be the other way around. We might have *started* World War III by going in there."

Margaret took a sip of tea and thought for a moment. "Well, no, Rosalind, I *don't* know that. But we don't know what might have happened if we hadn't gotten in there. Saddam may have already fired missiles on Israel, or..."

"It's been proven there were no WMDs. The whole thing was Bush's..."

"I beg your pardon. The lack of evidence about WMDs doesn't mean a thing, except that that beast got them out before *we* went in. And I bet you he really had to scramble to get them out, too."

Bridget brought the salads.

"Anyway, Rosalind. Think about it this way. When Hitler was over there in Germany cranking up the German war machine, who was trying to draw the world's attention to what he was doing?"

"I suppose you're talking about Churchill."

"Right. But who wanted to listen? The British Prime Minister, Mr. Chamberlain, was playing diplomatic games with a lawless tyrant and didn't have a clue about what was going on. Most of the British Parliament thought Churchill was a fanatic."

"Or a drunk." Rosalind laughed.

"Well," Margaret looked out the window. "He had his problems...but we've all got our share of problems."

"So, Margaret, are you comparing Bush to Churchill?"

"Well, yes, if you want to put it that way. History doesn't exactly repeat itself. At least we hope it doesn't. But there *are* some parallels."

"So, you're comparing Saddam Hussein to Hitler?"

"They were both tyrants who had no respect for the lives of their own citizens. Thank God for leaders like Churchill and Bush who will stand up to dictators."

"You're right about that. Somebody has to draw the line in the sand somewhere."

Bridget brought their food: trout amandine for Margaret, roasted chicken for Rosalind. They said a short prayer, then Margaret continued:

"The truth is, Rosalind, we can't know how right or wrong our foreign policy is, until history is written. Case in point: again, Mr. Churchill...if history had been written in the mid-30's when no one knew yet what Hitler was up to, the history writers would have dealt unfavorably with Churchill. But history was written...it's always written, years later. And I think you can agree that history writers have shown conclusively that if Mr. Churchill hadn't roused his nation in just the nick of time, the Nazis would have used their *Wehrmacht* to *blitzkrieg* all of Europe."

"Margaret, that's true, but, do you really think that's what Saddam was up to?"

"We'll never know, will we?"

"Somehow I don't think our President will be considered one of the great ones."

"Only time will tell. There was only one *truly* great man in history anyway."

"And who was that? Jesus?"

"Yes."

Rosalind cocked her head for a moment and thought about it. "I agree. He's probably had more impact on the world than any other person. But...he certainly didn't go raising great armies to, you know, oppose the Romans or anything...."

"Well, that wasn't his job. And besides, the Romans weren't that bad anyway, at least, not at the time of Christ."

"Okay, so it wasn't his job to raise armies to defeat the forces of evil in the world...what was his job?"

"It definitely *was* his job to defeat the forces of evil, but, you're right, not by raising armies."

"His strategy was nonviolent resistance then, like Gandhi."

"Oh, it was much more than nonviolent resistance. It was resurrection from the dead."

"You believe that?"

"Yes. And think about this. It was his job to rise from being dead. But he couldn't have done that unless something had first killed him, right?"

"Right."

"So it was his job to die and then rise from the dead. What greater work could *any* man do than overcoming death? Even if it's just to, you know, show that it could be done."

Rosalind laughed. "Sounds good to me. Sign me up."

"Well, do you believe it?"

"Oh, yes. I do. I do believe it."

"Well, you're already signed up then."

Bridget dropped in to ask about dessert. They both ordered orange sherbet.

Bridget left the restaurant at 4:30, the same time that Kaneesha came in. When Hilda had heard about the Smiths coming from North Carolina to see Jonda, she insisted that Bridget work lunch, so she would then be free to meet Jonda's grandparents. Bridget caught the bus back to Kaneesha's house, greeted Jonda and Bernadette, and prepared (as if she knew how to) herself to meet these people.

Bernadette, bless her heart, was cooking a dinner for them, fried chicken, potato salad and green beans. Her home would be a pleasant setting for such an occasion as this.

Bridget and her young friend sat on Bernadette's sofa, in the living room, with the afternoon sun shining in. Bridget read *Winnie the Pooh*, and also used the occasion to introduce some consonant sounds to Jonda.

At 5:30, the doorbell rang. They had decided that Bernadette would answer it, since the house was hers. The couple that walked in the door seemed a perfect match. He was tall, gray-haired with a large, Romanesque nose and a serious look on his face. She was about a foot shorter than he, dyed blonde hair, plump, with bright blue eyes, just a hint of smile in her sad eyes. She was holding a brown paper bag.

"Hello." Bernadette smiled broadly at them. "Won't you come in?" They stepped in. He had a hat in his hand.

"I am Bernadette Michot." She extended her hand.

"Frank Smith." He smiled politely and shook Bernadette's hand.

"I'm Beatrice...so nice to meet you." Her accent was southern.

Bridget was rising from the sofa, Jonda with her. The Smiths, being guests, assumed nothing except that they had made it to their destination after many hours of travel. They were relieved, and thankful.

"I'm Bridget." She looked down at the child. "Jonda, do you remember your grandparents?" The little girl was in no hurry to do anything. Bridget looked at the Smiths and smiled kindly. "What do you wish to be called?"

"Grandma and Grandpa." Slowly, the gentle couple approached their granddaughter. It was evident that there had been little communication with them before this moment. Mr. Smith crouched, smiling. "Hi, Jonda. I'm your Grandpa Smith. I saw you when you were born...when your mama brought you into the world."

Jonda was being shy. Her other hand was holding Bridget's skirt.

Then it was Grandma's turn. She deftly picked up a nearby wooden chair, set it a few feet in front of Jonda, and sat on it, not leaning back, but forward, so that her face was quite close to the child's, but not *too* close.

"Jonda, have you ever seen a giraffe?"

"No." The child relaxed a bit.

"I'd like to show you one now. Can I do that?"

"Yeah."

Beatrice kept her eyes on Jonda's eyes. Without looking down at the paper bag, she reached into it, pulled out a stuffed giraffe about two feet high, brown, yellow and soft. The giraffe had a goofy smile on its face.

And then, like a ray of sun that suddenly breaks through after a rainstorm, there was a smile on Jonda's face. She reached out for the giraffe, for she knew it was hers to keep. Beatrice bequeathed it to her, the first gift that had ever passed between them.

Success. This is what life is all about.

Bridget spoke into the silent celebration. "That fried chicken smells mighty good, don't ya think?"

Bernadette knew her cue. "Well, come on in here and get ya some of it."

But Frank Smith couldn't make it into the kitchen; instead, he began weeping. His wife embraced him; they stood together for a few moments in mutual mourning.

Bridget had 17 questions running through her mind, but could reach no peace in her mind about how to present any one of them. *What about the funeral? What were their intentions regarding Jonda? What can I do to comfort them? What can I do to help them begin a relationship with Jonda? What arrangements do I need to help them with? What obligations do I have to them while they are here in Urdor? What should I do for them tomorrow? What should I do for them tonight? What should I do right now? What can I say to them?*

Since she could decide on nothing, she simply sat on an armchair; it was a seat where she could be available to them, in the same room with them, but not demanding any response, not requiring anything by her presence. Waiting for these gentle people to finish their crying, or waiting for herself to decide what she should now do...she didn't know, in this awkward moment, what it was that she waiting for as she sat. Jonda crawled up in her lap. That didn't make it any easier. The child had this attachment to her, and not to them. There was something wrong, but she didn't understand it.

The *something wrong* was a gulf of estrangement that had widened between the Smiths and Wanda over the last seven years. But Bridget didn't know that. She didn't know anything. She had never taken the time to *know* Wanda. It was just a party thing. They had partied together. The chaotic existence that Wanda had shared with Buzz had been founded on partying, recreational drug-use, sex; but it had deteriorated into a life of confusion that was ill-fitted for the needs of a mother and daughter. Wanda had never really figured it out...*that her life had changed, that she needed to be a mother now instead of a party girl. She never figured it out. Perhaps she had begun to understand that truth when she sought respite with Bridget in the motel room.* But then, because of Buzz's violence, Wanda never had the chance to make those adjustments in her life.

The tears now lubricating the Smiths' grief were a flood of pain that they had dammed within themselves for all this time. Now there was no reason to maintain the dam. The flood gates must open. No longer could they restrain themselves, in fear of further alienation, from speaking to Wanda, No longer could they plan for a future reconciliation. No longer could they pray for her, or wait for her to show some sign of softness toward them. No longer could they hope. Nevermore could they hope for reconciliation with their estranged Wanda. *Quoth the raven: 'Nevermore.'*

The only hope that now remained lived within the breast of a five-year-old girl, whom they barely knew, and who didn't know them. *What hope could be in that? They had blown it. Jonda was not their daughter; she could never be. They had been given one chance, and now it was over. Nothing left...*except a child who hardly knows them.

From all the wayward, wanton, recklessness of Wanda Smith's life, there remained but one thing: Jonda. *We will ask her what she wants to do. We will give her the choice...to go to North Carolina, begin a new life with us, or...or what?...stay here with this nice young lady. Who is she anyway? What right does she have to take our granddaughter? But she's not taking our granddaughter. She's making it possible for us to make this connection. She's helping us. If it hadn't been for her compassionate intervention, we would be in a much worse situation now. I should thank her.*

Beatrice Smith relaxed her embrace from her husband. She walked over to the couch, sat down, looking at Bridget and Jonda with tears in her eyes.

"I want to thank you for helping us. Thank you."

"I haven't done anything. But please tell me: What *can* I do to help you?"

"We'll be going to the coroner's office in the morning. But after that, I don't know what we'll do We can...we can take Wanda home for burial."

The statement seemed, to Bridget, more like a question. At last, she had something to offer: affirmation. "That would be best."

Now here was one question answered. It wasn't so hard. Very simple really.

Bridget wanted to make conversation. Now she had an opportunity.

"You raised Wanda in North Carolina, is that right?"

"Yes, in Greensboro."

Bridget wanted to ask what had gone wrong between them, but she dare not.

"Wanda was very kind to me; she took me in when I needed a place to stay."

The teary woman managed a smile. It was a pleasant thought to her...her daughter helping someone in need. "Oh, and when was that?"

"Just a few weeks ago."

"Oh." They were silent for a moment. Grandma gazed at Jonda, sitting peacefully on the floor, her arms around her legs. "And that's when you got to know Jonda?"

"Yes."

Then Jonda was surprised when her grandmother addressed her: "Jonda, what would you like to do?"

The child looked up at Bridget, as if seeking assistance. But Bridget merely smiled, and touched Jonda's hair, pulling a strand of it out of her face.

"I want some fried chicken."

Bernadette emerged from the kitchen. She had heard everything, and had been waiting in the wings for her opportunity to assist in this transition in any way possible. "Come and get it. Dinner is served," she announced with a smile.

They all sat at the kitchen table. Frank Smith looked at Bernadette and asked: "May we pray?"

"Let us pray," agreed Bernadette.

"Lord, we thank you for this food tonight, this food that smells so good. We thank you for the generosity of this woman, Bernadette, who has prepared it. We thank you for Bridget, and the help she has given. We thank you for Jonda, Lord. And we ask that you bless our time together, and help us to become friends. In Jesus name."

"Amen."

Bernadette spoke. "I've been here all my life. My husband and I raised two kids in this house before he passed away, and I want you to know that I appreciate having company."

"Where are your children now?" asked Beatrice.

"My daughter, Kaneesha, works at the restaurant with Bridget. She's been there for two years. My son, Andre, is a senior at Radford College."

"When did your husband pass away?

"It was three years ago...lung cancer."

"Kaneesha says that he was a good father," said Bridget.

"Bridget, how long have you lived here in Urdor?" asked Mr. Smith.

"I came here two years ago from Cleveland, Ohio, to study at Lincoln University."

"You're still a student?"

"I'm not taking classes now."

"I know a little bit about Lincoln. We like to keep up with basketball in North Carolina. Last year, your basketball team knocked Carolina out of the NCAA tournament.

"I remember that," said Bernadette.

"Anyway, Bridget," said the genteel man, "maybe you'll get back around to school someday."

"Perhaps," agreed Bridget. "Being in school and taking it seriously takes a lot of time."

"Where's mommy?" interjected Jonda, out of the blue.

Who knew what to say? No one. There was an awkward silence. Bridget was thinking: *This one's for the grandparents.*

But it was Bernadette who came to the rescue. Being the hostess, she felt the need to manage any potentially awkward situation.

"Jonda, did you hear me say a minute ago that I had a husband?"

"Yes."

"Well he died, and your mama went to be with him."

"Oh."

Beatrice volunteered further comment. "We hope they're in heaven, Jonda."

Bernadette said, "Well, I know my Willie is in heaven, so your mama must be there with him."

"That's right," said Beatrice. "You know, Jonda, before you were even born, your mother lived with us, and we loved her."

"Did she love you?" asked Jonda.

"Yes, she loved us. When she was your age, she lived with us. We raised her from a little bitty baby."

"Buzz is mean to me," Jonda interjected.

"I'm sorry you had to put up with that, honey," offered Beatrice. "He won't be mean to you any more. You won't have to go back to him."

"He shot my mama."

Bridget had hoped they could get through the meal without the subject coming up. A sudden remembrance of Wanda's body lying fetus-like on the hotel-room floor disturbed her, and robbed her of composure. She could feel the tears coming.

"Yes, he did, Jonda," Bridget managed to say, "but he's not gonna shoot anybody else, because he's in jail, where mean people belong." Bridget felt panic coming on. "Excuse me." Covering her mouth, she hurried out of the room, and into the bathroom.

Beatrice studied her granddaughter's sad, puzzled face. "Jonda, what do you want to do?"

"I don't know. I don't want to do anything."

Bernadette, the facilitator, knew that this was a moment for tenderness. She spoke softly to the child, "Miss Bridget was crying because she was sad about Buzz shooting your mother. But you know what, Jonda?"

"What?"

Bernadette put her hand gently on the back of Jonda's neck. "We're all sad. We're all sad about it. But you could make us all feel better right now, if you'd go give your grandma a big hug."

Beatrice could see willingness in the child's eyes, but no initiative. Beatrice had what she needed now, thanks to Bernadette's careful intervention. She had what she needed now to make the leap of intimacy that this whole tragic circumstance had been crying out for. Hesitantly, she rose from the seat, walked around the table, extended her arms to the orphan. Jonda responded without inhibition. They had not embraced since Jonda's third birthday, until now. Grandmother held onto granddaughter for dear life. This is what life and death is all about.

Stars
18

The receptionist ushered Helen Olei into the office of assistant District Attorney Madeleine Skepto.

"What can I do for you, Ms. Olei?"

"I'd like to file a formal complaint. On Friday night, a week and a half ago, I was raped. I want to charge Moa Grindell with the crime of rape."

Madeleine raised her eyebrows in mild surprise. "Did you call the police after the crime was committed?"

"My suitemate called the police less than two hours after the incident. They sent a team of investigators. There is a police report and a case file is underway."

"Let me ask you, first of all, Ms. Olei, what is your job or profession?"

"I'm an emergency RN at Wessex County Medical Center."

"That explains your forthright demeanor. This is unusual for a rape case."

"I'm sure it is. I've seen this kind of thing before, but I've never, until recently, been on the receiving end of it. And believe me, I was not so 'forthright' about it for the first week or so. But then something happened that contributes to the unusual nature of this rape case."

"And what is that?"

"Monday night, two nights ago, I was at work. A deputy sheriff, Eddie Wheeler, brought in a man whom he had just arrested. The prisoner needed treatment for a broken leg. When I saw him, I recognized him immediately as the man who raped me. His name is Moa Grindell."

"Well, that's pretty amazing, Helen. And you're right...it is unusual. Most of the time these offenders are identified after a whole lot of investigative work and forensics that takes a long time."

"I know how long some of these processes take, Ms. Skepto, and that's why I'm here. Considering my sure identification of the rapist, the case should move expeditiously. Am I right?"

"Well, let's hope so. There are numerous facts that we need to establish beyond reasonable doubt before a jury will convict."

"Like... what might some of those facts be?"

"Well, for starters, your identification of the rapist. On a scale of 1 to 10, what is the number that would indicate the surety of your identification?"

"Ten."

"Oh yeah? How can you be so sure? Where did the crime occur?"

"In my bedroom."

"About what time?"

"Midnight."

"Was it dark in your room at midnight?"

"Yes, it was dark, but after it happened I got a full view of him, because he tripped in the living room on his way out. And in the light of a living room lamp I saw a tattoo on the back of his neck which identifies him without question. When I saw it on him at work the other night, I knew exactly who he was, no question about it."

Madeleine paused for a minute, writing on a legal pad.

"Okay. That sounds pretty convincing. What kind of tattoo was it?"

"It was a red dragon."

Madeleine's eyebrows raised slightly. She leaned back in the chair, tossed her pen on the legal pad.

"Oh? We've actually seen quite a few of those lately."

"Hmm...must be a fad of some kind. Anyway, I got a good look at him. He was thin, with a receding hairline, about 35, ruddy complexion. When I saw him in the emergency room a couple of nights ago, I recognized him immediately. I asked the deputy to turn his wheelchair around so I could see the back of his neck. I knew it would be there—a red dragon. I'll never forget seeing it the night of the crime. He was down on my living room floor, writhing. He was actually a pretty stupid rapist. There were a lot of things he could have done differently to cover his crime. He could have turned the light out before he came in my room, could have been more careful leaving, could have...well...he could have killed me." Helen was getting a little upset. "He could have...not had a tattoo. Why would a rapist get a tattoo that would so readily identify him? Pretty stupid."

Madeleine was listening with interest, swiveling in her chair. "Helen, lately we've encountered a group of white power racists in our area who wear a red dragon tattoo."

Helen didn't say anything, she was seething. After a minute or so, Madeleine resumed their interview. "So, anyway, he got away. Then what happened?"

"The next thing I remember was waking up and seeing Rachel, my suitemate."

"Who called the police?"

"Rachel did."

"And how much time had elapsed?"

"I don't know...30 minutes? I must have passed out."

"But I remember talking to Rachel. Then she left the room to get the phone. I did something then that I realized I shouldn't have done—I took a shower."

"I understand."

"But later on, when the Nurse Examiner was interviewing me, and gathering samples for evidence, she said the samples they got looked very reliable. I must have been lucid enough while showering to not wash all the evidence away."

Madeleine looked at Helen thoughtfully, then admonished her. "You know, its very likely that you'll have to talk about all of this on a witness stand in the courtroom. Are you prepared to do that? Can you handle it?"

Helen's face assumed a vicious expression. "If it's what I have to do to put that guy under the jail, I can handle it. And they better not give me a hard time about taking a shower. The Nurse Examiner said there was enough evidence recovered to support my testimony."

"If the DNA sample matches."

"It'll match. Once again, Ms. Skepto, that's why I'm here. I can identify this criminal beyond reasonable doubt."

"What you need to prepare for, Helen, is the relentless inquisition that a defense attorney could inflict on you."

Helen was annoyed. "It's no damn crime for a woman to take a shower after someone has raped her, okay?"

Madeleine sat back in her chair, stopped swiveling. She spoke softly. "No, it's not. It shouldn't matter anyway." She paused for a moment, writing on the pad. "Helen, I couldn't help noticing...are you pregnant?"

"Yes."

"How far along?"

"Four months. And that's why they oughta put him under the jail...raping a pregnant woman. He could have done serious damage to the baby."

"He probably didn't know you were pregnant. I doubt that was a factor."

Helen was mad. "He didn't *know?*" Whose side are you on anyway? You think he chose his victims according to minimal collateral damage?"

"No, no, remember...I'm only preparing you for what a relentless defense attorney will throw at you on the stand."

"And you think they'll raise the pregnancy issue, as if...to question my—"

"They always do."

"Yeah—if the woman knows the guy. I never saw him—"

"Hey, hey...don't get so defensive. We won't let it come to that. Anyway, Helen, the police are conducting a full investigation?"

"Yes."

"And I can read all about it in their report?"

"Yes."

"I'll read their report when it comes through, and then we'll talk some more. Okay?"

"Okay."

"Is there anything else you'd like to tell me before I go to a scheduled meeting?"

"Only...thank you for taking the time to hear my complaint."

"Well, we'll do what we can to have this guy brought to justice. Do you have a lawyer?"

"You're my lawyer. You represent the people against criminals, don't you?"

"Right. Just checking. We'll see to it he gets what's due to him. I'll call you in a couple days after I've seen the police report."

"Thank you." They shook hands. Helen walked out of the office.

That guy didn't know who he was messin' with when he chose her for his victim.

***

On Thursday afternoon, Big Photon Phil, a member of the Solar Electromagnetons Energy team, traveled 93 million miles through the void of space in about 8 minutes with his buddies. Phil and his teammates hit the stratosphere traveling at a pretty good clip, the speed of light, and merrily radiated their way through the atmosphere, waving at everyone as they went along catching all the lights just right, until they finally managed a safe landing on a slab of freeway for a pit stop and a bite to eat. Old Mother Earth, sitting in an oily-looking worn-out toll booth, reached out her hand and collected the dollar that Photon Phil stuck out the window of his supercharged-quantum-leap, wavelength-jumpin' mean-lean-running machine. She handed him some infrared pennies for change. "Thank you. Have a nice day." She raised the bar; the green light went on. Photon Phil hightailed it back skyward for the return trip. But about ten miles out he started feeling a little sleepy, and he heard a lilting little tropospherical blues song that was kinda lulling him to sleep. So Phil stopped and hung out for awhile, but then decided *well this just wasn't happenin'* so maybe he'd just drift back down to Earth and check the place out, maybe even stay for awhile, and see if he could stir up a little heat or sump'n. When he finally landed the second time, he was in a parking lot in Urdor. He whipped out his cell phone, gave his buddy Pete a call.

"Hey breaker one nine good buddy. Where ya at?"

"Punxtatawny. Looks like a nice place. I could get into it. I think I'll hang out for awhile, maybe six weeks or so…see if things warm it up a bit."

"Awesome, dude! Yeah, well, it looks like I'm in Urdor, just outside of DC…think I'll have a look around this parking lot. Yo! Totally cool! Ya oughta see these wheels, man. Well, take it easy, Pete. I'll catch ya on the flip-flop."

"Roger that, Phil. Over and out."

Phil slipped the phone back into his BTU light-saber-valence pouch and started radiating the concrete. He felt right at home, very comfortable. It had been a long ride. He started to sink into a deep sleep.

People walking through the parking lot saw him, but they hadn't noticed.

In fact, Frank Smith stepped right on Phil while he was pressing the remote to open the rental car. The kind man assisted his granddaughter into the front seat, reminded her to snap the seat-belt. He opened the back door for Beatrice and she got in.

"This is a nice car," said Jonda, "not all dusty like Buzz's van."

"What's really nice, Jonda, is having you in it with us. Thank you for coming with us. It has been a very hard thing...what we did this morning."

They had just left the morgue, where they had seen Wanda's body. It was not an easy thing to do. Frank and Beatrice had spent years hoping, in the back of their minds, that someday, somehow, Wanda would turn her life around, or change her attitude, or something, and *at least come and visit them.* But it had never happened. *This* happened instead. She would never more enter their home back in Greensboro. *Quoth the raven: 'Nevermore.'*

But there was a surreal quality that enshrouded their time now. It was partly due to the unprecedented experience of seeing their only child *like a patient etherized upon a table. What a waste her life had been. I shouldn't say that...shouldn't even think that. There had been some bright moments in her childhood. It had been good, generally. It had been good until...she fell in with those druggies.* Everything had changed then. Even her personality changed. She had become another person—someone they no longer knew.

But there was something else that cast a surreal palor over this day and time. It was the presence of the young girl. And both of them felt it...*as if Wanda were not gone...she's right there, six years old again.* No, that's Jonda, not Wanda. *That's another person, another human being, that Wanda left to take her place.*

"Wanda..no..." Beatrice mumbled.

"What's that, dear?" asked Frank. He knew what was going on. He felt it too. They would have to *consciously* keep it in their minds that *this child is somebody else. This is not Wanda. This child has had a nativity and environment that is totally different from the sheltered one we gave Wanda.*

"Let's go get some lunch, Jonda. Are you hungry?"

"A little bit."

Frank was not very hungry. Bernadette had served breakfast. Bridget had left for work. They had set out for the morgue, and to make arrangements for Wanda's body to be flown back to North Carolina where they would bury her. Bridget had suggested that they come to the restaurant for lunch. Although he wasn't very hungry, Frank saw a lunch at the restaurant as a constructive way to spend time on such a day as this. If they didn't include some destination besides a morgue in the itinerary, their day could turn quite depressing. So, as Bridget had suggested, they stopped at the Jesse James Gang Grille for lunch. The place was crowded. As soon as they walked in, a friendly woman approached them:

"Hello. I'm Hilda Hightower. Bridget said we might expect you, Frank and Beatrice...and Jonda. Good afternoon, Jonda. Y'all have a seat over here."

Bridget was thankful for the opportunity to serve them. It would be easier than last night. In this setting, she had something to keep busy with. She would not have to awkwardly plan what the next move, or next word, would be. It was easier to say something like:

"Hello. It's good to see you again. I know...it must have been difficult...what you had to do this morning. I was thinking it would be good for Jonda to come here, after an experience like that."

"This is a popular place," observed Frank.

"There's a convention in town, at the Belmont, a few doors up the street."

"Well, that's good for business. They sure like this place."

"A lot of people do. Do you want something to drink? How about you, Jonda?"

"Coke."

"Okay" She looked at the Smiths.

"Iced tea for both of us," said Beatrice.

Bridget walked away, busy. Hilda returned.

"Mr. And Mrs. Smith, please order whatever you want. I want you to know that your lunch tab will be paid by a secret benefactor, a person who understands that you've had to incur a lot of expenses for this trip."

"That's wonderful," said Frank. "I would like to thank this person myself."

Hilda just smiled and shrugged. "Are you finding your way around pretty well? Can I answer any questions about Urdor, or locations of places?"

"We found the morgue this morning, no problem, and did what we had to do there. Then we talked to the airline on the phone about arrangements to get back to North Carolina for the funeral. I don't know what else we'll do here. We're not flying back 'til tomorrow."

"What about Jonda?" Hilda, uninhibited, posed the big question.

Frank smiled and looked at his granddaughter. "I don't know. What *about* Jonda?" He looked at the child. "Jonda, what do you want to do?"

"I'll have a hamburger."

They laughed. "Well, there you have it."

Hilda was a little puzzled. "So, Mr. Smith, you won't be going to the sheriff's office?"

"No. Our only concern now is Wanda's burial, and Jonda's welfare. As far as the law goes, I suppose we'll hear from them sooner or later. There's nothing we can do, nor anything we *want* to do about the law. What's done is done." He paused for a moment, looked right into Hilda's compassionate eyes. "There's no bringing her back."

Bridget brought their drinks and took orders.

***

A basketball bounced on the rim twice, then finally settled into the net, and out the lower end, falling straight down to the wooden floor. Isaac grabbed it, took two steps away from the goal and, as if it were all one arabesquish motion, tossed a hook shot over his head into the basket again. Eighteen shots in a row he had made...using every improvised position that occurred to him, until...number 19.

"It didn't go down, bro," said Wes, his teammate.

"Eighteen in a row is not half bad," said Isaac, "for a little point guard."

But the missed shot did signal a change of regimen. Isaac began popping them in from behind the 3-point line, starting at the base line, moving around the circle in increments of 10 degrees. Wes was passing it back to him each time, until he'd gone all the way around.

The two Lincoln players, Isaac the point man and Wes the post man, had lingered beyond the practice session that the team had just completed. *You could never get enough practice to get ready for the first conference playoff game.* And the Eagles were the #1 seed. That's a lot of expectation to live up to. And that's a lot of *payback* lurking in the minds of their first opponents, Marianna College. Sure, the Wildcats were a #12 seed, but *anything* could happen in a conference tournament. Especially in *this* conference, which was famous for making overconfident #1 seeds eat humble pie.

Although, such a thing did not usually happen in the first round.

But it *could*. The Eagles were going to be ready for Saturday night, and Isaac was going to make sure of it. And he *himself* would be ready, to begin this postseason strong, and *finish* strong. They had won the regular-season conference title outright; now it would be time to make the title official by sweeping the tournament.

"I guess I better hang it up, Wes. I've gotta get dressed up for dinner at the FEF convention."

"The *what* convention?"

"Family Education Foundation. My mother signed me into it when I was in kindergarten, because, you know, she's a teacher and all."

"Oh, yeah? What is it?"

Isaac took a shot from a point just short of half-court, but missed. "It's a national organization to...I guess you could say, protect the interests of families in the school system."

"Tha's cool."

"And they've asked me to speak to the young people."

"No kidding. That's even cooler. What are you gonna tell em?"

The two friends couldn't stop shooting. "I'm gonna tell em to stay in school, learn how to read and write well." He did a reverse layup. "I'm gonna tell 'em to work hard, stay straight, and 'do unto others as you would have them do unto you.'" He popped in another hook shot. "I'll remind them how fortunate they are to be attending good high schools in a place where everybody's pretty safe and secure." Missed a 3-pointer. "A place where you don't have a bunch of smartasses coming in tellin' ya what to do with your life, where you can go or can't go." Made a 3-pointer. "What you can say or not say." He tossed up a foul shot. "I'll remind them that there are guys like my brother on the other side of the world protecting the rights of oppressed peoples." He dribbled the ball under his legs a few times. "Guys who are not much older than them, putting their lives on the line so that people all over the world." Another foul-shot in. "...Including us, can have some peace and a constitutional government."

"And a dependable supply of oil," said Wes, laughing.

"That too."

"Just thought I'd throw that one in, bro'."

Isaac missed a 3-pointer. "Yeah, all that stuff--that's what I'm gonna tell 'em." He threw the ball over in a rack, headed for the shower. "So I'll see ya later. Thanks for hangin' with me, bro. We'll do it again tomorrow."

"Right." Wes dunked a basketball, *jammin'*.

Atrocities
19

Butch Gremillion was thinking about his son back in Abbeville. He was worried because Maynard was running with a pretty loose crowd. It seemed like things had been heating up a little lately. The boy was coming in at all hours of the night, sleeping late, smelling like booze. And now here was Butch, suspended again, for four days, fifty feet above the murky waters of the Gulf of Mexico, on a natural gas rig.

Nothing he can do about it now, except pray. A not-quite-grown boy weighing in at 200 pounds seemed like a little heavier burden than what his sweet Suzanna could handle at home. So he was praying for her too. This troublesome maelstrom in Maynard's life had started to spin out of control a few months ago. It seemed to Butch that he could keep a pretty tight rein on the boy when he was home.

But he was not home, and that's what worried him. *Well, if the boy can live through Thursday, I'll straighten him once and for all when I get back.*

But that was four days ago. Immediately after having his little worry/prayer session, Butch had spun the wheel that opened a valve far below him, in the depths of the Gulf waters, and a few thousand cubic feet of natural gas escaped from the bowels of the earth. After bouncing around in chaotic boredom for a few million years, these molecules of rarified organic detritus, or dinosaur farts as Butch called them, hit the open road like Mario Andretti on a mission, raced each other out of that rotten, substrate prison where they'd been locked up all that time by some ancient earthquake, and then lit out like a bunch of bats outa hell, hissing through that pipeline like nobody's biznez for 1500 miles or so, all the way to Virginia and points beyond.

On this particular March evening some of them escaped through a gaslamp that hung on the outside wall of the Belmont Hotel in Urdor, Virginia. But, alas, though their miniscule gaseous molecule-bodies had been unsealed from beneath Gulf waters four days before, their fates were nevertheless sealed as soon as they escaped into Urdorian air. They had been yearning to be free; now they yearned no longer. They burned.

Maudy was watching the flicker of the gaslamp as she waited for her son to show up at the hotel entrance. She appreciated the little wavering flame. It seemed so...quaint, so classy, as if, this were 100 years ago.

People had been arriving from all over the place for the *Family Education Foundation* convention. As the talkative crowd walked past her, the gaslamp illuminated a diverse collection of faces, most of them eager to touch base on a convention's first night. *Gathering together...people we've not seen since last year...Mary from Missouri, Jack from Jackson, Chuck from Chicago,* all of them uniting once again to talk about the great things we've done and the greater things we're going to do, some drinking coffee, getting primed up for an evening of conversation and catching up, some having a little wine, sampling mellow relaxation in the ambiance. Name tags, hugs, laughter, hors d'eovres on silver trays, dinner, guest speakers, one of whom would be her own Isaac. And the gaslamp on the wall setting the mood of old-world elegance. She loved it.

Family Education Foundation. She had been a member since 1978, when she was teaching 4th grade at Dubois Elementary School. A loose federation of educators, parents, rich people, poor people, mostly Afro-American people whose mission was to pool resources to enable greater literacy among its membership and among those associated with its membership, and whose mission was also to ensure the continued presence and vigilance of families in public and private education at all levels.

And then there came Isaac, smiling, walking toward her, all dressed up. *My, doesn't my boy look grand tonight.*

The theatrical point guard stopped curtly, clicked his heels.

"Good evening, mama."

"Good evening, son."

He held out his arm. "Are we ready for a convention tonight?"

"Yes, sir." She eased her arm into his. They began walking toward the hotel entrance.

Just in front of them, Aleph Leng was also preparing to enter the building. But in the flash of a neuron a visual signal imposed upon his mind a vague memory: *What was that? Something wrong here? What was it? Behind the trash can!*

Just as suddenly as the African had seen something peculiar, he stopped.

Isaac, looking over at his mother's smiling face, ran right into Aleph's tall frame.

"Excuse me." Aleph turned around abruptly, pushed Isaac in a rude gesture, ran over to a trash can that was off to one side. *There! Behind the trash can was...*

Explosion. Confusion, Smoke. Glass, Choking. Stumbling. Isaac was stumbling, trying to find his mother in the smoke.

***

Laura Zenakis spoke sharply to the medical secretary at the nurse's station.

"Florence, call Pat, call Hester and Jamal...Terry...anyone you can get. There's been an explosion at the Belmont Hotel. The Police Chief says there will probably be twenty, thirty, maybe more people over here in the next few minutes. A bunch of them probably critical, and coding. Have Myron make as many emergency kits as we can put together before they start getting here."

***

Heat and Light. Heat: sudden, searing pain. Light, bursting too rudely, too hotly on unprepared skin...tearing, mincing, obliterating, explodng sudden splotchy, spitting incineration on all in its uncaring path of what flesh is heir to...

"Number nine...take him to number nine..." Aleph heard.

Wha...? What?

Confusion, voices, motion. Pain.

Why am I moving?

"Get a central line going"

Who?...Wha? Unguilty...I am unguilty. Take me somewhere else.

Blood, shed, already dried.

Blood, yet dripping...

In my eyes...I can't see...red

Confusion, voices, motion. Pain.

"Sidney, open another carton."

Khartoum... Ahmed? Wwas I there...no...why?...where?...who?

"Get his leg elevated."

Slipping.

"Stay with us, Aleph"

Sliding. *Saliva*

"Get suction in his mouth"

Saliva slathering.

Slavery, and all that flesh is heir to.

"Eject it...take it out...yes."

Wha? Who? Egypt. We are leaving Egypt...slipping out undetected, under cover of night. Don't go back. Tom is waiting up ahead. All passengers for Cincinnati....

"Aleph, can you hear me? Stay with us."

Spitting saliva...slavery...Let my people go!

"No not yet. Hold that higher, Joyce."

Gaping wound.

"Close it up."

Gahenna...no...unguilty

"But clear the airway...***Now!***...clear it."

Clear? Clear to go? St.Clare? Just believe, St.Clare.

"Clear the area, please. Liz, get that out of here."

"Now, relax pressure."

LAX. Fasten your seatbelts, adjust your seats into the upright position, prepare for landing...attendants prepare for crosscheck.

Cross.

"Aim higher, Joyce."

Aim...Ominous...Amistad

"Wrap it up, Liz...encircle in with gauze."

Cirque...the circle of the earth...I see it.

Light.

Long light.

"He's flatlining."

***

"Maudy?" Helen could see her coming around. Her eyes were opening slightly, although the left one was badly swollen, with a two-inch laceration along the cheekbone, apparently from a flying object.

"Maudy? Can you hear me?"

"Isaac. Where's Isaac?"

"He's here, Maudy. He's in the next room. You're at the hospital."

"What happened?"

"An explosion. You're going to be all right."

"Is Isaac all right?"

"He's fine. He's waiting in the next room."

"I can't move my leg."

"Don't try to move it now, Maudy."

Helen was looking into the woman's eyes as they spoke. At the same time she was swabbing the wound just below Maudy's eye, preparing it for stitches.

"In just a few minutes we'll be sending you to X-ray. Do you remember falling?"

"Yes."

"We're going to X-ray your hip. Can you feel this?" Helen reached down to Maudy's feet, gently squeezed her toes."

"Yes."

"How 'bout this?" Helen squeezed her ankle slightly

"Yes."

"What about this?" Checking the knee.

"Yes."

"Great."

Then Dr. Winger was standing over Maudy, taking Helen's place. He looked into her eyes and spoke: "Mrs. Jones, I'm Dr. Winger. You've got a nasty cut below your eye. Helen has gotten it cleaned up, and now I'm going to sew it up so it can heal.
Okay?"

"Okay. Did you see my Isaac?"

"Yes, ma'am, I did. I just talked to him. He is hardly hurt at all. He was protected from the blast by someone else."

"Who? Who protected us?"

"We'll tell you more about it later. Now, you're going to feel a little pinch on your cheek." He injected local anesthetic, then nimbly switched places with Helen again. Helen was swabbing the wound again.

"Mrs. Jones, now I'm going to ask you to lift your knee a little bit, if you can. Can you lift it?"

"No. It's too painful," wincing.

"Okay, don't try anymore. Mrs. Jones, you *may* have broken your hip in the fall, but we won't know for sure until we get the x-ray. Do you understand?

"Yes."

Helen spoke again. "Maudy, I'm going to put this patch over your eyes while we sew your cheek up. Are you ready?"

"Yes."

***

Marcus opened a can of turpentine. He tipped it slightly so that its upper contents would spill onto a rag that lay on the parking lot next to his car. With the rag partially soaked, he began rubbing on the driver's-side door. Someone had painted a black swastika on it while he was working late. His cell phone rang.

He opened it, looked at the mini-screen, saw "Grille," which stood for Jesse James Gang Grille. In the last few days, however, whenever he would see "Grille" displayed as the caller ID, it registered in his mind as "Girl," meaning Bridget, because she would often call from there.

"Hi."

"Marcus, have you heard about the explosion?"

"No, where?"

"At the Belmont Hotel, about 20 minutes ago."

The Belmont was just two blocks from the restaurant.

"That's where the FEF convention is. Aleph told me he would be going there tonight. Has anybody been down there to see what's happening?"

"Kaneesha left here right after we heard it, but she hasn't returned. I don't think anybody's getting in there for awhile. The police have got the whole block barricaded."

"I want to find out if anything has happened to Aleph. Don't you think he would have left there by now?

"The TV News says the police aren't letting anyone in or out except rescue workers."

"I'm headed over there in a few minutes, as soon as I get the car-door cleaned up. Someone painted a swastika on it. I wonder if it was that Dexter Bisto guy."

"You mean the one who threw the red paint on the Lincoln statue?"

"Yeah."

"I don't know, Marcus. But when you do get over here, you should probably park a few blocks away. Nobody's driving on State Street now."

"Okay. I'll see you in a about thirty minutes."

Marcus put the phone in his shirt pocket, then continued scrubbing the black paint away until it was gone. He threw the rags and turpentine into a bucket, brought them into the old drug-store building. After setting the bucket in a closet, he walked through the unfinished kitchen, out into the large space that would soon be the main dining room. He stood and looked at the progress that had been made since they had started work a week and a half ago. The front end of the building was enclosed now, with four bay windows where only transoms had been before. Lucido's crew had expedited the work well. They didn't mess around. Aleph's progress with the ceiling grid was impressive. Marcus had hoped that Aleph could run electrical conduit at the same time, thereby gaining some time. But that had not happened. The electrical work was still mired in Bryan's sluggish refusal to either get it done or turn the contract loose. Marcus' threat to Bryan had been a little presumptuous. A contractor can't just pick up the phone and find a company to follow behind another electrical contractor's mess. Consequently, no electrical work had been done this week. Aleph, licensed only in California, couldn't legally do any electrical work until the old contract was voided and a new one undertaken with a person or company licensed to work in Virginia.

Why did Bryan have to be such a bastard? His foot-dragging was inexplicable. Or at least, irrational. There was no good reason (that Marcus could ascertain) for Bryan to drop this job. He had brought the rage of Lucido's crew upon himself. Marcus suspected that Bryan was simply refusing to work with the Mexicans. And Bryan had spoken about Aleph in a hostile way. *Bryan was just mired in his own little hate world. Maybe he was the one who painted a swastika on the car. What is happening around here? This is a noose of hate slipped around this project, cutting off the electrical work. How long before the whole project would be delayed because of it?*

There was something rotten going on. Marcus had encountered it face to face ten days ago on the steps of the Lincoln Memorial. It had hit him in the face, and even gotten him arrested. Now it was hitting again, this time right in the middle of his work.

How long had it taken the Park Service to get Lincoln's limestone feet cleaned up? Or were they even **able** *to get it cleaned up?*

Suddenly, Marcus was frantic with worry about how they might not have gotten the red paint out of those monumental shoes. *The porous limestone surely didn't release red oil-paint as freely as his enamel-finished car-door released black* paint. But that's a miniscule problem—a red stain on the President slain. The weightier question would be: How long before the destructive effects of that civil war would be eradicated? The slaves were emancipated, but the hate was not eradicated. *'Jerusalem, Jerusalem, who kills the prophets and stones those who are sent to her! How often I wanted to gather your children together, the way a hen gathers her chicks under her wings, and you were unwilling. Behold, your house is being left to you desolate!'*

Splotches of hate from that two-hundred year debate—the monster of slavery, having been allowed to slither away from Philadelphia unsubdued, reared its multiple heads in Gettysburg, Savannah, and numerous points between, slinging blood and offal as it went...slinging, like Dexter Bisto flinging scarlet stain upon the President slain.

And what hideous hydra-head had struggled from fettered Austrian imprisonment, then absconded with the ancient swastika, splaying its red and black alarm upon every whitewashed wall and shattered-glass storefront of central Europe? And what hideous chimera of human hate had now implanted that same crooked cross upon the door of Marcus' car?

How long would mankind be slashing at serpent heads? How long would mankind be scrubbing against the red and black stain of sin?

Bridget called again.

"Yeah."

"Kaneesha just got back here. She knows one of the cops. He told her one of the victims fits the description of Aleph. We think he's been taken to the hospital."

Marcus couldn't say anything. He looked at the scaffold upon which Aleph had stood earlier that day. Lying on the scaffold was the tool belt that Marcus had loaned to Aleph.

"Marcus..."

"What?"

"Did you hear me?"

"I heard you. That means I'm going to the hospital. Let me know if you hear anything different from what you just told me. Okay?"

"I will."

"I'll call you when I know more. Bye."

"Goodbye, Marcus."

He looked up at the ceiling, at the last piece of ceiling grid that Aleph had put up, just a few hours ago. He was hoping that Aleph would be there tomorrow to put the next piece up. Somehow, it didn't seem likely.

Marcus sunk down to his knees. He prayed for the African, a man he hardly knew, but whom he had recently come to admire and love.

And he prayed for himself.

When Marcus drove into the parking lot of Wessex Medical Center, he hadn't expected to see a spinning blue light, but there it was. The flashing intermittently illuminated the crowd of people around the hospital main entrance.

He parked the car, walked over to the crowd. The police were screening entrants to the hospital; there were more people congregated than the waiting room could safely accommodate. A pall of sadness hung over the gathered people. Low conversations and weeping drifted into his awareness while Marcus carefully excused himself through.

When Marcus came near the door, he found a policeman and a policewoman screening those who were seeking entry.

The woman was speaking to a man who was just ahead of Marcus. "I do not have Rex or Sylvia Johnson on the list, sir. That's probably good news. They have not been admitted to the hospital or treated in the emergency room. Most likely, they are both still at the hotel. I suggest you go to the hotel."

The man walked away, exasperated.

The policewoman looked at Marcus and asked him, "Are you looking for someone?"

"Yes. I am looking for a man who works for me, Aleph Leng."

She checked her list. "Mr. Leng has been admitted to the hospital. What is your name, sir?"

"Marcus Derwin."

The woman nodded to the officer at the door. He stepped aside. Marcus entered. It was obvious why the two officers had been posted at the door. The emergency waiting room was full of people. Most of them Afro-Americans, most of them sharply dressed for the opening night of a convention. None were smiling. These people were gathered with one shared, unwelcome mission: to find someone they knew or loved whose life or health was in question.

The similarity of this scene to a funeral was discomfiting.

Just as Marcus' approach to the entrance had required careful navigation through a solemn crowd, his movement toward the reception desk demanded a similar tact, except that now he was in a lit-up room. The darkness outside had been forgiving. In here, he could see plainly the contortion of faces weeping, the quivering of uncertain lips. He could hear the low, guarded moans, laments, the rumblings of a spirit troubled with injustice, injury and probably death.

Shock. These people were in shock. Marcus sensed that most of them had been there at the hotel when the bomb exploded.

When he got to the main desk, there was no one there. After a moment, a thin, white-haired, distinguished woman appeared from a door behind the desk.

She looked at Marcus with weariness in her eyes. "Can I help you?"

"I'm looking for a man who works for me, Aleph Leng."

"Mr. Leng was brought in two hours ago." The woman hesitated. "He did not survive."

Without a word, Marcus wandered through the grief-stricken convention, looking for a place to sit. All the seats taken, he sat on the floor, against a wall. He was numb.

He could see no one in particular; the room was full of dark faces and fine clothes. A grave murmur cast all sound into a hushed non-presence, like the whisper of a distant surf.

Why am I here? Who are these people? I don't know a single person here. They must be wondering why the white guy is sitting on the floor. I came here looking for one person, and he is dead. I have no reason to be here. I better leave.

A cloud of fear was forming over Marcus's mind. *Here, I've been through twenty-seven years of life, with very little knowledge of death, except for Joey Calhoun in high school, and a few acquaintances I hardly knew. Now, in the same week, two people close to me die. They were not close to me, but they were close to me.*

Then out of the stupor that engulfed him, one image flashed before Marcus's eyes, captivating him: the face of a woman. Incredibly beautiful, with a long, graceful neck, white pearls strung across her perfectly smooth, black skin, she was an essence of dignity. Lips tight with tension, nose slightly flaring with each breath, as if righteous anger were seething beneath the carefully restrained countenance, yet her eyes were brimming with tears, as if she might erupt at any moment into unmitigated grief. Then she spoke:

"This *cannot* happen here. This *cannot* happen here. In Fallujah, it was a car-bomb that got Joseph. In Fallujah, that God-forsaken place...how many thousands of miles from here, an ocean away from here. *How* did they bring it here?"

A man was speaking softly to her: "We don't know who did this, Diana. It's got nothing to do with Fallujah, nothing to do with Joseph's death—"

"Daddy, daddy..."

"Daddy's gonna be all right, Diana. You'll see."

The receptionist's voice rang out: "Alexander Reece."

The man who had been speaking looked over at the woman who was calling out. He raised his hand and answered her: "That's me."

The lady motioned for him to come over to her.

"Come on, Diana. They're calling us now. Let's go see how dad is doing now."

He took her gently by the arm; they walked away, disappeared through a door that the receptionist had opened for them.

As soon as they cleared out, Marcus saw in front of him a face that he recognized. *"Who is that guy? I've seen him somewhere."* A young man was sitting, speaking to an old couple. Marcus watched him, sure that he would know before long who the man is.

As Marcus was observing, the man looked down, as if he were contemplating the next words that he might utter. As the young face turned downward, Marcus' brain immediately supplied a thought that the man was looking down at a basketball, that he was about to pass a basketball. *Isaac Jones.*

As Marcus' brain registered the fact that there was someone in the room that he knows, or at least, *knows of*, his sense of well-being began to return to him. He could do this now. He could get through this, *Don't need to go anywhere just yet. There's Isaac Jones. I'm on a winning team here.* Marcus' attention narrowed onto Isaac. He watched him closely; after a few seconds, he could hear what Isaac was saying to the older couple:

"No, no, I wasn't moving at all. In fact, I ran right into him. He stopped suddenly. I ran right into his back. Next thing I know, he's pushing me aside. It was *déjà vu* for me, just like being knocked around on the court. He made an abrupt left turn, about 120 degrees, and started moving back past where we had just been. Then the bomb went off. When it hit, Aleph was standing between me and it."

"Who?" Marcus erupted.

Isaac looked over at him without a second thought. "Aleph Leng, the man who saved my life."

Perspectives
20

Mona Lisa was smiling at Sylvia, or so it seemed.

Sylvia hit a button on her cell phone. She waited for a few moments for her sister to answer. Then Rachel did answer.

"Hello."

"Hello, Rachel."

"Sylvia, where *are* you?"

"Can you believe this? I'm standing in the Louvre, looking at the Mona Lisa."

"Does she live up to her reputation?"

"In some ways, yes. In others, no. I mean, she's no cover girl or anything, you know, but she is *pretty well-known.* I'm standing in this room with about a hundred people looking at Mona Lisa. All of these people, just gazing. I mean, it's strange. We walked down a really long hall of Italian masters...Raphael, Donatello, Boticelli, and there would be, you know, someone looking at every fifth painting or so. Then we get to the end of the hall, turn the corner...and it's like, 150 people standing like a herd of sheep looking at Mona Lisa. I don't get it...but, anyway. This is our second day in Paris, and I thought I'd call and say hi. How are you doing?"

"I'm doing fine. You won't forget to bring a bottle of wine, I hope."

"Oh, sure. What kind is it you want?"

"It doesn't matter. Just pick something out. I want to see what you come up with. Oh, and, about the Mona Lisa...you know the reason so many people are interested in it is because Da Vinci's use of perspective in the background was unprecedented at the time. He was the second Renaissance painter to use perspective in that way."

"Oh, yeah? Who was the first?"

"Alberti, Leon Battista Alberti, but nobody knows who he is. He had the first serious thoughts about perspective in painting, using Pythagorean principles and so forth, but he didn't develop the techniques much. That's what Da Vinci did, and that's why all those people are looking at Mona Lisa right now."

"Oh, I doubt if these people know anything about that stuff. They're probably here for the same reason I am...just to see what the big deal is all about Mona Lisa. Now that I'm here, though, the big deal is how many people are here looking at it. Maybe the next great artist would paint a picture of these people looking at the Mona Lisa."

"That's a great idea, Sylvia, maybe I'll try that if I get over there. Where are you staying?"

"We're at a hostel just a few blocks from here, actually. It's one that Janice knew about. We like it all right. It's clean. We had a continental breakfast there this morning with a couple of French guys, but we decided to lose them. Ha Ha."

"Be careful, Sylvia, and stay away from dark places at night."

"They say it's safer around here than at home, Rachel."

"I might believe it. There was a bombing right here in Urdor last night."

"Oh? Where was it?"

"A hotel, the Belmont Hotel. Helen was there until two o'clock this morning treating the victims, after she was supposed to get off at eleven."

"Was anybody killed?"

"One man was killed."

"Do they have any clue about who set the bomb?"

"Not that I know of."

"Here in Paris it's a little testy. Some of the French don't take too kindly to foreigners. There were riots out in the suburbs yesterday...some ethnic group, Algerians or some such group...mad because they're getting a raw deal from the government. People here expect a lot from their government, and I guess every group needs to get their share of the pie."

"Hey, Sylvia, there's someone at the door. Can you hold on a minute while I answer it?"

"Go ahead. I'm gonna go now...just wanted to say hi. These minutes are expensive you know. And there's a guy here telling me in French not to use cell phone."

"That's about typical for you, Sylvia. Thanks for calling, and don't forget my Beaujolais."

"Right. Bye now."

Rachel clicked the phone off and answered the door.

"Good morning. I'm Lee Nguyen, with the Wessex County Sheriff's Department, and this is Sergeant Luke Mendez. We'd like to speak with Helen Olei and Rachel Vinnier for a few minutes."

"Come on in. I'm Rachel. Have a seat and I'll be right with you." Rachel knocked on Helen's door. "We have visitors, Helen."

Rachel went in the bathroom, tied her hair back, returned to the living room. "Okay, gentlemen, Helen will be with us in a minute. What can I do for you?

Nguyen began. "Rachel, our records show that you called 911 to report the sexual assault that occurred here March 22. Is that right?"

"Yes. Were you able to determine how much time elapsed between that incident and the phone call?"

"I reported the incident about 1:00."

Helen walked in the room, aware of the question. "...and the crime occurred about midnight, so that would be about an hour." Her hair was wet, wrapped in a scarf. While taking a seat in the armchair across from Nguyen and Mendez, she greeted them. "I'm Helen Olei. Thank you for coming. I'd like to help in any way I can to get this case wrapped up in court. I've talked to the DA's office and registered a complaint."

"Good, Ms. Olei. Thank you for being so forthright. Let me confirm. Last Monday night, you were working in the emergency room, when Deputy Eddie Wheeler brought in Moa Grindell, whom you identified as the rapist. Is that right?"

"That's correct."

"Later that night, based on your identification, he was charged with sexual assault. Since that time, we obtained a search warrant to check his home for evidence that might support this case, or perhaps some other rape incidents that have not been solved. This is fairly routine for rape investigations."

"I understand; some of them have committed several crimes before they're caught."

"And when we searched Grindell's place, we did find information pertaining to other rape crimes. There was, in fact, a list recovered with the names of nineteen women on it."

Helen opened her mouth with disgust and ire. "No! He hasn't gotten away with that many?!"

"No, no. There were only two names on the list who have been assaulted to date. And both of those assault cases are still open. With those two turning up on his list, and this case being as tight as it probably is, it seems likely we'll be able to establish his guilt in those cases as well. We're waiting now on reports to come back on those cases, one about 5 months ago, the other about 2 months ago."

"It sounds like you've got a lot of evidence to convict him then."

"True. However, there is one little question mark about the list, and its relationship to victims or potential victims."

"And what is that?"

"Your name is not on the list." There was a silence.

"It must have been an impulsive act—one that he had not planned," said Helen, seeking explanation.

"Perhaps. But what is strange is this: Rachel, your name is on the list."

Rachel's jaw dropped. She was speechless for a moment. Then she blurted: "So, he might have been coming after me when he…"

"…when he found me instead," added Helen.

There was silence for a few moments. Everyone was dumbfounded, even the two detectives. Rachel stood up and paced around to the back of the couch. She sounded mad when she asked, "Why in the *hell* would I have been on a rapist's list?" I've never heard his name until this week. And I've never seen him…or I don't know that I've seen him. Do you have a picture of him?"

Sergeant Mendez, who had anticipated this question, handed the mugshot to Rachel. She looked at the photo with an expression of stupefied puzzlement on her beautiful face. She handed it back to him. "I haven't a clue."

"Crime studies show that many rapists and other serial criminals plan their assaults with quite elaborate premeditation and precision. He may have had an eye on this place for awhile," speculated Nguyen.

"I don't…think that's likely in this case. If he had been watching this place, he would have known that I work late most nights, especially Fridays and Saturdays."

Nguyen shook his head. "Who knows? We learned a long time ago, you can't second-guess a criminal. The crime statistics are just indicators of generalities. They don't mean anything really, when we get down to individual cases. But we have been looking at all the names on the list, including the sixteen names of women who have not suffered an assault. Assuming, for instance, that the names represented a list of potential victims, we were looking for common elements or characteristics among them."

Helen, curious at this unanticipated twist, spoke up, "Well, did you find anything?"

Nguyen leaned back on the sofa and sighed. "Uh...they all live around here, within about a thirty mile radius. But possibly more significant than that is the one characteristic that is common to every woman on the list: they are all Jewish."

Now Helen was upset. She stood up. "So you think this guy wanted to make a career out of raping Jewish women, and he hit me instead of Rachel because...because she wasn't home or something."

"It's just a hypothesis. This is how we solve crimes sometimes, by thinking hypothetically. But all theories aside, we do know this: There *was* a list found in his bedroom drawer with the names of nineteen women on it, two of whom had already been assaulted, and, Rachel's name was on the list, and, all the women listed are from Jewish families. *And that's not all, ladies.*" Nguyen was himself getting upset at the perverted consistency of criminal minds. He sat forward and put his head between his hands for a few seconds. "He's got a room full of anti-Semitic and Nazi crap...books, clothes, flags, bookmarked websites on the computer, white power literature. It's just, a rat's nest."

Nobody spoke.

"He's got a chain-link fence around his house with two Dobermans in the yard."

Sargeant Mendez nodded. "He's a fanatic, all right. I saw the stuff, too. He was living in his own little *Mein Kampf* world."

Rachel, alarmed at the prospect of such a person walking around undetected for so long, said: "I don't think it's very likely he was living in his own little world. If he had bookmarked websites on his computer with that stuff, he was probably communicating with others. I'll bet you he's in a network. He might have even bragged about some of his crimes to his buddies."

Helen agreed. "It's been shown in the histories of some psychopaths that they have a deep need to share their torrid little triumphs with others...bragging."

"We've got his computer, and we have specialists looking at his records now. There may, indeed, be some kind of network around here. We've had several hate crimes around here in the last few months," said Nguyen.

"Duh!" Helen exclaimed, incredulously. "Last night! the bombing at the Belmont Hotel, a convention of mostly black educators. We must have treated thirty people last night. One of them died."

"And there have been others...the bomb at the Holocaust Memorial Museum," said Rachel.

Helen asked, "You think they're connected?"

Nguyen cocked his head and squinted. "These days, with the internet and such, those associations can be pretty loose. There are a lot of wild ideas floating around out there on the fringe. They can feed off of each other's extremity, and maybe not even know the effects of their own fanaticism until they hear about it in the news."

Helen spoke. "You think there could be a connection between this guy and the bombings?"

"That's a long shot. Our specialists are checking out his connections. And we're working with the guys in DC and other places. We have quite a network of our own, you know. And there's no end to the possible ways that criminals are connected to each other. Well, this case right here is an example. When Wheeler brought Grindell in the hospital and you then identified him—that was just a fluke, right? We didn't know we had a serial rapist. He was picked up on suspicion of arson and assaulting an officer in the investigation of a murder case."

Helen had been considering many angles in this discussion, but the true-north that her consciousness kept turning back to was the rape itself. She had been pondering why this sick man might have purported to despise Jewish people, while at the same time targeting the women of that group as his victims for an act—coitus—that was considered, in its proper context, to be an act of *love*. This was the height of perversion. She tried to voice her thoughts. "It just seems so extremely perverse that this rapist would be *attracted* to the women of the group that he claims to despise."

Rachel looked sharply at her friend, and spoke decisively, "Don't even go there, Helen. It's perversion to the nth degree. Don't analyze it. Just overcome it."

"Hey, I'm with you. I was the one who caught the full force of that perversion. Remember?"

"Yes, my friend, and for that I am so sorry."

"It's not your fault," said Helen. They embraced. One woman, propitiating, had unknowingly taken the brunt of the dragon's perversity against the other.

***

Marcus had always wanted to believe this: The brutal law of the jungle is being supplanted by life-giving Spirit.

This Friday morning, he wanted to believe it, but the weight of Thursday night's events was too much to bear. He hadn't even gone to the job. Needing *shabat*, he had asked Daniel to cover those responsibilities. Instead of the usual routine, he was sitting in the railway station with a ticket for his destination, Philadelphia.

Watching a silver-bullet train ease up to the platform, Marcus' memory was jarred at the sight of a man who waited there, reading the *Wall Street Journal. Where have I seen him before? ... sitting on a wooden barrel by a steam locomotive in the old photograph at the Rathskellar.* Why would a well-dressed man reading the *Journal* make Marcus think of the 120-year-old railroad worker whose face he had contemplated while looking at an old photograph two weeks ago? *It must be the train—there's a train here; there was a train there, in the old photograph.*

The words to an old tune jangled in his head like copper coins in a tin cup: "*Once I had a railroad; I made it run. I made it run against time, Once I had a railroad; I made it run. Buddy, can you spare a dime?*"

He wondered why. The fellow reading the *Journal,* dapperly dressed in coat and tie, certainly didn't need a dime. And Marcus didn't need one either. He had a pocket full of plastic.

But there's something that everybody needs. None of us are complete. There's that hollow space inside...the hidden God-shaped void that wants to be filled up. Did we dream up that irksome empty space deep inside the soul? *Or was it placed there? Was it put there deliberately by One who would hope to fill it? What is this presence inside of me, that cries out for someone to break the law of the jungle, to outlive the survival of the fittest? Who would conquer the Nephilim? Who could supplant the cruel Cro-Magnon? Why does this soul refuse to accept the randomness of bombarding atoms? Why does it insist on seeing order amidst the chaos?*

How many Alephs have been fatally bitten by senseless explosions of unyielding vendetta against the world? How many torn victims have fallen to the ground, their innocent bloods now crying out with ancient, unsatisfied voice for justice?

Marcus is on the train now, sailing beyond the city, out into farms and fields of Maryland, rolling, sliding along sleek steel rails, beyond the pallor of death, beyond the cares of this forsaken place. A troop of crows flies up from a field...

And there's the sudden image of Wanda's dead body, lying on the floor of that crummy hotel room, the raven of death upon her brow, pecking at her sparkless eyes, dragging out the worm of visceral flesh from its abysmal home, as if it were a dragon playing in the mud.

Is there release from this sentence of death ?

The tin cup of memory rattled: *"Quoth the raven: 'Nevermore.'"*

"All out for Baltimore," would have been the cry of the conductor when his grandfather rode this rail. Now it was a recorded message: "Next stop, Baltimore terminal."

The old tin cup rattles once again with copper coin memories of some half-forgotten song: ***"Engine, engine, number nine, coming down the railroad line. I know she got on in Baltimore..."*** Then...

Rolling, riding, sliding across the sleek steel rail rumbling toward Philadelphia, Marcus finds his thoughts caught up in a whirl of idle madness, unrestrained by any rails of reason, untethered by any ribbons of linear sense or rhyme. *Buddy can you spare a dime?* How could so wild a mental ride be instigated by the sight of a businessman reading the *Wall Street Journal?*

Outside the city once again, wintry fields of brown punctuated by leafless trees fly past, cascading panorama of disappearing rural innocence being overtaken by relentless march of urban sameness, human saneness, and history's nameless appetite for obscurity, obliquity.

When Marcus arrived at Philadelphia, he got off the train, found a bus that took him to an old neighborhood where, as a child he had visited the home of his grandparents. Stepping off the bus, he walked four blocks to that old house. Someone else was living there now. *Houses sure have changed in the last 50 years. Were they all this small back then?* The expectations that people had about their houses were smaller. Their homes were smaller. Their incomes were smaller.

Marcus walked back from the direction he had come. He passed the bus stop, walked ten blocks beyond it. When he reached an old cemetery, in the back of a churchyard, he pushed back the squeaky, iron gate. Wandering across stone-dappled memories of where his grandparents' grave might be, at last he came upon it. There they stood, eternally announcing in chiseled letters on white marble streaked with gray:

Charlie Derwin	Louisa Derwin
1928-1998	1933-1999

Marcus stood for five minutes or so, looking at the two graves in sunshine. Then he sat down, on somebody else's grave. The household where these two had domiciled together for fifty years had been a steadfast presence in his childhood: a fixed place in time, a stake driven in the ground, a defining place in the wherewithal of his young existence. Now there were only two stones and a house that somebody else lived in. *Why did I come here?* In the bare tree-branch above him, a blackbird stirred, and squawked. *Quoth the raven: 'Nevermore.'*

Marcus looked at his hand. He had picked up a rock from somewhere, a little chunk of the white marble. He threw it errantly at the blackbird, which promptly flew away, squawking.

Then the wandering man stood up and walked out of the graveyard, carefully closing the old iron gate behind him. He headed back to the bus stop. By nightfall, he was back in Washington, but with little consolation.

***

Silverware was clattering, glasses were clinking, faces were drinking, eating, laughing, crying, thinking at the Jesse James Gang Grille on Friday night.

"The ink of the scholar is holier than the blood of the martyr," said Shapur. "The jihadists do not represent true Islam."

"Well, where are they getting their theology of violence from?" asked Morris.

"Every religion has its extremists—fanatics on both ends—who become so zealous for their own view of holy writ that they think they're doing god a favor by killing others who are not as pure as they. Look at Catholics and Protestants in northern Ireland, or Sunnis and Shiites in Iraq. But, *true* religion doesn't shed blood in order to make its point." As he finished his discourse, Shapur looked up at Kaneesha, who had just walked up to their table.

Having overheard their discussion, she tossed in her two cents worth. "In my religion, the holy blood was shed once and for all at Calvary. And there is no longer any need to be fighting about such things."

"I do wish, Kaneesha, that that event had settled the issue," remarked Morris. "Apparently, though, it didn't settle the issue, because people are still fighting about these things."

"Yeah, well, anyway...what are you guys having for dinner tonight?"

The two men ordered food.

"The point is," continued Shapur, "people can't be jumping to conclusions about small-time terrorists who set off home-made bombs—"

"IEDs, 'improvised explosive devices' is what they're calling them now," Morris inserted.

"Whatever. People in this country can't assume that Islamic militants are doing all of this. There are *all kinds of extremists* out there. Look at Oklahoma City, Waco, Idaho. This country has its own version of fanatic terrorists."

"I suppose you could be right. I had forgotten about McVeigh and all that..." said Morris.

"What we would need to prevent is extremist elements from outside *teaming up* with extremists inside. Then we'd really have a problem. It could lead to a bunch of little 911s." Shapur paused to take a bite of his salad. "Just look, for instance, at these two IED events that we've had here in the Washington area in the last couple of weeks. The one last night, down the street here at the FEF convention, must have been racially motivated, although we don't really *know* that. The point is that racism against blacks is a firmly-entrenched, *homegrown* kind of virus. So it's probably an inside job, right?...that is to say American extremists of some kind, a white power group of some kind maybe. Whereas, over in the city, at the Holocaust Memorial Museum, the perpetrators are more likely to be linked with international elements like the Nazis. Anti-semitism is very old, and its pretty much all over Europe and the Middle East, not as pervasive here."

Morris had a few things to say. "As near as I can figure, Shapur, there have been, for a long time (think of Haman in the book of Esther) some people somewhere in the world who didn't like the Jews. And it's because it was *their* scriptures that began the process of wrenching the human race away from the depraved cave-man worldview that all of life is just forces acting upon, and against, each other—and the stongest physical force wins out all the time."

"The law of the jungle, so to speak," observed Shapur.

"Or survival of the fittest, to put it another way," continued Morris.

Kaneesha brought their dinner. "What you're talking about is 'do unto the other guy before he does unto you.'" She set their steaks and potatoes on the table.

Shapur was extremely amused by Kaneesha's comment. He was laughing energetically.

Kaneesha, on a roll, thought she'd balance the sarcasm with a little nugget of truth. "Of course, that little proverb is more accurately spoken: 'Do unto others as you would have them do unto you.'"

"That's a point well-taken," said Morris. "It's really a quite revolutionary concept. And at the time it was spoken by Jesus, the Jewish ideas about spirituality overtaking raw force in the world were just being skimmed like dross off the top of a culture that had been cornered into one little stronghold by four empires: the Assyrians, Babylonians, Greeks, and Romans. In fact, Jewish culture was about to undergo a huge metamorphosis as it was cut off from its moorings—the temple, and everything associated with it. It was about to be transformed into a worldwide distillation of its very essence. Jesus foretold that when he predicted that the temple would be torn down."

"Titus, the Roman general, tore it down in 70 AD, and the Jewish people were scattered to the four winds," said Shapur. "And if I'm not mistaken, the Wailing Wall beneath Al Aqsa is a part of that temple compound that was torn down when the Romans ran them off."

"I think that's right, although it's just a section of the wall that surrounded the temple area. It's not part of the temple itself," said Morris. "What's pretty amazing is that after 1900 years they came back in large numbers to resurrect their culture in its birthplace."

"Yeah, and they made a lot of people mad in the process."

"Well, at that point, they had absolutely nothing to lose. Hitler had cornered them again—he thought he was in a position to wipe them out with his Aryan bullshit and loathsome, genocidal tactics. And when they survived *that* tribulation—nothing was going to stop them. I think that's why the Zionists are so adamant today. They were, as Isaiah put it, 'tried by the fire.' But that gets back to the dross thing. Before all that, the essence of their religion was a message that man was capable of, and destined for, a spiritual life that would transcend worldly origins. However, as ambitious as that message was, Jesus took it to an even higher level when he told them that it wasn't really about what's going to happen on earth, which is passing away. He drove home the message that there *is* a life after death."

"Marx later called all of that religion the 'opiate of the people,' " observed Shapur.

"Well, you either believe it or you don't," said Morris. "Either there's life after death or there isn't. *Or perhaps there's a third possibility*—there is life after death *if* you believe it."

"Well, *he proved* it," announced Kaneesha.

"Who? Marx?"

"No, you clown." Kaneesha laughed and poked Shapur in the arm. "Marx didn't prove anything, except that people are as gullible as he was accusing them of being. I think *his* ideas were opiates." She became very still and looked at Shapur, then at Morris. Then she continued, "Jesus proved it...life after death."

"How did he do that?" asked Shapur.

"He died and came back from death," stated Kaneesha. "It's as simple as that."

She filled Shapur's half-full water glass.

Shapur looked at her with mounting curiosity. "You believe that?"

"Why sure I believe it, honey. Don't you?" She smiled at him.

Shapur reciprocated with a chuckle. "I never really thought about it. How about you, Morris?"

"Makes sense to me. I'd much rather believe that life goes on after death. And as far as I can see, he's the only one who's come close to proving it."

"Well, you have to believe it," said Kaneesha. "It's part of the process, you know, faith." Morris' water glass was half-full. She filled it.

Errors
21

Leah Tullery didn't particularly like working late, but on this Friday night it would be worth it. Her employer, First Potomac Bank, was being bought out by EastBank. Today, the deal had been sealed; negotiations between the two corporations stretched into the evening hours. Here it was eight o'clock, and she was just leaving the office. Stepping off the elevator into the parking garage, she bid farewell to coworkers and located her car. She got in and drove out of the garage, headed for her apartment in north Washington. Leah, an administrator in the consumer loan department, had a brain-full of thoughts knocking in her head. Based on the deal they had just made, the two consumer loan departments would be merged together as one. That would probably mean that twenty of her employees would be turned loose, but her job seemed secure enough. She had, after all, been invited to the last two merger meetings.

Driving home, the possible combinations of different people in the two banks were linking and unlinking in her brain. But it was too much to try and figure out while driving home on Friday night after a long week. She couldn't do the permutation formula in her head while sitting at a red light. So she released it, and started thinking about her grandmother who was laid up in a hospital in Baltimore. Tomorrow, she would visit her.

Twenty minutes later, Leah turned the key in her apartment door and walked inside. She tossed her coat and briefcase on the sofa, went in the kitchen and popped a frozen diet meal into the toaster oven. She poured a glass of Zinfandel, took a sip, set it on the counter.

Entering her bedroom, she reached toward the lightswitch.

A dark intruder grabbed her arm and flung her to the floor. Immediately she felt the clumsy impact of his body upon her. She screamed once, twice, loudly. His frantic attempts to silence her with a wet a rag in the mouth were only propelling their struggle into a loud, disruptive confrontation.

Then the doorbell rang, and someone was banging on the door. In panic, the intruder knocked Leah out with a wooden club that had been tied to his leg. The doorbell was ringing, door knocking, jangling his nerves and his *modus operandi*. The intruder stepped into the living room, switched off the light, went to the kitchen and switched those lights off. The apartment was dark, and its resident quiet on the floor in the next room. He snuck over to the entry door and peeked through the viewer. The hall was dark. He couldn't see anything, but whoever was there was still knocking loudly and ringing the doorbell. He couldn't allow the noise to continue. Confusion was overtaking him; loud beating of his tell-tale heart inside *must be alerting to the world what his intentions were.* Then the knocking ceased and was replaced by the sounds of footfalls.

Unexpectedly, the visitors, whoever they were, were running fast in the hall, away from the apartment. The noise of their retreat subsided into silence. The intruder stepped into the hallway, closed the door behind him, headed for the red exit sign where he knew there would be a stairway. In the stairway, harsh with fluorescent light, he raced down two flights of stairs, slowed, stepped gingerly into the parking garage at ground level, as if he were a normal person on a normal errand. Finding the garage empty of people, he picked up the pace, hurried through the cavernous semi-lit space to the main vehicle garage exit, and slipped out, undetected, or so he thought.

Walking briskly on the sidewalk outside the apartment building, he saw, at first glance, maybe ten people scattered about. What the intruder didn't know was that standing in a shadow on the opposite side of the street was a DC policeman who noticed him. Having gotten a call about an attempted assault, the cop began pursuit.

"Stop," yelled the policeman.

But the intruder didn't stop. Instead, he began running, as fast as he could. The policeman pursued. After running a block or more, the criminal reached a parking lot and promptly threw himself on the ground, rolled under a parked car, and listened while his assailant ran by, perplexed. Assuming the cop's confusion, he rolled from beneath the car, took off in the opposite direction, and headed for a cross-street, which he reached in a few seconds. He hung a quick right turn and trotted along the dark, quiet street until he reached a worn-looking, twenty-year old BMW. Deftly unlocking it, he got in and drove away. He had escaped.

Officer Ron Patoli of the DC police had indeed lost sight of his charge for a few seconds, but only a few. When the suspect's running had stopped, he had also stopped soon thereafter. Officer Patoli had then slipped into a shadow in order to survey the scene of his last sighting. A minute later the suspect became visible again, heading in a perpendicular direction. Patoli had called for assistance; now he adopted a strategy of stealth rather than speed. With the suspect unaware, Patoli was able to get close enough to the BMW to get the license number before the criminal could drive away. Then he wrote the Virginia tag number: RD 00666.

So the vigilant cop had his number, but the criminal didn't know that. He proceeded cautiously through the dark streets of North Washington, attracting no attention. At a main thoroughfare he turned north and drove another 20 blocks. He got on the beltway headed southwest, cruised along at 65 for fifteen minutes, then took the Pretoria Parkway exit, headed west through Urdor. He breathed a sigh of relief.

***

Daniel had worked late at his office. Since Marcus had taken the day off, Daniel decided to finish his day's work with a visit to the construction site to check on the progress. He had assured Marcus he would keep an eye on it, but had not been able to get to it. Having just recovered his Ford Esposito from the repair shop today, Daniel was driving it west on Pretoria Parkway, toward the site.

A sudden, glary red brake-light brightness alerted him to a stopping in front of him. Daniel slammed on the brakes, just in time to avoid collision. But behind him, the screech of brakes was still alarming his consciousness. In the rear-view mirror two headlights were bearing down on him at a speed too fast to be interrupted by anything except another object.

Big Bang—it happened, like the intersection of entropy and order in the universe.

The rear end of Daniel's newly-repaired Esposito, suddenly violated by a barreling-down, bullysome BMW, *had become a roadblock in the fleeing would-be rapist's ill-planned escape route.* "What in the *hell* do you think you're doing?" he shouted loudly through the windshield.

Reacting impetuously to the rude question, Daniel responded with a philosophical question: "What do you mean—'what the hell am I doing?' What the hell are *you* doing, you asshole?"

Now, now, Daniel, says the Spirit, *no need to get belligerent.*

For the second time in as many weeks, Daniel stepped out of his wrecked Esposito. This time it wasn't necessary to exit through the passenger door. He whipped out his cell phone with great confidence that this time he was not at fault, and called the law.

The would-be rapist sat in his car, perplexed, not comprehending the significance of this simple twist of fate that might, through a simple twist of bumpers, somehow lead to his detention after such a *clean* getaway. Yet this delay *was* unfolding before his very eyes. Since getting in the BMW, he had *not*, to his knowledge, been assailed; yet he felt somehow that something had just gone askew; and he was feeling a little uncomfortable about this improbable turn of events.

That a simple bumper confrontation could haphazardly enable the long arm of the law to capture a would-be rapist is grounds for belief that possibly not all occurrences are random. Some events may occur through a providential propensity toward criminals getting what they deserve. *Is this possible? Nah...it's all just coincidence.*

Though the would-be rapist's heart was within him perverse, the universe is true; when all is put together, it is plumbed to perfection, in spite of the adverse intentions purveyed by malicious people like rapists, racists and other offenders..

It's not that duality is not a component in the design of the universe, mind you. Certainly there is something rotten in Denmark, and also in Antwerp, and Urdor, or anywhere else in the world you could think of. But every now and then something can happen to render a little correction to something else that has gone astray, so that the ultimate outcome, by and by, may contribute to the working out of all things to accomplish the purposes of the one who had set it all in motion to begin with.

Just then the long arm of the law pulled up, blue light spinning.

The rear-end collision, as usual, was self-evident. The officer issued a ticket to Barney Bluntell for following too closely. But that wasn't all he did. With the collision appropriately documented and the fault assigned, the cop looked at Barney and informed him: "Mr. Bluntell, you are under arrest. You have the right to remain silent. Anything you say can and will be used against you." He whipped out a pair of handcuffs, was about to slap them on the criminal's wrists.

Barney stepped back. "What's the charge?"

"Attempted rape."

"That's ridiculous. What the hell are you talking about?"

"Don't make me add the 'resisting arrest' charge."

"What the *hell* are you talking about?"

"This car is registered to you, Barney Bluntell."

"Yeah. So what?"

"Virginia license RD 00666."

"Yeah. What of it?"

"You just drove from the Snapdragon neighborhood of Washington."

"This is crazy. I don't know what you're talking about."

"I can get help to bring you in if need be. Are you gonna cooperate or not, sir?" The policeman's voice reflected an escalating tension.

Suddenly, Barney was off like a shot, foolishly fleeing the long arm of the law. He ran through the nearby parking lot, disappeared behind a video store.

The officer spoke into his radio transmitter. "Suspect has fled on foot, Pretoria and Skyview vicinity. I'll be in pursuit, but still expecting tow-truck. Request backup."

"Copy that, 409. But we need you to stay put at the scene of the accident. Backup is on the way to apprehend the suspect."

"Copy that. I'm stickin.'"

***

Saturday morning, Detective Derrick Trent of Washington Police took a drive to Wessex County. At 9:35, he walked into the Sheriff's office to meet Detective Lee Nguyen. It was time for a brainstorming session.

Nguyen spoke first. "Here's what we've got: Nineteen women on Moa Grindell's list, all within a 30 mile radius, all of them from Jewish families. Grindell's DNA is a match with the samples taken from the assault on Helen Olei. We're waiting on the lab for possible matches with those other two on the list that have been assaulted."

"Those two being Mimi Swann of Grahamton, and Karen Sherwin of Anacort. Right?"

"Correct. One in Maryland, the other in the southern end of your district. And I think this indicates that this guy (or guys?) really gets around. But here's the puzzle: With Grindell in custody, we might have thought that the list would become inert—that is, no more victims. However, and I'm thinking that's why you're here, one of the names on Grindell's list turns up as a *victim* last night. *He* couldn't have done it while in custody. So who did? *And*, is there some connection between Grindell's list and this Barney Bluntell fellow who tried last night to rape a woman whose name was on that same list?"

"Yep. That's it. Now...what about this guy Bluntell? What do we know about him?"

"He was identified by one of your patrolmen, who had gotten a phone tip from a resident in the apartment building where the intended victim lives."

"That victim being Leah Tullery of North Washington?"

"Yeah," affirmed Nguyen. "Our deputies apprehended Bluntell about 10 o'clock last night, after he fled the scene of an auto accident. They identified him on the basis of the license ID that officer Patoli had provided. That was some good police work on Patoli's part. Has Bluntell's identity as the attacker been established?"

"Leah Tullery never really got a look at the guy in any light. One reason for that is that he knocked her out. The medical examiner's opinion was that he used a blunt object. We did, in fact, find a billy club in the victim's bedroom with Bluntell's fingerprints on it. It seems that this guy is *not* an habitual attacker. He made a lot of stupid mistakes."

Trent continued: "Until the fingerprints were checked this morning, Bluntell's identity was based almost solely on Officer Patoli's sighting of him as he walked out of the parking level of the apartment building just minutes after the attack. Our precinct had gotten a call from another resident of the building. These brave people, a couple from two doors down, had intervened by ringing the doorbell and knocking loudly on the door. They oughta get a medal; they may have saved Tullery's life. Anyway, when Bluntell snuck out of the building, Ron Patoli had just gotten the heads up call from our dispatch. The officer's verbal attempt to halt Bluntell was ignored. The suspect ran. Patoli was able to keep a tail on him until Bluntell got into his BMW. Fortunately, our man was able to see that license tag. Half an hour later, the freak auto accident enabled the Urdor police to get him."

"That's strange. He wrecked himself right into an arrest after escaping. He *really is* a novice at this kind of thing," said Nguyen.

"Or a very unlucky one," followed Trent. "Anyway, he must have been pretty shaken up... he ran *again*, when your patrolman, acting on probable cause, initiated the arrest for attempted rape."

"Yeah, the guy's a runner for sure...must be guilty of *something*." The two detectives laughed. The logic behind this last inference was a bit of a stretch; but it was familiar to a couple of seasoned cops.

Trent was wondering: "What have you got on him?"

"He's owns a chain of convenience stores...lives here in Urdor, at..." Nguyen leaned back in his swivel chair and inspected the written report that was in his hand. "...at 784 Cedarcrest Lane...hmmm...nice neighborhood."

"And do you think the Grindell list could have *anything* to do with his choice of Tullery as a rape target?"

"It is a hell of a coincidence. Isn't it? You want to talk to him?"

"Yes. That's why I'm here, actually."

"Let's go find out what Barney Bluntell was up to. But first, Derrick, you gotta tell me about that tattoo on your arm...let me see it." Nguyen gingerly pulled the short sleeve up so he could see the figure that was pigmented between Trent's elbow and shoulder. He peered at it, cocked his head to read the name that was tattooed beneath the figure of a woman. "Dolores...is that your wife?"

"Nah, just an old flame. I couldn't get her off my mind when I was in Kosovo. I'm retired Army. I had this done in Pristina, where our Kosovo base was. But the thing with Dolores didn't work out. I found my wife, Penelope, about a year after I retired."

"And Penelope didn't make you erase the picture of Dolores that's on your arm?"

"Nah. It's no big deal. Just putting up with me is harder than putting up with the tattoo, a youthful indiscretion. And it's not an easy thing to fix anyway. Tattoos are *pretty permanent*. The only way you get rid of one is with a lot of pain. Penny (Penelope) said not to bother. She said, 'I know you love me, and not her; that's what counts.'"

Trent laughed softly. "Yeah...Penny's a good one, worth her weight in gold to me. And she puts up with much more than just an old tattoo in order to keep me around."

"So you married her after you retired from the Army?" inquired Nguyen.

"Yes, in '98. I was married before, but we split up after nine years."

"Sorry to hear that Derrick. Any kids?"

"No."

"Well, I'm glad you finally got hold of a good one, when you met Penny."

"Yeah. I'd have been a real mess by now if she hadn't come along." Trent gazed out the window, lost in thought, uncharacteristic for a DC detective. After half a minute or so, he looked at Nguyen's seasoned, Vietnamese face. "How 'bout you? Do you have a family?"

"I have two," said Nguyen. "My wife, Grace, has been with me for seven years now; we have a four-year-old daughter. But I had another family before that. I lost them during the Tet offensive in 1968. My wife was sixteen. We had a baby girl. But I never saw them again after our village was attacked and I joined the militia."

"And you don't know what became of them?"

"No. They disappeared."

Derrick Trent pondered for a few moments. "Ironic that you had a wife and daughter, and now you have another wife and daughter."

Nguyen's face lit up. "Yes...ironic, but very fortunate. In spite of the ordeal of losing the first, I am thankful for my *second* family. It's great to have second chances in life."

"You got that right. Me and you both."

Another pause.

"You must have seen some bad shit during that war," mused Trent.

"Yes. It's tragic what men do to one another."

"We saw a lot of that in Kosovo. What was really terrible, though, was what we heard about Bosnia, just across the border. There was some *really bad blood* between Muslims and Serbs in that part of the world. And it had gone on and on for generations. That kind of enmity doesn't just go away. It's gets worse and worse through generations. And the politicians were trying to put the different groups together as a nation--Yugoslovia. But we heard about incidents that had happened fifty, sixty years ago...some renegade Serbs, during the big War, had gone to Srebenica, rounded up young Muslim men and shot them. Then, as if that wasn't enough, they dumped the bodies, a dozen or more of them, *down into the wells where the town got its drinking water.* It's pathetic, and, according to what I heard, these acts were perpetrated in response to similar atrocities from the Muslims in times past."

"It's a vicious cycle," observed Nguyen. "It's almost as if there is no stopping it. There's something wrong with the human species."

"We're all damned to hell," chided Derrick. A slight smile turned on his ruddy face.

"Speak for yourself, good buddy." Nguyen reciprocated the smile.

"Well you know what I mean, Nguyen. Groups of people are always blaming other groups of people for what's wrong with the world. But when you get right down to it, we're all to blame."

"Some more than others," replied Nguyen, with raised eyebrows.

"Well, yeah, but you know what I mean. People are always looking for a scapegoat, like the Nazis blaming the Jews for all their economic woes."

"It looks like that scenario is still happening, based on a few things that we've uncovered lately."

"It seems to be worse, I think, in older cultures, where different factions have had more bad blood between them for generations, like I was telling you about in Bosnia. And these days...the French, for instance, blaming their economic problems on Algerians who've moved in from down south," said Trent.

"I hear what you're saying about older cultures, but we've got the same thing going on right here. A lot of folks are building up resentment against Mexicans because they think they're taking jobs away from other, traditionally-American groups that are more firmly established," said Nguyen.

"Like the Irish."

"Yeah. Europeans, basically...the ones that came in boatloads around the turn of the last century. They came on boats. These days, the immigrants arrive in a truck from Juarez or wherever, and when we turn them back, they come on foot, at night. You can't negate the attraction that people have for freedom and prosperity. It's been going on for thousands of years. People go where the action is, where they can find better opportunities."

"There are some real issues, though. It's complicated. A lot of Americans are on welfare because they can't get jobs... because the low-wage earners from Latin America or wherever are getting the jobs. They're willing to work for less."

"But those low-wage earners are keeping a constant deflationary force on our economy. As long as we let them work, their presence works constantly against inflation. Did you ever think about that? I know workers, and unions, in this country don't appreciate that, but it's true. By letting them work, we're assuring ourselves of an economy that can compete with the developing countries in the rest of the world."

"I never thought about it that way, Nguyen. I'll have to think about that," said Derrick. He was starting to get a little antsy. There was work yet to be done on this Saturday. "But let's go see what the hell we can find out from Barney Bluntell."

***

The Wessex County jailer led the suspected rapist into a windowless room to be interrogated. Detectives Nguyen and Trent sat at a conference table. Stenographer Gladys Meachum accompanied them. The wiry, middle-aged, bespectacled suspect with receding hairline sat down.

Nguyen began. "Barney, you were pretty intent on getting away from us last night. Why?"

Barney's long face registered an unyielding message of resentment. He said nothing.

"I have something here, Barney, that was found at the scene of an attempted rape in Washington last night. Is it yours, Barney?" The deputy set a sealed plastic bag on the table. Inside it was a wooden club, dark brown with varnish finish, about eighteen inches long. The suspect said nothing.

"I respect your right to remain silent, Barney. It is, after all, your right, as we explained to you on the way in...Let me just repeat that. You do have the right to remain silent. And you need to understand that any statement you make can, and will, be used as evidence against you in a court of law. You have the right to have an attorney present in any interrogation. Do you want to call your attorney?"

The pitiful suspect said nothing. His droopy eyes merely reflected an extreme loneliness, as if he had been forsaken by everyone in the world. But it was he who had forsaken those dear to him. Deep down inside himself he knew this. There was no defense. There would be no lawyer. There would only be a wriggling out. *If there was some way to just slide out of this...*

It just might have been a factor that Mr. Bluntell had more to hide from his wife than he did from the police. He had been unsuccessful in his attempt to accost Ms. Tullery. If no great attention was brought upon this turn of events, it might just work itself out. Finally, he spoke, in a very low, exasperated voice: "Whatever...I don't need your kikey court-appointed lawyer." He looked blankly at the wall.

"Barney, can you tell me why your fingerprints match the fingerprints we found on this billy club?"

No answer.

"Barney, you're not very adept at this rape business, leaving behind a weapon with fingerprints on it. Who taught you?"

Silence.

"Barney, why did you choose this woman as your victim?"

Nothing.

"Barney, do you know Moa Grindell?"

A flicker of alarm ran across the suspect's eyes, then subsided.

"Who made the list, Barney?"

"You people just don't get it, do you?" Barney replied with abrupt indignation. He fidgeted with annoyance.

"What is it we're supposed to get, Barney? What kind of statement are we supposed to read into the fact you and your employee, Moa Grindell, tried to rape two women whose names were on a list that Moa had at his home?"

Bluntell turned his head and looked directly at Nguyen for a second, then turned away again.

"You're right about one thing, Barney. We don't get it. But we're gonna get it. We know *why* you made the list, and we know it was either you or Moa who assaulted Mimi Swann and Karen Sherwin. And Barney, you're only digging yourself deeper by not giving us the information we need."

Barney growled: "You don't have a fucking clue what's going on."

Nguyen leaned back in his swivel chair, stretched his arms, then folded them behind his head. He looked into the suspect's eyes, then stood up.

Derrick Trent spoke slowly, convincingly: "On the contrary, Barney, we do know what's going on. We know about the list. We know about Dexter Bisto at the Lincoln Memorial. We know what happened at the Holocaust Museum. We know about your connection to the *Family Education Foundation* bombing. We're taking a look at your involvement in the defacing of Temple Beth Shalom. We even know about Buzz Townsend and the meth connection. You can run, Barney, but you can't hide."

"You don't know shit," came the defiant reaction. The rage within him had turned Barney's face red. The arteries in his neck swelling, eyes flashing, his countenance contorted with unfocused anger. "They've got you by the balls. You know that don't you?"

"Who's that, Barney?" Trent shot back at him. "It's the other way around. We've got *you* by the balls. We've got this club with your fingerprints on it. You never should have attempted a rape last night, Barney, because you've botched it up *bad*."

Trent stuck his face into the would-be rapist's face. "You should have left it up to some of the other guys in your group...some of the ones who have a little more experience with criminal activity." Then Derrick Trent couldn't suppress a thin smile.

So he stood up. He was laying the pressure on thick and heavy now. He pointed at the cowering prisoner and lowered his voice while adding a new tone of urgency. "You probably should have stayed at home with your wife last night, Barney. Do you think she's going to appreciate all the crap that's gonna fall on you when this stuff hits the fan? But you know what, Barney? It's not too late to save your skin. You can come clean right now. These bombings are serious stuff—felonies. You can help us break this ring open right now, and maybe, *maybe* get out of prison before you're too old to make love to your wife again." His voice was rising in volume again. "That's something' you should have been doing last night instead of trying to knock up somebody's daughter." It was a tongue lashing. The detective was ranting like an irate father to an errant teenager.

"You keep my wife out of this, you communist bastard." The suspect's voice was quiet and controlled, but desperate, quivering with indignation.

Trent's eyes narrowed. Again, he stuck his face right into the other man's. "Tell me something, Barney. Why were you out trying to knock up a nice Jewish girl instead being at home with your wife? Why? Was it personal? Or is there something going on with this list between you and Moa Grindell? Let me tell you something. We've been to Mo's place. We know about the Fascist bullshit that he's feeding on and propagating. We know about the porno, the methamphetamines, the snuff films."

Then Barney spoke seriously, looking right at the intimidator. "You've got the wrong man. I've stayed away from the IEDs. I've got nothing to do with them."

Derrick Trent sat down, poured himself half a glass of water. He looked at the prisoner, but didn't say anything.

Nguyen spoke calmly to the prisoner. "If you've got no direct connection to the bombings, you can prove it now by revealing the identities of the bombers."

"I didn't say I know who it is."

"Okay. Put it this way. What *do* you know about the bombings?"

"You make this out to be like some kind of crime syndicate or something," said the prisoner, defensively. "It's not. We're trying to bring this country back to its roots."

Nguyen and Trent were stunned by the improbability of this statement. Trent started to speak. Nguyen quickly set his hand on Trent's arm, motioning for silence. The two of them looked with askance at the strange man who sat at the table in front of them. But Barney Bluntell looked lost, as if he were a deer in headlights. His deep-set eyes, encircled with flaps of dark skin, betrayed a flash of eccentricity, or even schizophrenia. He was tottering on a decision to speak or clam up.

Nguyen decided to risk tipping the balance with a serious question. "Barney, what roots are you trying to bring this country back to?"

"This country has a history of decent people, white people, who can make it run right without interference from the communists and Jews who've taken it over."

Trent gave a low whistle and shook his head. He was trying to respond to the statement with a reasonable rebuttal, but could think of nothing right away.

But Nguyen spoke, calmly. "And did these decent, white people keep a list of young women and then rape them?"

"Women have to know their place. If men don't keep them in their place, then other men have to rise up and set things right."

"By raping them?" Trent was incredulous, getting irate. Nguyen touched his arm again, signaling restraint. He wanted to ask another question, prime the pump, get to the source of this perversity. He probed further:

"So, are *you* going to put these women in their place?"

"You're damned right." Barney was on the soap box now, showing his true colors, almost unaware of his prisoner status, lecturing the cops on what would have to be done to get society straightened out.

"And how did you know who these women are...the ones that need to be put in their place?"

"It's the Jewish women. They started the whole thing. Now its infecting everybody. The men don't know how to handle their women. They've fucked everything up. The Jews started communism. Marx and Lenin were Jews. You know that, don't you?"

Now Nguyen thought he'd take a chance. "Is that why you bombed the Holocaust Memorial?"

Barney looked at Nguyen, surprised at the question. "That whole damned holocaust never happened. You know that don't you? They made the whole thing up so they could get sympathy from everybody else...just like the niggers."

"Oh yeah? What did *they* do?"

"They didn't do a damn thing, except pick cotton. The Jews raised a bunch of hell until they got Lincoln and the rest of that nigger-lovin' crowd worked up enough to fuck the whole country. It's been a mess ever since then."

Nguyen's voice became calm, professorial. "The last time I checked a history book, Barney, it said that it was a bunch of Christian abolitionists who got that movement going."

But the detective realized he was getting off track. He paused and thought for a moment. "What do you think it's gonna take to get this country straightened out?"

"It'll take a major rearrangement of power," said Barney, now overconfident in his own psychopathic harangue. Having lost sight of the criminal implications of his actions, Barney was misinterpreting Nguyen's interest in his activities. Barney was not an habitual criminal, but an idealogue who had gotten sucked into a criminal fringe of fascism. "These days, people don't know what real power is."

"What is it?" Nguyen inquired, now spreading the net of inquiry over Barney's self-laid trap of fanatical egocentrism.

"Power is whatever is taken by those who are unafraid to be strong." Barney smiled, lost now in his own self-incriminating screed, as if he were talking to himself. "Power is what you are going to see very soon, when the obstructions to it are taken out of the way."

"What obstructions?"

"The weak and inferior elements. They're dragging the whole evolution of the human race down. It's just a matter of time before power will be put back where it belongs. The Jews were the ones who fucked it up to begin with, with their worship of weakness...then the niggers, spicks. Some people were born to be slaves. What we need is a caste system. The Hindus had a few things right, but they missed it on the animals thing, and the *untouchables*. It's better to just extinguish them altogether."

Nguyen looked over at Trent, amazed at the unbridled fanaticism that had just passed from the prisoner's lips. They were at a loss for words for a minute or more. Derrick Trent stood, stretched, began pacing around at one end of the room. Then he asked, "So that's why you moved on the Holocaust Museum?"

"That was only a wake-up call. The next time, it'll be *much* more effective."

"Says who?" Trent shot back.

"Says me...and about 100 other people," declared Barney, not even thinking now of the legal implications of his diatribe.

"How do you know? Were you there?"

"The *fuhrer* was there."

Trent stopped his pacing, incredulous. He was about to react. Nguyen, sensing discovery, shot a look of caution in his direction—an almost-indiscernible shaking of the head. Now was not the time for an outburst. This could be the mother lode of their line of questioning. Nguyen spoke carefully, "And what did the *fuhrer* say about it?"

"He said it was a good beginning."

Nguyen, playing devil's advocate, continued, "But it didn't really accomplish much, did it?"

"It didn't need to. It served its purpose. Just like the *first fuhrer*—it took him another 10 years to take the power that was his all along."

"When did he tell you this?"

"It was that same day."

"Is the *fuhrer* going to make himself known?"

"When the time is right."

"The time is right now. The world *must* know who the *fuhrer* is. It is his destiny," Nguyen said.

"Wendall Foggerty," proclaimed the prisoner.

Nguyen, flabbergasted, sat in the chair that was next to him. He put his right hand on the irksome bandage that swaddled his left hand. He hadn't known two weeks ago that it was the *fuhrer* who had shot him while an old barn went up in smoke and furious flames..

Destinies

22

Saturday, April 6, a bough of cherry blossoms hung over a corner of the parking lot at Sanderson Park. Marcus had to lift the branch up slightly to avoid closing his car door on it. Then he walked around to the back of the car, removed his bicycle from its rack, mounted it, did a few laps around the parking lot while waiting for Bridget.

About five minutes later, there she was: the light of his life, wavy, dark brown hair glistening with a hint of red highlight in the spring sunshine, winsome brown eyes that viewed the world in such a different perspective from his that he now felt incomplete at the passing of any day in which he could not look into them. On this Saturday morning, it had been more than two days since he *had* seen them.

She rode up next to him on the bicycle that he had given her. In her presence, all the burden of life and death was suddenly featherweight. They got off their bikes and embraced. "Will you marry me?" he said, impulsively.

She began giggling, and leaned back, looking at him with an ocean of mirth sloshing inside those soft brown eyes. "I'm thinking about it. I'll get back to ya."

He felt her hips pressed against his. *This is how life begins*, he thought.

"What'd you do in Philly?"

"Wasted time...saw my grandparents' graves, then came home."

"Aleph's death kind of threw you for a loop, didn't it?"

"Yeah. I hardly knew the guy. I can't figure out why such a good person would be taken out by--"

"By such an evil thing as a bomb in a trash can."

"It's just...wrong. And that night when I got home, I looked in the room where he had been staying. There was his stuff, not much really... I've never had to do that before: dispose of someone's personal possessions because they just got killed."

"What did you do with it?"

"Nothing, yet. I guess I'll give it to Goodwill or something like that. There's an address book with names of his friends in California."

"Have you called any of them?"

"No. Well, I called the people he was staying with—the fellow who works at the Kenyan embassy. I told his wife about Aleph on the phone. I suppose I should call someone in California. I didn't know Aleph well at all, never had time to know him really. But from what little I did know about him, his friends in California probably considered him a dear friend."

"Yes. He was a very special person."

"And also on Thursday night, when I was at the hospital, I met Isaac Jones, the basketball player. He says...this is amazing, Bridget...he says that Aleph had walked right over to where the bomb was, to check it out or whatever, and that Aleph was standing right next to the bomb when it went off."

"It's no wonder, then, that he was the only one who died."

"Yeah. But Isaac told me that when Aleph got into that position, he was the only thing.... He said that Aleph saved his life by stepping between the bomb and him."

"The blast hit Isaac too?"

"Not really, Aleph pretty much caught the whole thing. The other people around there had minor injuries...Isaac, and his mother. Isaac's mother was admitted to the hospital because she fell and broke her hip. Isaac called me this morning. The *Family Education Foundation* has asked him to speak at the funeral tomorrow. He never even met Aleph, and yet is asked to speak about him. It's strange. There will be hundreds of people there at the funeral, but nobody who really knows Aleph."

"What about his friends at the Kenyan Embassy?"

"Oh, yeah, they'll be there: the Acacias, Joshua and Asumbi Acacia. I suppose they'll be asked to speak as well, since he lived with them for a while. And she told me they would call one of the people in California." Marcus paused for a second. "That's enough about that, though. What about you?"

"Jonda's grandparents took her back to North Carolina with them yesterday."

"That's really good news, Bridget." He squeezed her tightly. "That's the best thing that could have happened in that situation."

"I think they were hoping all along that they could take her."

"How was it for Jonda? Was she into it?"

"I think she was, yes. Her latching on to me was a natural response in that terrible situation. There had been some estrangement between Wanda and her parents. I never got into it with them. Wanda had only taken Jonda to her parents twice, and that had been several years ago. Jonda's memory of them seemed to be very dim, but there was enough there to build upon. Bernadette said the Lord worked it all out. Looking back on it, I guess you could say that's what happened."

"If the Lord is working on anything at all, it's a mystery to me what he's working out and what's just working itself out," said Marcus.

"I know what you mean. I said something like that to Bernadette. She said he'll work on anything you ask him to."

He squeezed her again. "I'm gonna ask him to talk you into marrying me."

"Go ahead and ask him, wild man. We'll see what he comes up with. Are we gonna ride today or what? I've got to go to work at four."

"Let's hit the trail then."

"Look." Bridget pointed toward the grassy field nearby. A flock of swallows was swirling in a circular path—twenty or thirty of them, all together, moving in unison like synchronized swimmers. They would make a big arc, with a radius of about twenty yards, rising slightly in the air as they went. Then suddenly they would, all together, swoop downwards in a graceful freefall, slowing. Then the cycle would start again. Time after time they repeated the maneuver. *Is one bird leading, setting the path with the others immediately following? Or are they all on some identical wavelength, some genetic command or flight plan? How could their movements be so perfectly tuned together, making the flock appear to move as one organism?* Marcus marveled at the sight. "Cool," said Bridget. She hopped on her bike and rode away.

***

Hester Prynne was walking through a forest dappled with spring green and sunshine. Her daughter, Pearl, walked beside her, their hands enfolded. The moving picture was one of pure mother-daughter love in sylvan bliss.

"That's a scene from *The Scarlet Letter*," said Bridget, as she paused while walking by a storefront TV on display, "a scene from ages past. How times have changed since the 19th century." Lost momentarily in thought, she stood gazing at the tube, waiting for Marcus to catch up after locking the bikes. Then she took his hand and they walked to Starbucks next door.

When they were sitting at a table drinking coffee, Bridget spoke. "Marcus, when Wanda was staying with me, she told me that Buzz had been making methamphetamine and selling it. She said that the process of making the stuff required a lot of cold medicine. He would get large quantities of it, and heat it up in some special way, and the meth crystals would form as it cooled."

"Yes. I've heard of people doing that. Did you know that Buzz was doing that when you stayed at their place?"

"Not really. I figured out, after a couple days, that something strange was going on there. That's when I had to get out."

"Did you do some of that stuff?"

"Twice. It's potent stuff. It really scares me to think about it now—to think of how close I may have come to ending up like Wanda."

Marcus took her hands gently in his. "But you know what, Bridget?"

"What, Marcus?"

"At a freaky party you met me. And now we're ridin' on a totally different road than what might have been if you had gone in that direction."

"I *know*." She leaned her head on his shoulder. I'm just amazed when I think of it...how close I was to that...that *underworld*...that secret little paranoid drug world that Wanda and Buzz existed in." Bridget shivered.

"So that night we met, you decided to make use of your dad's funds?"

"My funds, a trust fund that my parents had set up for me."

"And why hadn't you used it before?"

"My father and I had had a big fight when I didn't go back to school after three semesters. After that, I wanted to make a go of it on my own...to see where it would take me. When I was sleeping on that filthy couch at Wanda's trailer, I realized that *that's* where it had taken me."

"Can't hardly blame your dad for being concerned about that."

"He never knew about any of it. He was always just a silent presence in the background. I think he was just waiting patiently for something to happen, something *he knew would happen*, to bring me back to my senses."

"Like the father in the parable of the prodigal son."

"Yeah, the prodigal *daughter*. That story is not a part of our tradition, but I've heard the story. I'm kind of glad he didn't come snooping around. It might have freaked him out pretty bad...me sleeping on a grungy couch in a broken-down trailer with a couple of meth freaks. One of these days, pretty soon, I'll have to go up to Cleveland and see them, thank them for hanging with me through that time."

"And they never knew how close you came to being a derelict."

They laughed. Life is grand on a spring day when you've survived such perils, and outlived others who didn't. They sipped lattes.

"But that whole dangerous encounter with the drug world started with me dropping out of school. I just didn't have any direction. I couldn't come up with any reason for anything I was doing there."

"Do you have any direction now?"

"*You're* the only direction I have now."

"So you *will* marry me?

She slapped him playfully on the cheek. "I've only known you for two weeks, you fool."

"Love at first sight, don't you know."

"So, you're saying you know what love is," she challenged.

"Yes, it's what I have for you."

"Did your parents love each other?"

"They did, until my father's death when I was twelve—the plane crash. I told you about it. But my mother did a pretty good job of teaching me about love. And there were grandparents—whose graves I saw yesterday—together for almost fifty years."

"Your father's parents were in Philadelphia?"

"Yes. And that's where we lived until my dad died. Then mom took us to Dallas, where she had grown up. It was a pretty good combination: Dallas and Philadelphia. We got the best of both worlds, city and suburbs. I guess that's why Daniel and I gravitated to this place. It's like a cross between the two. There's only one thing wrong with Urdor."

"What's that?"

"It's kinda lonely here."

"You, silly...you've got me to keep you from loneliness."

"Yeah, until 4 o'clock. Then you're gone until almost midnight."

"Well, this job is great. It's one of the best I've ever had. If I had been at the Grille when I got out of school, I might not have fallen in with Wanda's crowd and had a close call with derelictism."

"I guess you never would have met me."

"Oh, we would have crossed paths."

"How do you figure that? You probably never would have been going to a freak party at Blimp's house."

"Yeah, but if I had been working at the Grille all along, then we would have met when you and Daniel got the contract on the new building."

"Well, that's true. You've made my point for me. You see, it was destiny all along that we should get together. Now that we've proven it, will you marry me?"

Bridget giggled, put her head on his shoulder. "You fool. What do you want with a mixed-up girl like me?"

"You can't argue with destiny, Bridget."

"We're just two ships passing in the night."

He laughed out loud. "No, no. If that were so, we wouldn't be here in Starbucks right now. We would have *passed each other*. You might be out in the middle of Virginia somewhere, and I'd be--"

"You'd be getting arrested on the steps of the Lincoln Memorial." She squeezed his hand playfully.

"Well, that's a perfect example of what I'm talking about. I got out of jail, nowhere to go, feeling suicidal."

"Oh, yeah, *right*." She twisted his arm with mock cruelty.

"And there I was, just out of jail, the loneliest man in the world, lost, no reason to live...and you hooked us up with that old couple from Gaithersburg, and they brought us back to Urdor. That was pretty good the way you bailed me out of a bad situation."

"Aw, go on...."

"Yep. We make a good team, all right. And I think it's destiny."

"Marcus, you're oversimplifying everything. The problem is...you're not a nice Jewish boy."

"Oh, I get it. Well, that shouldn't matter. You were about to write off your folks anyway, right?"

"Yes, I was, but I shouldn't write them off. I owe it to them."

"You owe what to them? Your life?"

"Well, yes. They brought me into the world."

Marcus was nodding his head with exaggeration. "Yes, you do owe them *something*, but not your life. They gave your life back to you when you left home. From that time on, your life was your own, and it's still your own, to do with what you see fit to do. You can't live to please them; you've got to do what's right for you. But there *is* something you owe them: your love and respect. *Honor your father and mother, that it may go well with you.* I remember that one from way back somewhere."

Bridget smiled. "It'll all work out."

"Is that a 'yes?'"

She just smiled again, suddenly feeling melancholy, but not knowing why. "I *am* glad you're here." She kissed him gently. "Marcus."

"What is it?"

"I don't like the fact that Aleph was such an innocent guy. He didn't deserve to die. It's not right." Marcus was at a loss for words. "And Wanda...look at her life. She was no saint, but *she's* dead, and that reprobate boyfriend of hers is alive. *He* should have been the dead one. There's no *justice.* That's why I can't buy this destiny business."

Hesitating, Marcus offered: "Wanda made...some bad choices in her life, and it caught up with her. It killed her. If she had pulled out of her dive earlier, before Buzz had such a grip on her, it might have been different. See. That's what *you* did. You were on a downward spiral, but were able to correct your course before it became critical, before it became *fatal.* That's destiny."

"You're so optimistic, Marcus. You're irresistible."

"I *hope* you find me irresistible."

"Maybe it is destiny, Marcus. But I was talking to a fellow recently who described it in a way similar to what you just said. But he didn't call it 'destiny.'"

"Oh? What did he call it?"

"Providence."

Marcus thought about it for a moment. "Hmmm...I could go with that. Providence. I like that. Who told you that?"

"Sid, the guy who sells vegetables to the restaurant. He also said that Jesus is the source of that Providence."

"I could probably go with that too, now that you mention it."

Bridget stretched a hair band around her hair. "Come on, let's ride some more, Marcus. I've got to be at work in an hour and a half."

"Okay. But first—one more question."

"Shoot."

He pointed to his water glass on the table. "What is that?"

"What do you mean?"

"I mean: What *is* that on the table?"

"It's a glass half-full of water."

"Great. See. You qualify as an optimist too. Providence has put us together."

"You mean because I said it's half full, not half-empty, I am an optimist."

"Yeah. You're a believer."

"Oh, psshh, you clown!" She pushed him out the door.

***

It had been a long day for detectives Lee Nguyen and Derrick Trent, but they were still hard at it. About 4 o'clock, Trent had come close to calling it a day. But the Sheriff's office got an email from a sheriff in Idaho that contained surprising news. It was something they wanted to discuss with the rapist, Moa Grindell. So they had him brought in from the jail.

In the same drab room where they had questioned Barney Bluntell earlier, the two men were seated at the table, watching the criminal as he entered the room and sat down.

Derrick Trent spoke: "Mo, we got some unexpected news today...thought you'd like to know about it."

Moa Grindell didn't say a word. He pretended to look out a window that wasn't there.

"The *fuhrer* is dead."

The criminal's eyes, in spite of his role-playing aloofness, betrayed a sudden surprise. Still, he said nothing.

Trent continued presenting facts. "When the *fuhrer* left Wessex County four or five days ago, he must have been in a big hurry. We put out an APB on him, because, you see, he had taken a shot at Detective Nguyen here. But then you probably knew that, because you were there at the barn when it burned down. Weren't you?"

Stubborn silence.

"Actually, Mo, excuse me, you weren't there at Wendall's barn when it burned to the ground, because you hightailed it the hell out of there. That's why we found you stranded like a crippled cat in a catalpa tree, with a broken leg in Buzz Townsend's meth lab trailer. Anyway... we wanted to charge the *fuhrer* with the crime that we knew he had committed— assaulting an officer with a gun, with intent to kill."

Trent paused. Looking intently at the criminal, he continued: "Well, like I said, he must have been in a hurry, because in just a few days, he made it all the way to Idaho. Do you have any idea, Mo, why he would have been going to Hoffish, Idaho?"

"What the hell are you telling me this for? I'm sick of this bullshit."

"I'm just giving you the news, Mo. Anyway, when he got out there to Hoffish, Idaho, he must have had a little argument with Max Bronf, because Max shot him dead. Wendell Foggerty is dead. That leaves you with...who else? Barney Bluntell? He's a bumbling idiot, Mo. You're on your own, by yourself. We've got your DNA matching three rape victims, one of them dead. You'll be lucky to get off with three life sentences. You need to come clean on all of it. If you know anything about bombing at the Holocaust Museum, now's the time to make it right."

Silence.

"You think about that. We'll be back. Next time, we'll have the court stenographer."

Revelations
23

At 7 o'clock Saturday evening, Rachel Vinnier was comparing two wine labels, one from the Bordeaux region of France and the other from Napa Valley, California. She was making wine selections for a wedding rehearsal party that would be coming in very shortly.

The Jesse James Gang Grille was bursting at the seams with hungry people. Glancing up, she noticed the two detectives, Nguyen and Trent, entering through the front door. Rachel recognized Nguyen, having spoken to him a couple days prior, at her apartment. Although the role of hostess was not her official one this evening, she greeted the two men. "Good evening, gentlemen. Thank you for choosing the Jesse James Gang Grille."

Nguyen observed, "It looks like a couple hundred other people chose it too."

"How perceptive you detective-types are," she commented, smiling. "Had I known in advance that you would be here, Mr. Nguyen, we might have reserved a table for you. As it is...."

"No problem. We're in no hurry. We'll have a seat at the bar here for a little while, since we're off duty."

"I'd estimate about a 45-minute wait. Would you like something to drink while you're waiting?"

"That'll be fine. We'll have a couple of lager drafts." The detectives walked to the far end of the bar. They noticed a small table right next to the bar and sat down. They began unwinding, analyzing in a more relaxed way the interviews they had been conducting in the last few days. There seemed to be some connections between disparate persons and events that they could not yet discern.

Derrick Trent spoke in a hushed tone. "As I was saying, there's quite a difference between these two guys. Once we got Barney going yesterday, he was really singing. You did a great job of getting him started, Lee. This other guy, Grindell, the one whose case is pretty-well wrapped up, has such tight control over his mouth. He seems more like a hardened criminal, even though he had no record until now."

" I think he's been raping women for a long time. His DNA matches with the samples from the Swann and Sherwin cases. He must have thought he was pretty good at it, then got overconfident and screwed up," said Nguyen.

"It doesn't pay for these criminals when they get cocky. It often leads to their screwing up. I think we've seen a pattern of it in DC, especially for serial criminals. They get away with a few crimes, then get sloppy...or vain. Ms. Olei was commenting the other day about the tattoo on the back of Grindell's neck. It's really downright stupid for a rapist to identify himself in that way. That same tattoo, by the way, showed up on another neck recently."

"Oh, yeah? Whose was that?"

"Did you hear about the desecration incident at the Lincoln Memorial a couple weeks ago?"

"Yeah. I read about it."

"The guy that did that, Dexter Bisto, also had a dragon tattoo on the back of his neck. I didn't see it, but I heard about it from the arresting officer."

"You have to wonder if there's some kind of identity there...common identity...or maybe it's just a fad," said Nguyen.

"Well, I'm thinking there's *some* kind of connection. Here we've got a couple of rapists who are sharing a list of victims, all of whom are Jewish women. So there appears to be some racist vendetta going on there. And one of the guys has this dragon on the back of his neck. Then over in DC, you've got another guy who turns up with a dragon tattoo...and he's defacing a national monument while mouthing off about white power or some such thing. It's obvious he's racially motivated, though his vindictiveness is directed toward a different ethnic group, African-Americans."

"Two different bigots blasting at two different racial identities, but both men having a dragon tattoo on their necks."

"It could be a loose association, based on ideological, or internet connections, or it might be a gang of some type. You think maybe they know each other?" asked Trent.

"We should talk to Grindell again on Monday, and ask him if he knows this Dexter guy."

"It's not likely we'd get much response from him. You saw how tight-lipped he was today."

"I was also thinking about motives," said Nguyen. "It was obvious that Bluntell had ideological motives, whereas Grindell's are, I think, overtly sexual ones."

"Yeah. Barney's a real fanatic. But Grindell seems more like a regular horny bastard who decides to rape women because he can't get one of his own," said Trent.

"Bluntell is philosophical about it, and involves himself with the terrorist element. Did he admit to being *with* Foggerty at the Holocaust Museum?"

"I think so. We need to go back over that tape."

"That reminds me, Derrick. When we were interviewing Bluntell last night, and you hit him with all those 'we know about this' and 'we know about that,' you were, in effect, linking a bunch of these events together. You must have known something I didn't."

"Nah. It was just a hunch." Derrick Trent laughed. "I think his interview confirmed connections between some events, but it wasn't until I brought his wife into it that he started talking. It was guilt about going out on his wife that penetrated his defenses. Once he started feeling bad, well, he whined pretty freely."

"It was almost as if he slipped into another personality."

"Yeah. These criminals have identities that they have to keep secret so they won't get caught. After a while, though, they can't keep them straight. *Oh, what a tangled web we weave, when first we purpose to deceive.* That kind of shit can't stay wrapped up forever. Sooner or later it comes out." Suddenly, Trent looked up. "Did you hear that?" He was gazing at a fellow sitting at the bar.

"Hear what?" asked Nguyen.

Trent lowered his voice. "That guy right there, at the bar. He said something about a red dragon. Listen for a minute."

Morris Schroeder and Shapur Kabir were having one of their usual discussions. Morris was saying: "Modern minds don't comprehend the metaphorical truth that is imparted through the use of archaic symbolism. Ancient writers didn't have the use of cinema, or photography. And they didn't have the benefit of scientific inquiry. They would use symbols, based on creatures or elements of the natural world, to represent entities in the spiritual world. Anyway, this serpent, or dragon, spews water out of his mouth. It's a desperate attempt to drown the woman, or extinguish her influence. But then the earth helps the woman, by swallowing up the flood that comes from his mouth. Maybe that flood is rhetoric, because it comes out of the mouth—you know, like the hate message that Hitler spewed out. But the symbolism could be more inclusive than that. At any rate, this pregnant woman is given wings like an eagle, and is taken to the wilderness. I suppose that could be related to the expanding use of aircraft as the 20th century progressed. Or it may be more specific—the Allied powers used air power to overcome the Nazi war machine and afterwards to transplant the woman--Israel-- to Eretz Israel, the land, which is a wilderness. But of course there were people already living there in Palestine, and many of them were displaced with bloodshed, so another cycle of the old grudges were set into motion. It's a mess, always has been."

"Excuse me, sir," interjected Trent. "I couldn't help overhearing your fascinating treatise. May I ask what it is you're talking about?"

Morris turned toward Trent. "Oh, I'm glad to be of service. I was talking about the flood of anti-Semitism that is metaphorically prophesied in the book of Revelation."

"You were saying something about a red dragon?"

"Yes, the dragon (or sometimes it's rendered as a serpent) is an ancient symbol, possibly based on historical encounters that humans had with certain animals now extinct, or on mythologized tales about snakes or whales. It can represent many characters or entities in human experience: evil, wisdom, power, depending on the cultural context. In the specific context that I was referring to, Revelation, the dragon depicted in chapter 12 is often considered to represent a spiritual entity that spews out a tide of hate against the Jewish people. The scene is presented in which a pregnant woman, classically interpreted as the Jewish nation, is about to give birth to a child, a Messiah who will overcome the evil that is in the world. The dragon spews forth his tide of hate in opposition to the woman and her child that is about to be born. In this historical context, then, the dragon entity manifests itself as hate speech and action against the Jewish people, but also against those men and women who follow the Messiah child who is born to the woman."

"So you would associate the dragon with the Nazis, the Third Reich?"

"Most definitely, and it was indicated prophetically, 1900 years ago."

"What about today? What would this dragon be associated with today?"

"Well, as I mentioned before, it's a very old symbol. The Chinese dragon, for instance, the new year and all that, may have nothing to do with its Western counterpart. The dragon has, in certain cultural contexts, represented wisdom and/or power. It's not necessarily a symbol of evil."

Trent was pursuing a line of thought. "If you were to see on a person, say, a dragon tattoo, what would it suggest to you about that person?"

"Nothing really. People these days will wear tattoos of just about anything. Maybe...rebellion?...mystery...or, cultish associations, perhaps, but that would be a stretch. It may be that the tattooist showed them a bunch of samples, and they chose the dragon because it meant rejection of authority to them, or desire for power. Actually, if we were to settle on any one *thing* that the dragon represents, it would be *power.* Maybe a person who is coveting power, power that they do not have, would have a dragon tattooed onto their body somewhere."

Nguyen thought about what Barney Bluntell had said: that a rearrangement of *power* would be necessary to "make things right."

Morris, who loved to expound on just about anything, still had more to say, and was profoundly grateful for this unexpected audience of three. He continued, "What's interesting is that the child, the Messiah, whose birth is threatened by the dragon's flood, is *truly* an antithesis to the power principle...the will to power, as Niechtze called it. After his birth (the dragon having been unable to prevent it) the Messiah child *refused* to play the power game. His friends tried to get him to take up the sword against the Romans, who were the bullyish authority of that time and place. But he wouldn't do it. He had plans of his own. Instead of extending the cycle of violence, he *broke* it. By spreading his arms wide to be crucified on a cross (instead of raising a sword) he insured that his message would be told from that time forward to all generations. He must have been a genius...or God himself. That such a strategy of submission would metamorphose into the most widespread drama in all of human history is simply a miracle."

Nguyen thought of Barney's statement about doing away with the "weak and inferior elements" of humanity.

Bridget approached the men, and, looking at Shapur, she said: "I've got a table for you guys now."

Morris looked at Bridget and asked: "Which table is it?"

"Number twelve, by the window."

"That can accommodate four, right?" asked Morris.

"Yes."

Morris looked at Derrick Trent. "Why don't you gentlemen join us?. We've got a table, now that we've been here for an hour."

Trent looked askance at Nguyen, who shrugged his shoulders.

Morris extended his hand to the detectives. "I'm Morris Schroeder, with the physics department at Lincoln University."

"Derrick Trent." They shook hands.

"Shapur Kabir." They shook hands.

"Lee Nguyen." They shook hands again, and all moved into the main dining room of the Jesse James Gang Grille.

Bridget seated the four men at the table by the window, took their drink orders. Trent and Nguyen had never received their beers. But now they would.

Morris, as always, was anxious for more discussion. He looked at Trent, and asked, "What provoked your interest in the red dragon?"

Trent laughed, stalling. He looked at his partner. A police officer had to be careful. Nguyen smiled and shrugged his shoulders. Every now and then, a detective would have to relate to people on a regular basis...not cop to citizen, but man to man. Trent had been playing the interrogator role for a few days now; he was worn out. He thought that now, just *now*, the citizenry of this great land might impart something to him that could help him do his job better...some information or perspective that would help him to be a better detective, detecting truth on behalf of the people...

It's time to relax and be a normal guy. Take off the mask. These two guys are not criminals or terrorists. They're citizens. "We're detectives. I'm with the Washington Metro department. Nguyen here--"

"I'm with the Sheriff's department here in Wessex County. We've been working on a few cases together. The bombing incident over here at the Belmont Hotel on Thursday night is one of them."

"Have you figured it out yet?" asked Shapur.

"Oh...the Belmont Hotel? No. We've got a few clues we're working on."

Shapur looked at the two detectives to get their attention. He said: "Well, you know what?"

"What?"

Shapur pointed at the TV screen in the corner. The basketball game was on—Lincoln University Eagles vs. Marianna College Wildcats. "Do you see that fellow playing point guard for Lincoln?"

"Yes," said Nguyen. "That's Isaac Jones. He was right there where the bomb went off two nights ago, at the Belmont. It's a miracle that he's in good enough shape tonight to be darting around on a basketball court."

"He was shielded from the blast," said Shapur.

"Yes. I heard that," said Nguyen. "There was a man there who was about to examine the bomb when it went off."

"Aleph Leng," said Morris.

"Right," said Nguyen. You seem to have kept up with this event."

"Our waitress, Bridget, has a good friend, Marcus. Aleph was staying at Marcus' house before he was killed."

"He's an African, isn't he? From Sudan?"

Bridget brought their drinks. Shapur asked her, "Wasn't Aleph from Sudan?"

"Yes. He was an American citizen. But he had come from Sudan, via Kenya, about three years ago. That's what he told me and Marcus."

Trent was interested. "That fellow had also been at the Holocaust Museum when the bomb went off there two weeks ago."

"Yes. He showed us, at the Holocaust Museum, where he was standing when the bomb exploded there," said Bridget.

"It kind of makes you wonder. That's an incredible coincidence, whether he wasn't involved--" Trent was speculating.

"Oh, you needn't wonder about Aleph," said Bridget. "Don't forget. He was killed in the Belmont blast."

"You don't think he might have been a suicide bomber?"

"No way!" Bridget was visibly annoyed. "I'll be back in a minute. You guys decide what you want to eat."

Trent raised his eyebrows. "She's a little testy, huh?"

"Aleph was *not* a suicide bomber," stated Shapur. "From what we've heard about him, he spent half his life running away from such people in Sudan."

"We've got to examine these events from every possible angle," said Trent.

"I understand," said Shapur. He pointed up at the TV screen. "The Eagles are up by twelve at the half."

"That's what we'd expect with a number one seed facing number twelve," observed Nguyen.

Morris was curious. "Have you guys been able to see any connection between those two bombing incidents?"

Nguyen glanced at his partner. "Not really, not yet."

"Could that be related to your question about the red dragon?" asked Morris. Morris had an intellect that wouldn't stop.

Trent offered, "We don't know enough yet. We're looking into it." Ambiguity was the safest course for detectives to take when talking about their cases.

"Our lovely waitress, Bridget, told me that the fellow who splattered red paint on Lincoln's feet had a dragon tattoo on the back of his neck," said Morris.

"Oh yeah?" blurted Trent. "How does she know that?"

"She was there when it happened. Her friend Marcus was the guy that put a stop to it."

Trent looked baffled. "He was the guy that got into a fight with Dexter Bisto?"

"Well...yeah, he tackled the guy who was shouting about white power. That's what Bridget told us. Isn't that right, Bridget?" Morris lifted his arm to be sure that Bridget would stop as she was passing. "Marcus wrestled that white power wacko on the steps of the Lincoln Memorial, didn't he?"

"He did," assented Bridget.

"You were there with Marcus, weren't you?" asked Morris.

"I was there. It was one of the strangest experiences I've ever had. Marcus and I were looking at the Gettysburg Address and the next thing you know this guy is making a racket and shouting that Lincoln was a traitor. It was weird."

Trent was amazed at what he was hearing. "And the guy had a dragon tattoo on the back of his neck?"

"Yes. I didn't see it, but Marcus told me about it."

"What color was the tattoo?"

"Marcus said it was red."

Shapur had been thinking about all of this. "It's just a tattoo...probably nothing to it. People have all kinds of crazy things tattooed on their bodies these days. The only significance would be...if you found the same one on another person who is connected to one of these racist incidents."

Trent and Nguyen looked at each other. Nguyen laughed.

"What?" Morris was laughing, looking steadily at the two detectives. "You *do have* another tattoo somewhere in all of this. That's why you were interested in the dragon to begin with. You're wondering what the beastly symbolism will lead to."

"Who knows?" quipped Shapur, "could be a cliffhanger."

"What?"

Rachel walked up to their table, smiling. She asked: "Will you gentlemen be having any wine with your dinner tonight?" Nguyen gazed at her in wonder. The other dragon tattoo had been on the neck of the attacker who had probably been after her when he had assaulted her roommate.

"Yes, Rachel. How about a bottle of good white wine to go with the flounder that I'm going to order?" said Nguyen.

"Liebfraumilch, perhaps?" suggested Rachel, with a funny little smile on her face.

"That will be fine."

Bridget stopped in and took their orders for dinner. On the TV in the corner, Isaac Jones was penetrating the Marianna defense with skillful assists.

"Oh, Bridget," said Shapur, "could you bring us some bread with that wine?"

"Yes, sir."

Unseen by the diners at the Jesse James Gang Grille, the ancient dragon crouched outside in darkness, waiting to implant his image upon the necks of all men and women everywhere. But a newborn child was waiting in the wings to oppose him.

Ends
24

Isaac Jones had not delivered the speech that he had prepared for teenagers at the *Family Education Foundation*. A monstrous act had prevented it.

But now, this Sunday afternoon, he ascended a podium brightly decorated with lilies and chrysanthemums, to speak on behalf of a man whom he had never met.

The young athlete surveyed the questioning faces of this mournful assembly. The convention that was being called to order on Thursday night when Aleph died should not have ended this way.

He saw his mother, who had been protected, like him, from the blast by Aleph's last-second maneuver. He saw Kaneesha, who had been a regular companion for his mother these last few years. He saw Marcus, who had told him more about Aleph's life than any other person. He saw Joshua and Asumbi Acacia, the last people to truly know the deceased. He saw his coach, Sid, and his best friend, Wes. He saw the mayor of Urdor, and Lili Kapua, President of *Family Education Foundation*. He saw the families of many whose lives had been disrupted by the explosion.

Isaac considered the tragic circumstances of this stranger's death, and he spoke.

"Four thousand years ago, our ancestors stood upon this earth and declared that, by the command of a loving Creator, no man should kill another. Yet there are in this depraved world, some who shamefully disregard the laws of God and man.

We are gathered here today to honor a man whose life, though untimely ripped from him, was given sacrificially in an attempt to protect others.

"Thirteen days ago, curiously enough, Aleph Leng had survived the bombing that took place at the Holocaust Memorial Museum. Three days ago, his awareness of impending danger to our Family Education Foundation members moved him to act on our behalf to remove or disable an explosive device. That impulse to protect us cost him his life.

"Now we honor Aleph Leng, though we hardly knew him. Inspired by his example, we take increased devotion to that cause for which he has given his last full measure of devotion—the resolve that the dignity and improvement of human life shall not perish from the face of the earth.

"Aleph was a native of Africa, Sudan. He was a man whose youth had been spent escaping the foul entrapments of evil men. Yes, there is evil in the world, and this occasion is evidence of that fact.

"As a young man, Aleph chose the sanctuary of America because he knew our country to be a place where human dignity and freedom is valued. For his sake, and for the sake of our children, we declare here today: human dignity and freedom will not perish from the face of the earth.

"But I want to tell you of another choice that Aleph Leng had made: eternal life. It was *because* of his belief in eternal life that he could so willingly risk his mortal life. I stand today on behalf of our fallen brother and announce to you: though he was slain, yet does he live, eternally, because of his belief in the resurrection. There is one who went before him to establish that way of eternal life, by defeating death itself.

"So Aleph Leng did not live, or die, in vain. He still lives. And I ask you: Will you live eternally as he does? The choice is yours to make."

Isaac stepped down from the podium and walked slowly to the back of the room.

In the third row from the back of the auditorium, a retort came forth. "Jeez, what was he trying to say?"

Isaac smiled and exited through the back door. He left it wide open, the noonday sun shining prism-bright.

***

A fiery red sun was just now slicing into the Pacific horizon like a ruby wheel.

Lili Kapua was appreciating its brilliant hue as she thought about what Isaac had said at Aleph Leng's funeral. The flight from California seemed like a mere blinking of an eye, so lost in thought was she. Isaac Jones, the basketball player, had been her rather impulsive choice as a speaker for the "young people" at the convention. Through the intense cascade of improvised events that had followed the bomb blast, Isaac's eulogy of a man whom no one knew had crowned their tragedy with an aroma of victory.

Suddenly, the plane was out of the clouds. A luminous panorama of Honolulu was splayed beneath them...from golden Waikiki strand to steep, green, serrated Ko'olau mountain range...from Diamond Head crater to the ruby-wheel sunset.

Lili's thought was always the same when returning from anywhere to her Hawaii home. *This is as close as you can get, on earth, to having a place called Paradise.*

Her eyes settled upon Diamond Head, as the plane's banking presented a spectacular view of that extinct volcano. She knew that, when viewed from the city below, that precipice could be seen protruding at its seaward end like a mounted jewel upon an o'er-rimming volcanic crown. The apex had formed during eruptions as a windblown accumulation of spewing lava and ash 300,000 years ago. Looking at it now, a person could somehow affirm within its angular form the name "Diamond Head." With igneous starkness its jaggedness seemed to manifest, not a perfect diamond shape, but a jewel-like sculpting of perfect resoluteness. *The Creator has forged this pinnacle from the depths of a fiery earth, and in so doing could impress upon all visitors and residents this fact: Oahu is a very special island.*

It was an outcropping of earthen majesty, within a royal Hawaiian archipelago, strung out upon the vast Pacific as a gem-studded tiara upon a sapphire princess: Oahu. Offering its windswept countenance to a jaded world, the precipice awaited with stately geologic dignity a coronation in the hearts of all Oahu-comers as the very crown of creation.

Hawaii! Where east and west hemispheres meet, where Japanese agrarians and American cowboys exchanged the fruits of their labors along lava-laden roads.

Hawaii, the only state in the Union with a heritage of kings and queens.

And it was this heritage--this royal Hawaiian blood--that coursed through Lili's veins—this sovereign pulse that propelled the beating of her queenly heart. She began to reflect upon the long sojourn that was now ending.

Sadly, a deep scar within her dominated the outcome of this trip. A malevolently-constructed explosive device had ripped into that royal heart, shattering with it the philanthropic optimism of her beloved Family Education Foundation. The noble burden of responsibility that she bore as president of a great organization now weighed upon her with heavy tragedy.

The bombing had robbed one brave man of his life, and had robbed the Foundation of its precious annual agenda.

Lili's thoughts once again descended to the dead volcano below, now hidden from sight as the plane began its final descent. Its earthen center had once been a fiery caldera spewing molten lava. Her home island had been formed eons ago when such calamitous activity had deposited millions of acres of new earth upon the ocean bed miles below. One volcano after another over hundreds of thousands of years had formed the Hawaiian ridges.

Explosive heat—such a creative force. Perhaps whole continents had been formed by this process. A few hundred miles away, the big island—the one named "Hawaii," was still growing larger by these volcanic processes. Eyewitnesses who had seen the explosive eruptions overflowing those active craters had reported seeing fire and brimstone as if viewing hell itself.

Even Paradise had a "hell" of its own.

Explosive heat—such a *destructive* force. Perhaps whole civilizations had been destroyed by this process, especially since depraved humans had devised ways to harness that perilous power to inflict vengeance and enmity upon themselves.

The big bang that both begins life and ends it is happening somewhere at every moment, and could indeed exalt itself above human order and propriety at any given moment.

Lily thought about the IED that had decimated their convention. It was but one miniscule atrocity amid cataclysmic cascades of human abomination. Murder and rape and cruelties without number strung back through the shadows of human experience. Thoughtful men and women in ages past had forged images of their species' own depravity upon the fires of this hell.

This most recent embodiment of hate had raised its dragon head of homicidal insult and ripped away the heart of an innocent man. It had also torn hers asunder, slinging sulfurous tongues of mayhem upon her people's collective good intentions to have an edifying time together. What would have been a productive convention had become a somber assembly of mourning and solemnity.

But now the plane was landing, the time for reflection suspending. Life must go on.

The first familiar person that Lili saw on the ground was her housekeeper, Pao, who had dutifully secured a cart for their luggage. Pao was smiling broadly, glad to see them. After David had gathered their baggage and stacked it on the cart, she directed their attention to a Chinese woman who had watched their reunion activities while patiently sitting nearby. As the young lady stood up to be introduced to them, Lili could see that she was pregnant.

Wang Chuanxin had managed to do what few women have done: she had escaped the draconic bureaucracy that sought to extinguish the prenatal life of her second child. By the ministrations of a devoted husband and a few well-placed bribes, she had managed to board a plane out of China, to Honolulu, and so the child was still alive within her. Now she was in a foreign land with a foreign fear and nowhere to go. But at least her child was alive. She had been sitting in the baggage claim area for three hours, waiting for someone she didn't know.

Pao introduced her as Wang Chuanxin, who had just arrived from Beijing that very day.

"Chuanxin is a friend of my friend Chen. She has eluded the party officials in her home province; they had conspired to abort her child."

Lili had not expected an encounter such as this in a routine airport arrival. She looked at the waifish mother with alarm and curiosity. "How did you manage to get out of there?" she wondered aloud.

"She speaks no English. I will translate," Pao said.

As Pao spoke to her in their language, Lili noticed the fearful look on Chuanxin's delicate face as she responded to Pao's question with rapid Mandarin.

"She says that her husband bribed some officials in order to get her on the plane that brought her to Honolulu. She still doesn't know how the situation will be resolved, or how she will reunite with her husband."

"Ask her where she is going to stay."

Pao's translation was followed by a quick, two-word reply.

"She doesn't know."

Lili looked directly into her housekeeper's eyes. "Pao, how did you know that she would be here today?"

"I received the phone call last night from my friend Chen. He asked me to help her."

"And who is Chen?"

"We are in church together."

"I see." Lili's queenly heart was moving her toward a response of compassionate action. *I was a stranger and you took me in.*

"Ask her if she wants to come stay with us for awhile."

Pao spoke to their new friend energetically. Her plan was actually working out just as she had anticipated, for she knew her employer well. Chuanxin replied happily, with a large smile suddenly appearing on her formerly-strained face.

Pao did not bother to complete the verbiage. She grabbed Chuanxin's two bags and slung them on top of the loaded cart, there being just enough space for them.

Then David spoke to Pao, "We'll wait here while you bring the car around."

"Yes, sir," she affirmed, and was off to get the car.

Lili sighed. It had been a long couple of weeks.

***

Back in Urdor, Virginia, Moses Reece lay, unresponsive, in a hospital bed at Wessex County Medical Center. The dragon had stretched forth its murderous will and snatched the passing pilgrim from beneath a canopy at the Belmont Hotel, in that same torturous instant that it had so rapturously hurled Aleph Leng into the next dimension. But Moses was still hanging on for dear life, as if on a precipice. For seven days he had lain there. Behind him was a life well-lived; before him...a half-full vision of heaven. Beside him stood his son, Alexander, and his daughter, Diana. Alexander was watching through teary eyes; Diana was praying.

He had no way to speak to them. They could not know that he was looking into the abyss; they could not know that he was rejecting it. They could not know that he was seeing, on the dark side, the unknown pane of infamous death's door...two paths diverging.

This was Moses' view from the precipice: two paths, diverging.

Soon, and very soon, he would be choosing the one that he had known all along would be there for him. And that (knowing) had made all the difference. Soon, and very soon, he would be going to see the king.

Now his time had come, and so Moses was lifted for the first time beyond the precipice.